Murder At The House On The Hill

Victoria Walters is a ... urrey.
Victoria writes the ... series
GLENDALE HALL, which has won wide reader acclaim.
She has been chosen for WHSmith Fresh Talent and
shortlisted for two RNA awards. Victoria was also picked
as an Amazon Rising Star. Her first cosy crime novel
MURDER AT THE HOUSE ON THE HILL was
published in 2021.

Follow Victoria on social media here:

Instagram: vickyjwalters
Facebook: Victoria Walters author
YouTube: Victoria Walters
Twitter: Vicky_Walters

Also by Victoria Walters

The Glendale Hall series (in reading order)

Coming Home to Glendale Hall
New Beginnings at Glendale Hall
Hopeful Hearts at Glendale Hall
Always and Forever at Glendale Hall

The Dedley End Mysteries

Murder at the House on the Hill

Standalone novels

Summer at the Kindness Café
The Second Love of my Life

Murder At The House On The Hill

Victoria Walters

First published in the United Kingdom in 2021 by

Hera Books
28b Cricketfield Road
London, E5 8NS
United Kingdom

A CIP catalogue record for this book is available from the British Library.

Print ISBN 978 1 80032 609 5
Ebook ISBN 978 1 912973 63 7

Look for more great books at www.herabooks.com

Printed and bound in Great Britain by Clays Ltd, Elcograf S.p.A.

I

A huge thank you to Anna Bell for helping me to come up with the name for the village (and the series!) — I'll be forever grateful.

Chapter One

Sleet danced past the window of the Dedley Endings Bookshop but Nancy Hunter paid it no attention – she was far too engrossed in her book.

Dedley End, nestled in the Cotswolds, was filled with tourists in the summer seeking out cobbled streets and hikes with stunning views but in December it was just the locals who spent time in the village. The days were drawing ever closer to Christmas and Nancy knew that there would be a last-minute rush from their customers to buy gifts. But today, it had been too cold for many of them to venture into the small High Street, so it had been a quiet morning in the shop. After doing all the admin and tidying that was needed, she had retreated behind the counter and pulled out the book she was in the middle of, thinking as she often did that she really did have the best job in the world.

'Fancy a cup of tea, love? It's so chilly,' her grandmother, Jane, called from the back office. Nancy called back that she would love one. Her grandmother was meant to be retired but she couldn't resist daily walks to the shop from their nearby cottage, needing her fix of local gossip – although so far today there had been none to enjoy.

Nancy closed her book when she reached the end of the chapter. She had read it before – it was one of her favourites passed down to her by her father, a murder mystery by bestselling author Thomas Green. She smiled over at their beagle Charlie who was fast asleep on the window seat. He always accompanied her in the shop and was beloved by the village. Nancy continued a sweep of the small, cosy shop with her eyes, and let out a wistful sigh. At this time of year, she missed her father the most. They would need to decorate the shop for Christmas soon and that had always been his favourite thing to do.

'Here we go,' Jane said, coming out with two large steaming hot mugs, taking her usual seat by the till. Although now in her late sixties with grey hair and wrinkles around her green eyes, she was still surprisingly sprightly. Nancy's father had passed on his bookshop to Jane after his untimely death and she had spent sixteen years at the helm before letting Nancy take over the day-to-day management of it earlier this year, but she hated being stuck at home so fully immersed herself in local activities and committees. 'What are you thinking about?'

'That we need to put up the tree, and how much Dad enjoyed wrapping books to put under it,' Nancy replied, pushing back a stray hair from her light brown bob as she looked over at the corner where the tree stood every year.

Her grandmother smiled. 'He really did. It's always hard at this time of the year without him, isn't it?' she said wistfully.

Nancy nodded. 'Because it's such a family time.' Her face clouded over as she thought about how her gran was her only family. Not only had she lost her father when she was ten, but her mother had long since left the village and neither of them had any idea where she was. 'Let's decorate on Sunday,' she added, trying to brighten the conversation up. 'Make it really special.' Nancy was twenty-six and had worked in the bookshop since she had left university five years ago and was excited to be running it now. She had lots of ideas for the place but they would need to wait until after the Christmas rush.

'He would love that. And we can move all the Christmas editions to the window, they always sell well, don't they?'

Nancy nodded in agreement, looking at the bookshelves. When Nancy's father had decided to open a bookshop in the village he had lived in all his life, there had really only been one choice of genre for him. If you lived in Dedley End, you had to embrace the murder puns or lose your sense of humour completely. The Dedley Endings Bookshop consequently only sold crime, mystery and thriller books and people came from far and wide for the novelty, especially as so many detective stories were set in the Cotswolds. The business had thrived for twenty years, and Nancy was determined that it would continue to do so for a very long time indeed.

The door opened then, making the bell on top of it jingle merrily. Charlie opened his eyes instantly and let out a bark in greeting. He didn't get up though; it was too cold for the dog to move from his warm sleeping spot.

'Morning folks,' Paul, the postman, said with a nod. 'Here's your post.' He placed two envelopes on the counter and then actually winked. 'Causing a stir in the village this morning, they are,' he said, giving them a tap.

'What are they?' Jane asked, standing and moving to Nancy's side to see.

'I'll let you see for yourselves but I will say this – I'll see you there!' And with that cryptic comment, he left the shop, pushing his post cart off down the High Street, whistling on his way as usual.

Jane and Nancy looked at one another. 'Well, what was that all about?'

'Only one way to find out,' Nancy said, picking up the envelope addressed to her. Her grandmother did the same for hers. Nancy opened up the envelope and pulled out the thick cream card within. It was the highest quality stationery – an invitation written in gold calligraphy. 'Oh my,' she said with a gasp as she read it.

'Knock me down with a feather,' Jane muttered as she too read her invite. 'I can't believe it.'

Nancy stared at the words just as stunned.

Nancy Hunter and guest

Please join us for an engagement celebration to honour Maria Roth and Charles Spencer at Roth Lodge on Friday 8th December from 7.30pm to 9pm.

Cocktails and canapés will be served. Dress code: Black tie

Please RSVP to Jessica Roth

'But the Roths never invite anyone in the village to their house,' Nancy said when she had read it, looking up at her gran, wide-eyed. She used the word 'house' but Roth Lodge really was a mansion. Although it stood just outside the village, perched on a hill, the Roth family never ventured into the High Street and kept the large gates firmly closed to anyone from Dedley End.

'Not for thirty years,' Jane agreed, shaking her head. 'I never thought I'd see the day again, to be honest.'

'I wonder why they've invited us to this,' Nancy said. 'I don't think I've ever even spoken to Maria Roth.'

'Perhaps she persuaded her parents, and grandfather, to let her invite locals. I mean, it is her party. Well, whatever the reason behind it, we *have* been invited. The question is, what do we RSVP?'

Before Nancy could answer her, the bookshop doorbell jingled again and she reluctantly tore her eyes away from the invitation to see who it was.

Chapter Two

'It's quiet in here!' a cheerful male voice called out as the door swung open to reveal Jonathan Murphy, Nancy's friend since childhood, giving them a cheerful wave.

This time Charlie did get up; he loved Jonathan and rushed over to greet him, his tail wagging. Jonathan bent down to rub his ears. 'I brought lunch!'

'Brilliant, I'm starving,' Nancy replied, turning back to the invitation.

'You always are,' he replied, coming over and putting a paper bag from the local café, The Teahouse, down on the counter. 'I bought enough for three, Mrs H,' he added, giving Jane one of his winning smiles. She tutted under her breath. Nancy hid a grin. Her grandmother always acted like Jonathan was a bad influence. 'So, what's the news?' he asked casually.

Nancy looked up and narrowed her eyes as Jonathan pulled out an egg and cress sandwich for Jane, a cheese and tomato for Nancy, and a ham and pickle for himself, three bags of crisps, three bottles of orange juice and three chocolate muffins. 'What's all this in aid of?' she asked.

He avoided her eyes. 'What are you saying? That I can't bring my oldest and dearest friend her lunch without an ulterior motive?'

'That's exactly what I'm saying.'

Finally, he looked up and smiled sheepishly at her. Jonathan was shorter than Nancy even though he was two years older, at twenty-eight, something that she had often teased him about while they were growing up. He had messy dark hair, and dark eyes, and always wore the same scruffy jeans paired with an array of cosy jumpers. Jonathan, in turn, had started her nickname of 'Nancy the vampire' at school thanks to her willowy figure, pale skin, and surname.

Really it was a wonder that they were friends at all.

'Well, yes, I suppose I did want to talk to you…' His eyes rested on the invitation in her hands again.

'Something to do with this?' she pressed, giving it a little wave.

'All right, fine, I need to ask you something. And you must say yes because my career depends on it!'

'Let's get the food out and sit down first. With all this excitement, I need some sustenance,' Jane said, rolling her eyes at their exchange. Jonathan dutifully handed out the food, and Jane sat back down behind the till, and he went over to the brown leather armchair kept out for customers.

Nancy walked to the window seat, which offered a view of the small, narrow shop, and perched on it. Charlie jumped back up beside her and put a paw on her leg. She smiled, breaking off a piece of her sandwich for him to eat. She loved the shop. Everywhere you looked were books; tall shelves packed with them from floor to ceiling. Customers often became confused with the ordering – her father hadn't been the most organised of people, after all – and even their part-time assistant, and Nancy's friend, Penelope was often calling for help to find a book, but Nancy knew where every title was. Keeping the system as it was helped her to feel closer to her lost father.

At one end stood the counter and till, the small office and toilet behind it; and in one corner stood a grandfather clock, passed on by George Hunter's father to his son, still ticking loudly and efficiently. On the walls were framed book covers – the greatest murder mysteries and detective stories of all time watching over them. And then, behind the counter, was a photo of her dad outside the bookshop on opening day, looking as proud as Punch. Nancy loved looking at that photo seeing him so happy, and the resemblance between them. From photos, it was clear she took after him and her grandmother, and not her absent mother, something she was relieved about. They all had the same green eyes but she was tall and slim like her father, and his father before him, whereas Jane was rather short and stocky if they were honest about it.

Nancy took a bite of her sandwich and patted Charlie as he curled back up in his bed next to her. She grinned at her gran as they chewed their food in silence with Jonathan watching them, tapping his foot on the floor. Finally, she gave in. 'Go on then, spit it out. What do you want to ask?' she called over to him.

'It's about the Roth party. I mean, what a scoop! For the first time in years the Roths are opening up their house again and inviting some of the village inside. What's it been – like, thirty years or something crazy like that? So, I need to be there to cover it.' Jonathan worked at the local paper, the *Cotswold Star*, as features editor, and was always looking for an article that might liven up the newspaper. Unfortunately, they lived in a nice, safe area, which was pleasant to inhabit, but rather dull when your job was trying to find interesting stories. 'When we heard that people in the village were starting to receive invitations, my editor Tony tried to secure me one but the Roths were firm – they may be opening up their doors to the village but not to the press.'

'I don't blame them,' Jane remarked dryly.

'I'll choose to ignore that comment, Mrs H,' he replied, turning again to Nancy. 'But they did confirm to Tony that all business owners in the village have been invited and I saw Paul the Postie heading your way and he said all the invites have a plus one…' he trailed off with a grin.

'You shouldn't call him that,' Jane told him.

'He likes it! Anyway, you have been invited, right? So, how about I escort you?' he said to Nancy.

She shook her head. 'The last event you escorted me to was the Rotary Club's Christmas party, and old Mr Andrew started rubbing my thigh,' she recalled with a shudder.

'Well, it's not like you can't handle yourself. If I remember rightly, you ended up pouring your drink all over him.'

'He deserved it,' Nancy replied.

'Quite right,' her grandmother agreed. 'Anyway, what makes you think we'll be accepting their invitation?' She grinned at Nancy when Jonathan couldn't see. They both enjoyed teasing him whenever possible. 'I, for one, don't want to be going anywhere with the weather like this,' she added, gesturing to the sleet that was thickening into snow behind them.

'It's going to be the social event of the year, and I know you've always wanted to get a look inside that house of theirs,' Jonathan replied, looking at Nancy.

That was certainly true. Nancy had passed Roth Lodge every day on her walk to and from school, and she had always wanted to know what went on inside such a splendid home but, like the rest of the village, she had never been invited in until now. She sighed. 'I can't pretend I'm not curious. I would love to see inside. I still can't quite believe they've invited the village. They never let any of us inside.'

'They used to years ago,' her grandmother said. 'They would hold all sorts of events there but I haven't seen inside those gates since their last garden party which, as you said Jonathan, must be about thirty years ago now. And that party will always stick in my mind, I can tell you.' She looked around the bookshop. 'If it's still there, you would love their library, Nancy. It was a dream back then,' she added, wistfully.

'They are inviting everyone deemed important in the village,' Jonathan said, clearly trying to flatter them both. 'Tony said the member of staff he spoke to told him it was a rushed decision, apparently. Maria insisted despite their usual closed-door policy and I guess her parents relented. I suppose she wants the whole world to know she's getting married. That's why the invites are so last minute.'

'Well, after all these years, we can't not go, can we, love?'

'I think we'd regret it if we didn't,' Nancy agreed with Jane. 'Although I have no idea what to wear to a black-tie party.'

'We'll find you something, I'm sure of it,' Jane said, excited now. 'I wonder who else will be there. I'm just going to ring Gloria now actually, to see if she's had one too.' She hurried into the office. There was nothing she loved better than being the source of exciting news.

'So, what do you think? Can I tag along? I would have the exclusive scoop on the event if I could be there,' Jonathan pleaded with Nancy once they were alone.

She smiled, unable to hold out any longer. It really was too good an opportunity to miss. And it wasn't as if her social calendar was anywhere near full. An engagement party at Roth Lodge a few weeks before Christmas would keep her entertained enough for months. And then she thought of another incentive. 'You'll need to wear a tux.'

Jonathan sighed. 'I hadn't even thought of that. I suppose I'll have to borrow Tony's.' His editor wasn't much better at dressing than him but he'd had to invest in a tuxedo for a wedding. He checked his watch. 'Right then, now it's all settled, I'd better get back to the office. I need to read up on the Roth family, make sure I know who's who, and think about what scandal we can uncover.'

Nancy raised an eyebrow. 'Scandal in Dedley End? You're going to be disappointed.' Everyone knew that nothing scandalous ever happened in their village.

'Maybe. We'll see. They have kept their doors shut for thirty years, but why?'

'It was after that garden party Gran just mentioned. You'll have to ask her for the details. I think she said something was stolen at it. Although if you listen to village rumour, it was anything from a police investigation into fraud, to them being part of the Illuminati.'

'Well, it's always the wealthy ones that have the biggest skeletons in the closet. I can promise you that.' He stood up and walked to the door, pausing to give Charlie a farewell pat.

Nancy twisted in the window seat to look out at the High Street. 'I'd wait two minutes if I were you.'

'Why?'

She nodded towards the small supermarket opposite the bookshop where a young woman had just come out, struggling with her shopping bag and umbrella.

Jonathan followed her gaze. 'Blimey. Well spotted.' He leaned back from the window in case she saw him.

'One of these days, the way you treat women is going to catch up with you, Jonathan Murphy, and I won't be around to save you.' Kate was Jonathan's ex-girlfriend and Nancy thought that she still loved him even though Jonathan ran from anything that came close to being a relationship.

Jonathan checked outside again. The coast was now clear. 'You'll always be around to save me, Nancy, that's why we're friends.' He yanked open the door. 'I'll pick you up on the night of the party like a proper chaperone.'

'As if you could ever be called that!' Nancy cried after him but he just whistled and walked away as if he hadn't heard her. She shook her head. She didn't like the casual way he treated women but occasionally she was envious about how easily he seemed to navigate relationships. She hadn't dated anyone since her university boyfriend Richard had ended their three-year relationship, and wasn't at all sure that she wanted to. A broken heart wasn't something she was in a hurry to have repeated.

Nancy heard her grandmother talking excitedly to the vicar's wife in the office. She couldn't help but feel the same shiver of excitement herself at the thought of this party. Of finally getting to see inside the grand Roth Lodge. And getting to dress up, too. She felt rather like Cinderella finally getting to go to the ball.

She picked up the muffin Jonathan had left. Charlie lifted his head to look hopefully at her. 'After all this excitement, I deserve this,' she told the faithful beagle, taking a big bite.

Chapter Three

After Nancy had closed the bookshop for the night, she walked with Charlie to the village green. Jane had left earlier to start cooking dinner at their cottage. Nancy watched as the beagle took off across the field, running joyfully after a day in the shop. They came to the green twice a day; he loved the space and it always cheered Nancy to see the dog so happy. The evening was bitterly cold so she kept moving to try to not freeze to death, throwing a ball for him, and thinking longingly of getting home for warmth and food. She turned to look at the village behind them, the wind whipping fiercely around her. At least the snow had abated for now.

A family waved to her as they walked past. Nancy knew pretty much everyone in their village, and everyone knew her. She adored Dedley End with its cobbled streets, stone walls and the rolling green countryside that framed it all and had never imagined living anywhere else – although she did wish that sometimes there could be a bit more excitement to be had there. Which was why there was a definite spring to her step since receiving the invitation to the Roth party. She was pleased for her gran too. They always needed a pick-me-up without their loved ones at this time of year. Not only had they lost Nancy's father, George, but her mother had left years ago. And Jane's husband had long since passed away too, so it was now just the two of them.

George Hunter had died when Nancy was just ten years old so her memories of him were fuzzy. He had named her after Nancy Drew and as an avid fan of mysteries, had instilled a love of books in her from a very early age. Jane always told her that she was so much like him, and that made her happy, as did looking after the bookshop, which had been his pride and joy.

Her mother, Samantha, had walked out when she was only six, leaving her father a note to say she couldn't cope with family life so Nancy didn't remember much about her at all. Her mother's image came from the few photographs Jane had of her. If Nancy was honest, she didn't try to remember that much about her. It only caused her pain to think of the woman who had made the decision to leave her daughter behind.

'Come on, Charlie, let's get some food,' she called out to the beagle, her nose now completely numb. Charlie came obediently and they set off down the road towards the cottage they shared with Jane. It stood at the edge of the village with a view of the green, opposite the church. It had been built in the eighteenth century and Nancy loved it fiercely even though it was draughty in winter and the roof occasionally leaked. She had lived there since she was ten apart from three years studying English Literature at university in Bath, where she had met her ex, Richard. Richard had wanted them to move to London together after graduation but how could she have abandoned both her grandmother and her father's bookshop? Richard had gone without her in the end, and she had returned home to Dedley End and had been there ever since.

'We're home!' Nancy called out as she let herself in, Charlie running eagerly ahead, smiling at the warmth and delicious smell of food that greeted her.

'In here!' Jane called back from the kitchen.

Nancy hung up her coat and took off her boots, put her bag down on the stairs, and went in to see her. Her grandmother was stirring a big pot on the cooker and Charlie was furiously drinking from his water bowl. 'I'm absolutely frozen.'

'Sit down and I'll bring over the food, you'll soon warm up.'

Jane was a brilliant cook and Nancy's stomach rumbled as she sat at the small pine table in the kitchen where they ate their meals. Jane gave Charlie his dinner then dished up two bowls of stew, mash and veg for herself and Nancy. Nancy poured them both a gin and tonic, their tipple of choice, and they tucked in happily.

'Jonathan was asking earlier about why the Roths stopped associating with the village all those years ago? I couldn't quite remember the whole story,' Nancy said when she felt warm enough to talk. Charlie finished his food then disappeared into their small lounge where a log fire burned, knowing they'd join him in there afterwards.

'The last time I went there was about thirty years ago, so before your parents met…' Jane broke off, clearing her throat. It was always a hard subject. Jane had told Nancy that her father, George, had loved his wife with all his heart and had been devastated when she left the village, never to be seen again. Nancy could never understand how anyone could walk away from their loved ones like that. Jane took a sip of her drink, then continued. 'Your grandfather and I were invited to the annual summer garden party as usual. The whole village used to be invited along every year. George came with us, too. Marcus, who is still the head of the Roth family and older than me, hosted the parties, with his wife Louisa. Everything was splendid as usual but then there was a sudden change in the atmosphere. Their butler came out and told us all that we had to go home. It was so sudden. We didn't know what was going on. Afterwards, the talk around the village was that their housekeeper had stolen a lot of money. The housekeeper was fired and disappeared from the village so I always assumed that was true. After that, the garden parties stopped.' She paused and leaned forward. 'In fact, they never invited any of us into that house again. I suppose they didn't know who to trust after that. She had been treated as one of the family and was a local woman. There were rumours that there was more to it, that Louisa Roth had health issues and her husband Marcus thought she needed peace and quiet. Which may be true as she died a few years later. Must be twenty years ago now – not long after your father actually, and she was still pretty young. Our GP back then said it had been cancer – he was a little loose-lipped down the pub sometimes but the funeral was private, of course.' Jane shrugged. 'Marcus's son went on to have two sons of his own and Maria, of course, but they all were sent to boarding school and I think most of them live in London or in their own houses now. Whatever the reason, they stick to their own kind now, you know? Social circles that none of us are part of. They stopped bothering to be involved with anything going on in the village; they even stopped using the local shops. They've never set foot inside the bookshop, for instance.'

'How strange. It seems so extreme,' Nancy said, helping herself to a second helping of creamy mash.

'Very. Who knows what's been going on in that house for all these years? But it'll be lovely to see it again. It's very grand. You'll love it. It's a house right out of a novel,' she said, her eyes twinkling at the very idea.

'That's what I hoped,' Nancy said. 'How do you even end up living in a house like that?'

'Well, the house has been in the family since Marcus's grandfather, I believe. The family obviously have inherited money but they also have an investment company, stocks and shares – buying up businesses and that sort of thing. They are definitely multi-millionaires, that's for sure. Money makes money, love, it's a rule of life.'

'Hmm, if only we knew what that was like.' They smiled though. They knew bookselling would never make them a fortune but they loved it too much to really care. 'But, seriously, what shall I wear to this party? I don't think I want to buy something for just one night. The invitation says black tie, though.' Nancy couldn't remember the last time they had got really dressed up for an occasion. Penelope's wedding three years ago perhaps.

'I'm sure I have something upstairs. Let's have a look once we're finished. We've still got some apple pie left for dessert, I'll make us some custard.'

Nancy smiled, glad she had a fast metabolism with her gran around. 'I'm so curious to see the house but also meet the family for the first time. So, Maria is Marcus Roth's granddaughter then?'

'That's right,' Jane confirmed, bringing over the apple pie. 'Gloria told me to look at the engagement announcement in the paper, and I'll be honest, she is a plain girl but I suppose when your family have millions then you're desirable to just about anyone.'

'Gran!' Nancy admonished, laughing. 'I'm sure she's a lovely girl and has found someone who really loves her.'

Jane looked sceptical. 'You may be right, but I don't suppose it was a hardship to discover what her surname was. And we'll finally get to see Lucy Roth too.'

'Who's that?' Nancy asked curiously as she tucked into her pudding, not as up-to-date on village gossip as her gran was.

'She's married to Harry Roth, the eldest of the boys. Apparently, they met in Paris when he was working over there and had a whirlwind romance before turning up at Roth Lodge married. Gloria said that by all accounts the family weren't too pleased about it. She's quite glamorous, though. I saw her driving through the village once, and she looked like a model. I bet she'll wear something stunning. We need to make sure you look the part.'

Nancy was unconvinced. She was tall and slim, yes, but could certainly never be described as glamorous. She looked down at her wool skirt and jumper and felt suddenly nervous that she'd be completely out of place at this party. Maybe she shouldn't have agreed to go after all.

Jane noticed she'd suddenly gone quiet. 'Don't you fret. You'll be the belle of the ball by the time I've finished with you.'

—

After they had eaten, they went upstairs to Jane's room, which faced the front of the cottage. Nancy's was at the back with its sloping roof, and view of their small, square garden. Nancy sat on the bed while her gran searched through her two wardrobes. She had loved fashion when she was younger and had kept all of her favourite clothes.

'I wish you weren't so much taller than me,' Jane said with a sigh. 'I'm not sure if any of these are going to work. Oh, I've had a thought.' She turned to look at Nancy. 'I mean, you might not want to wear it but it will look stunning on you.'

'What is it?'

Jane pointed to the shelf at the top of the wardrobe. 'See that box on top there? Can you reach it and bring it down?'

Nancy did as she was asked and laid the box on the bed, opening it up, and coughing a little from the dust as she did so. They both leaned over to see inside. Folded up inside was a gold dress.

'It was your mother's,' Jane said softly. 'She left it here when…' She trailed off and cleared her throat. 'So I kept it for you.'

Nancy stared at it. It was a heavy beaded gold knee-length dress, and it was beautiful. 'It was my mother's,' she repeated, unsure how to feel. She had very few of Samantha Hunter's belongings – although her mother's wedding dress was in the loft; clearly she hadn't wanted to take that when she fled their home, leaving six-year-old Nancy behind. Nancy had never seen this dress before. But she supposed she rarely asked her gran about her mother. When her dad died just four years after Samantha left them, she had hoped that her mother might turn up at the funeral, and explain why she ran away without her only child. But she hadn't.

Nancy knew that her father had tried to find her after she walked out. Jane had told her about it when she had asked but all he could find out was she had been seen getting the train to London and after that, there had been no trace. He had asked the police for help but as she'd left a note saying she was leaving, they were unable to do anything. And so Samantha Hunter had never returned to Dedley End.

When Nancy was a teenager, she made the decision not to think about the woman who so clearly didn't think about her, and refused to even wonder about where her mother might be or look for her in any way. She had googled her once a few years ago but hadn't even found a Facebook account so she had told herself to forget about her. It was pointless to dwell on the reasons why she had left; she was gone, and that was that.

It was her father's death that tortured her more. Because she had known he loved her and she had loved him too, and they had their shared love of books, and their beloved bookshop, to tie them together. And because the accident had been both a shock and a mystery. She had so many questions but very few answers.

Even though technically Nancy wasn't an orphan, she felt as if she was one. 'Would it even suit me, though?' she said, gesturing to the lovely dress.

'You'll look like a flapper in it with your bob.'

Nancy looked at her grandmother shocked. 'Excuse me?'

'Flapper,' Jane repeated more loudly. 'From the 1920s. Why, what did you think I said?'

She shook her head, deciding it was better not to answer that.

'It's up to you though, love.'

Nancy ran her fingertips over the fabric. 'Did you see her wear it?'

'Once. Your parents had a New Year's Eve party at your old house.'

Nancy had walked past it many times; it was the next road over from her gran's cottage, and it was strange to think it had housed her and her parents once upon a time. The fact she had once been part of a family of three felt like a fairy tale now.

'She was tall and slim and dark, just like you. She looked stunning in this dress, so glamorous. I remember your father looked like he'd never seen anyone so beautiful,' she said, her voice breaking a little bit.

'I can't wear it if it'll make you sad.'

'It won't, I promise. I was just feeling a little bit sentimental. I'm fine. You could wear it with your black heels and I have that gold clutch bag; that would go perfectly.'

Nancy looked at the dress. It was gorgeous. 'I just never thought I'd want anything of hers, you know?'

'I know. And sometimes I'm sentimental about things but I don't think we should be about this. It's a dress that hasn't been worn in years and you need something for this party. Let's face it; there's no time or money to buy something new. We should be practical.'

Nancy smiled. She liked looking at it like that. 'You're right, Gran. Thank you.'

Jane reached out to rub Nancy's arm. 'You have so many people who love you, never forget that.'

Nancy nodded. 'I won't.'

'Right, we're going to miss our soap if we don't get a move on.' Jane stood up to go downstairs. Nancy hesitated, but picked up the box and put it in her room before following her grandmother into the lounge, wondering if the ghosts of the past would ever really leave her.

Chapter Four

That weekend, Nancy and Jane walked to the one and only pub in the village as they always did for Sunday lunch, the only day they allowed themselves not to open up the bookshop. Once a week they treated themselves to a roast dinner at the White Swan, a thatched-roofed white building at the top of the High Street. No one was quite sure how it came by its name as they were nowhere near the river. Walking inside the warm pub, where a log fire crackled, they went over to the table always reserved for them by the window where Jonathan and Penelope already sat.

Nancy stopped at the bar to get her and Jane a drink and then she joined them, passing her gran a G & T, waving at Jonathan who was nursing his beer, and giving Penelope a kiss on the cheek before sitting down. She slipped out of her tweed coat and took a sip of her own drink, her cheeks warming up almost instantly.

'This drink is so needed,' Penelope said, gesturing to her wine, her blonde hair bouncing in its ponytail. 'Kitty hasn't slept well this week and I'm exhausted. It's horrible to say, I know, but I'm glad of the break today.' Penelope Gordon had been at school with Nancy and Jonathan and helped out part-time at the bookshop in between looking after her little girl. Kitty spent Sundays with her grandparents when her dad was away. He worked in the army and was currently abroad so his parents helped out to give Penelope a rest once a week. This meant she could often join them for lunch. Jonathan never needed an excuse to come into the White Swan so almost every week he sat with them too.

'Of course you do, don't be silly,' Nancy assured her. Nancy always admired how stoically Pen dealt with her husband being away so much. She was still the same fast-talking, petite blonde with sparkling blue eyes as she had been at school. Nancy had always envied her small stature. They had first become friends when a group of kids had been teasing Nancy about her height at the start of primary school.

'Can you help me?' Penelope had called over. Nancy had looked up to see a trainer on top of the wall nearby. 'My shoe is up there and you're the only one who can reach it. None of these boys are tall enough.' The boys had shut up when Nancy had got it down for her. 'I wish I could grow as big as you,' Penelope had said. 'You must feel so lucky.'

Nancy had never felt that way but that was Pen all over — optimistic and positive, even now all these years later. They had become friends instantly then and she'd introduced Penelope and Jonathan to one another; he had lived across the road to her when she lived with her parents. Despite him being a couple of years older than them, which as kids had seemed like such a big gap, and them all being so different to one another, the three of them had always been close.

'Thanks, Nancy. And once I've finished this wine and eaten a massive roast, I'll be ready to face another week, I'm sure.' She smiled brightly. 'Enough about me though, you need to tell me all about this Roth party that everyone is talking about. I'm not going to lie, I'm pretty jealous that you all get to put on your glad rags and mingle with society's finest.'

'Well, Jonathan will be there, don't forget,' Nancy couldn't resist saying.

'Hey, I'll have you know I scrub up very well,' he protested.

'I'm looking forward to seeing the house again. I wonder how much it's changed,' Jane said, ignoring their exchange as she often did. Their banter was well practised after all these years.

'I'm a little nervous though, I've never been anywhere that fancy,' Nancy admitted to them.

'Oh, you'll be fine! Think of all the people-watching you'll be able to do,' Penelope said with envy.

'And you will look stunning in your dress,' her grand-mother added. 'I would mostly be worried about Jonathan showing us up.'

'Why are you all picking on me?' he cried as they all laughed. 'You just wait, James Bond will have nothing on me in my tux.'

'I never thought I'd ever see you wear one,' Nancy told him. She was finding it very hard to picture. She had decided to wear her mother's dress. There really wasn't anything else and she was trying to look at it as just a piece of clothing and not part of the woman who ran away, but it wasn't going to be easy.

The waitress came over then and they all ordered their roast dinners. The pub had filled up now with people coming in for the famous roasts. Nancy recognised most of the people in there – without tourists visiting it was full of local families, and the atmosphere was cosy and cheerful, especially as it was now December, and Christmas was on the horizon.

The door opened and Nancy watched as a man and woman walked inside, and hurried over to a reserved table in the corner. He was wearing a suit, and she a smart dress, which was pretty rare in the White Swan. 'Do you know them?' she asked the others in a low voice, as she didn't recognise them.

Penelope glanced over. 'Isn't that one of the Roth grandsons? I saw him once at the bank in Woodley.'

Jane nodded. 'Yes, that's Will. Marcus Roth's younger grandson,' she said.

Nancy looked again. She knew that he was a couple of years older like Jonathan as his sister Maria, the one getting engaged, was the same age as her and Pen. She thought he looked rather handsome, with his tousled dark hair and smart suit. 'Is that his wife with him, then?' Nancy couldn't help but be struck by her. She was stunning with long, dark hair waving over her shoulders, and bright red lipstick. They ordered two drinks and once alone, leaned in close to talk.

'I don't think he's married,' her gran replied, looking over again. 'You know what? I think that's Lucy Roth. Remember the photo of their wedding in your paper?' she checked with Jonathan.

'You're right,' Jonathan confirmed after he'd taken a look himself. 'Harry married her in France after a whirl-wind romance. They sent in the announcement via email with a photo so we didn't get a personal quote from the family at all.'

'She's so pretty,' Nancy said, thinking the woman looked as if she would fit in well in Paris. 'They look like they're having a serious conversation,' she added. The pair of them were still talking in low voices, heads close together.

Penelope gasped. 'Maybe they're having an affair! You can find out on Friday. See if they look too friendly at the party.'

Jonathan rolled his eyes. 'Only you would jump from two people having a drink in a pub to *that*,' he said.

Then, they heard raised voices. Glancing back, they saw now that Lucy was gesturing with her hands as she spoke, clearly becoming heated about something. Will Roth seemed to be trying to calm her down and reached out but she shook his hand off, and jumped up.

'I will not stay here and listen to this any further,' the woman cried out then, in a cut-glass accent, her tone as chilly as ice. 'I shall try to forget this ever happened,' she added before turning on her heels, and storming out of the pub, her head held high.

Nancy's table wasn't the only one watching them by this point. Will Roth seemed to notice then that there were eyes on him, and he stood up too, flinging money down on the table, and hurrying out after her, his cheeks clearly pink.

'Well, what do you make of it now?' Penelope asked Jonathan pointedly.

'I really don't know,' he replied. 'That was quite a show, though.'

'Certainly not what we've come to expect from that family. I've never seen any of them act like that in public,' Jane said, looking shocked.

'I don't remember even seeing any of them in here before at all,' Nancy added. 'How interesting. Maybe you're right, Pen and we should keep an eye on them at the party.'

'See? I told you I'd be able to dig up a scandal,' Jonathan said, pulling out his phone to make a note. 'There's a story there, mark my words.'

Their roast dinners arrived then, putting an end to their speculation as they tucked in but Jonathan's words echoed in Nancy's mind. She was inclined to think he was right.

The party really couldn't come soon enough.

Chapter Five

The day of the party dawned crisp and dry, much to Nancy's relief. Her bob had a tendency to turn frizzy in the rain. As she hadn't had an occasion to dress up for a long time, she took her time, having a long soak in the bath first. She finally had an occasion to wear the red lipstick her grandmother had given her for her last birthday, and flicked her eyes with liner. She straightened her bob and added a gold clip to one side, and then spritzed herself with perfume. Pulling on her mother's old dress, and stepping into the only pair of heels she owned, Nancy stood in front of her full-length mirror.

She had to admit that she did feel pretty in the dress, and as she'd never seen Samantha in it, it didn't remind her of her mother. She was glad her gran had encouraged her to wear it; it made her legs look more shapely than usual and it fitted her slim figure well. She wondered for a moment what Samantha Hunter had looked like in it at the New Year's Eve party her gran had said she'd worn it to but it was impossible to imagine. She only had old photos of her mother and hadn't looked at them in a long time. Nancy knew though that she looked far more like her father anyway.

She turned from the mirror, determined to make the most of this party and have fun. She picked up her clutch bag and threw on a smile before heading downstairs, not about to let thoughts of things lost prevent her from enjoying the here and now.

Her grandmother was ready and waiting in their small hallway, wearing a black sparkly pleated skirt and matching blouse, her grey hair tucked neatly behind her ears, a black fake fur coat wrapped over her shoulders. 'Oh love, you look stunning,' Jane said, breaking into a smile. 'Just perfect.'

'You look lovely, Gran,' Nancy replied, pleased, pulling on her coat. She peeped into the lounge to check Charlie was okay – he was fast asleep in his basket after his long walk earlier and large dinner.

The doorbell rang. 'There's Jonathan then. Let's get going.' Jane opened the door to a suited and booted Jonathan. Nancy noted he had combed his hair, and polished his shoes too.

Jonathan whistled. 'Well, Nancy and Mrs H, you both look gorgeous! That dress is stunning, Nancy!' he said with a grin, stepping back to let them come outside.

'No need to sound so surprised,' Nancy replied but she was pleased he had noticed the effort she had made. She locked the cottage behind them.

'What about me?' he said, gesturing down to his shiny shoes.

'You scrub up better than I thought,' she replied.

'Well, there's a backhanded compliment if I've ever heard one but I'll take it. Come on or we'll be late,' he said, waving them forwards. They climbed into the waiting taxi, and drove towards the house on the hill.

The village rolled past the window, the stars above bright and twinkling in the clear, inky black sky. As the taxi drew near, the road became a lot busier; people were walking to the house from the village or taking taxis like them but there were also limos and all sorts of fancy cars. Even their driver whistled at the sight. They drove through the large, imposing iron gates that were usually kept shut, up to the grand house. Roth Lodge sat high above the village, a large, elegant stone building with ivy climbing over much of the front. Tonight, the white door was thrown open and people decked out in their finest were passing through into a hallway filled with light.

'Here we go, then,' Jonathan said when the taxi pulled up to a stop. He helped Jane to climb out, paid the driver and moved around to Nancy's side but she was already standing, and chuckled at him. 'I'm just trying to be a gentleman,' he said, holding out his arm for her and Jane.

'When that happens, hell will freeze over,' she said cheerfully but took his arm as she was wearing heels after all. Her gran was on his other side and they walked forward together. Nancy looked up at the Victorian mansion, brightly lit, towering above them on the hill, hearing music inside, and a thrill ran down her spine. Her grandmother had been right – she felt as if she had stepped into a novel.

They walked up to the brightly lit open doorway where a man wearing black and white was checking invitations. When he nodded at theirs, they wandered into a vast reception hall. Nancy tried not to gasp as she took in the black and white chessboard stone floor beneath her. A grand piano stood to one side and was being played by a man dressed in a tux. Then she looked up to see an ornate ironwork balustrade ringing the first floor, looking out onto the space below. A dazzling chandelier hung from the ceiling above it, casting a kaleidoscope of light down on them. Nancy could hardly believe her eyes.

A woman dressed in black and white stepped forward then and slipped Nancy's coat from her shoulders, gesturing to the door ahead, thrown open into a formal reception room full of party guests.

As they continued on into the drawing room, another server wearing black and white immediately came up to them with a tray of champagne, and each of them took a glass.

The drawing room itself was long and narrow with a high, ornate ceiling, and the same chessboard flooring as the hall. Another chandelier sparkled above them. At the opposite end of the room to where they had entered, was another door that Nancy could just see opened to reveal the first-floor staircase. Nancy eagerly drank in the scene – the people milling around, their laughter ringing out merrily, looking so glamorous in their cocktail dresses and tuxedos. Champagne corks popped and servers milled around dishing out drinks and canapés. It felt like a fantasy to Nancy.

'Hello all!' They were greeted by a voice behind them. They turned to see Dedley End's vicar, Reverend Williams and his wife Gloria. 'What a party, eh?' Despite living in the Cotswolds for almost forty years, he had a Jamaican twang to his accent, which everyone enjoyed when listening to his sermons. He was wearing his dog collar tonight and Gloria wore a blue satin dress. She leaned in to greet Jane with a kiss. There wasn't anything that happened in Dedley End without either Jane or Gloria knowing about it.

'It's like nothing I've ever been to,' Jonathan agreed, pulling out his iPhone to take a couple of snaps.

Nancy saw him trying to do it discreetly so no one caught on to the real reason he was there; she hoped they wouldn't get thrown out. She nudged him as a startling red dress caught her eye. They moved slightly away from the others. 'Look, there's Lucy Roth.'

Jonathan followed her gaze. Lucy was standing with two other women, and she looked no less than mesmerising in a red silk dress, with her long black hair curled down her back. Her lips were the same colour as her dress, and she was smiling at something one of the other women was saying. 'She really is attractive. There's Harry, her husband. Let's face it, she can't be with him for his looks,' he said.

Nancy gave Harry a glance; he definitely didn't match his wife in looks but Nancy was sure there must be something special about him. She was secretly a romantic, not that she'd admit that to Jonathan. 'I wonder what she and Will were talking about. Can you see him?'

'Not yet,' he replied, looking around. 'Let's have a selfie,' he suggested, turning to face her. 'While we look this good,' he added with a grin.

'You can't take a selfie here,' she admonished him, certain that would be on the list of uncouth things to do.

'If I take the photo then it's not a selfie,' a smooth, cultured voice said from behind them. They turned to see Will Roth holding his hand out. Surprised, Jonathan handed over his phone and Will took a photo of them, champagne in hand, the fireplace behind them, hasty smiles arranged on their faces. 'I'm Will Roth,' he said, giving the phone back to Jonathan then holding out a hand for him to shake. He had a very charming smile. His floppy hair reminded Nancy of Hugh Grant in the nineties and he was wearing a tux that looked as if it had been made just for him. Which was highly likely considering the money the family had, she realised. 'And you two are...?' he asked, his accent as posh as his sister-in-law's.

'Nancy Hunter,' she replied when he turned to shake her hand. 'This is my friend, Jonathan Murphy.'

'I haven't seen you here before, are you one of the village guests?' Will asked her.

'Yes, I'm not usually invited to this sort of thing,' she replied with a smile, taking a quick sip of her drink for fortification.

'What do you do then, Miss Hunter?'

'I run the village bookshop with my grandmother,' she said, gesturing to Jane a few feet away still chatting with the vicar and his wife.

'Doesn't everyone just use Amazon nowadays?'

Nancy didn't care that it was his house; she wasn't going to let anyone get away with that. 'What rubbish! Of course not. Can Amazon give you personal recommendations? Or help you find the perfect gift for a loved one? Besides, our bookshop sells only crime, thrillers and mysteries so we don't only have the well-known titles but hidden gems, forgotten classics, out of print stories – anything you could ever want, really,' she replied hotly.

Will stared at her for a moment, then threw his head back and laughed. 'I have never been put in my place so superbly. Come on, I must introduce you to my family.' With an arm firmly around her waist, Will steered Nancy towards a group standing close to the fireplace. She looked over her shoulder in panic at Jonathan who narrowed his eyes but followed quickly, hoping no doubt for something he could use in the newspaper.

'Everyone, this delightful creature is Nancy Hunter, our local bookseller, and her friend, Jonathan Murphy,'

Will Roth said to them. 'And this is my mother, Jessica, my father, Peter, and my grandfather, Marcus Roth.'

'How do you do? You have a stunning home,' Nancy said.

Peter Roth was dark-haired like his sons, and was what Nancy supposed might be called 'dashing'; his wife was an attractive redhead in a long, black dress. Both were clearly unimpressed to be forced to meet them.

'I know your name,' Peter said shortly to Jonathan. 'You're press.'

'We made it clear that we didn't want reporters,' Jessica began angrily until Marcus laid a hand on his daughter-in-law's arm and she stopped speaking.

'I assume Jonathan is here as Nancy's plus one,' he said. 'So, I'm sure he won't be working tonight, am I correct?'

Jonathan hastily put his iPhone away and nodded, looking terrified. Marcus turned to Nancy with a warm smile. She knew he was older than her grandmother – she guessed he was in his seventies – and had salt and pepper hair but still had a handsome face and, like the other men in his family, wore a crisp, tailored dinner jacket. 'My dear, I have heard of your bookshop, of course. It's always wonderful to see a local business do well. My wife Louisa would have loved it, she was an avid reader. We have a library here, of course, and it was her pride and joy.'

'I would love to see it,' Nancy said eagerly.

'Maria will be arriving any minute. I really don't think—' Jessica began again in her haughty tone, turning to Marcus.

'I'll show you,' he interrupted his daughter-in-law again. 'This way,' he said.

'I'll be circulating,' Jonathan called after her retreating back, walking quickly away from the group as Marcus whisked her out of the drawing room, giving her no chance to resist. They walked back into the chessboard-floored hallway, now empty, crossed it and entered double doors opposite the drawing room.

'This is actually rather fortuitous,' Marcus said. 'My wife, as I said, curated our library and to be honest, since her death the room has been rather neglected.' Despite his age, Marcus walked briskly and Nancy was glad of her long legs as she kept up with him. He pushed open the heavy doors to reveal the long, narrow library. Nancy couldn't contain her gasp of pleasure as she walked into the room filled with books, two leather armchairs by the fireplace in the centre of the room, large French windows at the other end looking out to the vast garden.

'What a wonderful room,' she said, walking to the shelves. Mrs Roth had certainly built up a marvellous collection of hardback books.

'I haven't bought anything new for a long time,' Marcus told her. 'I should try to sort it out for future generations. The family keep telling me to but I wouldn't know where to start.'

The books did indeed all look pretty dated and dusty to Nancy's eye. 'I would be delighted to offer any help,' she said, twirling to look at the other side of the room. 'If you ever did want to update the collection.'

Marcus clapped his hands. 'What a perfect idea! Let's arrange for you to cast your professional eye over the books without delay and you can tell me what we need to order. Monday, maybe? Are you free?'

Before she could respond, a voice made them turn in surprise. 'Come on, you two bookworms,' Will Roth said, suddenly appearing in the doorway, smirking at them. 'Mum and Dad are having kittens – they want to start the speeches. The couple have finally finished having their photos taken upstairs and are about to make their grand entrance.' He rolled his eyes.

'Ah, well, I'd better go back, then. Let me know about Monday though, Miss Hunter.' Marcus hurried out of the room. Nancy could barely believe her luck – she would not only get a chance to return to Roth Lodge and look at all the books they had, but the Roths might very well become customers, too.

'You look like the cat who got the cream,' Will remarked as she walked out with him.

'There is nothing like books to put a smile on your face.'

'I'll take your word for that. Personally, I prefer a stiff whisky.'

Chapter Six

Nancy and Will walked into the path of Lucy Roth then, who stood in the middle of the hallway, hand on her hip, eyes narrowed, watching them walk towards her. 'What are you up to, Will?' she asked, somewhat haughtily.

'The couple of the night have finally finished taking pictures upstairs and are ready to make their grand entrance. So, we've all been summoned into the drawing room,' Will told her, cheerfully.

Lucy sighed with barely concealed annoyance, her eyes roaming over Nancy, who was watching their exchange with interest. 'That's a stunning dress.'

'Thank you,' Nancy replied. 'I love yours, too. I've always worried red is too daring for me.'

'You should never worry about that,' Lucy said in a softer tone. 'You should always wear a dress, not the other way around.' She glanced at Will. 'I need to get something upstairs if anyone asks,' she told him, coldly, before spinning on her heels and hurrying across the hallway into the drawing room, disappearing from their view.

Will watched her go, shaking his head. 'That'll go down like a lead balloon.'

'Oh really, why?'

'Let's just say, Lucy hasn't exactly fitted into this family,' he replied, darkly. He turned back to Nancy. 'You can find your way now, can't you? I need to locate my aunt,' he said, walking off across the hallway in the other direction to Lucy, past the front door where they had all entered the house, and down a corridor where Nancy supposed the kitchen might be.

Nancy was intrigued by the conversation between Lucy and Will. It had appeared frosty, making her think that perhaps their row in the pub stemmed from dislike and not an affair, as Penelope had thought it might be. She wondered why Will, who appeared friendly and charming, had taken against Lucy, or vice versa. Her curiosity was most definitely piqued by them.

As Nancy crossed the stone floor to the drawing room, something in her peripheral vision caught her eye. She looked upwards to see Lucy leaning over the first-floor railing, looking lost in thought. She made a somewhat lonely figure, if stunning with it. Nancy smiled but Lucy didn't see her, so she continued on into the drawing room wondering what Lucy could be thinking about.

She thought about what Will had said about Lucy not fitting in. The Roths had closed ranks for a long time, it perhaps wasn't a stretch to think they may not have welcomed a newcomer with open arms. Nancy hoped Lucy was okay and vowed to try to speak to her again later. Perhaps she could try to befriend her – after all, she had been invited back to look at the library so their paths might very well cross again.

Once back in the drawing room, Nancy searched for the others. She spotted Jonathan who waved from the middle of the room where he was standing with her grandmother. She weaved through the guests to reach them, and took the glass of champagne Jonathan offered her.

'Marcus Roth asked if I might look at their library and order them in some new books, as they haven't updated their collection in years,' she said to her grandmother.

'Oh how wonderful,' Jane replied. 'I bet they have some rare books, what luck.'

'I know, I can't wait to see. He said something about me coming over on Monday but I don't know, it feels too good to be true after they've kept away from us for so long. So, have you given up reporting on the party?' she asked Jonathan.

'Of course not. I'm keeping my ear to the ground and I've managed a few photos, enough to put together a news story – whether the family like it or not.'

'Well, make sure you don't burn our bridges,' Jane scolded him. 'If the family become our customers, it'll do wonders for the business.'

Will Roth suddenly appeared beside them then so they stopped talking. Nancy assumed he had come in through the hallway door behind her. Nancy looked around but couldn't see any of the other members of the Roth family in the room. Will stopped a server and took two glasses of champagne from his tray. He drained one in seconds and gave the server back the empty glass and then sipped the second one. He shrugged when he saw Nancy looking. She was about to ask him if anything was wrong when a man in a black and white uniform stepped forward and cleared his throat. The room slowly fell into silence. 'May I announce Maria Roth and her fiancé, Charles Taylor,' he said, grandly, stepping back to allow the couple to enter from the door at the other end of the drawing room arm-in-arm, their smiles dazzling.

Maria looked a lot like her mother, Jessica, with auburn curls to her shoulder and porcelain skin, and wore a sparkling silver dress. Her fiancé was tall with thinning hair but he had warm, dark eyes.

'Oh, how lovely,' Jane murmured.

'My sister,' Will said in a low voice, 'has finally found someone stupid enough to marry into this family.'

Nancy raised an eyebrow. 'What's wrong with your family?'

He smiled but it didn't reach his eyes. 'How long have you got?'

Nancy and Jonathan exchanged an intrigued look. Before Nancy could ask him any more though, Harry walked through the same door the couple had come in with his grandfather Marcus Roth, greeting the beaming couple. Then, moments later, Jessica Roth swept into the room as well. Another woman followed her, smaller and dowdier than the rest, her hair in a tight bun, and then Peter Roth came in, striding as briskly as his father had with Nancy.

'My aunt,' Will whispered, seeing Nancy looking at her. 'Where's Lucy? Still powdering her nose?' he asked, looking behind them, craning his neck. Nancy did the same but the glamorous woman was nowhere to be seen. 'They won't forget this,' he said with a sigh, turning back.

'Why doesn't she get on with your family?' Nancy asked him, curiously. Jonathan leaned in closer to listen.

Will shrugged. 'No one was happy that my dear brother married a girl they hadn't pre-approved.' He swigged his champagne glass dry, looking pretty indifferent about it all. Nancy wondered if that was what their row in the pub had been about – her marriage to Harry and the fact that his family weren't happy about it. Was Will trying to get Lucy to leave? Before she could probe any further, Will turned to greet someone.

'Oh hey there, Bank, glad you could make it,' Will said then, shaking the hand of a tall, blond man. 'Not seen you at the club for a while.'

'Been working flat out on a new account,' a Danish-accented voice replied. The voice jolted Nancy. She looked slowly up although she already knew who it was – that voice was far too familiar. When she lifted her face, she was met with bright blue eyes staring back at her.

'Nancy, is that really you?'

She could barely stutter a response before he leaned in to kiss her cheek, enveloping her in a cloud of his musky aftershave – aftershave she had once bought him.

'What are you doing here?' he asked.

'You two know each other?' Will asked, watching their exchange with interest.

'Old flames,' Jonathan replied, taking a long swig of his champagne. Nancy couldn't miss the bite to his words but her gaze was fixed on Richard's. Richard Bank – her university boyfriend and the only man she'd ever loved.

'Well, we didn't think you'd ever come back to Dedley End,' Jane tutted at him, arching an eyebrow.

'Will and I have done some business together in London,' Richard explained, seemingly oblivious to the hostility from Jonathan and Jane, smiling down at Nancy. 'I hoped you'd be here,' he added softly. Nancy couldn't help but smile back.

The sound of clinking glass drew their attention to the front of the room. Nancy was relieved that Richard moved his gaze away from her; she had forgotten how piercing those blue eyes of his were. She glanced at him, though. He was still handsome with his floppy hair and designer stubble, his tailor-made suit and the way that he was one of the few people in the room taller than her.

She looked away, forcing herself to focus on the speech. She sucked in a deep breath and tried not to notice her grandmother giving her a concerned look or Jonathan glaring at Richard's back. She wondered how well Will knew her ex, who was still standing too close for comfort. She hadn't seen Richard for five years, since they'd left Bath University and parted. It was most unsettling to see him again. He must have known she'd be here. Why had he come to Dedley End after all this time? And why was seeing him again making her heart race so much?

'Shouldn't you be up there too?' Jonathan asked Will. Will just grinned in response. Nancy really wasn't sure what to make of the youngest of the Roth family.

'Shh you lot,' her grandmother hissed. A dutiful silence descended over the room as the Roth family faced them – Marcus the head, his son Peter and his wife Jessica to one side of him, and to the other the happy couple, his granddaughter Maria and her fiancé Charles, with Harry on the other side of them, frowning at the room, perhaps looking for his wife. He was shorter and fairer-haired than his brother, a little on the stocky side, not as handsome, but just as smartly attired. And then there was the aunt, who had stepped back from the group a little, and looked somewhat out of place. Lucy and Will were the only family members not at the front of the room. Nancy wondered if the others had realised that they were missing or not. Or if they cared. Their family dynamic felt rather strange to her.

'Welcome, everyone,' Marcus Roth said, his deep voice commanding the room instantly. Despite his intimidating appearance, there was a softness to his eyes and smile that Nancy liked. She had already warmed to him. His fondness for books had made a strong case in his favour.

'I am delighted to welcome you all here to celebrate the engagement of my beloved granddaughter, Maria.' There was a scattering of polite applause. 'Maria and Charles have been together for a long time now and I think we all know that they are perfect for one another. We were delighted when Charles asked Maria to marry him, and we are all looking forward to welcoming him to the family. They are very touched that so many of you came out here tonight to toast their engagement with us.'

'As if we had any choice,' Will muttered next to Nancy. He reached for another glass of champagne from a waiter's tray. 'At least I can be back in London tomorrow.'

Nancy shook her head at him, unsure if he was joking or not, as Marcus continued speaking. Will definitely had a cheeky charm about him; she was sure he had the gift of the gab. Could he have charmed his sister-in-law then? But he seemed firm about his intention to get out of the house and back to London, which would take him away from Lucy. Nancy thought that Pen's idea about them having an affair was looking less and less likely, which made the possibility of Jonathan uncovering a scandal tonight extremely uncertain.

'We are looking forward to the wedding this summer, which I am told will be the event of the year,' Marcus continued. There was some polite laughter at that. 'Anyway, my dear, late wife always told me that my speeches went on far too long so I will leave it there. All that remains is for us to raise our glasses to the happy couple and wish them a lifetime of joy. To Maria and Charles!'

The room echoed the toast, everyone reaching for a sip of champagne. Nancy followed suit, thinking that she was starting to become a little light-headed already.

'Excuse me, I'll find you in a minute, I need to speak to my boss,' Richard said to Nancy then, hurrying through the crowd and disappearing into the sea of suits and glamourous dresses. She felt her shoulders sag as if they had been filled with tension – which they likely had after seeing him again.

'Well, that was unexpected,' Jonathan said. 'What was old Richard Bank doing here?'

Will looked surprised. 'Our family business works with his company, they look after our accounts, and we frequent the same club in London. How do you all know him, then?'

All eyes turned to Nancy and she felt herself blush. She opened her mouth, unsure quite how to explain, when a piercing scream cut through the room.

Conversations paused as people looked around, confused. Nancy wondered if they had imagined the sound but then a second scream rang out, sounding louder than the first in the hushed room. It was so chilling that the hairs on Nancy's arms instantly stood on end. Jane gasped beside her in shock. When Nancy looked at him, Jonathan's eyes were wide.

Everyone turned around. The scream had definitely come from the hallway. It took a second and then everyone started moving in unison towards the door.

Nancy felt Jonathan reach for her hand, and pull her along. She looked behind her but lost sight of her gran in the rush. She hurried after Jonathan, hardly having time to even guess what could be the matter.

It was soon tragically clear.

Nancy stopped, frozen on the stone floor as people crowded around, their faces draining of colour when they saw what had happened. Jonathan moved to the edge to get closer. And then she felt a hand on her shoulder and was startled to see Richard behind her, shaking his head gravely. She was glad of his support though; her knees suddenly felt unsteady as she surveyed the scene, unable to quite believe what she was seeing.

'No!' a man's voice cried out behind them.

Nancy watched as Harry Roth pushed past people to get to the front. She followed his gaze, moving from the waitress, her hands covering her face in horror, clearly the source of the screams, to the sight a few feet away. His mouth fell open and he sank down to his knees, not caring about the cold, hard floor. He let out a moan that sent shivers down Nancy's spine.

She looked up to the railings where she had seen the stunning woman in the red dress just a while ago and then she moved her eyes slowly down. She blinked but it was still there. It wasn't a nightmare; it was really happening.

Lying on the stone in the middle of the hallway, in striking contrast to the black and white chessboard floor beneath, her red dress billowing out around her and a pool of blood seeping slowly from her head across the floor, was the lifeless body of Lucy Roth.

Chapter Seven

'Are you okay, Gran?' Nancy was relieved to have finally found Jane after the past few minutes of confusion in the house. Once Lucy's body had been discovered, the main lights went on, the music stopped, the guests were ushered back into the drawing room by the serving staff, and the police and an ambulance were called. When Nancy had turned around, Richard had disappeared again and she couldn't see Jonathan anywhere so she had gone into the drawing room and found Jane sitting down at the edge of the room. The Roth family had all stayed in the hallway with… well, the body. Nancy still couldn't believe that Lucy was dead. She had watched as Harry had crouched over the body of his wife until his father and grandfather had pulled him back. She didn't think she'd ever forget the look of devastation on his face.

'I think so, what a shock,' her grandmother replied.

'It really was.' Nancy rubbed her arm and Jane smiled up at her gratefully. Nancy saw Maria walk past them, clinging to her fiancé, and heard her hiss, 'I can't believe our party has been ruined like this!'

Nancy had to force herself not to gape openly at such an unfeeling comment. Charles was shushing her, evidently feeling much the same about her statement as Nancy did. She stood on her tiptoes to see what was happening out in the hallway but it was impossible. Servers moved around offering tea, biscuits, and brandy for those in shock.

'There you both are,' Jonathan said, finding them then. Nancy was relieved to see him. 'I just phoned my editor, Tony, and we've put up a news alert on the website. He wants me to try to get some quotes from the family or the police.'

'Do you think she could have fallen?' Nancy asked him in a low voice. She knew deep in her bones that was impossible but she clung to some hope. She couldn't get the vision of Lucy leaning on the balcony railings earlier from her head.

Jonathan shook his head. 'Not over that railing, no. Did you see how tall it is? Plus, you can't stand on the railing so she couldn't have – well, jumped, either.'

'I saw her leaning up there,' Nancy said. 'So, did someone just come up behind her and...' She trailed off, unable to finish. It was a sheer drop down to the hallway, and given that stone floor, she hadn't stood a chance of surviving.

'They must have done. This is a murder, mark my words. I can't believe my luck.'

Nancy stared at him. 'What?'

He caught her gaze and shrugged. 'I'm sorry for her, of course I am, but this is my chance finally to get Tony to take me seriously. No more parties and fluff, I can finally write a serious news piece and he'll have to let me as I was the only reporter here when it happened.'

'Honestly, Jonathan, thinking of yourself at a time like this,' Jane scolded him. 'What about the poor family?'

'They didn't look too upset, just shocked if you ask me. Apart from Harry, anyway.'

'Why wouldn't they be upset? Oh, the police have arrived,' Jane said as they all turned to see the police moving in. Jonathan held up his phone to take a photo. Nancy tried to feel angry at him for thinking of himself at a time like this, but she knew how passionate he was about his career and it was so unexpected for something like this to happen in Dedley End, she couldn't really blame him for seizing the opportunity. 'You wondered if you'd uncover a Roth scandal,' she said to him.

'I certainly didn't think we'd get anything as good as this. So, Nancy...' He leaned in closer. 'Who have you got your eye on? I know you don't miss anything.'

She smiled at this attempt at flattery and thought of all the mystery novels she had devoured in her life. 'I hardly know. I mean, it's usually someone close to the victim, isn't it?'

Jonathan nodded. 'The family must be the prime suspects, right? Harry's sudden marriage to Lucy didn't go down well by all accounts, and now look at the result of it.'

'It could be anyone here, though,' she reminded him.

'Although hardly anyone here has set foot in this house for years, and none of us had even met Lucy,' Jonathan said.

Nancy had to admit that was a good point. Certainly no one in the village would have cause to hurt Lucy as they hadn't known her. She knew there were business associates at the party, like Richard, and presumably family friends but they were a reclusive lot after all. She pictured the family she had just met and tried to see one of them as a murderer but it was impossible. The Roths were wealthy and respected; had one of them really pushed Lucy to her death? And if so, then why?

'Honestly, what a morbid conversation,' Jane said to them. 'Can you see Gloria and the reverend? I wonder how close they were when it happened.' She craned her neck eagerly. Nancy looked too but couldn't see them. She also couldn't help but look for Richard. She remembered the feel of his hand on her shoulder and shivered involuntarily. Where had he got to? Maybe he was supporting the family out in the hallway?

A man cleared his throat then and conversations around them ceased. He was a tall gentleman in a grey suit with short, greying hair, and he stepped into the centre of the room, another man in a suit and a uniformed woman standing slightly behind him. 'I'm Detective Chief Inspector Brown,' he said in a commanding voice. 'Thank you all for being patient. While I speak to the family, my officers here will go around the room and take down all your details and initial statements. I ask you to continue to be patient and wait until we have done this before you leave tonight. I hope I will have your full cooperation. Thank you.' With a brisk nod, he went back into the hallway where the Roth family still congregated, away from the prying eyes of their guests, and where Lucy Roth's body lay still. Conversations started up again, a buzz running through the room now the police were there.

'See? They've brought in DCI Brown. You'd only do that for suspected murder, right? I'll call my editor and tell him,' Jonathan said, stepping into the corner.

'A murder! Right here in Dedley End, I can't believe it,' Jane said, shaking her head.

'I don't think there's ever been one in the village before. Well...' Nancy trailed off, unable to stop herself thinking about her dad. The worst thing to happen in Dedley End had always been his car crash – he'd died instantly when his car hit a tree. There had been another car on the road but the police had never found the other driver. There had only been one piece of evidence at the scene but that hadn't led anywhere. The tyre tracks had indicated that the other car had been on the wrong side of the road but the driver had failed to stop, leaving Nancy and her grandmother never knowing what really happened that night. Was it an accident? Had the other car caused Nancy's dad to crash? They had never found out. And here was another mystery. What if the police failed to solve this one, too?

'There you are.' Richard approached then. Even though there had been a murder, he looked as calm and unruffled as ever. 'I've been trying to find you. Are you both well? Mrs Hunter, do you need anything?'

Jane shivered even as she glared at him. 'I'm a little cold.'

'I'll find your coats,' he said quickly, hurrying off again.

'That's another shock, seeing him again,' Jane said. She took Nancy's hand in hers and squeezed it.

'It is,' Nancy agreed. She had thought he was long gone from her life. She couldn't believe that the night she saw him again for the first time there had been a murder. She shook her head, telling herself not to wish for more excitement in the village ever again. She shivered. Someone in the room was a killer.

'Well, what do we make of this?' Rev. Williams appeared at her elbow then, with his wife. 'What a business, what an awful business.' He had been the vicar in Dedley End ever since Nancy could remember. Her grandmother attended church every Sunday, and often had meals at the vicarage. She and Gloria had been close friends for years and the vicar and his wife were both warm and kind, and well-loved in the village. They were approaching retirement age now but Nancy tried not to think about that too much; she couldn't imagine how the village would run without them at the helm.

'My hands are shaking,' Gloria admitted.

'Here.' Nancy found another chair and pulled it over so Gloria could sit next to her grandmother. 'I wonder how long we'll have to stay? I'd like to get Gran home.'

'We can give you a lift back to the cottage when they let us go. I drove here,' the vicar replied.

'Oh, yes, thank you.'

'What a fright that scream gave me,' Jane said to her friend, putting her hand to her chest.

'Me too. What a thing to happen!'

'Do you know the family at all?' Nancy asked the vicar.

'I used to. Marcus and his wife Louisa used to attend church before they stopped coming into the village. They were a lovely couple but they've just kept to themselves for so long. Until tonight...' He trailed off. It was surely not the village comeback the family had planned.

'Lucy and Harry hadn't been married that long, had they?' Nancy asked.

'Just six months. They met in Paris. We believe that the family were all quite stunned when Harry came back from France with a bride. But Harry was madly in love with her,' Gloria told them. 'Right, darling?'

The vicar nodded. 'He really was. A dreadful business all round.'

'What did Lucy do before she met Harry?'

'Worked in a bar, apparently,' Gloria replied.

Nancy raised an eyebrow. Lucy hadn't spoken like someone who had until recently been working in a bar in

Paris. Had she affected her cut-glass accent to fit in with the Roths? It was very interesting. She had to admit she wouldn't have put Harry and Lucy together – she being so stunning, and Harry not really, but he *was* extremely rich. If Lucy had been attracted by his money, did that explain her untimely death? Had someone got her out of the way before she stole her husband's fortune?

Nancy's mind was suddenly whirring with possibilities, and then she remembered the argument they had witnessed in the pub. What if Will Roth had had something to do with this? It was hard to believe when she thought of how charming he had been with them at the party but he had seemed very hostile towards Lucy...

Richard returned then with their coats and Nancy draped hers over her shoulders, feeling chilly too. Jonathan came back after his phone call and they all looked at one another, an awkwardness settling over the group. Nancy was about to introduce the vicar and his wife to Richard when he touched her arm. 'I need to go and check on the family. I'll find you again,' he said and then disappeared once again. Nancy was about to call after him when one of the plain-clothed police officers came over. She looked at Richard's retreating back – he had been running around all night, what exactly was his role here? She was very confused. But then the whole night was disorienting. She hoped it would be over soon.

'I'm Detective Constable Pang,' the officer said, notebook at the ready. 'I need to take down your details please, and ask you what you saw tonight.' He went through the group, speaking first to the vicar and his wife who had been too far away to see anything, and then to Jane who could only describe the shocking scream that they had all heard.

'I work for the *Cotswold Star*, have you got any initial thoughts as to what happened?' Jonathan asked the constable then, holding his phone to take his own notes.

DC Pang sighed. 'No statement for the press yet. Inspector Brown will be doing that later. Can I take your details first?'

Both Jonathan and Nancy gave their names and addresses and the same account of watching Marcus's speech and then hearing the scream behind them in the hallway as Jane had.

Pang nodded when they'd finished. 'We'll be in touch if we have any further questions,' he replied, dully, moving away.

'Wait, there's something else…' Nancy began. 'Something we saw in the pub…'

'Oh, yes, Nancy, that could be important,' her grandmother agreed.

'Lucy Roth was in there with—'

'I only need to know what happened tonight,' DC Pang cut them off. 'I've got a lot of people to get through. If you think of anything else, call the station, okay?' he said, already moving away.

'Wait, are we free to go?' Nancy called after his retreating back. He gave a go-ahead gesture. 'Well, that was rude,' Nancy said when they were alone.

'Quite, love, you were trying to help,' Jane agreed.

'And it could be important. Lucy was arguing with Will, we all saw it,' Jonathan said. 'Well, looks like my news article will be more informed than the police are. But let's face it, our police haven't ever had to investigate something like this before. Let's wait until we can talk to DCI Brown,' Jonathan said. 'Mind you, not sure he's much more capable, to be honest.'

'Why don't we head off now?' Rev. Williams suggested. 'It's late and we've all had a shock. We should get some rest.'

Nancy nodded. It was clear their information would have to wait. And she was keen to get her grandmother home. She was just as tired herself – the night's events had erased all party spirit, and she longed for her bed. She glanced around for Richard as they made their way out of Roth Lodge but there was no sign of him.

It had felt like a dream seeing him again after all this time. In fact, the whole night had taken on a surreal feel to it. It was hard to shake the image of Lucy Roth's lifeless body from her mind. She was sure she'd never forget it. She glanced at the grand house once more as she followed the others outside to the vicar's car. She'd finally been granted her wish to see inside Roth Lodge and she was certain in that moment that she'd be quite happy to never see it again.

Chapter Eight

Nancy was surprised to find Jane up and about when she rose on Saturday morning. 'I'm coming to the shop with you, I don't want to be alone today,' Jane explained. 'And I don't want to miss out on anything.' Despite all that had happened, Nancy had to chuckle at her grandmother not wanting to lose out on any gossip. So, after a quick breakfast, they left the cottage with Charlie trotting along the pavement beside them. Nancy took him for a run on the green and then joined Jane in the bookshop.

'I hope it warms up in here soon,' Jane said as she brought out two mugs of hot tea and Nancy turned around the bookshop sign to 'open'.

It was a frosty morning, a layer of sparkling white covering all the surfaces outside, and Nancy could see her breath in the air when she exhaled. She switched on the heater but it always took ages to do anything. Charlie laid down in his bed in the window seat, positioning himself directly in a shaft of weak sunlight coming through the window. Nancy joined Jane behind the counter and eagerly sipped the tea her gran had made them. 'I'm so tired, I took ages to get off to sleep,' she said.

'Me too, I kept thinking about that poor girl.' Her gran shuddered. 'When I woke up this morning, I hoped it had just been a nightmare.'

'I'm afraid not. It's just so hard to take in. Did someone at the party really push her over the railings? But who was it? And why?'

'Just horrid. Maybe we shouldn't think about it.'

'I think it's all I'm going to be able to think about for a long time,' Nancy said. She felt unsettled right down to her bones.

They went about their usual first checks of the day, making sure the shop was presentable, but neither of their hearts were in it. Nancy couldn't stop wondering what was happening with the Roths. She tried to ring Jonathan but he didn't answer.

A few minutes later, though, the bell on the door sounded, and in walked Jonathan himself, looking as if he hadn't slept a wink.

'Please say there's coffee for me, I've been up half the night,' he said, flopping in the armchair, unshaven and pale, still wearing his suit from the night before, covered with his overcoat.

'Here you go.' Nancy brought him out a mug. 'Maybe you should go to bed.'

'I can't, I'm too wired.' He took a long gulp of the black coffee. Nancy could never fathom how he could drink it; she was a tea woman through and through. 'DCI Brown just released a statement confirming that they're treating Lucy Roth's death as murder. How can I possibly sleep when the most exciting thing to ever happen in Dedley End is afoot?' he asked, cheerfully.

'I wish you wouldn't look so happy about murder,' Jane said with a sigh.

'I can't believe it's really true,' Nancy said, shaking her head. 'She was murdered.'

'She was,' Jonathan confirmed. 'My post about her death has gone viral online. I can't believe I was on scene to break the news. And now the police have confirmed it was murder, my phone won't stop ringing. All the national press are on their way. The village is going to get very crowded. The Roth name is so well known, everyone wants a piece of this story.'

'You might be right about that,' Nancy said, looking out of the bookshop window.

Jonathan and Jane came over to join her. They watched as cars and people started arriving in the High Street. People were setting up cameras, the police were walking about in their uniforms, villagers stopped to watch and chat – it was the busiest the High Street had ever been in December, Nancy thought.

'Well, look what I've set in motion,' Jonathan said with a whistle.

'Blimey,' Nancy said.

'Oh my,' Jane added. They watched in silence until Jane pointed over the road. 'Look, here's Penelope.'

The bell jingled again a minute later when Penelope walked in. 'Well, what a to-do! It took me forever to find somewhere to park. Why is the village so busy? We haven't added another fete to the annual list, have we?' she asked, taking off her coat with a puzzled look. She helped out most Saturdays, as it was their busiest day of the week. She saw their faces. 'What's up?'

'You'd better grab a coffee and we'll explain,' Nancy told her. After they all had refills and Pen had a mug, they sat down and Nancy explained what had happened at the Roth party, leaving Penelope stuttering in disbelief at the news.

'Trust you all to be right at the centre of all this. God, I'm so jealous!' she said at the end.

'Penelope, the poor woman was murdered! We had to see the body and everything,' Jane admonished her. 'You're as bad as Jonathan, seeing it as his chance to get promoted.'

Jonathan shrugged. 'It's not as if I had anything to do with her death so why does it matter if I try to benefit from it? In fact, I've come to beg a favour on that score from you, Nancy.'

'Another favour? Look where the last one got us.'

'How could we have known how the party would end? Don't complain though – not only were you there to witness the first ever Dedley End murder, but don't forget you got a gig out of it, too.'

'Oh, yes,' she replied, remembering. She explained to Penelope about Marcus Roth wanting her book advice. 'I doubt he'll remember though, after what happened last night.'

'Well, I need you to make him remember,' Jonathan said. 'Think about it – how perfect would it be if you got to hang out at the house and spend time with the family? You could see if there are any clues as to who did this. Imagine if we could solve it before the police. I'd have the biggest news story of the year!'

'You think you can solve a murder before the police do?' Penelope turned to him, raising her eyebrow. 'I knew you were arrogant, Jonathan Murphy, but that takes the biscuit.'

'Nancy, help me out here. Our police have never had a murder on their hands before. Oh—' he stopped short, looking up at the picture on the wall of Nancy's dad on the bookshop's opening day. 'I'm sorry.'

Nancy sighed. 'They certainly didn't do a good job of investigating Dad's accident.'

'If it was an accident,' Jane replied darkly. She had always held the other driver who had fled the scene that night to blame. 'You have a point, Jonathan, how can we trust them to solve this murder?'

'And they certainly didn't want to listen to us tell them about the argument we witnessed in the pub last week. Remember, Pen, between Will and Lucy Roth?' Nancy said.

Penelope nodded, her eyes wide. 'Do you think Will could have killed her, then? They did look very angry with one another, didn't they?'

'I don't know but it's something to investigate, surely?'

'Especially if they were having an affair,' Penelope agreed. 'Did you get any hints last night?'

'None at all. He didn't seem to like her much at the party,' Nancy said.

'A crime of hate then, perhaps,' Jonathan mused, making a note on his phone. 'Or the husband, Harry, could have discovered the affair and killed her in a fit of rage. Or... there have been rumours she was a gold-digger – anyone in the family could have taken against her if they thought she was after the family fortune. Her marriage to Harry was a whirlwind romance, after all.' He looked up. 'Well, whatever happened, the truth is somewhere inside the house on the hill. We just have to find out what it is.'

'Do you think it could have been one of the guests and not the family?' Penelope asked then.

'We can't rule that out at the moment, I don't think,' Nancy mused. 'But hardly anyone had even met Lucy and certainly no one in Dedley End had been inside that house for so long, I wonder what the motive could have been for someone else? Will, however, indicated the family weren't particularly fond of her, and we know he had argued with her.' Nancy sighed. 'I felt sorry for Lucy last night. She looked, I don't know, kind of alone.'

'We know how the Roths shut the whole village out for years, it really wouldn't surprise me if they had done the same to Lucy too,' Jane said. 'You're right, love, I do feel like she didn't have anyone in her corner. We need to make sure that isn't the case now too.'

'But how do we do that?' Nancy questioned. 'How do we make sure she does get justice?'

'You have a solid in with the family, Nancy. It's our best place to start to try to find out who could have done this, and why. They are the people closest to her. And they're more likely to reveal something to you than the cops. You could finally put all that murder and mystery reading to good use,' Jonathan said.

'I know I do like a murder mystery, and I am named after a detective, but be serious – it's not like we can actually investigate a murder.'

'We do know a lot about murder mysteries, though,' her grandmother said then, her eyes twinkling a little. 'And if we don't trust the police to get justice for Lucy…'

'We take matters into our own hands?' Nancy finished for her. They looked at one another, uncertainly.

'You know, on second thoughts, maybe this is silly,' Jonathan said then. 'I mean, could you really find a killer? Perhaps it's ridiculous to think you can find the truth. The police, although they haven't proved themselves capable in the past, probably should just be left to deal with this. I mean, if they don't get justice for Lucy, why should it really bother us?'

'Because someone shouldn't just get away with murder!' Nancy cried. 'We know what it's like to never know the real truth, to always wonder… We can't let that happen again,' she added, fiercely.

Jonathan smirked. 'I think you should put your money where your mouth is, my dear Nancy.'

'Huh?' She stared at him, wondering why he was looking so pleased with himself.

He grinned. 'I bet you and Mrs H fifty quid that you can't find the murderer before the police do.'

'Now you're betting against us?' Nancy cried in outrage.

'Well, you said yourself that you're no experts in crime-solving, didn't you? Maybe you should just leave it to DCI Brown, after all.'

'What rot,' Jane said crossly. 'Of course we can solve the crime,' she said, playing right into his hands. 'Can't we, Nancy?'

'Well, I think we can, and we need to get justice for Lucy. And I don't want a killer living in my village, do you?' She turned to Jonathan. 'But a bet sounds a little distasteful, doesn't it?'

'There's true intentions behind it though,' Penelope said. 'I think you should do it. I know how hard it's been for you both not knowing what happened to your father, Nancy,' she said. 'We can't let that happen to Harry Roth as well. And if you can wipe that grin off of Jonathan's face while you're at it,' she added, 'then I'm all for it.'

'Hey!' he cried.

'Well, I've never backed down from a bet,' Nancy said. 'But I'd want to do this anyway. For Lucy.'

Her grandmother nodded. 'For Lucy.'

Nancy reached out to shake Jonathan's hand. His hand was warm and strong in hers. 'Fifty quid we find the killer before the police do then. You'd better start saving.'

'This is fifty quid I'll be willing to lose,' he said. 'That's the first time in my life I'm saying that!'

'It won't be dangerous, will it?' Jane asked then, biting her lip as if she had suddenly realised what had just happened. 'You two always used to get in such trouble when you were little.'

'But you're going to help, aren't you, Mrs H?' Jonathan asked. 'Then you can make sure that I don't lead Nancy astray.' He winked at Nancy when her grandmother couldn't see.

'Well, that's true. And I'm sure dear George would want us to after what happened to him. And this place.' She gestured to the bookshop. 'His pride and joy, all about mysteries, what would he have done in our position?'

'He would have wanted to solve it, Gran,' Nancy replied, certain about that. 'I can't believe we're doing this but I think we have to.'

They all nodded.

'But where do we start?'

Before anyone could answer, her phone buzzed in her pocket. When she pulled it out and saw the name on the screen, she froze.

'What's wrong? Who is it?' Jonathan asked, seeing her face.

'It's Richard,' she said, moving into the office to answer it.

'Richard?' she heard Penelope say from behind her.

'There wasn't only one shock event last night,' Jonathan replied. 'Nancy's ex-boyfriend is back in Dedley End.'

Chapter Nine

'Hello?' Nancy paced the office, too on edge to sit down. She could hear the others in the shop talking in low voices and she knew they were talking about her. She tried to focus but her mind was whirring with everything that had happened over the past twenty-four hours so it wasn't easy. 'Richard?'

'I'm relieved you still have the same number. I didn't get a chance to say goodbye to you last tonight, I wanted to check in on you. How are you?'

'That's sweet of you,' she replied, wishing that she didn't remember how kind he could be. 'I'm doing okay. I mean, what a shock! In the cold light of day, it's hard to believe it even happened.'

'Tell me about it. I was meant to be staying at Roth Lodge but I booked into the White Swan instead, I thought it was best.'

'You're still in Dedley End?' She couldn't help but think back to the one and only Christmas she had brought him home to the village with her, and how strange it had been to have him there. It hadn't been a successful visit, and he'd never returned, no matter how much she had wanted him to. That had been their final Christmas as a couple.

'I am. I wondered if you wanted to join me at the pub for lunch? It's been so long, I'd love to catch up. I know the circumstances aren't what I had been hoping for when Will invited me to the party but I don't want to let this opportunity to talk to you pass.'

'Oh.' She was surprised and flattered, nervous and excited. 'I mean, I guess I could…'

'Excellent. That's sorted then. See you at twelve thirty, okay?' He hung up briskly and she remembered then how hard it had been in the past to argue with him. But what harm could a lunch at the pub really do? She went back into the shop, conscious that her neck was flushed beneath her jumper, hoping the others wouldn't notice.

In her absence, the bookshop had become busier. Gloria had come in, along with Mr Smith – one of their regular customers – and a local family, all of whom were in the middle of the shop talking to Jane and Penelope, making no pretence that they were there to browse the books.

'Everyone wants the scoop,' Jonathan said, standing up and walking over to her. 'So, what did Dicky want?'

'Don't call him that, you know he hates it,' she said. Jonathan and Richard had not exactly hit it off when they met that time. 'He called to invite me for lunch before he leaves Dedley End.'

Jonathan raised an eyebrow. 'And you're actually going?'

'I haven't seen him for five years, I can't turn down an old friend.'

'Old friend?' he scoffed. 'I can't believe he even deigned to set foot in the village again, I thought we were all beneath him.'

Nancy sighed. 'That was five years ago, people change and move on.'

'Do they?' They stared at one another. Jonathan looked away first. 'I need to go home and change.'

'Don't be like that. Richard might be able to help us.'

'How?'

'He knows the Roths, he might have some insight for me. I mean, where do we even start investigating this murder?'

'By finding out as much as we can about the victim,' Jonathan declared, as if he was an expert on the subject.

'Well, it's as good a place to start as any. And Richard might be able to help.'

He sighed. 'I suppose so. Just be careful okay, Nancy? I know how upset you were when you broke up.'

Nancy nodded. 'I promise.' She watched him go, wishing things didn't suddenly feel rather complicated.

'Nancy, come and tell Gloria about the argument we witnessed in the pub,' Jane called her over then.

Nancy knew she'd have to tell the story repeatedly today but she didn't really mind; she needed the distraction from thinking about the lunch she had agreed to have with Richard.

–

The White Swan, like the rest of the village, was busier than ever when Nancy walked inside at lunch time. She spotted Lisa, who worked in the newsagent, sitting with her friends near one of the news crews, taking selfies with them in the background. Mrs Taylor, Nancy's old school headmistress, was staring out of the window and calling out everyone who walked past to no one in particular. A police van pulled up in the car park and they all craned to see it from the window. The butcher

Pete waved to Nancy as he walked through with a tray of pints for a table of men in the corner talking loudly over one another. She even saw Rev. Williams in the back with a sherry talking to Mrs Wood, the village florist. It seemed like everyone wanted to talk about what was happening in the village.

'Nancy, over here!' Tanya, the landlady of the pub, called to get Nancy's attention as she stared around her. She turned and went over to the bar, weaving around people to get there. 'Can you believe this place today? I'll make a fortune out of this murder at this rate,' she said, as cheerful about it as Jonathan had been. Nancy knew she didn't mean any harm but she couldn't help but wince at her words. Lucy seemed far from their thoughts, although Nancy had to admit none of them had known her, thanks to the Roths keeping their distance from everyone in the village. 'You were at the party last night too, weren't you?'

'That's right, I can't believe what happened.'

'I could hardly sleep, thinking about what I saw! But, just between us, I'm not as shocked as some. There was always something odd about that family, if you ask me. Why hide themselves away from us for all these years? Eccentric is just another word for crazy!' Before Nancy could respond, Tanya was called away by a customer.

Nancy knew it was true that they knew very little about the family. She resolved to find out as much as she could. She carried on into the pub, trying to find Richard amongst all the patrons. Finally, she spotted him at a tiny table at the back. He waved when she got closer, and she smiled to see him again, more pleased than she had thought she'd be.

Richard rose to kiss her on the cheek, dressed today in dark jeans and a shirt, slightly less formal than last night but still smart and freshly shaven. 'Is it always this busy in here?'

'No. This is because of last night. The whole village is talking about it.'

'I suppose in a place like this there isn't much to talk about usually,' he said, looking around with disdain. Nancy's hackles rose as they always did if anyone said anything disparaging about her beloved Dedley End. She wondered if the wedge that had grown between them was still there after all, but then he chuckled. 'Only joking. This is news everywhere. Proper newspaper fodder – a family worth millions, a name as old as this very building, involved in such a scandal. Doesn't make for a very cosy lunch though.'

Nancy slipped her coat off. 'I was so surprised to see you there last night. But you work with the Roths, is that right?'

'My company took over their company account last year, so I've been working with them since then – that was the only time I've been to their house, though,' Richard said, confirming what Will Roth had told her at the party.

'They hadn't invited any of the village to the house in years. What a night to choose.' Nancy found it easier focusing on the Roths. It made it easier not to notice the way he was smiling at her, or the sexy Danish lilt to his voice she had always loved, or that familiar smell of his. Not a lot easier, if she was honest, but a little bit.

'No one could have seen that coming. Poor Lucy!'

'Did you know her well?' she asked, leaning forward eagerly.

'No. She and Harry Roth only got married six months ago. I have been dealing mostly with Will. Harry had been running their office in France until his marriage.

67

I met them once when they first came back to the UK and stayed in London for a couple of nights, but then they moved back here and I hadn't seen them again until last night.' He called the waitress over then and ordered a bottle of wine without asking Nancy. She preferred gin and tonic now but didn't like to argue. She ordered the pie and mash, and he ordered the steak.

'What did you think of Lucy when you met her?' She picked their conversation back up once they were alone again.

'Obviously very attractive but she didn't seem like the bride Harry would have chosen. I was surprised Marcus Roth hadn't fixed him up with the daughter of another established English country family.'

'This isn't the 1950s,' she replied with a laugh.

He shrugged. 'You know I still don't understand some of your strange customs!' He had grown up in Denmark but had lived in England since university.

'Did Lucy and Will seem close?'

He frowned. 'Not that I noticed, but we were only together for a couple of hours over a drink… you're asking a lot about them.'

'Just intrigued. I mean, as you say, it's not often there's a murder in our midst.' She kept her tone light, not wanting to tell him about her bet with Jonathan. She didn't want him to laugh at her or anything. 'You went into accounting, then?'

He nodded. 'The Roth account was a big scoop for my company, I can tell you. Their investment company is worth a fortune as I'm sure you know.'

'So I gather.'

Richard had always been career-focused and it seemed he had achieved what he had always intended to. She

68

thought back to them meeting at Bath University, living in the same Halls of Residence. She had done an English degree, and he studied Economics. They had soon started dating and had been together for three years when they broke up.

Everything had changed between them their final Christmas at uni when Richard had come to Dedley End for the holidays. It hadn't gone well. He hadn't made an effort with her gran or friends, had appeared to look down on her village, and had kept on making disparaging comments. When she'd confronted him about it back at uni, he had admitted that he didn't see the point in getting to know everyone as he'd be moving to London after uni and he thought she should come with him. He had assumed it, basically.

After their final exams, she had told him that she couldn't leave her gran or the bookshop; that she intended to take it over when Jane retired after all, and they'd had a big row. She had pleaded with him not to end their relationship, saying that they'd make it work somehow, but for him it was London or nothing. He'd gone without her and her first and only love had ended. Nancy shook her head to clear those thoughts. She had to focus on the here and now and not what might have been.

'What do you think happened last night? I mean, someone at the party committed murder,' she asked him in a low voice. 'Who do you think did it?' He knew the family much better than she did, maybe he had an insight that would help her out.

Richard sighed. 'I told you before, you read too many murder mysteries,' he said. Then, seeing the look on her face, he smiled. 'All I mean is, I'd rather not talk about the Roths all afternoon, and waste this precious time with you.' Nancy hadn't forgotten how charming this man could be. 'I want to know what you've been doing.'

'Oh, you know me, same old, same old. I'm still working in the shop – I run it now – and living in the cottage with Gran, and I have a dog now too.'

'And you're still friends with Jonathan.' He drew out the name, raising an eyebrow. She nodded, at a loss what to say. 'I wondered if I might find you married.'

She gave a nervous laugh. 'Me? No, I'm single.'

'So, you and him…'

She sighed. 'I told you, we are just friends,' she said, firmly. When Richard had met Jonathan, he'd been convinced Jonathan was in love with her. She had dismissed his jealously but the two of them had definitely locked horns and it appeared that time had not healed that particular wound. For either of them. 'What about you?'

'You proved harder to get over than I thought,' he replied. She was saved from having to reply with the arrival of their wine and decided she would need a large glass of it.

'To getting reacquainted,' Richard proposed as a toast when their glasses were full. Nancy clinked hers against his and took a long sip.

'Have you spoken to the Roths today?' she asked him then, unable to leave the subject alone altogether.

He sighed. 'I popped in to the house. There are police everywhere, and Harry is hysterical. Will has been told he can't go home to London, which he wasn't very happy about.'

'He lives down there now?'

'That's right; he runs their London office, which is why he is the one I know best in the family.'

'And is he married?'

'Single, as far as I know.' Richard arched an eyebrow. 'Why are you asking about Will? You don't think he had something to do with what happened?'

'Oh, I have no idea, but the family must be under suspicion.'

'I suppose they must be.' He frowned. 'Well, as I said, I really don't know them all that well. And I'll be quite happy to leave them and go back to London. Although it means our reunion will be brief.' He leaned in closer. 'I hope now that we're back in touch, we can see each other again soon. I don't want to wait another five years, do you?' He touched her hand again and she wished she could ignore the current of electricity that travelled up her arm but it was impossible.

She shook her head and he smiled, and she forgot all about the Roths for the rest of their lunch.

Chapter Ten

With all the excitement after the murder, Nancy and her grandmother had forgotten that they needed to bake cookies for the annual Christmas fair held every year in the church hall. Jane and Gloria organised the event so local businesses could sell produce and Christmas gifts, and there was always a cake stall. So that evening, they holed themselves up in the kitchen. Jonathan came around to discuss the case while they worked, sitting at the table, and pulling out his laptop and notebooks.

'Crime-solving and baking – only in Dedley End!' Nancy said with a laugh as she started to cream the butter and sugar. Charlie came in and laid down under the table, close to her feet, likely hoping she'd drop some cookie dough on the floor for him.

'Fine with me as long as I get to taste a couple of these cookies.'

'You'll have to help us ice them,' Jane told Jonathan. 'We have to make about a hundred.'

He grimaced. 'So, Nancy, did Richard have any insights into the Roths that we should know about?' he asked casually although Nancy didn't miss his eye roll when he said Richard's name.

'Only what we kind of knew from village gossip anyway – that Harry and Lucy married six months ago after a whirlwind romance and he was surprised at the pairing. Thought it was strange that Harry hadn't married someone his family knew.'

'Hmm. I think he's right, and I can't believe I'm saying that. But it must have been a real shock for the Roths when Harry turned up on the doorstep married to someone they'd never met before.'

'I certainly would be shocked if Nancy did that,' Jane said, passing Nancy baking trays and cookie cutters. 'And the Roths strike me as people who would care a lot about who joins their family.'

'Plus, Lucy worked in a bar,' Nancy said. 'Gloria said that, remember? She met Harry working in a bar in Paris. And it always felt like the family thought they were above us, you know? Too good to socialise or even set foot in our village so I wonder how his choice of bride went down with them?'

'I can see how they would have been angry with Harry but wouldn't they be more likely to consider cutting him off from the family money then to actually murder Lucy?' Jonathan mused.

'Does Richard know them well? What did he think happened?' Jane asked her, sitting down to line the baking trays.

'He didn't have many insights; he was confused about why I was so interested and I didn't like to tell him about our investigating, you know,' she said, not meeting either of their eyes. She saw them exchange a look. 'He really doesn't know them well. They started working with his accountancy firm since last year and that was the first time he'd been invited to Roth Lodge. He'd only met Harry and Lucy once for drinks when they stopped off in London before moving into Roth Lodge; usually he deals with Will.'

'Who we know didn't like Lucy much, if we go back to their argument in the pub,' Jonathan said. 'Maybe Will was suspicious of Lucy's intentions? Maybe he didn't like the fact that she'd got his brother to marry her?'

'Maybe he'd found something out about her. What if she had a shady past?' Nancy asked, spooning the cookie mixture into the cookie cutters shaped like Christmas trees and snowmen on the baking tray.

'So, this might have nothing to do with the Roth family after all?' Jonathan frowned at his laptop. 'Lucy's social media is all set to private. Let me dig out their marriage announcement, see if there are any clues we can work with. Here we go,' he said, reading it aloud to them both.

> The Roth family would like to announce the marriage of Harry Roth to Lucy Lewis. Harry Roth, 30, of Dedley End married Lucy Lewis, 28, in Paris. Harry had been setting up the Parisian office of the family business, and met Lucy through her work in the hospitality industry. They married a month later then returned to the UK. After a short stay in London for their honeymoon, the couple have returned to the family home in Dedley End where they plan to spend married life together.

'It's very brief, and doesn't exactly scream delight and happiness from the family, does it? It confirms they had a whirlwind romance of just a month before they married, and that they came back to live at Roth Lodge six months ago,' Jonathan said.

'It was all very fast. How much could he really have known about her?' Nancy mused.

'You know what? We haven't tried her name before she got married.' Jonathan checked the announcement again. 'Here it is – Lewis. Let's try googling that then…'

'It was a big step-up: from working in a bar to joining the Roth family,' Jane commented as she helped Nancy. 'A real rags-to-riches tale.'

'Maybe Lucy was after Harry's money,' Nancy wondered aloud.

'I can't find Lucy Lewis online. At all,' Jonathan said, frowning at the screen. 'As if she doesn't exist.'

Nancy sighed, feeling somewhat defeated. Lucy Roth seemed to have become even more mysterious by the minute. 'What if that wasn't her real name?' she asked, slowly.

'What, she used a fake name to marry Harry?'

'It's possible, right?'

'I guess so. You'd need fake ID for the marriage certificate, though. And if she did use a fake name, that makes this even more perplexing. Perhaps the Roths found out she was lying about who she really was? Maybe they looked into her like I just have, and realised she had lied to Harry?'

'Maybe but would they go as far as to kill her for lying about who she was? I mean, even if she did marry Harry to get hold of his money, I'm still not convinced that's motive for murder. The family could have just had the marriage annulled or they could have got divorced,' Nancy said.

'They would have had to give her money though, if they did that.'

'Maybe but they must have a great lawyer, and even if they did have to pay her off, they are mega rich. I'm sure there must be more to it than that.'

'Could it be anything to do with their business?' Jonathan suggested.

'Richard said they make a fortune; he didn't suggest any problems there. And Lucy didn't have anything to do with the company as far as we know. Will was working at the London office but Harry was here with his wife. Running the Paris office remotely, perhaps?' Nancy said. 'Besides, there was something in Lucy's expression at the party...' She explained how she had seen Lucy apparently deep in thought. 'She looked lonely, to be honest. I think this is personal somehow. But more than that, I don't know.'

'I wonder if she invited anyone to the party,' Jane said. 'From her life before Harry?'

'I can try to find out when I go to the house,' Nancy said. 'But as I say, she seemed very alone at the party so it didn't seem like she did. If not, that leads back to the family as suspects again.'

'All we really know for sure right now is what happened at the party,' Jonathan said. 'Let's think back to where all the family were. Did any of them have the opportunity to do it? That might narrow things down.'

Nancy thought for a moment. 'Will came to get me and Marcus from the library but then he went off to find his aunt. Marcus hurried off, I didn't really see where to. But all the family apart from Will came into the drawing room from the other end to where we came in, which leads upstairs I think. Will came in from the hallway. I'll check the layout when I'm at the house.'

'So they all could have been upstairs where Lucy was. The only two that it couldn't have been were Maria and Charles. They were having photos taken with a photographer. There just wouldn't have been time for one of them to push her and then get down to the drawing room together plus the photographer would have seen them,' Jonathan said, writing everything down.

'And I heard Maria really upset that her party had been ruined,' Nancy added.

'Nice reaction.'

'I know but I don't see why she'd sabotage her own party.' Nancy shook her head.

'I agree,' Jonathan said, and he put a cross through their names on the list. 'That still leaves Marcus Roth, Peter or Jessica, plus Harry, and Will in terms of the family being able to have done it.' He frowned.

'You know who else it could be? The butler! The butler is always the one who's the killer,' Jane exclaimed excitedly.

'You two and your crime books,' Jonathan muttered. 'It's a good point about the staff though, we really don't know much about them. And of course, the house was full of party guests. Including Richard,' he added, looking at Nancy.

'We'll have to check if she invited anyone. It had to be someone who knew Lucy, you don't just kill a random person at a party,' she replied, shaking her head. She didn't tell them that she had been trying to remember exactly where Richard had been during Marcus's speech but he had kept disappearing during the party. All she knew was that he'd been with her when Lucy's body had been discovered; his hand had been on her shoulder.

'Well, we shall have to wait and see about that.' Jonathan interrupted her thoughts, and she was relieved about that. 'We need more information about the family and the household and any guest who knew Lucy – who has a motive? Nancy, I think it's all down to you on Monday to see what you can find out at that house.'

'Are you sure you should still go?' Jane asked, worriedly.

'They might not even let me in. The police could still be there, and Marcus Roth probably doesn't even remember asking me to look at their library.'

'Well, you can remind him. I'll ask the police as well what leads they're following. They know that everyone will be wanting to know what's going on. This is a safe, quiet place, people are going to be scared, and they need to be seen to be doing things. I think they'll want to keep me up to speed. Plus, one of the officers still owes me money from a poker night a few weeks ago so he needs to stay on my good side.'

'I think we will definitely be winning our bet then,' Nancy said dryly.

Jonathan grinned. 'Well, you'd better get started because the clock's ticking.'

'I hope we're not going to regret agreeing to this,' Jane muttered.

Chapter Eleven

After lunch on Sunday, Nancy took Charlie on the lead to the church hall where the annual Dedley End Christmas fair was being held. Her gran had been there since early in the morning helping to set up for the fair with Gloria and the rest of the village Events Committee. The fair always drew a healthy number of locals to it but this year seemed to be the best attended yet.

Nancy and Charlie walked into the church hall, which had been transformed for Christmas, and was already a hive of activity. Tables were set up around the perimeter of the square room loaded with all sorts of Christmas treats – handmade tree ornaments, stockings to hang on the fire-place, delicious-smelling scented candles, knitted scarves, and of course the cake table, run by the church, which Nancy and Jane had been baking for. In the corner of the room stood a tall, brightly lit Christmas tree, and Mariah Carey was playing from speakers at the back. Draped around the room were fairy lights and tinsel, and from the kitchen emitted the heady scent of mulled wine. The room made her determined to decorate the bookshop as soon as possible.

'Nancy!' her gran called over to her from the cake stall. 'Have you ever seen the fair so busy before? I suppose we can guess why so many people have ventured out this afternoon,' she said when Nancy went over.

Nancy looked around in interest. 'I think everyone within a ten-mile radius is here. Who knew murder could be so profitable?'

'Well, let's hope our book stall does well,' Jane said, nodding in the direction of the stall which Penelope was running for them as usual. 'Oh, Gloria, how much shall we charge for this lemon drizzle?'

Nancy left her gran to it and went over to the Dedley Endings stall.

Penelope had laid out a selection of books – some hardback fancy editions of Agatha Christie classics, perfect Christmas gifts, and the latest crime releases plus some Sherlock Holmes paperbacks, and all the festive books in popular series. She sat on a stool, blowing on her finger-less gloves. 'It's so cold in here. I've already had two hot chocolates to try to warm up.' She reached down to give Charlie a pat as he sniffed around with interest.

'It will heat up quickly with all these people here. I hope we can sell a lot of these.' The bookshop was doing fine but Nancy knew they couldn't rest on their laurels; bookselling was tough in this online era, and she didn't want to let her father down.

'I think we will. Murder is on everyone's mind, after all,' Penelope replied in a low voice.

'Will you need any help from me?'

'I'll be fine,' Pen replied cheerfully. 'You look around and find some treats for yourself and...' She leaned in closer. 'See if you get any titbits about the murder too, of course. We really don't want Jonathan winning this bet.'

'I know what you mean,' Nancy agreed. 'I like wiping the smug smile off Jonathan's face as much as I can,' she added with a laugh.

'You two have always competed. Remember when we were, like, ten years old and the two of you dared each other to knock on old Mrs Norton's house. You fell over and grazed your knee, and Jonathan got an ear-bashing from her when she saw you both out of her window.'

Nancy chuckled. 'Gran baked Mrs Norton a cake to say sorry. She was furious with us.' She and Jonathan had always got each other in trouble, and she really hoped that wasn't about to happen again.

'Have you two seen Jonathan anywhere?' A pretty brunette marched up to them then.

'Not today, no,' Nancy answered Kate.

'I thought he'd be here.'

'He said he might be working – you know, the Roth murder is a big story for him.'

Kate sighed. 'Always working. Okay, I'll see if he's at his flat, then.' She spun on her heels and weaved through the people towards the door.

'She deserves someone better than Jonathan,' Penelope remarked.

'He doesn't mean to hurt people,' Nancy said, loyally. 'He just doesn't feel the same way as she does.' She tried not to think again of Richard. He had left Dedley End but she couldn't help thinking about him saying they shouldn't lose touch again. What would it be like to have him back in her life? She really wasn't sure.

'I wonder why that is,' Penelope mumbled.

'Huh?'

'Nothing,' Penelope said louder. 'Oh, look, Mr Smith is coming over, I bet he'd like this edition of *Murder on the Orient Express*,' she said, picking it up and waving at him.

Nancy smiled and left her friend to it. She was great with their older customers and Nancy was sure she'd be able to sell quite a few books today, a definite bonus since they were usually closed on a Sunday. She decided to keep an eye out for a Christmas gift for Penelope. She deserved to be treated to something nice. She also needed a few more gifts for her grandmother. 'Right Charlie, where shall we start?' He pulled on his lead and she laughed when she saw the pets' stall he had sniffed out. She followed him over and bought him a new toy which he promptly put in his mouth, not wanting to wait until Christmas. She also got a bag of treats but hid those in her handbag for his stocking.

Then Nancy wandered over to the bath bombs, oils and salts stall, thinking she could get Penelope and her gran some bath treats for Christmas. It was always nice to pamper oneself.

'Hi there, Nancy,' Jenny greeted her from behind the table. She had lived in Dedley End since Nancy was a baby, although she travelled around craft fairs a lot selling her homemade scents. 'I heard you were at the party Friday night and I wondered if you were okay. Must have been dreadful seeing… that.'

'It was,' Nancy agreed. 'I don't think I'd ever have imagined that could happen here.'

'No, well, that's the problem when newcomers turn up, right?' Jenny said, sagely. 'You'll like this one.' She handed her a bottle of bubble bath to smell. 'I knew that woman would bring trouble in her wake, and so did my aunt.'

Nancy looked up with interest. 'Oh, yes, she works at Roth Lodge, I forgot.'

'That's right. For almost thirty years now. House-keeper. Lives there, too. She's in a dreadful state, the whole household is. You can imagine, the shock of it all, and everything.'

'And I expect the police have been all over the house,' Nancy said, trying not to act too interested. She examined a basket of bath bombs as she waited for Jenny to respond.

'They've been there all weekend. She's been interviewed twice. All very stressful for her. She's no spring chicken now. Although sharp as a tack still, runs in the family,' she winked at Nancy. 'Treating them all like criminals, she says. The police say that it must have been someone on the guest list because the doorman checked everyone had an invitation. No one else got in. And, of course, hardly anyone but the Roths knew Lucy – I mean, none of us had even met her before, had we? So, the whole household is under suspicion by all accounts.'

'They do say it's always someone you know,' Nancy replied. 'Don't they?'

Jenny shuddered. 'Doesn't bear thinking about. I only hope they give the family some peace soon. Although from what my aunt tells me I don't suppose they're losing much sleep over it, apart from Harry.'

'People do say they weren't particularly impressed with her.' She handed Jenny a lavender bath bomb. 'I'll take this for my grandmother, please. And a vanilla one for Pen. And a bottle of that bubble bath each for them, it smells incredible.'

'Lovely choices. I'll wrap those up for you.' She grabbed some tissue paper. 'No, they didn't much like her, so my aunt tells me. But you know what the rich are like, very closed ranks. I mean, look at how they kept apart from the village. So high and mighty. Probably looked down their nose at her, being a barmaid and all that. Poor girl.'

'Perhaps it was someone from her past and not the family, though?' Nancy handed over the money for the gifts. Nancy thought it was highly likely that one of the

Roth family were responsible for Lucy's death but she knew she should stay as open-minded as she possibly could to make sure she didn't miss anyone else it could have been.

Jenny passed her two prettily wrapped boxes. 'Why would they have been invited to the party, though? I just hope my aunt will be okay. Doesn't bear thinking about that she could be under the same roof as a killer. I told her to come and live with me for a bit but she said she'd get the sack so there she is.'

'Let's hope the police find the culprit soon then.'

Jenny looked unconvinced. 'That DCI Brown is another newcomer. He doesn't look like he could tell a prince from a thief, if you ask me.'

Nancy smiled. People who had grown up in the village were never trusting of newcomers, which was another point in her and her gran's favour when it came to investigating the murder. They were both Dedley End born and bred, surely they could sniff out the killer together? 'Thanks for this, Jenny. And I hope your aunt will be okay.'

'She's a strong 'un. If the killer does come after her, more fool them, if you ask me.' Someone else stepped up to the table then so Nancy took her leave, chewing her lip at the thought that the killer could strike again. She had agreed to go back to the house on the hill in the morning and she hadn't really thought about the fact that she could once again be under the same roof as a murderer. Adrenaline flooded through her veins, spiking her pulse, but she couldn't quite make herself feel fear. She did, however, feel excited.

Perhaps she had read too many murder mysteries growing up, after all.

Chapter Twelve

'Maybe I should come with you,' Jane said, biting her lip as she and Nancy finished off their breakfast on Monday morning. 'I'm starting to wonder if we were hasty in making this bet with Jonathan.'

'I'm only going to look at the library, like I said I would to Marcus Roth, and I'll just keep my eyes and ears open. I won't draw attention to myself, I promise.'

'It's so horrible to think there could be someone there who is capable of murder.' Jane shuddered.

'I know, and we need to make sure the person responsible is found out. Like you said, we can't let someone escape justice. Not like what happened with Dad.'

Jane nodded solemnly. 'You're right. I just wish you didn't have to go back to that house. Are you sure I shouldn't come with you?'

'I think that could arouse suspicion, and you need to open the bookshop. I'll come straight to the shop once I finish, and I won't take any risks, I promise. If it was someone Lucy knew then they had a personal reason to hurt her, didn't they? What reason would they have to hurt me?' She was trying to be brave but she was nervous; it was all very well hypothetically talking about who could have pushed Lucy over the railings but coming face-to-face with them was very different. She hoped she'd be able to channel the detectives she knew and loved and not chicken out of this. She would just focus on the books, as she promised her gran; they had never let her down before.

'Well, be careful and if anything seems amiss, get straight out of there.'

'I will,' she promised. 'Right, I'd better get going.' She gave her gran a kiss on the cheek and ruffled Charlie's fur before leaving their cosy cottage and heading out into the bitterly cold morning.

Even though she'd wrapped herself up in her wool coat, scarves and boots, she was freezing by the time the gates of Roth Lodge loomed large in front of her. Mist circled the quiet house, in stark contrast to when she had last seen it all lit up and merry for the party. The house looked like it was in mourning today, which she supposed it was.

She pushed the bell with her shaky gloved finger, the sound echoing all around her.

'Yes?'

'Um, Nancy Hunter for Marcus Roth,' she said into the speaker, hoping that he hadn't forgotten their plan for her to come to the library today. She breathed a sigh of relief when a buzzer sounded, and the gates began to open in front of her.

Sucking in a deep breath, pulling on all her courage, she walked up the driveway, gravel crunching underfoot. The front door opened before she got to it. 'Miss Hunter, come on in,' said a tall, thin older-looking man, dressed in all black.

She stepped over the threshold, and paused. A policeman stood near the centre of the hallway keeping watch by the taped-off scene of Lucy's murder. Nancy shivered. It was impossible not to flashback to the sight of beautiful Lucy Roth's face stripped of all colour and life on the chessboard floor, or the sight of the vivid red blood seeping over the black and white stones beneath. Nancy felt cold down to her bones standing there. She would perhaps forever be haunted by the sight of it.

'Most of the police work has been done over the weekend but they don't want us to touch it yet,' the man behind her explained as he closed the front door. The police officer was looking at her, his expression unreadable. She tried to give him a 'I'm not at all suspicious' smile, but was worried she actually came across as looking a little hysterical. He didn't say anything though.

'I'm Frank, Miss, the Roths' butler. Won't you come this way, please?' The man who had let her in asked, politely, calling her attention away. His accent was almost as posh as that of the family he served. She wondered what it must be like working for such a family. One that could afford to have a butler in this day and age. It was surely a strange way to make a living. She wasn't sure she'd be able to bear being at their beck and call. She hoped he was being paid well for it, at least.

'It's such a big house, it's hard to get one's bearings,' she said as he led her across the hallway towards the library. The house felt eerily quiet to her, and goosebumps pricked her skin underneath her coat. She wondered where the rest of the household was.

'Let me help you out,' he said, pausing. 'Ahead is the library and next to it is Mr Roth's study, down the corridor is the kitchen. There are stairs to the first floor that way too,' he said, gesturing to the direction Will had gone off in at the party. 'And behind you is the drawing room, which you know from the party, and at the other end is the second staircase up to the first floor.'

He then pointed to the door next to the library. 'And that is the downstairs powder room, and at the end there is the dining room. Upstairs are bedrooms for the family and guests and the top floor is the staff quarters. This way then.'

Nancy took in what he had told her as she followed him on to the library. She had been correct in thinking that all the family could have been upstairs and able to push Lucy over the railings before returning to the party in time for the speeches. She remembered then her gran's joke about the butler killing Lucy Roth. She certainly couldn't picture it. The man was clearly stiff and slow-moving, surely past retirement age. Could he have managed to push young and healthy Lucy Roth over a railing? Still, she had a chance to see if he knew anything. 'So, how long have you worked for the Roths?' she asked him.

'Forty years, Miss,' Frank replied, lifting his head with pride. He pushed open the double doors to the library.

'That's such a long time. What happened at the party must have been such a shock.'

'Oh, it was,' he replied, gravely. 'I was upstairs. Mrs Harper and I had the night off as they had brought in caterers and servers. We were sitting up on the third floor playing cards together when we heard the sirens, and came down to see what had happened. Such a shock.'

'I can imagine,' she murmured, sympathetically, thinking that this ruled him and Mrs Harper out as suspects – if what he said was true, of course, but he certainly seemed to be speaking sincerely. She supposed that even if you had worked for the family for as long as he had, you weren't invited to their parties but kept hidden from sight. What a strange world they all seemed to live in.

'Mr Roth will be with you shortly. Can I get you anything, Miss?' The butler asked, stepping back to let Nancy walk through into the library.

'I would love a cup of tea, please, if that's not too much trouble?' she replied, looking at the library, marvelling once again at how impressive it was.

'Of course not,' he said, briskly.

The doors closed behind her and she jumped a little. 'Get a grip,' she whispered aloud to herself as she spun around, taking in the empty room, trying to let the presence of her beloved books soothe her. Her phone buzzed in her bag so she took it out and read the message from Jonathan.

> Good luck with your snooping. I'm going to the police station to see if anyone will talk there. See you back at the bookshop later!

Nancy wished he was with her to help; she wasn't quite sure where to even start. It wasn't as if there was a manual for this sort of thing. She took off her coat and put her bag down on the chair, and decided she would make the best of being here. If she only got to spend the time with these books then that would be fine, but if she could find out anything to help solve the murder then all the better.

The doors swung open behind her once again, and she turned to see Marcus Roth striding in. He was wearing a sombre suit, was unshaven, and looked pale. 'Miss Hunter, I was surprised when Frank said you were here. In all the confusion, I quite forgot about asking you to look at our library. I wonder, perhaps, would you prefer to hold off until things are less… well, until things quieten down? I don't want you to feel worried about being here.'

'I'm not scared or anything,' she replied, hoping she sounded calmer than she felt. She wanted to be cool and confident but it was certainly disconcerting, knowing there had been a death so close to where they were standing. 'But I understand if I'm in the way or you'd rather be alone. I didn't think – I mean, I suppose I thought the distraction might help?'

Marcus walked in further and gave her hand a quick squeeze. 'I'm very glad you did think that. The past couple of days have been a waking nightmare, as I'm sure you can imagine. Time in here talking about books is exactly what I need actually, so thank you for coming.'

'Not at all,' she mumbled, suddenly feeling incredibly guilty about her ulterior motives. She tried to shake it off: she was here for Lucy. That's what mattered.

'Well, that's settled then. I've asked Mrs Harper to make us tea, so shall we sit and talk about what you might be able to do here?'

She sat down in one of the large, red armchairs that he pointed to. She thought of Mrs Harper's niece, Jenny, at the fair and wondered if there might be a way to talk to the housekeeper and see if she had any more insight to give. Nancy was certain that the Roths' staff knew a lot more than the family would ever suspect they did. 'How is everyone coping?' Nancy asked him then.

'It's been utter chaos. One never realises how much a murder disrupts a household until it happens to them.'

'No, I suppose not,' Nancy replied, surprised he could be so flippant when discussing what had happened. He didn't appear to be grieving for Lucy Roth at all, just the fact that the murder had interrupted their lives. Lucy's isolation in the family seemed to rear up again. Was it only Harry who cared that she was gone? Did that make the others just unfeeling or worse, killers? Which category did Marcus fall into? Did he need to go on their list of suspects?

He seemed to understand the expression on her face. 'Don't get me wrong, my dear, it's shocking and tragic, but I don't understand why the police seem so determined that one of us had a hand in it. Can you imagine? It's ridiculous! And it means that the real killer is just getting away with it.' He spoke crossly, incredulous that a Roth could be suspected of something like that, and Nancy could tell he really didn't believe it was at all possible. Was he just in denial, or could someone outside of the family be responsible?

'I suppose they assume it must have been someone close to her. Was there anyone at the party who knew her before she came to live here, I wonder?'

'My daughter-in-law, Jessica, handled the guest list, and I can't see her letting anyone... dubious into the house. As far as I know, Lucy had no family and all her friends are back in France so she really only had Harry.' He sighed. 'And us,' he added as an afterthought.

Nancy had been right then – Lucy had been isolated. She'd had no one but her husband and his new family, who hadn't welcomed her or cared for her. It was no wonder she had appeared lonely at the party. How awful. She felt a spark of determination to make sure that someone did care enough about Lucy to get justice for her. She would do for Lucy what she couldn't do for her father. Someone needed to be on her side even if it was too late to help her any other way now.

Before Nancy could dig any deeper, there was a knock, and the doors opened to reveal a young, petite blonde carrying in a tray of tea things. Nancy was disappointed it wasn't Mrs Harper herself so she could have tried to catch her eye.

'Thank you, Natalie,' Marcus said as she set the tray down between them. She nodded at him and then her eyes flicked over Nancy with interest before she ducked her head, and hurried out of the room again. 'Poor girl,' he continued, after the doors were closed again. 'She has been working here for about a year and helped Lucy move in, and worked closely with her, I think she has taken what's happened very hard.'

Nancy made a mental note to try to speak to her as well – if she had been close with Lucy, she might well have her suspicions about why she was murdered, and by whom. Marcus handed her a dainty cup and saucer, pretty bone china that she knew her grandmother would love, and took one himself. There was also a plate of biscuits on the tray. Nancy supposed one could get used to being waited on after all.

'Right then, enough talk of these unpleasant things – let's talk about books instead. A far better topic for conversation, I think,' Marcus said, sipping his tea. Nancy was disappointed but could hardly say so; he thought she was there for the library and the library alone, after all. He told her that his wife had fallen in love with the Roth family library as soon as she saw it. 'To be honest, I think it was one of the reasons she agreed to marry me,' he said with a small chuckle. Nancy wondered how he could speak of his wife so warmly but of Lucy Roth so coldly. 'She spent years adding to the library, and she was passionate about books, but once she passed away, it was hard to come in here without her. We haven't bought anything new for a long time, and I know that would have made her sad.'

'Libraries need to be cultivated,' Nancy agreed. 'It's not about just adding the latest bestseller but thinking about the heart of your library, the kinds of books you want to collect and which new books will build on what you already have.'

Marcus nodded. 'Exactly. I haven't a clue where to start so I'm glad you're here.'

'I think the best place for me to begin is to check your inventory, make sure it's up to date, and get to know the books you already have, then we can think about what you might like to add.'

'That sounds like an excellent idea.' He smiled. 'Now, we must discuss payment…'

'Oh no,' Nancy said quickly. She didn't mind lying about her true reason for being in the house to help Lucy but it didn't feel right to accept payment because of that. 'As you're buying the books through our bookshop, that's all the payment I need. I'll enjoy this, I promise.'

He frowned. 'But it might take a few days? I couldn't possibly not reimburse your time like that.'

'Well, let's see when it's all done, shall we?' she said hurriedly. Before he could argue further, the doors behind them opened again, and he turned. 'Ah, Will, Miss Hunter has come to help reinvigorate our library.'

Will Roth strode in. He wore jeans and a cashmere jumper, his hair pushed back, his chin unshaven. Like his grandfather, the past two days seemed to have weighed heavily on him as he looked exhausted. 'Lovely to see you again,' he said, politely. 'Our resident bookworm.'

Marcus stood up. 'Now, Miss Hunter, I'm afraid I have a couple of meetings. Will you be alright getting to grips here on your own for a while? The inventory books are on the desk ready, and there's a laptop as well if you prefer a more modern way of working,' he said with a look that suggested he thoroughly disapproved of modern ways.

'I'll be fine,' Nancy said. 'But I might lose track of time in here.'

Marcus chuckled. 'Just like my wife. I'll get Frank to let you know when lunch is ready. You'll eat with us, of course. And we shall discuss the matter of your reimbursement further,' he added with a firm look.

She smiled weakly.

'Will, let her get on with her work please, don't distract her.'

'As if I would,' Will replied with a grin.

Marcus sighed and with a nod at Nancy, he swept out of the room. He closed the doors, leaving Nancy alone with Will and wondering if she should be worried or not. Will looked perfectly relaxed, however.

'Well, I hope he's going to buy a ton of books through your shop. What a tiresome job, sorting out this dusty tomb,' Will said, sitting down in the chair his grandfather had just vacated.

She shrugged, although she hoped so too. 'I love books, this is fun for me.'

'I suppose it's a prerequisite to owning a bookshop. So, have you always lived in the village?'

Nancy nodded. 'All my life.'

'I left this house when I was eighteen, couldn't wait, if I'm honest. I went to Oxford and then I got my flat in London. And I can't wait to get back to it, and my work, my whole life there, but I'm stuck here for the time being.'

'Why did you want to leave? I mean, this house is beautiful,' she asked curiously.

'It is but the words "gilded cage" come to mind. You can't do anything here without everyone knowing about it,' he replied.

Nancy felt for Lucy all over again. Six months she had lived at Roth Lodge – had she felt as trapped as her brother-in-law? 'It must be hard for you all dealing with this,' she said, watching him closely. She was still trying to understand his relationship with Lucy. Had they been lovers or haters?

'Well, Harry is hysterical, and my mother has barely left her bed. My father and grandfather are trying to hold everyone together, and the police are in and out every day. I don't see what it's got to do with me but they won't let me go home. I feel for Harry, of course I do, but I told him when he showed up with her after knowing her for all of five minutes that it would all end in tears.'

Nancy raised an eyebrow. 'You imagined this might happen?'

'Well, no, but I could tell she was trouble. I don't know why the police keep asking us questions as if we know anything. As if it's anything to do with us. She brought this to our door, and we seem to be the ones paying for it.'

'I mean, she did lose her life,' Nancy reminded him, surprised again by how unfeeling the Roths were about her death.

Will sighed. 'I know, I know. And I feel bad for her, of course I do, but I can't pretend there was any love lost between us, you know?'

'You didn't like her, then?' He certainly didn't seem to be mourning a lost lover but was he hiding his true feelings? It was so hard to tell. She longed to ask him what they had been arguing about in the pub. She wondered if he'd told the police about it.

'To be honest, no. And that detective was shocked when I told him that but why lie about it? Harry married her after some whirlwind romance and couldn't see her for what she was – a common gold-digger. He'd only known her a month before their wedding.'

'How long had Harry been working in France?'

'For about two years so I hadn't seen much of him, it was a shock when he arrived in London with a wife, I can tell you, and then they moved in here. Which I couldn't understand. I hope they find whoever did it, naturally, but I for one will be glad when we can get back to the way things used to be around here.'

Nancy was struck by a resemblance to his grandfather in his attitude. It was a reminder that before the engagement party, the Roths had kept themselves apart from the village and everyone in it – a haughty reserve, you'd call it perhaps. It made Nancy think that whoever Harry had married, they would not have found the family easy to get on with. Did the Roths respect anyone outside of their world? She didn't suppose the list was that long. It reminded her not to fall for Will's apparent friendliness; it could be all pretence. She wasn't one of them and nor had Lucy been. As such, she thought it wise to trust no one here.

'Good luck, Nancy Hunter.' He glanced around the room. 'I think you're going to need it.'

And so did she.

Chapter Thirteen

Alone in the library, Nancy remained in her seat for a few minutes, stumped. She pulled out her phone to send a message to Jonathan.

> I just spoke to Will Roth. He says he was never a fan of Lucy – thought she was a common gold-digger! He can't wait to go back to London but the whole family has been told to stay at the house for now by the police. So, what was he arguing about with Lucy in the pub?

She fired off the message then got up and went to the desk to make a start on the library. She opened up the heavy, leather-bound inventory. It would take a few days just to go through the books they currently had, let alone start thinking of what to order in for Marcus. It was the perfect cover to dig for more information about the murder.

Jonathan replied a few minutes later.

Try to find out what the rest of the family thought about Lucy too. I spotted the doorman they hired for the party leaving the police station – he confirmed he checked all invites on the way in, and there was no chance for anyone else to leave the house without being seen by him, and according to him no one had left before Lucy was killed. So, it must have been someone at the party who did it! They killed her then mingled back in with the guests.

Nancy wrote back to tell Jonathan that Marcus seemed to think Lucy hadn't invited anyone to the party herself, and that he too was definitely not a fan of her. So far no one Nancy had seen had been at all upset that Lucy was gone. Nancy understood why the police were focusing on the family – everything was pointing in their direction at the moment.

Nancy hadn't found another suspect to add to the list yet. She very much doubted that in the short time the party lasted, Lucy could have upset a party guest who didn't know her enough for them to push her over the railing. She wondered about Harry. Could someone have done it to punish him? Or maybe he had a jealous ex in the picture? Nancy shook her head. Harry had been in France for two years, both those two ideas seemed unlikely. The only other person who had met Lucy before was Richard. But she knew him, didn't she? Surely there was no way he could be at all involved? What would his motive even be anyway?

Nancy felt certain it was one of the Roth family but she had no idea who it could be yet. She supposed the best way to find out who the killer really was would be to find out the reason *why* they did it.

As the answer was nowhere near being obvious to her, she went back to the books and worked for a couple of hours, going through the inventory. Marcus's wife Louisa seemed to have shelved the books according to her tastes, which would have pleased Nancy's dad – he had done the same in the bookshop, which was why customers were often baffled.

The clock in the corner chimed then, announcing that it was midday. Nancy supposed she'd be called for lunch soon and it felt as if the day was slipping away without her gleaning anything more to help the case. Her eyes fell on the tea tray. She grabbed it and hurried out of the library with it. She turned in the direction the butler had pointed out and soon her nose confirmed she was heading the right way as the smell of lunch filled the corridor. She found herself in the doorway to the kitchen.

It was the largest kitchen she had ever seen, all country wood and pretty china, offering a view of the grounds. She spotted a large Aga in the corner, and in front of it stood the housekeeper, Mrs Harper. Nancy had seen her out and about in the village for her whole life – she was always moving about briskly, on some errand for the Roths, no doubt. Nancy's grandmother knew her to say hello to and have a quick chat with, but that was it.

'Mrs Harper, I brought the tea tray back for you,' Nancy said, stepping into the warm room.

The housekeeper turned from stirring a big pot of soup. 'There was no need, dear, Natalie would have collected it. But thank you, just pop it down on the table there. You're Nancy, aren't you, Jane Hunter's granddaughter?' She had grey hair and light eyes, an expression that recalled her niece Jenny, and a thick local accent.

'That's right,' she replied, popping the tray down. 'Marcus Roth has asked me to take a look at the family library and order in some new books for him.'

'Oh yes. It has been rather neglected since Louisa passed away. She used to spend a lot of time in there. I'm glad he's trying to revive it again. We need something positive around here,' she said with a heavy sigh.

'Marcus said the police have been all over the house.' Nancy seized on that opening, hoping she could lead Mrs Harper into giving her some useful information.

The housekeeper tutted. 'And making a right mess of it, too! I've been clearing up all morning and there's so much more to do. What they think they're going to find, God above knows.'

'I suppose they might find something to help the case – perhaps in Lucy's room?'

She turned back to the stove to stir the soup again. 'Well, I don't know what. She hadn't lived here for that long, and she didn't have many belongings with her. Said she hadn't wanted to bring much over from France, had a big clear-out before they came, but I think she just didn't have many things to bring, you know?' She turned back to Nancy and pursed her lips. 'After all, she only worked in a bar in Paris and Harry mentioned she shared a small flat with a colleague. Despite her cut-glass accent, this was most definitely unlike anywhere she had lived before. Harry bought her a lot of clothes when they moved in, all designer of course, so she didn't need her old belongings anymore.'

Nancy sensed the judgment from the housekeeper. It appeared that, like the family, she too thought Harry had married beneath him. Nancy had never met so many snobs in her life before. It irritated her. What did where Lucy work and live have to do with what kind of woman she was? If Harry loved her and was happy, why should that matter? 'So, were you surprised when Harry arrived home with a wife?' she prodded, wanting to know more about Harry. All the focus was on Lucy but he had chosen her as his wife. She sat down at the table, tilting her head curiously.

'I practically raised that boy, I've known him and Will their whole lives. I was hired just before Harry was born. Will has always been a charmer, he has the gift of the gab, that boy, and always had a ton of friends and girls around him but Harry was different – more sensitive, you know, more caring. I always thought he'd make an excellent husband. So, I wasn't surprised he got married, no, but it was out of character for him to do something so important without his family knowing. Without talking it through with his father and grandfather.' She shook her head. 'I think that's what put the family's noses out of joint. That they weren't consulted about something so important. But I have to say, it was clear that he was head over heels in love with her, Nancy. Written all over his face. Besotted, he was. I always say it's not good for a man to be that infatuated with his wife. Stops them thinking clearly, you know, and look where that leads.' She raised an eyebrow and started slicing up some crusty bread.

At least Harry had loved Lucy. That was something. She hadn't been welcomed into his family but at least she had had him on her side, Nancy supposed. 'What did you make of Lucy?'

'She seemed to care for him too, I've always said that, but she made it plain she thought she was the lady of the house now. Wanted to get involved in the running of things. And that, of course, put Mrs Roth's nose out of joint. Take the engagement party: Lucy tried to organise it but we have a way of doing things here.' She turned then, seeming suddenly to realise that Nancy was hanging off her every word. 'Why all the questions anyway?' she asked pointedly.

'I suppose because I've been looking at all the family books, it's made me curious about them, you know?' Nancy stood up, sensing she had outstayed her welcome. 'I'll remember you to my grandmother.'

'Please do.' She bent down to take something out of the oven, and Nancy knew she had been dismissed. Slipping out, she made her way back to the library. She was starting to understand the tensions in the house leading up to Lucy's death better. Harry had turned up after a whirlwind romance, putting his family's noses out of joint that he'd got married in secret. Not only that though, he'd married beneath him in their eyes to a woman from a much humbler background who then tried to make her mark on the household, causing more tension in the process. But it all still seemed rather petty when it came to considering a motive for murder.

Nancy had barely got back to her work when there was a knock on the door, and Frank, the butler, stepped in to tell her lunch was ready. She wasn't sure what to expect as she followed him to the dining room – a room she had not yet seen. She walked in and faltered for a moment in the doorway as a bunch of faces all turned to look at her. It was an ominous sight, and Nancy wondered briefly if she should just turn around and make a run for it.

'Miss Nancy Hunter,' the butler announced, foiling her plan, before disappearing, and leaving her alone.

'Come here, my dear, and sit by me so I can hear about how you're getting on,' Marcus called out to her, pulling back the chair next to him. Nancy had to walk the length of the long, shiny mahogany table to get there. She passed by Peter, Marcus's son, at the head of the table, his wife Jessica next to him and drinking a rather large glass of wine, Harry opposite her, slumped glumly in his seat, Will next to him, giving Nancy a grin, the newly engaged couple Maria and Charles, and opposite them a woman she recognised as the aunt who she had seen during Marcus's speech, but hadn't spoken to yet. That left her seat, Marcus at the head of the other end, and one empty chair. Nancy shivered a little as she looked across at it, realising that if she had come any other day Lucy Roth would likely have been seated there.

'Here you go,' Will said, leaning over the table to pour her a glass of wine. Nancy decided she would probably need it.

'You remember everyone from the party?' Marcus said in a low voice. 'My son Peter, his wife Jessica, Harry and Will, their boys, Maria and her fiancé Charles, and that's Jessica's sister, Annabel. She has been staying with us the past couple of months but usually lives down in Cornwall.'

Nancy glanced at her. She definitely looked nothing like her sister – dowdy almost, with mousy, long hair streaked with grey. She was much shorter and curvier, too.

'How have you found our library, then?' Marcus asked as the door opened and Frank came in followed by Natalie, the girl who had brought in the tea earlier, both laden with trays. They placed a bowl of soup in front of everyone, and then handed around a bread basket. When Natalie placed Nancy's soup down, the liquid sloshed a little as if her hand was unsteady. Nancy tried to give her a reassuring smile but the girl refused to meet her gaze. Nancy wanted to try to speak to her, as Marcus had said she had worked mostly for Lucy. She might know something of import.

Nancy felt the whole table was listening as she responded to Marcus's question even though they busied themselves buttering the bread, and picking up their spoons. She tried not to notice and just looked at Marcus. 'Well, your wife certainly knew a lot about books. She had a great eye. And kept immaculate records.'

'She would spend hours in there.'

'Her system doesn't seem to have much order to it. I think she just shelved according to her taste, exactly like my dad did at the bookshop,' she added with a smile. 'You have an impressive number of books for a private library. I've been making notes as I go about what you might look at acquiring, though. You have a lot of history books.'

Marcus nodded as he tore apart his bread. 'That was my father's doing – he was a real history buff, and collected most of those books. My wife was more into her novels and poetry so that side might have been a bit neglected lately.'

Nancy nodded. 'I can see some gaps. Some of what you have must be worth a fortune.' She had noticed a lot of rare books and first editions, some signed, and knew that they were sought after.

'They are indeed. Why, once my father paid a hundred thousand pounds for—'

'Father,' Peter interrupted then from the other end of the table. 'Must you talk about things like that? You would have thought you'd be more careful after recent events.'

Marcus sighed. 'I hardly think anyone at this table is going to run out of the door with one of our first editions.'

Nancy felt her cheeks turn pink at the insinuation that she might have her eye on one of their books.

Will noticed and gave her a smile. 'My father is on the look-out for criminals now, Nancy; he wasn't suggesting you were about to pilfer the library.'

'I should hope not,' Marcus said, throwing his son an angry look. 'She has kindly agreed to help us today and is our guest in this house.'

Peter pushed back his chair, and stood up. 'If this family had been more particular about who they invited into this house, we wouldn't be in this mess. You'd have thought we would have learned our lesson by now but clearly not. I'm going to my study, I do not wish to be disturbed,' he said, before walking out.

'I'm very sorry for my son's appalling manners,' Marcus said then to Nancy.

'He's only saying what you're all thinking,' Harry said miserably then. 'As if it was Lucy's fault for being killed, and mine for marrying her in the first place and bringing murder into our house. Well, I'm sorry we didn't see this coming,' he said, before getting up and leaving as well.

'Harry!' Jessica called, jumping up and hurrying out after him.

'Well, then there were six,' Will said, picking his spoon back up. 'This is delicious.'

'It really is,' Aunt Annabel agreed, looking up for the first time.

Maria sighed. 'Come on, Charles. I don't know why we stayed all weekend. Let's go home,' she said, standing up then as well. Charles dutifully got up and followed her out.

'She's taking it hard that a murder interrupted her party,' Will observed.

'Will,' Marcus sighed, wearily.

'They live in Woodley,' Will explained to Nancy. 'And I can't say I blame them for wanting to go home. I only wish I was allowed to leave too.'

Nancy picked her spoon back up, stunned. She had never seen a row like that in her own family, let alone in front of a stranger. Did the rich always behave like this, or was it just the Roths? No wonder Lucy had found it so difficult to fit in.

'It isn't usually like this, I assure you,' Marcus said then.

'Come on, grandfather,' Will said with a shake of his head. 'It's always like this.'

The door opened again, and back in came Frank and Natalie, bringing the second course even though they had barely touched the first one with all the drama. Nancy watched Natalie. The girl was studying her, biting her lip as if nervous. She wondered what she was thinking.

Nancy hoped that they could finish lunch quickly so she could get back to the peace of the library, as her mind was buzzing with questions.

Chapter Fourteen

'Mind if I join you?'

Nancy turned to see Jessica Roth's sister, Annabel, poking her head around the double doors to the library. She had been back at her work for an hour, thoughts of the disastrous lunch forgotten as she lost herself amongst the books once again. 'Of course,' she called back, rubbing her neck after looking down at Louisa Roth's record books for too long.

'I am at a loose end and Marcus suggested I see if you would like some help,' Annabel said, walking in and closing the doors behind her. 'It's so peaceful in here,' she added with a grateful sigh. Like her sister, she spoke beautifully although their looks were quite different.

'Nothing quite as peaceful as a room full of books,' Nancy agreed, trying to contain her glee that one of the family had come to her so easily. 'Do you come to stay up here often?' she asked, with an encouraging smile.

Annabel walked over to the desk and pulled one of the armchairs closer to Nancy. 'Yes fairly often, we are close, Jessica and I. She wanted help with the engagement party and the wedding planning so I've been here for almost three months now.' She smiled. 'This house is very different to my small cottage by the sea, I can tell you.'

'Do you both come from Cornwall?' Nancy asked, noting the difference between the sisters – one living in a cottage on the coast, the other in this grand house.

'No. Our family home was in Oxford but after our parents died, I bought my cottage down there, I've always wanted to live by the sea. Jessica met Peter at Oxford.' She chuckled. 'I'm yet to meet my Prince Charming.'

'Same here,' Nancy quipped. They smiled at one another. Annabel definitely appeared more down-to-earth than the other members of the family, perhaps because she usually lived far away. 'Lucy was very lucky to meet Harry,' Nancy said, trying to lead Annabel into talking about her.

'They made a lovely couple. I know that my sister wasn't so sure but Lucy and Harry seemed very much in love so I didn't see the harm. I tried to make peace between them as much as I could when I arrived. I sensed tension in the house but then we all got so busy with the party, so everything seemed okay, you know? I just can't believe what happened. Poor Lucy,' Annabel said, shaking her head.

'Did Lucy invite anyone to the party herself? Any family, or a friend?' Nancy wanted to check if what Marcus had thought about Lucy not inviting anyone was true or not.

'No, she didn't have any family, and any friends were back in France as far as I know,' Annabel replied, confirming what he had said. She looked around the room. 'Would you like some help in here? I do like to be useful.'

Nancy nodded. Annabel might reveal something else that would be useful if she spent more time with her. 'I'm checking off all the books in the inventory to make sure it's all up to date. If I read out titles, you could look at the shelves and then we can make sure they are there, and we have the right location for them written down. Would that be okay?'

'Perfect. I'm just twiddling my thumbs at the moment. Ever since the night of the party, I've felt as if I shouldn't be here, you know? But the police have asked everyone to stay for the time being,' she said, getting up, and going over to the shelves.

'Will said the same. Maria and Charles are going home though?'

'As they only live in Woodley, that inspector – I forget his name – said that would be okay but he wants us all nearby for questioning. I don't mind as I can support the family, you know? But I do miss home.'

'Of course you do. Did Maria get on well with Lucy?'

Annabel considered that. 'I think so. Lucy had good taste and was helpful with the party and wedding planning. I think Maria admired her style. She's perhaps not quite as stylish, if that's not untactful to say.'

Nancy nodded; Lucy had been incredibly elegant and she had admired her style at the party too.

'And perhaps, as she was about to get married, she liked the idea of Lucy and Harry's whirlwind romance.'

'Like something out of a book,' she agreed, gesturing to the books around them.

'Quite.'

Nancy mulled over everything she had found out. Maria and Charles were occupied at the party and Maria admired Lucy so she was confident they weren't suspects. Harry appeared to be devastated by his wife's death and she didn't sense that was an act but she couldn't rule out any of the rest of the family. None of them seemed to either have approved of or liked Lucy apart from Annabel. Although it was a big leap in her mind to jump from hostility to murder. There must have been more to it, surely?

'Where shall we start, then?' Annabel prodded her.

Nancy decided that she had better focus on the books for a while so as not to arouse suspicion; she had asked a lot of questions today. She started to reel off book titles and they lost an hour working through the list together. They were therefore startled when Frank, the butler, came in with a tray of tea and biscuits, slipping out again discreetly. 'I think we'd better take a break,' Nancy suggested, and the pair of them sank gratefully into the armchairs for some refreshment. 'We have got a lot done, actually. Thank you so much for your help.'

'Oh, it's been lovely to have something to do, so I don't sit around and think about everything, you know,' Annabel said, sipping her tea. She shivered. 'I still can't believe what happened.'

'Me neither,' Nancy replied. 'Nothing like this has ever happened in Dedley End before.'

'I suppose you must feel unsafe now?'

Nancy sipped her own tea as she considered how to reply. 'I suppose it depends on the outcome.'

'What do you mean?'

'Well, most often murder is connected to someone you know, isn't it? So, we needn't be worried about someone stalking the streets looking for their next victim.'

Annabel stared at her. 'You mean that they would be looking for their next victim in this house instead?' she squeaked, her tea sloshing over the cup as she jumped a little.

'I didn't mean to worry you! You have nothing to worry about, I'm sure. There must have been a reason for what happened to Miss Roth. Don't you think?' Nancy tilted her head and looked at her, hoping that if Annabel had any suspects in mind she would share who they were with her.

The question hung in the air. Annabel took a deep breath and drank more of her tea. She took a bite of a chocolate biscuit, which was always helpful in calming one down and only then did she seem up to answering Nancy. 'I suppose it was a shock to the family when Harry showed up married to Lucy, and she hadn't really been welcomed into the fold. But the Roths are a respectable family, you can't really be suggesting that they have done anything...' She leaned forward, her voice dropping to a loud whisper. 'Untoward?'

'I wasn't suggesting that at all, no, only that most victims know their killers. In books,' Nancy said, hastily, gesturing around them. 'So, it is possible that she did know the person.'

Annabel nodded once. 'Yes, I do see exactly what you are saying.'

'Did she mention that she was worried about someone, did she seemed scared of anyone do you think?'

'I don't believe so,' Annabel said, slowly. 'But I'll think about that. Yes, yes I will.'

'You can always tell one of the police officers if anyone springs to mind – or me, if you're not sure who to trust,' Nancy added, casually.

'I will. Goodness, I shall be glad to get back to Cornwall, I don't mind telling you that.'

'I completely understand.'

They returned to their work after that and Nancy thought about how Annabel hadn't thought that one of the Roths might have killed Lucy. She felt it didn't signify much though – after all, did anyone actually think that someone in their family could be capable of murder? At least Annabel seemed to be an ally so if anything did come to her mind, Nancy was hopeful Annabel would come to her, and that was the best she could hope for that afternoon. She was conscious that the light was fading, and she really should get back to the bookshop in case her gran was getting worried about her.

Nancy read out the name of a book that struck her as she did so. *The Man in the Brown Suit*. It was one of her grandmother's favourite Agatha Christie novels, as it had much more of an adventurous romantic slant to the murder mystery than was typical of the author. She had loved it as a girl. There was a hesitation from Annabel so she looked over at the shelf she stood by. 'Is it there, Annabel?'

Annabel quickly glanced back and nodded. 'Oh, yes, there it is. I wasn't sure for a moment... tick!' She smiled at Nancy who dutifully ticked it off as found, and then looked down at her watch. 'Goodness me, look how late it is!'

Nancy looked at the clock on the mantelpiece. 'Yes, I really need to get going. My gran has been on her own in the shop all day.'

Annabel quickly walked away from the books. 'Well, thank you for letting me help you.'

'We got through so much more together, I should be thanking you,' Nancy replied, carrying over the inventory log to the desk. 'I suppose I had better say goodbye to Mr Roth?'

'I'll find Frank, he always knows where everyone is,' Annabel replied, hurrying out, eager to help.

Nancy marked the page they had got to. She glanced at the shelf they had reached, wondering what edition of *The Man in the Brown Suit* the Roths had collected. She knew she'd get a kick out of seeing a fancy edition of it – maybe a first edition or even a copy signed by the author. Nancy grabbed her coat and bag and pulled out her phone ready to snap a photograph to show her grandmother at home. Hurrying back to the shelf, she found where Annabel had been standing, and ran her fingers along the spines.

Frowning, she stopped and checked again. Despite Annabel saying she had found it, Nancy couldn't see the book there.

Stumped, she slipped on her coat and glanced at the doors, remembering Annabel's hesitation. Had Annabel taken it out of the library with her? And if not, then she had lied to Nancy about the book being there. But why would she have done that?

'I hear you've been busy bees in here,' Marcus Roth said cheerfully as he strode in. Behind him, Annabel hovered and Nancy noted that there was no sign of the book in her possession. 'I can't thank you enough.'

'It was fascinating,' she replied, honestly. 'I can come back later in the week?'

'Whenever you're free. Goodness knows, we all need the distraction of you being here, Miss Hunter. Natalie will show you out.'

Annabel gave her a friendly wave before hurrying after him. Nancy stepped out of the library where Natalie stood, shifting her feet from side to side.

'What do you do here then, Natalie?' Nancy asked pleasantly as they walked across the hallway.

'Miss, I saw you here at the party, didn't I?' she asked, ignoring the question.

'That's right.'

'And you were with that friend of yours, I've heard of him, the reporter?'

They reached the doorway and Natalie hung back, glancing behind her as if checking they weren't being overheard.

'That's right. Jonathan Murphy. He works for the *Cotswold Star*.' Nancy reached into her bag and fished out his business card. 'Did you want to talk to him about something? Here are his details.'

The girl hesitated for a second before snatching the card and slipping it into her pocket. 'Thanks, Miss.' She spun around and disappeared into the house.

Nancy wasn't quite sure what to make of that at all.

She glanced at the policeman still on guard; he nodded at her and she walked quickly to the door, stepping out of Roth Lodge into the darkness outside. She shivered as she hurried up the drive. She couldn't breathe a sigh of relief until she passed through the gate, and made her way towards the village.

Chapter Fifteen

Nancy walked into the bookshop to find Jane, Jonathan and Charlie inside. The shop was light and warm, a welcome sight after the ominous mansion she had spent the best part of her day in. 'I'm so glad to see you all,' she said, smiling as Charlie bounded over to her, standing up on his back legs to greet her.

'We were getting worried,' Jane said with relief. 'You look pale and tired, are you okay? Sit down, I'll make us all a cup of tea. Jonathan, turn the sign to closed, we can shut a bit early today,' she said all in a rush, hurrying out into the back.

Nancy sank down on the window seat, taking off her coat. Charlie jumped up beside her and laid his head on her lap. She stroked him happily. 'I feel like I've been on tenterhooks in that house, it's so lovely to be able to relax.'

'I think we need chocolate biscuits too, Mrs H!' Jonathan called over his shoulder as he shut the door to the shop. 'Get some food and drink inside you and then we want to hear everything that happened.'

'I have news too,' Jane said, coming back into the shop with a tray of tea and biscuits. 'We've been so busy. Everyone wanted to come in and talk about the case, we've sold double the books we usually do on a Monday. Who knew murder would be so good for business?'

Jonathan grinned. 'It's the most exciting thing to ever happen in Dedley End.'

'Can we really call murder exciting?' Nancy questioned but the other two just gave her a despairing look, and she smiled, unable to deny that she too found it all rather thrilling, if taxing on one's nerves.

When they had re-fuelled themselves with tea and biscuits enough to begin talking, Nancy started to tell them everything that had happened at Roth Lodge. 'None of them seem to have been particularly fond of Lucy,' Nancy concluded. 'Apart from Harry, who seems genuinely devastated. They are treating her death more like an inconvenience at the house than anything else.'

'What did you make of Will?' Jonathan turned to her. 'After all, the argument between him and Lucy we saw at the pub must be relevant, no?'

Nancy sighed. 'It certainly seems like there is more to find out there but I found Will rather funny and charming, so it's hard to believe he'd be capable of anything like that. He was honest that he didn't like her, and thought she'd married Harry for his money, but he didn't mention the argument to me. We must tell the police and see what they make of it, I suppose.' She wasn't exactly sure why but she still felt unsure that Will felt strongly enough about Lucy, love or hate, to kill her.

'If he can charm you then he may have charmed Lucy too,' Jonathan suggested, frowning at the thought. 'It could all be an act.'

'Perhaps,' Nancy replied, although she still couldn't quite get herself to believe it.

'Maybe they all saw Lucy as a threat to the family. Will thought she was a gold-digger but his brother was blind to her faults so he decided to get rid of her himself?' Jonathan made a note in his book but even he didn't seem all that convinced.

'Do you really think she was a gold-digger?' Jane asked. 'I hate that expression, I must say.'

'She was a lot more attractive than Harry,' Jonathan pointed out.

Nancy felt a little angry on Lucy's behalf. 'People get married for lots of reasons. It's clear Harry really loved her; we'll never know how Lucy felt but even if she didn't love him as much as he loved her, that doesn't mean she deserved to die.'

'Quite,' Jane said. 'And people like the Roths assume everyone thinks about their money because they have so much but not everyone is interested in being rich. I mean, I married my husband knowing he didn't have a penny. I didn't care, I loved him.'

'I'd be the same,' Nancy agreed. That sort of thing had never motivated her either, so she felt an affinity with Lucy. Maybe the poor girl really did just fall in love and want her happy-ever-after. What an unfortunate ending to their whirlwind romance.

Jonathan cleared his throat to get her attention. 'What else happened at the house? Anything of any use to us?'

Nancy told them then about the row she'd witnessed at lunch. 'They don't seem to be a close family, to be sure,' she said, imagining that there might be a whole host of secrets being kept under that roof. 'The only thing though that really stood out was the book.' She explained who Annabel was and how she had helped her in the library, and what she had told her about Lucy, before either lying about the presence of *The Man in the Brown Suit*, or swiftly removing it from the room afterwards. Nancy shrugged helplessly. 'But that of course could be quite irrelevant to Lucy's death. Annabel could have just wanted to read it.'

'Was it worth any money? Maybe she took it for that reason?' her grandmother asked.

'I spotted a lot of books that would be worth a fair bit if sold so I don't know why you'd choose that one in particular, though. Still, write it down, Jonathan, and if I can find it when I'm next there, I can look it over just in case.'

Jonathan did as he was told.

'Oh, Jonathan, you might be contacted by the maid.' She told him about Natalie and how she took his card. 'I think she might want to tell you something.'

'Let's hope so because we really don't have all that much to go on yet,' he replied with a sigh. 'The police were really tight-lipped when I spoke to them. All they would say was that they're "exploring a number of different avenues". Which in my mind means they are clueless. Then again, so are we. Are we missing something? What if we're looking in all the wrong places?'

She shook her head. 'We can't be. The answer must be at Roth Lodge. It's just a case of finding it.' She turned to Jane. 'As we've closed early, shall we put up the decorations? Jonathan, you can give us a hand.'

'Oh, can I?' He folded his arms across his chest.

'Yes, I was out all day because you need us to solve this murder for your career so you can help me put the tree up.'

'Okay, fine. But this isn't just for me. Lucy Roth deserves her killer to be caught, especially if no one seems to care she's gone in that house.'

Nancy nodded. 'I agree. Someone needs to be on her side.' They went to get the boxes of decorations from the shelves in the office and set about making the shop look festive. Jonathan put the tree up next to the door and Jane wrapped some books up to put under it while Nancy hung the baubles and fairy lights on it. They had a small tree for the counter where the till was too, and they draped snowflakes across the window and added fairy lights to the window display, swapping the books for festive-themed ones. Once they had finished, the bookshop looked full of the cheer of the season, even if the three of them didn't quite feel it yet. But with a murder mystery on their minds, it wasn't any wonder.

'And now, for the final flourish,' Jane said, passing the star to her much taller granddaughter. Nancy stood on her tiptoes and positioned it on top of the Christmas tree. It was the star that had been on her Christmas trees at home every year growing up until the bookshop opened and her dad used it in the bookshop instead. It had been a tradition to him, and she was determined to continue it. 'The shop looks wonderful, love.'

Nancy stared at the star. 'I wish we could solve the mystery of Dad's death. Looking into Lucy's murder just brings it all back.'

'It does.' Jane put her hand on her shoulder. 'The trail may be cold on one mystery in Dedley End but let's make sure the other one doesn't go the same way. For Lucy and for George.'

Nancy felt a lump rise up in her throat. She looked across at Jonathan, reflected in the fairy lights, and he nodded in agreement. 'Definitely,' Nancy agreed. 'We do this for Lucy and for Dad,' she said, making a silent promise to the star that they would make sure justice was served this time around.

Chapter Sixteen

Tuesday was another busy day in the bookshop. And everyone who came in had a comment to make about the murder.

Mrs Sarpong came in to pick up a Ruth Rendell book. 'I always knew there was something off about that family,' she confided in Nancy and Jane. 'Too much money makes people act funny. Think they're above us all in the village and now look!'

And then the head teacher of the local school, Adam Perkins, came over, having heard them talking about it. He didn't think their whirlwind romance had helped matters. 'You should never marry someone you haven't seen in their natural habitat. How do you know what they're really like until you see their family and where they grew up, huh?'

'Well, I think they both made excellent points,' Jane said when the shop was empty again.

'But speculating as such doesn't get us any closer to catching the murderer.' Nancy looked out of the window. 'The police are out and about again,' she said, noticing them walking around the High Street. 'Oh, they're coming this way.'

Jane hurried to her side behind the till to have a look.

Sure enough, DCI Brown, accompanied by DC Pang, walked into the shop. 'Good morning, we were hoping you'd have a few minutes to go through your statements from the night of the party at the Roths' home? We're trying to talk to everyone who was there,' DCI Brown said after they had shown their badges and repeated their names.

'Of course, any help we can give. Can I get you tea?' Jane asked. 'Would you like to sit down?'

'No, thank you, this won't take long,' he replied with a wave of his hand. Pang had an electronic pad to take notes. Nancy wondered what it was about being interviewed by the police that made you feel like you'd done something wrong even when you hadn't.

'Can you tell us what happened when you got to the party, who you talked to, where you were? Miss Hunter, shall we begin with you?'

Nancy nodded. 'We arrived with our friend Jonathan Murphy and we went into the drawing room when we got there, where everyone was, really. We soon got talking to Will Roth.' She told them that he introduced her to the rest of the family and how she was taken promptly to see their library by Marcus Roth once he knew what she did for a living. 'He was hoping I might offer some help in sourcing new books for their library so we had a look at it together. We were probably in there for twenty minutes or so until Will found us and told us that they wanted to start the speeches. Marcus hurried out of the library and then I followed with Will Roth. And then we saw Lucy Roth…' The two officers listened more carefully then as Nancy told them how Lucy had said she'd be back soon, and had then disappeared upstairs.

'And she was alone at that point?' DCI Brown checked.

Nancy nodded. 'Yes. Then Will said he wanted to find his aunt and walked off in the direction of the kitchen.'

'But you didn't see what direction Marcus Roth went in?'

'No,' she confirmed. 'I carried on to the drawing room, and then I saw Lucy again.' She told them about seeing her leaning on the railings. It still made the hairs on her arms stand up to remember that. 'Then I walked back into the drawing room alone, and found my gran and Jonathan.'

'Did you see any other members of the family in there?'

'No, they all walked in after me.' The officers exchanged a look and Nancy was sure they had realised, as she had, that there had been enough time for any of the family to push Lucy before the speeches began. But which one had it been?

'And what did you do while Miss Hunter was in the library?' Inspector Brown turned to Jane.

'I was talking to the Reverend Williams and his wife, they are old friends of mine, and Jonathan Murphy was with us, too. We didn't see anyone else we knew. Well, apart from Richard,' she added to Nancy.

'Richard?' DCI Brown asked.

'My ex-boyfriend, he's an accountant for the Roth family business, Richard Bank.'

The DCI nodded, the name was evidently familiar to him. Pang jotted that down. 'Can you talk us through what happened when the family came into the drawing room?'

'All of the family walked in from the door at the end of the drawing room, which I believe leads to the first-floor staircase,' Nancy said, remembering what the butler had explained to her. 'Will Roth came in from the hallway door and he stood with us through the speech. Harry went up to the front next with his grandfather, Marcus. Then

I think Jessica and her sister came in together, and Peter Roth was the last one to walk up there, I believe.'

'And there is another staircase next to the kitchen so they all could have come down from the first floor for the speeches,' DCI Brown said. 'We know that Maria and Charles were upstairs with a photographer.' He leaned forward. 'Are you quite sure about where the family came in from, Miss Hunter?'

She checked her memory. 'Yes, quite sure.'

'Right, please tell us what happened when the speeches started.'

'The family were all at the front apart from Lucy. We commented on her absence and I definitely saw Harry Roth searching the room for her but Marcus Roth started his speech then, I'm not sure the others had noticed she wasn't there, or perhaps weren't concerned by it. And so, Marcus was talking and then we, well, we heard a scream.' She stopped, remembering how the scream had echoed through the room. She shivered before continuing. 'And then it was chaos. We all moved into the hallway, trying to find out what was happening. And that's when we saw the... body.'

'I lost sight of Nancy in the rush to get into the hallway,' Jane picked up. 'I can't move as fast as I used to. I was at the back so I couldn't really see anything, I just heard what was happening,' she added, shaking her head.

'I know it's hard but can you describe the scene for us, please?' DCI Brown turned to Nancy who had seen more than her grandmother.

'Of course. Well, the waitress who had screamed was standing out there, her hands covering her face. And on the floor in middle of the hall was Lucy Roth. There was blood everywhere. She was clearly dead. And then

I heard Harry shout something and he rushed towards the body; someone shouted to call an ambulance but I heard someone else say it was too late for that. And then I think it was Marcus Roth who told everyone to go back into the drawing room.'

Brown nodded. 'And is there anything else that you can tell us that might be important? Anything at all?'

'Well, yes, we did see something before the party that could be relevant.' She told them then about seeing Will and Lucy Roth in the White Swan arguing before the party.

DCI Brown frowned a little. 'And you didn't think to mention this to us before, Miss Hunter?'

'Actually, I did. I tried to tell DC Pang at the party but he said he had to talk to someone else,' Nancy replied, pointedly.

'He was quite rude to us,' Jane added. The policeman looked up in dismay, the tips of his ears turning pink.

'I see,' Brown said, glancing at him with a frown. 'I do apologise, it was a hectic night, and we were trying to get the details of everyone as quickly as we could. Thank you for telling us now. We shall look into that. And if you do remember anything else, you'll let me know, won't you?' He slid a business card across the counter to them. 'It's taking a while to talk to all the guests as I'm sure you can imagine but your account matches up with everyone else's, that's for sure.'

'So, you have some leads already?' Nancy couldn't help but ask.

'We do. Don't worry, Miss Hunter, we'll have this all sewn up very soon. Very soon indeed.' He gave them a brisk nod, and the two policemen swept out of the bookshop. They watched DCI Brown talking to DC Pang, looking annoyed, as they walked away.

'Well, I'm not at all convinced that they will have it sewn up as quickly as they believe, do you?' Jane asked. 'I'll put the kettle on, I'm gasping after that.'

Nancy shook her head. She was sure they were all missing something important but what that might be, she hadn't a clue. She looked at the book shelves, which were home to all the mystery novels she had loved through the years, and willed one of them to tell her what their next move should be.

Chapter Seventeen

Nancy closed the bookshop by herself on Wednesday – Jane had wanted to do some bits in the house, and she had looked after Charlie so Nancy walked back to the cottage alone, a rare occurrence. As she walked away from the shop, her phone rang inside her bag. She struggled to find it in the darkness of the December evening as it buzzed incessantly, and she muttered with annoyance, stopping in the empty High Street to dig around inside her bag. Finally, she found it and saw it was Jonathan calling. 'Hello?' she answered, breathlessly. She started walking again, her hands already freezing, picking up the pace to try to warm herself up.

'The maid that spoke to you at the Roths', Natalie, she phoned me and asked if she could speak to me. She said that she has important information about the murder. So, I've arranged to meet her in the pub, do you want to come and talk to her with me?'

Nancy's pulse picked up as she nodded even though he couldn't see her. She had sensed the maid was wrestling with something. She knew the staff there would know everything that went on at Roth Lodge. Perhaps she held the key to solving it all. 'Yes, definitely.'

'Great. I'm heading there now.'

'I'll just pop home and then I'll be right there,' she promised, hanging up, and stuffing her phone back into her bag. After she had stopped talking, she was struck by the silence all around her. All she could hear was the sound of her boots walking over the cobbled road. She sped up, walking faster than usual, eager to get home.

The High Street was still and silent after all the shops had closed for the night and everyone had gone home to find warmth. The only light came in pools from the lampposts she passed. Even the stars weren't out tonight, hidden by dark clouds.

A shiver ran down Nancy's spine, which was silly as she had never felt unsafe in Dedley End before but then again, there had never been a murderer in their midst before now. She was relieved when she turned into her road and passed familiar houses lit up with fairy lights and saw her cottage bright and welcoming ahead of her.

'Only me!' she called out as she let herself in to the cottage, her heart beating rapidly in her chest from her hurried walk and nerves.

'In here!' Jane called back. When Nancy walked into the living room she found her grandmother sitting with Rev. Williams, a cup of tea in each of their hands.

'Good evening, Nancy,' the vicar said, cheerfully. 'I just wanted to check on you both with all this awful business still going on.'

'That's kind of you,' Nancy replied, hoping she wasn't panting too much as she spoke. 'I am going to nip out again though, Jonathan wants to meet me,' she said, giving her grandmother a significant look. 'I just wanted to make sure you're okay first, though?'

'Oh, perfectly. I've had visitors all day. I don't think anyone will want to stop talking about what happened until next Christmas,' her grandmother said happily.

'Why don't you come back to the vicarage with me for your tea if Nancy is going out?' Rev. Williams suggested. 'Gloria is cooking a roast and she always makes far too much.'

'I can eat at the pub,' Nancy said, happy that her gran wouldn't be alone for the evening.

'I'd be delighted,' Jane replied with a big smile. 'I'll go and find my coat.'

'The police came to see me, have they spoken to you too, Nancy dear?' The vicar asked then. 'What a dreadful business this all is, I only wish I could have been more helpful.'

Nancy perched on the arm of the chair as she nodded. 'They came to see us at the shop. I'm sure you gave them all the information you could, that's all we can do.'

'Indeed. I told them that I was sure that things had improved between Harry and his wife since he came to see me,' he replied, taking a sip of his tea.

Nancy stared at him. 'Harry came to see you?'

'Yes. And really, I do keep people's confidences, Nancy, I assure you, but this is a murder case, you know.'

Jane came back in with her coat on and smiled at Nancy because they both knew the vicar enjoyed a little gossip like most of the village.

'Why did he come and see you?' Nancy leaned forward eagerly. As far as they knew, none of the Roths came near Dedley End usually, even the church.

'Well, as I told the police, he came to see me not long after he returned from Paris. He wanted to discuss the idea of having a church blessing for his marriage to Lucy. He said that his family were upset that they hadn't had a proper wedding. He said they had fallen in love so quickly that he had wanted to marry her right away but now was wondering if he had been a little too, well, hasty. The problem was, Lucy really didn't want to have a blessing. Not religious in the slightest, apparently and couldn't see why he was bothered. And things were frosty between her and the rest of the family, by all accounts, so she didn't feel like celebrating with them.' He sighed. 'He was quite upset. I told him that I could talk to Lucy if he wanted but he didn't seem keen on the idea. I told him to be patient and that marriage is about compromise after all. It couldn't have been easy for her to come to his home and be with his family, and everything, you know? But I didn't hear from him again so I assumed things had been resolved, and he had decided not to have a blessing after all.'

Nancy absorbed what he had told them. It further confirmed that the Roth family hadn't welcomed Lucy into the fold. And that had created tension between the newlyweds, that was now clear. But had that created enough tension to spill over into murder? 'I wonder why they stayed here if things were so difficult between Lucy and the family,' Nancy mused then. 'I mean, Will lives in London, they didn't have to stay in Dedley End.'

'I assumed that once the dust settled, things had become more amicable. It must have been a shock for him to turn up with a wife, after all. But I don't know that for certain,' he replied, getting up, and picking up his coat. 'That wasn't his only visit though,' he said with a smile, evidently enjoying their surprised reaction. 'Yesterday, I found him sat in a pew. He looked lost in thought. When I approached him, he got up and hurried out of the church. I thought he might have been crying. But that's to be expected. His wife's death must have hit him hard. Such a tragedy.' He shook his head. 'Right, Jane, are you ready?'

'Are you sure you'll be okay?' Jane checked with her granddaughter.

'Of course, you have a nice evening, I'll see you back here later.'

The vicar and Jane bid Nancy a good night and left her alone in the cottage. She sat for a moment, thinking through what he had told them. Lucy and Harry had remained in Dedley End for six months. Surely if things had been that bad at Roth Lodge they would have left? But based on the family's reaction, it didn't appear to have improved that much; they didn't seem upset that she was gone, and Will had been arguing with her only recently. Why not go back to France again, or go down to London like Will? If that's where the family business was, wouldn't Harry have been better off there anyway?

Or had they been determined to get the family to warm to Lucy? That had certainly not worked. Although perhaps the vicar was right and things had become slightly better with time. If so, then the murder made even less sense to Nancy.

What about Harry? If Harry was grieving in the church, did that mean that Lucy's murder couldn't have been anything to do with him? Or could he have been in the church to pray for forgiveness?

With a sigh, Nancy got up; she couldn't work it all out sitting in a chair, she had an appointment to keep, and perhaps things would become clearer after that. She went to the mirror and re-applied her lipstick, before pulling her coat back on, and slipping out into the night herself. She turned in the opposite direction to the bookshop to walk to the pub.

When Nancy reached the White Swan, she pushed open the door, enjoying the warmth from the crackling log fire and merry chatter that greeted her, shutting out the cold, dark night as she closed it behind her. Craning her neck, she soon spotted Jonathan sitting at a corner table, waving at her. She weaved through the patrons, some of whom said hello as she passed – she knew most people in the village, after all – and once she reached him, she shrugged off her coat and sat down beside him. 'Well, what a day,' she said.

'I got you a drink, I knew you'd be needing it,' he said with a grin, sliding a gin and tonic across the table to her. He was nursing a beer, a notebook ready and open in front of him.

'I really do. I have so much to catch you up on.'

'Well, you'd better hold that thought because here comes our interviewee,' he replied in a low voice. They watched as Natalie, her head down, walked through the pub towards them. She looked up nervously and hurried over to their table when she spotted them. She looked even younger than she had at the house on the hill, her wool coat wrapped tightly around her, her blonde hair tucked into it.

Jonathan stood up when she reached their table. 'I'm Jonathan, reporter for the *Cotswold Star*, and you've already met Nancy, of course,' he said, reaching out to shake her hand.

'I'm Natalie,' she replied, her voice soft in the noisy pub, her skin flushed. She gave Nancy a tentative smile in return to her welcoming one.

'Thank you for coming, Natalie,' Jonathan said with a warm smile. 'Let me take your coat.' He helped her out of it and pulled out a chair so she could sit down. He caught Nancy's eyes and smiled. She gave a slight shake of her head at how charming he could be when he wanted to.

'Would you like a drink?' Jonathan asked. Natalie shook her head. 'Well, why don't you tell us a bit about what you do for the Roths?'

'I help with the housekeeping mostly, some ironing, errands like the food shopping, anything that Mrs Harper – that's the housekeeper – needs me to do, really.'

'And how long have you worked for them?'

'A year. I live in Woodley. Mrs Harper and Frank, the butler, they live at the Lodge but I come in every day, except Sundays. I have them off,' she said, speaking in a nervous rush. She bit her lip. 'They won't find out that I'm talking to you, will they?'

'Of course not, don't worry,' he reassured her. 'You can trust us.'

Nancy nodded. 'We really want to help solve this crime, Natalie, and I think you do too.'

'I do,' she agreed. She hesitated then continued. 'Lucy – that's what Mrs Roth liked me to call her – she was kind to me. What happened to her was so shocking. Just awful.' Her eyes welled up and she pulled a tissue out her pocket and sniffed into it. Nancy and Jonathan exchanged a look – this was the first person who'd had anything really positive to say about Lucy to them.

'When did you first meet Lucy Roth?' Nancy asked her eagerly.

'She and Mr Roth turned up at the Lodge one day. It was such a surprise. Everyone thought he was still in Paris and then suddenly he was back home, and with a wife too,' Natalie said, her eyes wide. 'The whole house was buzzing with it. Harry had never done anything without his parents' permission before. There were a lot of rows. I was told by him to look after Lucy and she got really upset in front of me a few times. She told me that they all seemed to hate her, and she hadn't expected that. And sometimes, she and Harry would argue too. She thought he wasn't sticking up for her enough.'

'And they'd been living there for six months now?'

'That's right. Things did start to get a bit better though – Maria wanted Lucy's help with her party planning and I think even Mrs Roth – Jessica, I mean – found her helpful with that. Marcus Roth seemed to calm down too. I heard him say his wife would have found the whirlwind romance wonderful so maybe he thought he should support it?'

Nancy nodded. That made sense and fit with what she knew of Marcus Roth herself. He had certainly been very much in love with his own wife. 'How were things between them all these past few weeks?'

'I noticed a change in Lucy; she seemed stressed and was running around, trying to help with everything. She seemed a little anxious or worried but when I asked if I could do anything, she said she was fine. And I noticed Jessica Roth snapping at her quite a bit again. Like the past tensions were coming back. Perhaps it was just because of the party, you know? We all had a lot to do, especially after Marcus agreed to let Maria invite people from the village.'

'Why did that happen?' Nancy asked, wondering if that had anything to do with what happened.

'Maria had talked about it before, I think, she thought it was weird that they kept away from the village, but Marcus said that he had his reasons. Lucy, though, supported it too, she thought the family should be part of the village. I don't think Jessica or Peter were keen but Harry supported his wife and Charles agreed with Maria so in the end Marcus had to back down. I know that he asked Frank to make sure anything valuable was in the safe.'

Nancy's hackles rose at the idea that the villagers would want to steal from them but she knew she had to ignore that to focus on Lucy. She was trying to piece it all together. It all seemed rather petty, though – stresses and strains of organising a party, for goodness' sake! That was hardly worth killing over. 'And did Lucy have anyone coming to the party herself?'

'No. She seemed to not know anyone here. I never heard her mention anyone anyway, and she said she didn't have any family. She only had Harry.'

Nancy's sympathy for Lucy grew further. 'Is there anything else you can tell us? You didn't see anything at the party?'

She shook her head. 'No. I wasn't there. They had hired caterers to serve people so I wasn't needed. Mrs Harper called me first thing in the morning to tell me what had happened.' She sniffed again and blew her nose. 'I was so shocked. And upset. Lucy was so young and beautiful… I'm sorry.'

'It's quite all right,' Jonathan told her, gently. He reached out to give her hand a squeeze. 'Of course you're upset. Take a minute.'

'I'm okay,' Natalie replied, straightening up. 'I just want to help her. Well, I went to the house as Mrs Harper needed me, you know? It was in chaos. The police were due to come to do a search and that's why I wanted to speak to you.' She looked over her shoulder and then leaned in closer to them, lowering her voice even further. 'Mrs Harper told me that the family wanted some time alone before the police turned up. We – the staff, that is – we all went into the kitchen for about an hour before Marcus Roth came in to say the police were there and we needed to offer them any assistance required and clean up when they allowed us to.'

'What did the family do in that hour?' Nancy asked, her pulse quickening a little bit. It certainly sounded suspicious that the staff were shut away for an hour.

'I don't know but I had to show that detective, Brown I think he said his name was, into Harry and Lucy's room and when I opened the door, I could tell someone had been in there. It had been tidied up! Lucy was pretty messy,' she said, smiling at the memory. 'She used to apologise to me about it. When I had left before the party, she had things everywhere as she got ready and I told her I'd clear it all in the morning but it had already been done. Someone had been up there, I'm sure of it, but Mrs Harper swore faithfully she hadn't touched it.'

Nancy glanced at Jonathan, who was furiously taking notes. 'So, the family told you all to stay away and then one of them must have gone into her room? But why?'

Natalie shrugged. 'I don't know. I realised no one had told the police that. I heard Marcus tell the detective that the room hadn't been touched. He either lied about it, or he didn't know. I'm not sure. I haven't slept since, wondering what to do. The police, though, they scare me. But I knew you'd asked for information at the paper, and I thought you'd know what to do.'

Jonathan nodded. 'Quite right. You did the right thing, Natalie. Thank you. That's very interesting information.'

'You'll find out what happened to Lucy, won't you?' she asked, pleadingly.

'We will,' Jonathan promised. 'You can be sure of that.'

Nancy really hoped they could live up to that promise.

Chapter Eighteen

Jonathan dropped Nancy off at the cottage after the pub had closed. As she waved goodbye to him, and he drove off, she realised there was a car parked over the road, which she didn't recognise – an unusual occurrence in Dedley End at this time of year. She pulled out her house keys and hurried up to the cottage door, wondering why strange things in the darkness were so unsettling lately.

'Nancy!'

She froze in the middle of unlocking the door, hearing her name called out in an all-too-familiar voice. Turning slowly, she looked across at the parked car. The window had been rolled down and in the dim light inside, she could just make out someone waving to her.

'It's me! Come over,' Richard said, leaning further out of the car. 'Sit with me for a minute.'

Trying to contain her surprise, she walked over the road, and climbed into the passenger seat of his car. 'What are you doing here?' she asked. She wished she hadn't had two gin and tonics in the pub as she felt rather light-headed being in such a confined space with him after so long.

'I was driving back to London from a conference up north,' he said. 'It was only half an hour out of my way to come to Dedley End. I just couldn't resist. I've been waiting out here for a while – I thought for a minute you weren't going to come home tonight.'

She knew he was fishing to find out who she had been with. 'I went out for a drink,' she said, not giving in to his curiosity. 'I didn't think you'd ever set foot in my village again and now I've seen you twice in a week.'

'I haven't stopped thinking about you since our lunch,' Richard said, twisting in his seat so they were face to face. Nancy tried to ignore how close they now were. She was very glad of the gearstick providing a barrier between them. 'I've missed you.'

'You have?' She felt confused. After five years out of her life, he was back and during the strangest time her village had ever experienced. She couldn't quite work out if she was pleased to see him again so soon or not. Once he had said that their relationship couldn't work if she didn't move to London with him, she had wondered if they had really been the best fit after all. He knew how important her father's shop was to her, how her gran was her only family, and yet he had still expected her to leave it all behind and come to London with him. What would she have done in the city? She belonged in Dedley End. And now he was telling her he missed her. 'Richard, I…'

'It's okay, I realise that my showing up again has thrown you, and that you might not be in the same place I am,' he said, smoothly cutting over her. 'But I came to tell you that I want you back in my life.'

She swallowed hard. 'But we broke up five years ago, you said you couldn't stay with me if I didn't join you in London even though you knew my life was here,' she said, gesturing around them. 'You made a new life without me.'

He nodded. 'I did, but that new life is missing something. I didn't realise what it was until I saw you at the party, but now I know that it's you.'

Nancy was flummoxed. She was definitely regretting the alcohol now. She felt woozy, and was relieved to be sitting down. 'I don't know what to say,' she said, truthfully.

'I understand. How about we just get to know each other again? I could come back at the weekend and take you out? We could talk things through.' He touched her hand quickly, gently. 'Please?' he added, softly.

Nancy hesitated. Why was it so hard to forget someone you had loved?

'Just one dinner?'

It sounded so simple. She knew it wasn't but she nodded. 'Okay. One meal.' Then she had a brainwave. 'On Saturday night. Before we light the village Christmas tree. You can stay for that, if you want.' It was a test, and they both knew it. The annual event brought the whole of Dedley End out, the village he had never wanted to be part of. Just how would he handle that? She hopped out of the car and hurried into the cottage without looking back even though she desperately wanted to.

–

Nancy was up while it was still dark the following morning, after tossing and turning all night. Her gran came downstairs not long afterwards, in her dressing gown. 'I heard you were awake, everything all right?' Jane asked as Nancy let Charlie out in the garden.

'Just a bad night, my mind was buzzing with everything that's going on.'

'I'll make some tea,' Jane said, heading to the kettle as Nancy sat down at the kitchen table. 'I suppose you were thinking about Richard, as well as the Roths?'

When Nancy had gone inside the night before, she had told Jane about Richard being outside but had hurried to bed, not really wanting to talk about it.

Nancy nodded. 'It's been a crazy few days. The murder would have been enough to contend with but now Richard is back on the scene.'

Jane brought over two cups of hot, strong, sweet tea. 'How do you feel seeing him again?'

'Confused. I can't quite believe I've agreed to go out with him, and that I'll be bringing him to tree night.' Every year, the village celebrated the countdown to Christmas by lighting up the tree on the village green.

'I'm surprised he agreed to come to it,' Jane said, sipping her tea. She certainly hadn't warmed to Richard when he had come to the village that Christmas. Nancy knew that she had thought him a snob.

'I suppose it must mean he genuinely has missed me,' Nancy mused. Richard hadn't wanted to join in any village activities on that visit, turning his nose up at their village, making it clear he thought it was all beneath him. It had sealed the ending of their relationship but now he was willingly returning to Dedley End, so maybe he had changed? Grown up in the years they had been apart?

'Well, of course he has,' Jane said firmly. 'You are very miss-able.'

Nancy smiled. 'Thanks, Gran.'

'But the question is – do you miss him too?'

'I haven't thought about him for a long time but after seeing him at the party, I suppose I have been thinking about him a little bit. I did love him, Gran, for almost three years. It's hard to forget that. And there hasn't really been anyone else since.'

Jane sighed. 'No. It is hard to forget the love of your life.' She looked out wistfully into the garden where Charlie was running around. Her husband, Nancy's grandfather, had passed away before Nancy had even been born. He'd died of a heart attack and Jane had never loved again. They'd been childhood sweethearts, both born and bred in Dedley End, and Nancy knew her gran still missed him every day.

'You will be careful though, won't you? I don't want you to get hurt.'

Nancy nodded.

'You know I was never his biggest fan but no one knows what really makes someone else's relationship work. It's really only your business. I'll be here whatever happens. You know that, right?'

'Thank you, Gran.' She smiled. 'I don't know what will happen but I think I need to focus on our case, and try not to worry about it. How are we going to make sure that we don't have to fork out fifty quid to Jonathan?'

It was Jane's turn to sigh then. 'I don't know. Everything seems to point to the Roths but why would one of them do that? To protect their fortune?'

'We know they weren't happy about the marriage but Harry and Lucy stayed living here for six months, why did they do that if the family were making their lives miserable? It doesn't make sense to me.'

'What about the argument we saw between Will and Lucy? I wonder what the police have done about that.'

'Me too. I don't think they were having an affair, Will seemed pretty sincere when he said he didn't trust her, that he thought she was a gold-digger.'

'Do you think stopping her from getting her hands on their money was the motive, then? And if it was, why did they do it on the night of the party?'

'I wondered that. The first time they open up their doors, they choose to commit murder. It doesn't make sense. Unless they wanted someone in the village to take the blame? To increase the list of possible suspects?' Nancy said. 'Or they just saw an opportunity and took it in the moment when they saw her up there alone?'

'If we knew the motive then we would know,' her gran replied with a sigh.

'They're so rich, surely everyone who marries into that family is attracted by the money, even just a little bit?' Nancy wondered. 'Having met them all, it's so hard to picture one of them as actually killing her, you know?'

Jane raised an eyebrow. 'Does anyone really seem like they're capable of murder though?'

'I said I'd be back to look at the library again so I think I should go tomorrow and keep my ears and eyes open while I'm there and see if I can work out who it might have been.'

Her grandmother shook her head. 'I really can't say I like the idea of you being in that house again when there could well be a killer under that roof. I think I had better come with you. It's Penelope's day to work anyway so I'm not needed at the shop. And I can be looking at the books while you do some snooping.'

Nancy had to admit she felt better knowing she wouldn't be alone there again. 'Thanks, Gran. I need your input into this as I'm stumped. At least the killing seems personal so I think we're safe there.'

'As long as no one in that house realises that we're trying to track down the killer,' Jane said darkly.

Nancy shuddered. 'Yes, I suppose you're right. We'd better be careful not to draw too much attention to ourselves just in case.'

'At least we have our occupations on our side. Who would ever think that booksellers could be trying to solve a murder?'

'Who indeed.' They chuckled then, and finished off their tea in companionable silence. Nancy had no idea what the next few days would bring but she wasn't alone, and that helped to give her the courage she would need to face it all.

Chapter Nineteen

Friday morning dawned crisp and bright again, the promise of Christmas dancing in the air. The huge Dedley End tree had been put up ready for the lighting night and was standing in the middle of the village green, the church peeking through behind it. When Nancy and Jane reached Roth Lodge, they saw that they too had decided it was time to decorate. Fairy lights were being strung up outside by the gardener as they walked up to the door. It seemed even murder couldn't put a stop to tradition at the house on the hill.

Frank, the butler, opened up the door. 'Miss Hunter,' he greeted her.

'I brought my grandmother to help me today, she runs the bookshop with me,' Nancy explained as she walked into the hall followed by Jane. There was no longer a policeman standing guard so it felt more normal to Nancy now, and she felt slightly more at ease.

Frank nodded as he held out his hands for their coats. 'Go on through, and I'll have some tea brought in,' he told them. Nancy thanked him and led Jane to the library. They both looked curiously at the house as they went, neither having the courage to speak; it was so quiet, even their footsteps echoed despite the fact neither of them wore heels.

'What are you doing here?' A cold, cut-glass voice asked, making them both jump as Nancy reached for the library door handles. They turned to see Jessica Roth walking down the corridor.

Hurrying behind her was her sister, Annabel. 'She's here to help Marcus with the library,' Annabel called. 'Remember?'

'And this is my grandmother, Jane Hunter, she helps me run the bookshop,' Nancy quickly explained, relieved that Annabel at least seemed pleased to see her again. Jessica, on the other hand, glared at them both. Side by side, they looked so different it was hard to believe they were even related. Annabel was shorter and stockier, her mousy hair tied back, no make-up on, wearing a frumpy cardigan and skirt. Jessica was tall and graceful in an elegant twin-set and pearls, her glossy hair loose over her shoulders.

'Lovely to meet you,' Annabel said to Jane with a warm smile.

'I don't know why my father-in-law is bothering with that dusty tomb,' Jessica said with a roll of her eyes, ignoring the introduction.

'Probably because his wife loved it so much,' Jane replied shortly. Nancy stifled a laugh as she opened up the library. She always enjoyed it when her gran put people in their place.

'Yes, well, sometimes you need to let the past stay buried,' she muttered. 'I have a headache, I'm going to have a lie down,' she declared, sweeping past them, her eyes casting a fleeting look over her shoulder at them, making Nancy feel as though they had been found very much wanting.

'Don't mind her. The police have been here again, they searched the whole house, and spoke to everyone,' Annabel said, following as Nancy and Jane walked into the library. 'We're all feeling rather shaken up.'

'I can imagine,' Nancy replied, wondering who was the most shaken by it all and if that meant they were the killer.

'In fact, Harry and Marcus are down at the police station as we speak,' Annabel continued, looking worried. 'They've been there for ages; we have no idea what's going on.'

'I'm sure the police are just being thorough, dear,' Jane said, giving Nancy an enquiring look. Nancy was intrigued too. Had there been a development in the case?

She slipped off her coat and grabbed her phone, firing off a quick text to Jonathan to alert him to what Annabel had told them. 'Do you think it's okay that we're here?' she asked Annabel then.

'Yes, perhaps we should go,' Jane said, the disappointment clear in her voice.

'I think you should carry on,' Annabel said. 'Marcus keeps saying we should carry on as normal but it's so hard. Ah, here's some tea.' In came Natalie who glanced at Nancy, apparently a little startled at seeing her there again, as she put the tea tray down on the desk shakily. 'Thank you, Natalie.' The girl gave a quick nod before hurrying out, unable to meet Nancy's eyes, missing her reassuring smile. 'I can't help you today, I'm afraid. I need to pop into town but you'll be alright, won't you both?'

'Of course. Did the police say when you can go home?' Nancy asked her.

Annabel grimaced. 'No, not yet but at least I can look after the family while I'm here. I'll see you later.' She went out with a warm smile for them.

Nancy followed and leaned out of the library, peeping to see where she went. She saw her grab a coat from the cupboard and let herself out of the front door.

'What is it?' Jane hissed behind her.

'Just checking she has really gone. There's no sign of any of the family. What do you say to doing some snooping?'

'Isn't that a bit risky?' Her grandmother bit her lip, concerned.

'How else are we ever going to find anything out? If the police are interviewing the family, they might already have their suspicions as to who the murderer is, but we don't. By some miracle if the police are right then we're going to lose this bet with Jonathan. Do you want that?'

Jane shook her head. 'No, and I still don't trust that the police will be on the right track. Okay, let's see what we can find out.' They slipped out of the library, closing the double doors behind them, and went out into the hallway.

Looking up at the ornate iron balustrade, Nancy pointed. 'Lucy was pushed from up there, and I've yet to see the first floor. Let's go up.' They walked through the drawing room and up the staircase at the back of the room up to the first floor. They walked down the corridor past closed doors to the gallery in the middle where Lucy had been leaning, looking over the rails down into the hallway below. The corridor continued on beyond the gallery. 'I guess her killer could have come from either direction to push her,' Nancy said, in a low voice, pointing back the way they had come, and then ahead which led to the other staircase above the kitchen. Lucy would have had her back to her killer as she looked down into the hallway, hands on the railing, the party in full swing in the drawing room, oblivious that the end for her was nigh.

'Let's look around,' her gran suggested.

'Which way though?' Nancy whispered. Jane shrugged. Nancy decided to carry on down the corridor to rooms they hadn't passed with her grandmother almost touching her shoulder behind her.

The house was twisty and turny, richly furnished with high ceilings and shiny wooden floors, a carpet aisle running down the corridor, the light dim on the dark winter day. It was a world away from their own cosy cottage and Nancy wondered if she would actually like to live somewhere like this. It felt imposing and impersonal as if the very walls carried a weight of secrets inside of them.

'Look, Gran,' Nancy whispered, pointing to a door ahead that was slightly open.

Jane looked behind them. 'No one seems to be around,' she said, her eyes twinkling a little bit.

Nancy smiled; she enjoyed her gran's flashes of rebel tendencies. 'Keep an eye out though,' she said, walking through the door, Jane close behind her, checking over her shoulder.

They found themselves in a bedroom with a large, grand four-poster bed in the centre and dramatic heavy drapes at the window, beyond which the lush grounds were visible. Nancy could see it was definitely a woman's room – there was a dress laid out on the bed and on the dressing table by the window were perfume bottles and various skin creams lined up neatly, brands too expensive for Nancy to use herself. The wardrobe was half open, clothes, bags and shoes visible and spilling out. On the bedside table was a vase of red roses, lending their subtle fragrance to the room. 'Whose room is this, I wonder?' she said in a low voice.

Jane positioned herself so she could look out at the door. 'See if you can find any clues,' she instructed Nancy.

Nancy had no idea quite how to do that but she walked over to the bedside table and pulled open a drawer. It was strange to look through someone's belongings. Nancy didn't like the cold shiver that ran down her spine but how else were they ever going to find out the secrets in this house? In the drawer was a box of tissues, a phone charger, and a book.

'Oh my God!' Nancy gasped as she reached for it.

'What is it?' Her gran hurried over eagerly.

'Look,' Nancy said, showing her the copy of *The Man in the Brown Suit*. 'It's the book that was missing from the library inventory. Remember? The one that Annabel told me was there but when I checked, it wasn't?' She held it in her hands, stroking the cover of the leather-bound hardback. It was an old copy but not a special edition or anything. 'This wouldn't be worth anything to sell so why did she hide it up here?'

'You think this is Annabel's room, then?' Jane asked.

'Seems likely now I've found this book here. I just don't understand why she didn't want me to see the book or why she took it up here. One of the staff could easily see it.' Nancy opened up the book and flicked through it, but there was nothing slipped inside. She turned back to the first page and then paused. There was a dedication written there in smooth black ink. She tapped it to draw her grandmother's attention to it, and they leaned over to read it.

For Dolly – I will never forget this summer. Forever yours, John.

'Who's Dolly?' Jane whispered.

'I have no idea. None of the Roths are called Dolly or John. I mean, it could be a second-hand book so the dedication might have nothing to do with them.' She closed the book and looked at her grandmother. 'Why then hide it up here?'

'You think she wanted to make sure you didn't see the dedication?'

'Maybe, but it means nothing to me so I don't see why. Maybe Annabel simply fancied reading it.' She groaned in frustration. She hadn't realised that trying to solve a murder would be so perplexing. 'I'll take a photo to show Jonathan.' She snapped one on her phone and then put the book back. She took another scan around the room but there seemed to be nothing else in there that might help. 'Shall we try another room?' she asked Jane.

'Someone's coming,' Jane hissed, hurrying out of the room as Nancy froze wondering what her gran was doing by exposing their presence.

Chapter Twenty

'Who are you?' a startled voice cried out.

'Oh, hello dear, remember me from the party? I'm Jane Hunter, Nancy's grandmother, and I appear to have become lost trying to find a bathroom,' Jane replied to the man outside, putting on her old lady voice that she used when talking to insurance companies or suppliers trying to give them a raw deal.

Nancy tiptoed to the door and peeped out. Will Roth was outside. Her heart was thudding in her chest but she supposed he was the least likely of the family to turf them out. And Jane appeared to be winning him over, thankfully.

'There is one downstairs,' he said.

'Oh really, I didn't know, I'm so sorry!' Jane cried.

'Don't worry. Please, let me show you to a guest bathroom. Is Nancy here, too? Do you both fancy joining me for a cup of tea in the kitchen?'

'She's in the library, let's go and get her after I use the loo,' Jane said, firmly taking his arm and pulling him down the corridor. Nancy grinned and hurried out of the room, turning back the way they had come, creeping as softly as she could down the stairs, through the drawing room, and across the hallway into the library to wait for her gran and Will.

'Nancy?'

Nancy looked up from the desk where she had hastily planted herself to make it look as if they had been hard at work studying the library inventory. Will Roth stood in the doorway with Jane.

'Come and have a cuppa with us, I've just met your gran, she had got lost in this maze of a house. I bet Mrs Harper has some biscuits we can ravage too.'

'Lovely,' she replied with a smile. Her gran gave her a thumbs-up sign behind his back. As she followed them, she noticed Will looked tired. He had a thick line of stubble around his chin and dark circles under his eyes. Yet he still wore smart trousers and a shirt, his shoes polished, his hair slick. 'No sign of your grandfather and brother?' she asked him gently as they walked to the kitchen together.

'Still at the police station,' he replied with a sigh. 'I have no idea what's going on. It feels as if they just keep asking us the same questions over and over again. The problem is, they can't find any evidence, or witnesses.' He opened the door to the kitchen, which was empty. 'Please sit, and I'll make the tea. I keep needing things to do otherwise I will go mad thinking about everything.'

They dutifully sat down in the country style-kitchen. It felt far warmer and cosier than the rest of the house, maybe because it was mostly the domain of the staff, and not the family. Nancy watched Will making them tea and putting biscuits out on a plate. He certainly wasn't above serving them, and she wondered if his mother would approve or not; she seemed the biggest snob of them all. Objectively Will was a good-looking man – tall and handsome, and obviously from a wealthy family and yet he appeared to be unattached. She thought back to the argument between him and Lucy and Penelope's belief they could have been more than just brother and sister-in-law. Nancy couldn't believe it, based on the way he spoke about Lucy but she knew they shouldn't miss this opportunity of being alone with him to press him on it. 'How are you all coping?' she asked him as casually as she could. 'It must be a dreadful strain on everyone.'

Jane watched Will's response with interest.

He nodded as the kettle boiled. 'It is. My brother is feeling it most of all – he gets relentless questions, and yet the police are no closer to finding out who did this. And they're still saying that we should all stay put. I really need to go back to work. Which may sound callous but life does go on, doesn't it?' He carried over the tray of tea and biscuits and sat down with them. 'Harry told me off for asking if I could go. He thinks none of us care about what happened to Lucy.'

'And is that true?' Jane asked as she poured them all tea into the dainty china tea cups and saucers; Nancy was sure they were worth a lot of money.

Will looked up at her, surprised. 'Well, naturally we care! Someone was killed in our family home. I'm not a callous man, I promise, Mrs Hunter. There was no love lost between the two of us but I'd never wish anyone dead.'

'Of course. Can I ask though – why didn't you like her?' Jane sipped her tea as she spoke mildly.

Will sighed. 'I was suspicious, I suppose. Suddenly, Harry came back from working in France with a wife that none of us had even met. It was just so sudden, and very out of the blue for Harry.'

Nancy helped herself to a biscuit. 'Are you and Harry close?' She was always curious about sibling relationships, being an only child herself.

'We were. Growing up, I mean, we were very close, and with Maria too but as we've got older, I suppose not as much. When we were in London though, we did a lot together, work and socialising and all that and then Harry went to set up an office in France,' Will explained. 'He's been in Paris for a couple of years so none of us have seen much of him, just for the family Christmas really. So, I didn't even know he was seeing anyone but he turned up in London and came to see me with Lucy, to tell me their news. They'd decided to have a little break in London at a hotel before coming here to Roth Lodge.' He shook his head. 'My first thought was how stunning Lucy was. I love Harry but, let's face it, he's not considered a looker.'

Jane nodded. 'But my dear, he is very rich.'

'Exactly.' He nodded. 'She walked in, looking like a supermodel and the thought that entered my mind almost immediately was that she was a gold-digger. After they came here, I spoke to my family. I had more calls from them than ever before. They all thought the same as I did. But Harry was adamant they were in love, and I suppose she did seem to dote on him. But my parents weren't happy, and my grandfather was disappointed, although he did come around slowly, and Maria was on their side actually. It all gradually calmed down and the calls stopped. I don't pay too much attention to this house while I'm away to be honest.' He paused to sip his tea. 'But then I was summoned back here for the engagement party. Things seemed tense again. Lucy and my mother seemed to argue about the party details. They were both really stressed. My brother was trying to keep the peace but I don't think it was working. Maria and Charles had moved in too, to make sure everything was perfect for the party.

So the house was pretty chaotic.' He sighed. 'I heard Harry and Lucy arguing a few times, and Harry had definitely lost weight, he seemed to be strained, tired... unhappy. I asked him about it and he said they often seemed to want different things. He admitted he wanted to start a family but she didn't want that. He went to the London office for the day so I asked Lucy to have a drink with me to talk things through.'

Nancy and Jane exchanged looks. He was being open about the argument they had witnessed in the pub, which was surprising. 'And she agreed?' Nancy prompted him, eager to finally discover what they had talked about that day.

He nodded. 'I told her that my brother was clearly unhappy. I wanted to help but she took it badly. Maybe I should have minded my own business but...' He trailed off.

'You argued?'

'That's right. We went to the local pub, I'm sure you both know it, so none of the family would see us. I hadn't been in there since I was a teenager. Anyway, it was a bit embarrassing. Lucy was angry with me. Everyone in the pub noticed too. They told the police, which is why they don't want me to leave and go back to London. They think there was more to it but, I swear, I just wanted her to cut my brother some slack. Lucy told me I didn't understand their relationship and to butt out, basically, which maybe she had a point about. What do I know of married life? I begged her not to tell Harry about it, and she didn't. So now the police have told him and he's furious with me.'

Nancy felt somewhat guilty for having been the one who told the police about the argument although she knew they hadn't been the only witnesses, as Will had just confirmed. And it had looked suspicious, there was no denying that. 'Do you think she really did love your brother?'

Will thought for a moment. 'I'm honestly not sure if she loved anyone but herself.'

Jane leaned forward. 'So, then, there could be lots of people who wanted to see her dead?'

He flinched a little at her words. 'I really don't know much about her, which was the problem. None of us did. And look what she has brought to our family.' He looked at them. 'You believe me though, don't you? I'd never hurt anyone. I was just trying to help Harry. I had nothing to do with her death, I swear it.' He spoke fiercely and sincerely. Nancy and her gran exchanged another look. She knew her gran felt the truth in his words as she did. But if he didn't do it, then who did?

Before either of them could give him an answer, they heard the front door open and heavy footsteps, and the sound of bodies piling into the house. They all looked at one another in surprise, turning to the door. Voices grew louder, and then the kitchen door soon opened. Nancy straightened in her chair, hoping they weren't about to be thrown out.

Marcus Roth and Harry came in, followed by Inspector Brown and two uniformed officers. Everyone looked grave, and Nancy's pulse started to speed up. Marcus was looking at the ground, his face weary, whereas Harry glared at his brother. Nancy had a very bad feeling about what was about to happen.

'Will Roth,' DCI Brown said, stepping forward.

'What's going on?' Will asked, confused, looking to his grandfather and brother for answers, but he received none from them. It was DCI Brown who explained all.

'You are under arrest for the murder of Lucy Roth.'

Chapter Twenty-One

Nancy and Jane watched in stunned fascination as DCI Brown read Will his rights and a uniformed officer pulled him up from his chair and handcuffed him. Will's face was one of pure shock. He looked down at Nancy and Jane and seemed to sense that they were the only ones in the room to hold any speck of sympathy for him in that moment.

'You have to help me,' he pleaded. 'I didn't do it.' He turned desperately to his brother and grandfather. 'How can you think I've done this?'

He was pulled then by the officer, yanked from the room, DCI Brown marching after them. Marcus and Harry followed behind.

'Well, I never,' Jane said to Nancy.

'Come on.' Nancy helped her up and they hurried out of the kitchen. In the hallway, the butler, housekeeper, and Natalie the maid were all standing around, trying not to look like they were watching but failing miserably. Nancy and Jane joined them to watch as Will struggled in vain, the police leading him to the front door. Marcus shook his head. Harry followed, as though he was making sure Will really was being taken away.

'Will?'

Nancy looked up to the gallery. Up there stood Jessica and her sister, looking down on them over the railings in horror.

'It'll be all right,' Marcus Roth said then, speaking up finally, his voice heavy. He watched as Will was yanked out of the front door by the policeman. 'I'll call our lawyer.'

'Please, someone!' Will called back. 'They've got it all wrong! I swear!' His words faded as they left the house.

'How can they think my Will has done this?' Jessica said after a moment, her voice desperate in the silence. No one quite knew how to answer her.

'We need to go,' Nancy whispered to her gran. 'I'll get our things.' She had to tell Jonathan what had just happened. She hurried into the library and grabbed their coats and bags. When she came out again, she almost collided with Marcus. 'Oh!'

'Miss Hunter,' he said, looking flustered. 'I apologise… you're leaving?'

'We must leave you all in peace, I think.'

'Well, yes, I suppose so.' He sighed. 'I'm sorry you had to see all that. Perhaps we had better leave the library work, for the present.'

She nodded, trying to hide her disappointment. It had been such an excellent ruse. 'I understand, Mr Roth.'

He waved his hand. 'Marcus, please. Excuse me then, I must phone the family lawyer.'

'Of course,' she replied but he had already taken off at his customary pace, marching briskly past her into the library. She continued on to the hallway and passed Jane her things.

'Brandy, I think,' Annabel called down to the house-keeper, her face pale and worried, before hurrying away down the first-floor corridor. There was no sign of Jessica

Roth. Nancy assumed the brandy was needed for her. Even though she seemed a cold woman, it must have been a dreadful shock seeing her son arrested for murder like that.

Harry had disappeared as well. Goodness only knew what he was thinking and feeling. Nancy remembered the way he had looked at his brother – as if he believed he was the murderer. She pulled her coat on quickly and linking arms with her gran, they hurried out of Roth Lodge. She wondered if they were crazy to trust in Will and yet she couldn't help thinking of his face and words, so sincere, so shocked, so helpless and pleading. Was he really that good an actor?

'I'll go and tell Jonathan what's happened and meet you back at the shop,' she said as they turned away from the house and walked towards the village.

'I can't believe that just happened. They've got it wrong, haven't they?' Jane's question hung in the air, neither quite sure of the answer.

–

Nancy walked alone through Dedley End after leaving Jane at the bookshop, telling Penelope everything that had happened at Roth Lodge.

She walked towards Jonathan's flat, above their local convenience store. The newspaper offices where he worked were in the next town over, Woodley, but it wasn't far to go to work and he, like Nancy, had never left the village they had grown up in.

Hurrying up the stairs to the side of the shop, she rapped hard on the door, hoping Jonathan was there. He didn't usually work on Fridays but maybe she should have called to check; she'd been too eager to talk to him, though.

'Nancy?' Jonathan flung open the door. His hair looked messy and his shirt was unbuttoned. 'What are you doing here?' he asked, somewhat flustered.

'Who is it?' a female voice called from within.

'Who's that?' Nancy asked, frowning because the woman sounded familiar.

Jonathan sighed. 'It's Kate.'

'Seriously?' she cried, incredulously. After the way he had tried to avoid her, he now had her in his flat, doing goodness knows what? Well, she knew what but would rather not think about it.

'Don't look at me like that!' He stepped forward quickly, pulling the door closed behind him so Kate wouldn't be able to hear them. 'You don't understand.'

'No, no, I don't,' she replied, flatly. 'I always stick up for you, telling everyone that you never mean to hurt anyone, but you know how Kate feels about you.'

'I wish you wouldn't look so disappointed in me. She came over, she came to me…'

'And you just couldn't help yourself?!' Nancy wasn't quite sure why she felt so annoyed with him but she couldn't shake off the anger that had risen up so suddenly. 'One day someone is going to break that heart of yours, Jonathan Murphy, and it'll only be what you deserve.'

'Maybe it's already broken, did you ever think of that?' He snapped back. They stared at one another for a long moment, frustration now on both their faces, tension in the air that surprised them both. Finally, he sagged a little with a sigh, and she stepped back, feeling like she needed to put some distance between them.

Nancy chose not to respond to what he had just said. 'I came to tell you that the police have arrested Will Roth for Lucy's murder.'

Jonathan's eyes widened. 'Crikey. Why, though?'

'I think because he and Lucy argued that day in the pub. That's all they have to go on. But Will explained to me and Gran what that was all about, and I think we believe him.' She quickly told him what Will had said, and how he had pleaded his innocence as the police had taken him away. 'If he didn't do it, we need to help him.'

'I'm not sure how. Only finding out who the real killer is will do that, and we haven't got much more than the police to go on, have we?'

'Marcus has suggested I stay away from the library what with everything going on so I've lost my in with the family now.' She was frustrated. 'I'm really not sure where we go from here.'

'Let's sleep on it; there must be some avenue we can try. Something the police haven't thought of. Unless it really is Will who did it, after all.'

'I hope it isn't.'

'You really like him, don't you?'

'For some reason, he feels like the most trustworthy of the family, I'm not really sure why, though. Perhaps he seems different from them, somehow. Like he doesn't care about being a Roth in the same way they do.'

Jonathan looked back at his flat. 'I'd better go back in, Nancy. I—'

'No,' she said, quickly. 'It's fine, don't worry.' She started to turn away, not wanting to fight with him anymore. She felt very tired all of a sudden. 'I need to go back to the shop anyway.'

'Well, I'll see you at the tree night tomorrow, won't I?' he called at her retreating back.

'Yes, yes, you will,' she called back, knowing that he wouldn't be at all impressed if she turned up with Richard but deciding that, after catching him with Kate, she really shouldn't care what he thought. She hurried back down the stairs and outside again, needing the cool outside air. She wished she hadn't been so short-tempered with him but it was hard to fathom his actions. He had told her he didn't want anything serious with Kate but was just stringing her on regardless. Was he really so uncaring, or could he just not help himself? She tried to stop thinking about what he had said but it was impossible. She strolled slowly back towards the bookshop, his words ringing in her ears.

'Maybe it's already broken…'

Had Jonathan really got a broken heart? And if so, who had broken it? Nancy really wasn't sure whether she wanted to find out the answer to that.

Chapter Twenty-Two

The following morning, Nancy fed Charlie as her gran sat at the kitchen table with her tea, looking down at a large book.

'What's that?' Nancy asked, going over to switch the kettle on, gasping for a cup of tea. Nerves were already setting in ahead of her evening date with Richard, and she was hoping something would take her mind off it.

Jane looked up, her eyes glistening. 'I got out the family album. Feeling a little sentimental ahead of Christmas, I suppose. I don't want to upset you though, love.'

'It's okay.' Nancy made them both a cup of tea and joined Jane at the table. 'I understand. Christmas just brings it all back, doesn't it?' She looked down at the photo of her parents holding her as a baby at their house on the edge of the village. She wondered how long they had been happy, the three of them, before it all went so wrong. Her mother leaving, and then her dad's accident. 'I've been thinking about Dad more than ever this week. I suppose because of Lucy Roth's murder. I can't help but wonder whether I could have found out something about the crash if I hadn't been so young at the time.'

Jane reached over to squeeze her hand. 'I have always wished I could have done more. I do think the police tried hard but they just could never find any evidence of who was driving the other car that night. We'll never know if they made your dad swerve and crash into the tree or not. I hate not knowing. And most of all, I hate that someone was unfeeling enough to drive away and not help him. That he was alone out there...' She trailed off, her eyes glistening.

Nancy shook her head. 'What kind of person drives off like that? And there must be someone else who knew what they had done, too. Their family, partner, someone – they must have gone home in a right state, surely?'

'I suppose so but if someone knew, they decided to protect them and not come forward. And then it rained so tyre tracks and any other evidence was washed away. All we ever had to go on was that scarf they found near your dad's car but it never came to anything,' Jane said. Nancy remembered her gran telling her the scarf had come from the department store Liberty London – a vivid yellow and blue silk. It could have belonged to anyone. The police thought the other driver must have been a tourist, speeding, not knowing the roads... and it had been dark and rainy that night, too. 'I don't think they meant to hurt anyone. That's what I've always tried to have faith in.'

'No, but they could have stopped and called for help, then maybe, just maybe, my dad could have been saved.' Nancy looked at her parents' smiling, happy faces, holding their daughter, and goosebumps pricked up along her arm. 'Do you think my mum ever knew about the crash?'

Jane sighed. 'I have always hoped not. Because if she had then she would have come back for you.'

'Do you really believe that, Gran?'

'They both loved you, Nancy. Your mother did, she just couldn't cope. But you should still hold on to that love.'

Nancy wasn't sure if her gran was right about her mother but she would never know. 'I wish Dad was still here.'

'Me too, love. I'm sorry, I shouldn't have got this out, it makes one maudlin.' She closed the photo album. 'We can't change the past, can we? We'll never get over what happened but you have to learn to live with the pain, don't you?'

Nancy nodded and sipped her tea but she still felt frustrated. There was someone walking around who knew what had happened that night and she wished she could find them, and uncover the truth finally. 'I hope that we can find out the truth about who killed Lucy. I couldn't bear two unsolved crimes in Dedley End.'

'We're sure it wasn't Will?'

'I feel like he's telling the truth but if it wasn't him, then who was it? How can they just walk around and live as if they haven't taken someone's life? I'll never understand it.'

'Nor can I. I'm worried this is upsetting you too much, though. Maybe we should forget this bet. And leave it to the police after all.'

'I don't think I can, Gran. If Harry really loved Lucy then how can he ever move on if the killer isn't found? And we know what that's like, don't we?'

Jane nodded.

Nancy wasn't sure she could walk away from it now. She was too invested. And if she didn't do something, Dedley End's second crime would be another to go unsolved or, even worse, someone who didn't do it might well end up taking the blame for it. How could she ever rest if she let either of those things happen?

They sipped their tea for a minute in silence. 'How are you feeling about tonight?' Jane asked then.

'A bit nervous,' she admitted. 'Am I crazy to have agreed to this date?'

'I don't know, love. I know you loved Richard a lot but there was a reason you broke up. I know that people can change but often we fundamentally want the same things from life, don't we?'

Nancy sighed. 'How did you know my grandfather was the one you wanted to be with?' she asked. He had died before she was born but she knew that her grandparents had been happy.

'We grew up together here in the village. I always thought we'd make a life together. Most married women didn't work back then and he looked after me, supported me. And he was my best friend.'

'That's lovely,' Nancy replied. 'With Richard, it always felt like things had to be on his terms, you know? He wanted us to live in London, he never asked what I wanted. He didn't understand why I couldn't leave Dedley End.'

'Does he understand now?'

'I guess I'll find out tonight. I just hope I'm not making the same mistake all over again.'

'As long as you're careful, it will be okay, I'm sure,' her gran told her. 'It isn't easy keeping a level head when it comes to love though.'

'I don't want to be hurt again, that's for sure.'

'I know. There's that saying, isn't there? *Fool me once, shame on you; fool me twice…*'

'*Shame on me,*' Nancy finished for her, smiling at her gran's love of bringing up cliché phrases when dishing out wisdom, but knowing they were clichés because they were almost always true.

'I wonder what Richard makes of Will being arrested? He worked with him quite a bit, didn't he?'

Nancy nodded. 'I'll ask him. Maybe he has some more insight. I didn't get to talk to him a lot about the party before. Maybe he noticed something that we didn't? I lost track of him that night so I'm not sure where he was when it all kicked off. He might have seen something that might help us. We're a bit stuck at this point, aren't we?'

'We'll help Will,' Jane promised. 'I don't think he'll get much support from his family. There doesn't seem to be much love in that house. No wonder Lucy felt like an outsider there, poor girl.'

Nancy checked the time. 'I'd better get going, I need to walk Charlie before I open the shop. You're heading to the green to check on things for the tree night, right?'

'I am. We need to make sure the lights are tested and everything is in place. Let me make you something to eat before you head off, though.'

'I don't think I can face anything this morning.' Nancy was too nervous about later. She clearly didn't want to lay herself open to be hurt again but she also knew that she had been hiding her heart, keeping people at a distance, and not putting herself 'out there', and she didn't want that for herself either. Why was it all so complicated? She envied her gran, and Penelope too, for their love lives, wishing she had met her soul mate at school as they both had.

And then she felt her cheeks grow hot as she thought of Jonathan. Her best friend. That was all he had ever been. But she knew he always had her back in life, even when he annoyed her or teased or disappointed her, and she hoped that he always would have. She was worried about their argument, and about what he would think when he saw her with Richard.

'You're not alone, Nancy,' her gran said, firmly. 'You'll always have me.'

Nancy smiled. 'Thanks, Gran.' She leaned over and gave her a hug. Charlie barked and wandered over to them. 'I know, Charlie, we also have you too,' she said with a laugh, reaching down to ruffle his fur.

Chapter Twenty-Three

'All ready then?' Jane asked, giving Nancy a kind smile as she walked into the living room. It was almost six o'clock, the time Richard was due to pick Nancy up. Jane was finishing off a plate of leftover cottage pie before she headed back to the village green to get everything ready for the tree lighting ceremony. Charlie was on the floor by her feet having a snooze before their night out.

Nancy, who was wearing a long wool skirt, soft grey jumper and boots, wasn't at all sure she was ready for this but nodded. 'I think so.' There was a beep from outside, and they looked at one another. She took a deep breath. 'Right then. I'd better be off.' She might have known he wouldn't knock on the door in case he had to face Jane. She put on a smile. 'See you later for tree night, then.' She half wanted to stay with her gran but forced herself to leave the cottage.

'I'll see you on the green, love,' Jane called after her. 'I hope you have a good time.'

'Thanks!' Nancy grabbed her bag and coat, and slipped outside, shivering instantly. Winter was in full force, and she was glad of the layers she had worn in preparation for standing outside later. Richard had jumped out of the car to open up the door for her and she walked over, buttoning her coat as she went.

'Thanks for coming,' Richard said as she climbed into the warm car.

Nancy just smiled, inwardly hoping that she hadn't made a big mistake. Richard got in the driver's seat and they set off. Nancy had told him to book a gastro pub in Woodley. She didn't want to go to the White Swan, as there would be far too many people she knew there; it would have set tongues wagging and she really didn't want to do that quite yet.

'Have you heard the news?' Nancy asked as she tried to relax in the car seat. 'About Will Roth?'

Richard nodded gravely. 'I did. Everyone in the office was talking about it yesterday. I can't believe he's been arrested. He seemed the most down to earth of the family to me, we always got on well.'

Nancy nodded. She had thought the same about Will. 'I really didn't feel like he'd be capable of it, it was a shock to me. Do you think he did it?'

Richard glanced at her. 'I know that he didn't particularly like Lucy but it seems absurd to me that the police believe that's motive for murder. But they must have a reason to arrest him? Perhaps he was in love with her or they were having an affair?'

'I thought that at first but after talking to him, I don't think so. He thought she was after Harry's money and was worried about his brother.'

'When did he tell you this?'

'Oh well, Marcus Roth asked me to look at their library and order some new books in for them but that's been put on hold now, obviously. I spoke to him at the house while I was there.' Nancy thought of something then that Richard could help with. 'If Lucy had been after their money, would they have had reason to worry? I mean, surely they have millions?'

'Their company is very successful and they have inherited money too. Even if she divorced Harry and was able to beat the family's lawyers, she would have only been entitled to half of what Harry had. Marcus runs the family trust fund and the company is separate – there are shareholders. They really do have a fantastic legal team, too; I wouldn't want to go up against them in court.'

'I don't understand then why she was killed.'

'Why are you so interested?'

'Well,' Nancy thought for a minute then decided to tell him. She needed to know if he would support her or not. 'My gran and I made a bet with Jonathan that we could find the killer before the police. It sounds frivolous but that's not the real reason we're looking into it. We don't want there to be someone else who doesn't get justice. After what happened with my dad and everything…' She trailed off, unsure if she was explaining herself properly.

'And you thought that with your crime knowledge you might get to the truth first?'

'Maybe it's silly.'

'Not silly, but they have a lot of resources that you don't have.'

'We thought the family might be more open with us, I suppose.'

Richard nodded. 'I can see that.' He hadn't laughed at her. A good sign. 'But you haven't got anywhere?'

'I've met the whole family now and honestly, I can't believe any of them would be capable of cold-blooded murder but someone in that house did it.' She told him everything they had found out about Lucy so far. 'The police have arrested Will because of the argument he had with Lucy but he's explained it, and I'm inclined to believe him. Why have a public row like that if you were planning to kill her?'

'He must have known the police would find out,' Richard agreed. 'As I said, I've always respected him since we met. I felt he has better morals than most people in business. But he could be a good liar, I suppose.' He pulled into the pub car park.

'Or he's innocent.' She sighed. 'Did you know any other people at the party? The police seem focused on the family and apparently Lucy didn't invite anyone she knew to the party but there were a lot of people there. Perhaps they chose the party to do it so they could go unnoticed.' She now wondered if she'd missed a suspect while focusing on the Roths.

'I had the impression Lucy didn't have anyone close here in the UK. I'm not sure there was anyone at the party who would care enough to want to hurt her?' He parked and jumped out to open the door for her. Always the gentleman. She smiled as she climbed out, appreciating it.

'That's what I thought but perhaps it was a heat of the moment thing. I could get my head around that more than a premeditated attack.' Nancy and Richard walked into the pub. 'Lucy is still somewhat a mystery. She could have had a lot of secrets we don't yet know about that might lead us to her killer. I'm just not sure how we uncover what they might be though,' Nancy admitted.

'As I say, I only met her once before. I didn't talk to her enough to help you. But if you want to look into her past then I think you need to go further afield than Roth Lodge. Where did she live before coming here?' he asked as they found their table in the corner of the pub close to the log fire.

Nancy hung her coat over the chair and thought about his suggestion. 'That's actually a good idea. We don't really know her background. All we know is that she was working in a bar in Paris when she met Harry and after a month they were married and back in the UK.'

'Maybe one of the Roths knows more? She wasn't French, was she?'

'No, British,' Nancy confirmed. She hadn't really thought about where Lucy had been before France, or even how long she had lived and worked in Paris before she met Harry. 'It's a good thought. I'll see if we can find out,' she told him with a smile. She had been focused on Roth Lodge but perhaps Richard was right and the answers might lie somewhere else entirely.

Richard signalled for a waiter and ordered them wine again. They ordered their food and when they were alone, he smiled at her. 'I'm glad we're doing this. Even though it ended so tragically, I'll always be grateful to the Roths for inviting us both to that party.'

'I didn't expect to ever see you again.'

'I like to think it was fate that got me working with Will Roth and led me back to you. I've missed talking to you. When we broke up, it was like I had lost part of me. I didn't realise how different life would be without you in it.'

Nancy stared at him. 'Really?' At the time, it had felt as if he had walked away and forgotten all about her with no regrets. For her, it had been hard to watch him go and she had been wary of opening up her heart again ever since.

'Remember how we used to talk all the time? I have wanted to talk to you so many times.'

'I missed talking to you too,' she replied. They used to sit up in her room in the halls sometimes all night just talking, and she had felt so close to him at the time. It was so strange how you could do that with someone, but then have them walk out of your life and sever that connection completely.

Their drinks arrived then, and he poured them both a large glass, holding his up for a toast.

'Merry Christmas, Nancy, here's to you solving the case, and to second chances too,' Richard said, giving her the kind of smouldering look that in the past had made her feel like her knees could buckle.

'Cheers, Richard,' she replied, glad she was older and wiser, and stronger now, too so there would be no knees buckling tonight but she did return his smile, and felt their old chemistry crackle in the air between them again. They clinked glasses and she took a long sip of her drink before speaking again. 'So, tell me about London, and your life there. How have you spent the past five years, I wonder?'

'I still can't believe it's been five years! They've mostly been spent working, to be honest. I'm now a qualified accountant and I work for a large company dealing with lots of clients. It's challenging and exciting too. I share a flat with a colleague in south-west London, which is ridiculously expensive but I love it,' Richard told her. Their meals arrived then – steak and chips for him, lasagne and garlic bread for her (she wasn't taking any chances).

She nodded. She had no desire for that kind of life, though. And he must know that. 'I'm glad,' she said. 'I have thought about you over the years and wondered what you were doing.'

'I'm pleased. I've done the same. So many times, I thought about contacting you but honestly, I didn't know if you would have wanted to speak to me.' He reached across and brushed her hand with his fingertips, warming her skin a little more than she would have liked. 'I don't suppose it will be at all easy for you to forget what an idiot I was in the past but I'm going to try really hard to make you see that I have changed. I shouldn't have expected you to want the same life as I did. I should have listened. I should have compromised back then. I know I hurt you and I'm so sorry for that. Do you think you can forgive me?'

'We were in different places, we had different dreams. I was hurt, I was upset, and I did miss you a lot – I was in love with you, but my life was in Dedley End and yours was in London.'

'And now?'

She shrugged. 'I don't know, do you?'

'No but I'd like to find out.' He smiled and she found herself smiling back. She had no idea whether they could start again but she was enjoying his company and she couldn't deny that. 'So, tell me about this tree night of yours...'

He was trying. He was showing an interest in her village, which he'd never done before. That was encouraging. She explained as they tucked into the delicious food and the meal passed quickly and more enjoyably than she had thought it would.

Chapter Twenty-Four

There hadn't been any hesitation from Richard about accompanying her back to Dedley End. He even seemed to be looking forward to it after she told him what to expect. It was certainly a change from the past when he had seemed to sneer at the quiet village she loved so much. She welcomed the change and hoped it would continue because she was having fun. They parked back at her cottage and walked over to the green together, close enough that their coats were touching. Nancy was warmer than she had expected to be thanks to the wine they had drunk, no doubt, but also the company for the evening – there was a colour to her cheeks that she knew couldn't only be blamed on alcohol and a roaring fire.

The green was filling up when they got there. Fairy lights were draped between trees around the edge of the grass, twinkling in welcome, and people were holding lanterns and sparklers, and there were two stalls selling mulled wine, mince pies and warm chestnuts, making the air smell deliciously like Christmas.

'There you are!' Penelope grabbed Nancy around the waist as she passed by her. Kitty, her little girl, was holding her hand and looking sweet in her duffle coat. She beamed in the dim light. 'Come on, we've nabbed a good spot!' She took her arm and pulled her along with them. Nancy looked back at Richard who shook his head with a laugh but followed them.

Penelope led them to the front of the circle forming around the huge tree where Jane stood, holding Charlie's lead in one gloved hand, and in the other a cup of mulled wine. Gloria and the vicar were with her, and beside them was Jonathan eating a mince pie, his coat collar turned up against the wind. All eyes turned to them as Penelope moved into the empty space next to Jonathan. Charlie wagged his tail as Nancy reached down to pat him and he sniffed Richard who gamely stroked him too.

'Hi, folks,' Nancy said with false brightness, trying not to meet Jonathan's eyes for fear of what she'd find in them. 'This is Richard. I think you know everyone from the party and, uh, last time but let me re-introduce you all.' Nancy said all their names to fill the suddenly awkward silence.

'Is this your first tree-lighting ceremony, Richard?' Gloria Williams asked him kindly.

'It is. Nancy said it's a big tradition here.'

'That's right. It started in the eighteenth century, so the legend goes.'

'I'll get us some drinks,' Nancy said, moving away towards the stalls. She felt someone close behind her, and sighed when she saw who it was, preparing herself for what he might say.

'Seriously, Nancy? You weren't going to tell me?' Jonathan hissed in a low voice as they made their way to the stall serving mulled wine.

'We don't have to tell each other everything,' she said, hating that his words stung so much.

'You didn't tell me this because you knew I wouldn't approve,' he replied, picking up a cup of mulled wine and handing it to her.

'Approve? I have to ask your permission about who I bring to the tree night now?' she countered, snatching another cup from the stand for Richard as Jonathan clearly wasn't going to.

He sighed. 'Don't be silly. But also, don't act like you didn't keep this from me for a reason. You know you're playing with fire, and that's why you didn't want to tell me about it,' he said, getting a cup for himself, and striding off, away from their group. She watched as he found his colleagues from the newspaper, pointedly turning his back on her as he greeted them.

'Well, that went well,' Nancy mumbled under her breath as she wandered back and handed Richard one of the cups. She gulped her mulled wine down despite it being quite hot, and burning her tongue in the process. Why was Jonathan being quite so unreasonable? She could have done with his support, like Penelope and her grand-mother, not his fury. But underneath her annoyance, she also knew he had a point. She had deliberately not told him about seeing Richard again because she knew he wouldn't want to support that. Did that mean that she thought Jonathan was right about Richard, or because she hoped he was wrong?

'Everything okay?' Richard asked her quietly.

'Of course,' she lied. She wasn't ready to open up about her feelings to him yet. They were only just back in touch. She looked across at where Jonathan stood and felt as though she was a million miles away from him. It was a feeling she wasn't used to, and she didn't like it at all.

'Good evening, everyone!' The mayor stepped to the front, and everyone hushed obediently. 'Thank you all for coming out tonight, a wonderful turn-out as always. Dedley End has had an unusual few days. I know that everyone is worried about what happened at Roth Lodge but rest assured, the police are doing all they can, and I know the Roths wouldn't want us to let the investigation dampen our festive spirit tonight. Our tree lighting ceremony has been a long tradition of this village, after all, and our community is as strong, and safe, as it has always been!' he said in his deep, loud voice, reaching even those at the back of the group. Nancy looked across and saw Jonathan's eyes meet hers. He looked as unconvinced as she was that they were as safe and sound as they had always been but it made her even more determined to find out what had happened to Lucy Roth. The mayor was right – it had threatened their way of life in the village she had always lived in, and which she loved, and she had to do something about it.

'Without further ado then, let's light up the green for another year!' He led them in a countdown, the kids shouting as loud as they could, and Nancy glanced at Richard who joined in too, smiling down at her. She could never have imagined him being beside her tonight.

They watched as the mayor flicked a switch and the tree lit up with dazzling gold light. There were whoops and cheers from the kids and a round of applause rippled through the group, as they all looked up in wonder at it. It didn't matter what was happening in the world, Nancy thought, there was always an opportunity for magic.

The church choir started up then, singing a Christmas carol, their voices echoing around the green, reaching up into the starlit sky.

Richard slipped an arm around Nancy's waist and she found herself leaning into his warm, solid body, as they all joined in with the choir, light as ever stronger than any darkness.

—

After the choir had finished their song list of carols, the villagers began to disperse in search of either the pub or warm living rooms.

'Right, let's walk back to the cottage,' Jane said after they had said goodbye to everyone. Jonathan had gone off to the pub, and Penelope had taken her very sleepy daughter home. Richard took Nancy's hand as they walked across the green together, Charlie bouncing beside them still excited by his night out, all feeling rather merry after the evening.

'What a beautiful night,' Jane said, glancing at the fairy lights above them.

'I love this time of year,' Nancy agreed with her. The village always looked so lovely at Christmas time, and it was impossible not to feel some festivity seeing it all lit up.

'You should come and see the lights in London,' Richard said to her then. 'You'd love them.'

'I haven't seen them since I was little,' she admitted, knowing she would enjoy it but feeling like it would be a big step to go and see him down there. The place that broke them. Talking of London reminded her of Will Roth. 'I wonder what's happening with Will at the police station. Will they charge him?'

'Surely not?' Jane asked. 'But I do feel as if we're at a dead end with it all. It's not as if we know who did it, if it wasn't really Will.'

'And Marcus Roth doesn't want me in their library anymore.'

'That's probably for the best. I really don't like the idea of you in that house if someone there is capable of killing another human being,' Richard said to her.

She quite liked him feeling protective towards her. 'But it means I have no idea how we can find out more about her past before she married Harry like you suggested.'

'Well, let's just wait and see what happens with Will. They can't keep him much longer without charging him.'

They reached the cottage then, lit up and welcoming.

'Right, I'm straight for bed,' Jane said as she opened the front door, letting Charlie off his lead. He ran inside straight for his bed. 'Goodnight, you two,' she said, slipping inside quickly to give them some privacy.

Nancy hovered on the doorstep, wishing her grandmother hadn't left them alone. She faced Richard in the dim light, looking up at him, unable to ignore the tender look he gave her. 'Thank you for tonight, I had a lovely time,' she told him, truthfully.

'I meant what I said, you know, about trying to make up for the past,' he said, stepping closer. 'What do you think about coming to see me in London? I'd love to show you the lights.'

She looked into his eyes and found herself confused. It felt like too much of a big step to stay with him in London but it had been a long time since she had been to the city, and she did want to see the lights.

Richard sensed her hesitation. 'Why don't you think about it? But I really do hope you say yes.' He leaned in and she hitched her breath, wondering if he was going to kiss her but at the last moment, he turned and kissed her gently on the cheek.

She smiled, pleased that he was moving slowly. She needed more time, and she was grateful he seemed to realise it.

'I'll miss you,' he said before turning and heading to his car with a warm wave in her direction. She watched him go, wondering if she would miss him too.

She found herself hoping that she just might.

Chapter Twenty-Five

The bookshop phone started ringing as soon as Nancy walked in early on Monday. She had decided to go in before opening to sort a few things out and hurried into the office when she heard it, wondering what kind of book emergency there could possibly be at that time. 'Hello?' she answered somewhat breathlessly.

'Miss Hunter?'

'Speaking.'

'Ah, good. I'm Charles Edwards. I represent Will Roth.'

'Oh,' Nancy said in surprise.

'Mr Roth is being released from police custody this morning. He was hoping that you might come and collect him from the station in Woodley. He would like your help with something.'

'Oh.' Nancy wasn't sure why she wasn't capable of saying anything other than 'oh' but she was taken aback. Will wanted her to pick him up? Why not someone from the house on the hill? He must want to speak to her about Lucy. 'Yes, yes, I will,' she said, firmly, not wanting to miss this opportunity. And surely, if he was being released then he wasn't the murderer? She hung up after they had agreed a time and she grabbed her phone to message Jonathan, assuming he wouldn't be awake just yet, to ask him to come and get her as soon as he was. Then she leaned against the desk to steady herself. Talk about twists and turns, she could barely keep up with everything. But she smiled, feeling somehow that she was getting closer to the truth. 'We won't give up, Lucy,' she promised.

–

Nancy and Jonathan drove to the police station together an hour later, leaving Jane and Charlie to open the bookshop for the day. They drove through Dedley End to Woodley, the next town over, where the police station that covered theirs and the surrounding villages was situated. They passed through the High Street and drove up the hill out onto the winding road that led to Woodley. Nancy always felt a nervous tingle whenever she was in a car on this road, the same road that had snatched her father from her. The crash was the reason she had never wished to learn to drive herself, and she wasn't that keen on being a passenger at the best of the times, but this spot made it worse. Thankfully, theirs was the only car out on the road that early on such a chilly morning.

'What do you think Will Roth wants to speak to me about?' Nancy broke the silence in the car. She hated it when she and Jonathan argued; he was practically family. It was a rare occurrence which was usually quickly resolved, thanks to their mutual good humour and years of friendship, and she hoped they would get past this disagreement the same way.

'I really don't know. If you're right about him being innocent perhaps he knows who did do it.' Jonathan glanced at her. 'It shows you've won his trust, though, which is a really good thing if we are ever going to get to the bottom of all this.'

She smiled. 'I suppose a bookseller is far more trusted than a reporter.'

'I think it's more about you than what you do.' He sighed. 'About last night…'

'You were right,' she interjected quickly. 'I shouldn't butt into your love life, it's none of my business.'

'Did you just say "butt into"?' He raised an eyebrow in her direction, smirking a little.

Nancy was relieved he was teasing her again. 'Poke my nose into then, if you prefer a more English way of saying it. And I should have told you I was bringing Richard to the tree night.'

Jonathan focused on the road again. 'Like you say, it was none of my business. I just don't want to see you hurt again, that's all.'

'I know.' She gazed out of the window for a moment. 'We're not back together or anything, just so you know.' She looked at him but couldn't tell what reaction he had to that. He could keep a poker face when he wanted to.

'But he wants you to be?' he asked quietly.

Nancy nodded. 'Yes,' she half-whispered. 'But, actually, he did have a good thought about the case,' she said, brightly, steering the conversation back onto safer ground. She told him about Richard's suggestion that they look into Lucy's past more. 'I'm not sure how we find out about that though, given her lack of online presence, but perhaps Will knows something? If we could find out where she lived before she went to France maybe that could help?'

'We can ask him,' Jonathan agreed. They smiled at one another, the air thankfully cleared.

They reached Woodley, passing cobbled streets and cosy pubs, heading towards the grey stone police station slap bang in the centre of the small town, parking over the road from it. When they climbed out of the car, they saw DCI Brown striding towards the building. He paused when he saw them.

'I keep on seeing you,' he said to Nancy. 'You were at the Roths' when I arrested Will. And I keep telling you,' he added to Jonathan, 'that I won't be making another statement on the case yet.'

'We're here to pick up Will,' Nancy said. 'He's been released, hasn't he?'

DCI Brown looked annoyed. 'For now, yes. He'll be out shortly.' He paused before moving on. 'If there's anything pertinent to the case that the pair of you know, you'll be sure to tell me, won't you?' He gave them a rather stern look.

'Of course, Brown, you can count on us,' Jonathan replied cheerfully. He glanced at Nancy as if to say 'yeah right'.

He shook his head and carried on walking inside.

A couple of minutes later, Will Roth shuffled out, blinking at the sunlight. Nancy waved and he came over. 'Miss Hunter,' he said looking relieved to see her.

'I think you'd better call me Nancy after this,' she said with a smile.

'Thank you, Nancy. I'm so relieved to be out of there.'

'They didn't charge you then?'

He shook his head. 'I told you I didn't do it. Can we go somewhere to talk and where I can clean up? I need to gather my strength before I even think about going home.' He glanced at Jonathan. 'If we can talk off the record.'

Nancy and Jonathan shared an intrigued look. 'Of course,' Nancy said quickly. 'I don't drive so Jonathan bought his car,' she explained his presence.

'We just want to help find out who really did this,' Jonathan added.

Will nodded at Jonathan. 'Okay then.'

'We can go to my cottage,' Nancy said. Will looked pretty rough compared to how she had seen him before; she supposed a couple of days in a police cell would do that to a person. 'You must be hungry too. Come on.'

'Thank you, most kind,' he replied politely. They piled back into the car and set off again for her cottage.

They drove for a minute in silence before Nancy could stand it no longer and twisted in her seat to look at Will. He gazed out of the window looking pale, tired, unshaven, and rather shell-shocked. 'Was it frightful, Will? Are you okay?'

'It was pretty scary even though I knew I was innocent, I kept thinking, what if they don't believe me? But Edwards is a good sort; he made sure they checked my alibi and once they had that, demanded they release me. I had no time to do it, and no motive, although they didn't seem to care about that. Just kept on about that damned row in the pub. Clutching at straws, I think.'

'You had an alibi all along?' She was confused. Why hadn't he said so before? She remembered how he'd left her at the party; the police must have thought he'd had time to follow Lucy upstairs.

Will sighed. 'I didn't say before because I didn't want my family to know. I didn't think it would come to this, though. I can't believe my family think I could be capable of anything like this. That's why I wanted to speak to you, Nancy. I was hoping you might help me talk to Harry, make him realise that this wasn't anything to do with me.'

'I'm happy to try,' she agreed. 'But what didn't you want them to know?'

They arrived at the cottage then so they climbed out of the car and Nancy let them inside. She showed Will the bathroom and gave him a towel, a razor, a spare toothbrush and a T-shirt of Jonathan's from the last time he had stayed over after having too many G & T's to drive home. She told Will to meet them in the kitchen when he was ready. She followed Jonathan through to the kitchen and made them all a cup of tea, and she also started to make scrambled eggs and toast for Will.

'Well, if he has an alibi we really are back to square one,' Jonathan said as he sat down at the table with his tea.

'He might know more than he's let on to us before.'

'Let's hope so.'

A few minutes later, Will joined them, looking much better. Nancy brought over his food and tea to him. 'I can't thank you enough for this,' he said, tucking in. 'I just needed time to face my family.'

'Why, Will?' she asked. She knew the Roths a little bit now and knew they weren't the easiest family to deal with but surely it was a good thing he hadn't been charged by the police?

Will took a long gulp of tea. 'I know that in this day and age, in this country, a lot of people don't see it as a big deal, as something they have to hide, and I wish I didn't but... my family... well, Nancy, you know a little of what they're like now. My grandfather especially would not be happy at all. So, I kept it quiet I'm afraid and it's led me here.' He rubbed at his hair nervously and glanced at Jonathan. 'I am ready to tell the truth but I'd still rather it didn't find its way into your newspaper. It's rather... personal.'

'You have my word,' Jonathan promised. 'When we print you've been released, we'll just say the police have confirmed you have an alibi.'

He nodded and turned to Nancy. 'At the party, when I left you, when the police think I killed Lucy, I was greeting someone. Someone I care about very much.' He looked so vulnerable then, with none of the easy charm of the man Nancy had first bumped into at the party. 'My boyfriend.'

'Oh.' Nancy let that sink in for a moment. 'So, your family didn't know?'

'Well, Harry did. He saw me and Rupert together once, in London, before he went to work in France. I suppose that might have contributed to the cooling of our relationship. He was upset I'd never confided in him, that I hadn't told him. I can't blame him. I was a coward. A total coward. I should have sung it from the rooftops. Poor Rupert, putting up with me hiding him from my family for years.' He shook his head. 'I've been very weak but I want to do better.'

'So, the police spoke to Rupert?' Jonathan asked him.

'Yes, he confirmed we were in the utility room. Classy, I know.' He grimaced. 'But it was the only room I knew no one at the party would be in. I work with him so he was on the invite list. I just wanted a few moments alone with him. So there was no way I had time to then go upstairs and find Lucy.'

'You should have told them straight away,' Nancy said. She was relieved though; she had really warmed to him. It was a shame he had felt he needed to keep such a part of himself hidden from those close to him. She thought, not for the first time, that having so much money hadn't seemed to make life at Roth Lodge any easier for its inhabitants to navigate. If anything, it appeared to have made it harder for them all.

'I know.' He hung his head. 'If only I'd been honest at the start, they wouldn't have needed to waste their time looking into me. They could have found the real culprit by now. I feel terrible about that.'

'Who do you think is the culprit, Will?' Jonathan steered them back to business.

'Honestly, I don't know. But Harry needs to know it wasn't me. I just wanted to help when I spoke to Lucy that day in the pub, to make sure she really did love him. I should have kept my nose well out, though. The mess I've made of my own love life, what right did I have to get involved in theirs?' He shook his head. 'What do you think, Nancy? Do you know who did it?'

'Honestly, I keep changing my mind,' she replied. 'But I want to find out.'

He nodded. 'Try, if you can. I haven't got much faith in Brown, between us.'

'Maybe it was someone from Lucy's past. Do you know anything else about her that might help? Something about her life in France?'

Will frowned. 'Not really, no. But she hadn't been there long before she met Harry, he told me. She lived in London before that. I think she shared a flat there. Some post came for her once at the house.'

Nancy's eyes lit up. If she had had post then maybe they could find out her old address, and maybe there would be something there that might finally shed light on who Lucy Roth had really been. And she knew just who might help with that. 'Don't worry, we'll figure it all out.' She glanced at Jonathan who nodded in agreement. They couldn't give up now.

'And you'll come with me to tell Harry? I'm not sure he'll listen to me otherwise.'

'Of course.' She had to ask. 'You don't have anyone else, Will?'

He shook his head. 'You've seen what it's like at Roth Lodge, that's why I rarely come back from London. My life is there, I have no one here.'

Did he realise how much he had in common with Lucy? If only he hadn't followed his family's example and got to know her. They both might have been a little less lonely in that house. 'You do now,' she replied, firmly. It was too late to befriend Lucy but she wanted to help Will if she could. Even if it did mean returning to that house again.

'Thanks, Nancy.' He looked up at her. 'Were you ever really at the house to look at our books?'

She smiled. 'I am a bookseller, Will.'

'Not like any I've ever met before.'

'Have you actually met one before, though?' Jonathan asked, raising an eyebrow.

Will grinned, a hint of his usual demeanour returning. 'Good point.'

Chapter Twenty-Six

Rupert phoned after Will had finished eating so he took the call in the lounge, leaving Nancy and Jonathan discussing in low voices what he had told then.

'Blimey, I can't believe Will had been keeping that secret for years,' Jonathan said.

'I know! It's no wonder Harry and Will aren't as close now. I can't blame Harry for feeling upset when he found out about Rupert. I think when the police started looking at Will as a suspect, Harry wasn't sure what to think as he knew Will had lied to him before. Which I can understand. Although murder is in a completely different league but Harry is grieving. What a mess.'

'If we discount both Will and Harry as suspects then we're really left with nothing to go on.' Jonathan tapped the table in frustration. 'Someone out there is feeling pretty smug right about now; they must be sure they've got away with murder, and they may well be right. I'm beginning to think neither we nor the police are going to catch them.'

Nancy shook her head. 'Something will trip them up. It has to. There must be a reason Lucy was killed. Once we find that out, we'll know who did it. If we can find out where she lived in London, I could do some digging there.' She hesitated. 'Richard could come with me.'

'Richard?' Jonathan asked, his expression annoyingly blank so Nancy had no idea what he was thinking.

'He already mentioned about me going down, to see the lights,' she mumbled. 'So, I could look into her past. It's really our only lead at this point, don't you think?'

Jonathan didn't look at all happy.

'He has answered all my questions, he's been helping about the case, he knows the Roths and more importantly, he knows London and so he can help me while I'm there.'

He sighed. 'I suppose so but I just worry about you, Nancy.'

'There's no need,' she assured him. 'So, when I go with Will I need to find Lucy's address while I'm there, and then I can go to her old flat with Richard and see if we can find out anything about her past. I feel like this is the right thing to do,' she said firmly. She didn't want him to argue; she knew that this was their only shot now.

Jonathan took a moment to answer but seemed to understand that arguing against it was fruitless. 'Okay. Just make sure you don't tip the Roths off that we're looking into all this. I know Will knows now, but he's innocent. One of them must be guilty and they can't know you're going to London to look into Lucy's past. They might hide something that could help us.'

'I won't let on anything.'

'If the person who did this realises Will is going to be released by the police, they might get nervous. And nervous people do desperate things.'

His words sent a shiver down her spine. 'Don't worry, I'll just act as Will's friend in there. There's only one person in that house who can help me now; I just hope I can get Natalie on her own.'

Will returned then, his mouth set in a grim line. 'Right then, I suppose we'd better go.'

Jonathan drove them to Roth Lodge and said he'd wait outside for Nancy. She felt better having him out there just in case, and besides, it looked like rain so she didn't fancy walking back to the bookshop. Will looked pale as he unlocked the door. She reached out and gave his hand a reassuring squeeze and he smiled gratefully at her.

'Sir, Miss Hunter,' Frank said, walking into the hallway at the sound of the door opening. 'Everything all right?'

Will nodded. 'I've been released, Frank. We'd like to speak to Harry. Could you have him come into the library? Only tell him Nancy is here, I don't want him legging it or anything.' Will strode off towards the library. Nancy hurried after him giving Frank an apologetic smile; she'd never get used to having a butler but if she had one, she hoped she'd be more polite to them than the Roths were with Frank.

'Yes, Sir,' Frank said to their retreating backs, disappearing dutifully to find Harry.

Nancy felt slightly more relaxed once in the library; somehow it felt like her domain now. She perched on one of the armchairs while Will paced, glad that the log fire was lit and crackling, providing much-needed warmth on the cold day. It did feel like nothing bad could happen in a room with a log fire in it.

Presently, Harry let himself in, frowning a little, clearly wondering what Nancy wanted with him. He, like the other men in his family, still seemed to prefer to wear a suit even though he was currently nowhere near the office. She wondered what he'd look like in jeans and a soft jumper like Jonathan favoured but it was difficult to imagine. He closed the doors behind him and then stopped short as he realised they weren't alone.

'Hello, Harry. Please, don't go,' Will said hurriedly, seeing his brother reach for the door handle. 'I've been released. I didn't do it, Harry, and I can prove it.'

'He can,' Nancy added. 'Why don't we all sit down and talk about it?'

'It's about Rupert,' Will said. 'Please, Harry.'

He still looked uncertain but he sat down gingerly in the other armchair. Will, however, continued pacing, too agitated, it appeared, to be seated.

'What about Rupert?' Harry asked shortly.

Will haltingly explained meeting Rupert in secret at the party. 'I had no time to follow Lucy upstairs. I should have told you straight away but I was scared about everyone finding out about him, about me,' he said. 'I'm so sorry, Harry.'

Harry shook his head. 'All I wanted was support from you. After hiding Rupert for years then you refused to support me when I brought home the woman I loved—' He broke off, his voice breaking at the end. He tried to compose himself. 'I needed you.'

Will looked stricken. 'I needed you too.'

Nancy hid an eye roll. Honestly, men could be so difficult. Why did they find it so hard to talk to one another? 'You need to be there for one another. You have both made mistakes, that's true, but you're brothers – isn't your relationship worth saving?' Nancy asked them.

'Why did you argue with Lucy, though? The police said you must have hurt her because of that,' Harry blurted out.

'I honestly believed I was looking out for you by talking to her. I thought you seemed upset and worried. I wanted to find out why but she was upset, she said I clearly didn't trust her so why should she trust me? She knew that I was suspicious of her intentions in marrying you and she got upset. I handled it badly, I know that now. I should have spoken to you. I really regret that, Harry.'

'You should have talked to me, to both of us, got to know us. Then you would have seen why we worked, why I loved her,' Harry said with anguish. 'All I wanted was for the family to accept Lucy.'

There was a short silence. Nancy decided to see how much she could get Harry to open up. 'How did you two meet?' she asked.

'I used to go to this bar near the office after work sometimes. I didn't know many people in Paris, just colleagues and clients, you know? It was on the way back to the apartment I rented and it was summer, so it was nice to stroll back and stop off for a beer. I'd have it at one of the tables outside, and watch the city go by. And then one night Lucy was there, serving. She quite honestly took my breath away.' He smiled at the memory, transported back to that hot Paris summer where love came as easily as the sunshine.

'What was she like?' She leaned forward, trying to paint a picture in her mind of this woman who had come into his life and changed it forever.

'She was unlike anyone I'd ever met before. She was stunning. Well, you saw her that night…' He trailed off, shaking his head. 'She was so charming, everyone was charmed by her. They all hung off her every word. She was passionate too. She showed me around Paris, she loved it all, and I found myself loving it there for the first time. I suppose she lit up my life.'

What a wonderful thought. But as Nancy thought of a love that burned so brightly, she remembered how it had been extinguished so violently.

'I'm sorry,' Will said again. 'I didn't see any of that, did I?'

'What do you think happened that night, Harry? Who did this to Lucy?' Nancy asked.

'I keep trying to work it out. I can understand how people were jealous of her, but hatred, pure hatred... I just don't understand it.' He sighed in frustration. 'She made me feel special. How could anyone hurt someone who was able to do that?'

Nancy could see he genuinely couldn't think of anyone who would have wanted to kill his wife. Blinded by love perhaps but she couldn't be angry at him for that. She felt sorry for him. He had lost the woman who had made him feel alive. 'Why were your family so distrustful of Lucy?'

Harry sighed. 'My family just didn't understand why I'd married her so quickly, and in secret. I suppose I've always been a careful sort of person, sensible and all that. I've worked hard, put the family first but Lucy was a one-off. I knew that if someone like that wanted to be with me, I had to grab hold of it as tightly as I could. Perhaps I even knew somehow when we met that I could lose her. I don't know. It was the craziest thing I've ever done getting married after only knowing her for a month but somehow, it felt like the sanest thing too.'

'Did you wonder whether you'd done the right thing when you came back here with her?'

'I suppose a little. Coming back here, it was like a bucket of cold water had been poured over us. It wasn't like the giddy, carefree days in Paris. Everyone looked at us as if we were mad. I knew we had each other but it was harder, definitely. We argued for the first time. She didn't think I stuck up for her enough, especially with my mother – they are both such strong women. I didn't know what to do for the best. I wanted everyone to see what I saw in Lucy but they just didn't want to. They thought she was after my money but she made me happy. I didn't care if she liked the fact I was rich. She could have had it all. As long as I had her, I was happy.'

Nancy wasn't sure she could fathom that intense kind of love. Was it healthy? She didn't know. But Harry certainly had loved Lucy. That was no lie. Whether Lucy had felt as intensely about him, there was no way for Nancy to know. She hoped she had loved him though, for his sake. 'I'm really sorry, Harry. That you lost her after so little time together,' she told him sincerely.

He gave her a small smile. 'Thank you.'

'I need you too, Harry,' Will said. 'I have to tell the family about Rupert. I know I'm asking too much seeing as I didn't support you with Lucy but will you be there when I tell them? Please?'

'You can't change the past, only what happens next,' Nancy said when she saw Harry hesitate.

Finally, he nodded. 'I just wish I knew what happened to Lucy.'

Nancy wondered whether to tell him that they were looking into the murder but decided the less people who knew, the better.

The double doors to the room were flung open unceremoniously, making them all jump.

'Harry, there you are. I've been looking all over the house for you,' his mother said sharply. She noticed Will then. 'You're home, thank God. Edwards said it was going to be okay but I was so worried.'

'I have an alibi, Mother, I couldn't have done it.'

'Well, of course not, darling. I never had any doubt.' She smiled, a little of her cold reserve evaporating but then she saw Nancy. 'What are you doing here again?' she asked with disdain. Nancy couldn't help but wonder what kind of mother Jessica had been to her sons; she certainly didn't give off an air of being capable of love and affection, even to her family. Was it any wonder that her sons had kept the people they loved secret from her?

'She brought me home from the station,' Will explained. 'I have something to tell you all.'

'Well, your grandfather wants to talk to us,' Jessica said. 'So, you can do it now. If you'll excuse us, Miss Hunter.' She gestured to the door, pointedly.

'Of course.' Nancy got up quickly, wondering what Marcus was going to talk to them about. She hoped he wouldn't be disappointed in Will. She wondered if Will hadn't given his family enough credit by not telling them about Rupert but she wasn't sure. The family still seemed to be keeping secrets, from her and from each other. 'I'll show myself out.'

Will stepped forward. 'Thank you, Nancy, for everything.'

'Good luck,' she said with a smile. She looked at Harry. 'I hope you'll be okay.' He gave her a nod and she walked out, feeling Jessica's narrowed eyes on her back as she went. She hoped Will and Harry could repair their relationship somehow. If only they could find Lucy's killer then they could try to heal together but with it hanging over the household, it was unlikely.

Nancy walked quickly across the chessboard floor, glad she had worn flat shoes so they weren't too noisy, but instead of making her way out of the front door, she turned and headed down the corridor that led to the kitchen. There was no way she was leaving without finding out where Lucy used to live. Will might not have killed her but someone did, and Nancy couldn't stop investigating now, she'd come too far, she was in too deep. Lucy needed her. She wasn't going to let someone escape justice as they had with her dad's accident. Seeing how upset Harry was had spurred her on even more. He needed closure. Something she and her gran had never had.

Managing to get to the kitchen unnoticed gave her a little spring to her step. She was starting to feel like she really was investigating this case for real now. She was nervous about being caught in there but she needed to get what she came for. Things were getting tough now, but that was no reason to give up – did any of the detectives in the books she loved give up when the going got tough? No, they just pushed harder.

Peeping through the doorway of the kitchen, she was relieved to find Natalie was there alone, sitting at the table with a cup of tea, evidently taking a break. 'Natalie,' Nancy said, softly, slipping into the room.

'Nancy, what are you doing here?' Natalie asked in surprise, glancing anxiously at the doorway.

Nancy got straight to the point, not wanting them to be interrupted before she got what she came for. 'Will told me that Lucy lived in London before she went to Paris, and he thinks she had some post delivered here. If you could get me her address, I could go down and see what I can find out about where she came from. It might help us to work out what happened to her,' she said urgently in a low voice.

'Do you think? But they're saying that Will had something to do with it.'

'He didn't. That I do know. But someone did. And this might help us find out who. Can you find it for me?'

Natalie hesitated for a moment then nodded and stood up. 'Anything to help Lucy. Wait here.' She half-ran from the room. Nancy hovered in the kitchen, her eyes keeping a fearful watch on the door, hoping no one would come in. Her pulse was racing. She was nervous, unsure if she could quite explain what she was still doing there if someone found her. If it was Jessica Roth, she'd probably be banished from the house for good but she finally had a clue that felt important and she needed to follow it through or she'd always wonder about it.

Natalie came back in record time, thankfully, and handed Nancy an envelope. 'This is it.'

'Thank you, Natalie. I'll let you know what happens. Can I go out this way?' she asked, looking at the back door.

Natalie nodded. 'Of course.' She opened up door. 'Hurry, in case Mrs Harper comes in.'

'Take care!' Nancy called back over her shoulder as she slipped out. She walked around the side of the house and stepped into the driveway triumphantly where Jonathan was still waiting for her, clutching Lucy's address in her hands, more determined than ever to find out who killed her, and why.

Chapter Twenty-Seven

It was Friday and Nancy was in the bookshop with her gran and Penelope, working after the shop had closed as they'd just had a big delivery ready for the final shopping days before Christmas.

'I'll do the gift wrapping,' Penelope said, smiling at the two of them, as they all knew Nancy and Jane were hopeless at wrapping but the service was popular with customers at this time of year. She settled herself behind the counter to wrap books while Nancy shelved the books that weren't already reserved for customers, and Jane gave the shop a clean, ready for the weekend.

'Are you sure you two can manage this weekend?' Nancy checked as she put the books out. She had arranged to go to London in the morning and this was usually their busiest weekend for customers as everyone hurried to pick up last minute gifts in the village. It would mark one of the first times she wouldn't be working the last weekend before Christmas but then it was already the strangest December, what with the murder that still hung in the air like a fog that just wouldn't lift.

She looked up at the photo of her father on the wall. She hoped he would be looking down on her this weekend in London and that he'd be proud of her for trying to get justice for Lucy. She sent him a silent 'thank you' for giving her a love of mystery books, without which she would never have even thought of getting involved in this case. She just hoped that she could see it through to the end.

'I actually still can't believe that you're going away for a mini-break with Richard,' Penelope said as she tied a gold package up with a red bow.

'It's not a mini-break!' Nancy protested. 'It's a fact-finding mission, actually. I'm going to find Lucy's old flat and see if there's something there that will help us get some idea of why she was killed. It feels like we're at a dead end but perhaps her past will give us something to go on. Richard lives in London so he's going to come with me. It's just a practical solution.'

Penelope snorted. 'Do you actually believe that, Nancy? Are you in that much denial? You'll be staying with your ex-boyfriend.'

'No, I booked a hotel,' Nancy said. She had been firm with Richard about that. She knew that staying in his flat could only lead to trouble. 'Why won't anyone trust me that I know what I'm doing?' Her grandmother had been similarly concerned when she had told her about going to London.

'We just want you to be careful,' Jane said as she dusted the shelf behind her. 'You were sad when things ended with him. And has the situation really changed? He lives there, you live here.'

'I have no idea what will happen but it's been nice to reconnect with him, that's all,' Nancy said, firmly.

'I still can't believe your ex shows up at the same time as a murder in the village, what are the odds?' Penelope said.

Nancy turned to her. 'Well, it was just a coincidence.'

Penelope looked up. 'Of course, what else would it be?' They all looked at one another.

Nancy shook her head. She was starting not to trust anyone. 'I have to go to London. We need a breakthrough in the case and this is the only lead we have right now.' She wanted to convince them as much as herself that this trip was all about digging into Lucy Roth's past. She didn't want them to know that she felt nervous about it. It was convenient, that wasn't a lie, but she knew Richard didn't see it like that. He had agreed to take her to Lucy's old flat but he wanted them to go out and enjoy the city too. She'd agreed and she was excited about having fun in London. She was flattered that he had missed her though, and it was hard to forget how much she had loved him in the past. Did she love him now? She supposed she would find out on this trip. 'I honestly have no idea how I feel about Richard.'

'I wish I could help but I was a fool who got married at twenty-one,' Penelope said with a smile.

'Any word on whether Oliver can come home for Christmas?' Jane asked about Pen's husband.

Penelope sighed. 'It's not looking good. Poor Kitty really has got her hopes up. If he can't then we won't see him until March now.' Sadness crossed her face, something Penelope didn't usually show.

'I can't imagine how hard it is for you guys. He misses you both just as much as you miss him, I know,' Nancy said. Penelope and Oliver had met at school like her gran had met her husband and were so in love, it was heart-breaking that they had to be apart so much.

'Listen, I know that I've been warning you about Richard,' Penelope said then. 'But, honestly, if you two still love each other then everyone will just have to get on board with that. Life's too short not to grab happiness when you can, right?'

'Well said,' Jane agreed. 'And we'll be just fine in the shop, everything will run like clockwork. And Jonathan said he'd have Charlie for us so we don't need to worry about him if the shop gets really busy. They'll go for a nice long walk. Don't worry about a thing, love. Now then, I think we need a cuppa.'

Nancy smiled. 'Thanks, guys.'

'What do you think?' Pen held up the gift-wrapped book.

'It's perfect.' Nancy turned back to the books and focused on the task in front of her, pushing her worries about the weekend away as much as she could.

–

Nancy took Charlie out on the green early on Saturday morning. She wanted to go for a walk to clear her head before Jonathan drove her to the train station. Her bag was packed, she wore a chunky knit jumper, jeans, boots and her winter coat, with gloves, hat and scarf as it was freezing cold. A layer of crunchy frost covered the ground and she could see her breath in the air. She smiled as Charlie chased after his ball. He didn't have any worries. She envied him.

'Morning, Nancy!' Mr Peabody, a retired police officer, walked past, a newspaper tucked under his arm. 'Got to keep abreast of all the news,' he called from the edge of the green. 'So, I hear they released Will Roth without charge?'

'I'm pleased they realised he was innocent,' she called back with a wave.

'I always said the Roths were too squeaky clean for their own good. Skeletons in those big closets of theirs, no doubt about it.'

'Were they ever in trouble with the police when you were working?'

He shook his head. 'Never. But you don't get that rich without doing something dodgy. Right, I'm off to have a cuppa! I'll be in the shop next week!'

Nancy waved as he walked off, whistling cheerfully as if they hadn't just been discussing murder but merely the weather. 'Come on, Charlie, time to go!' She whistled and the beagle hurried over to her so she could clip on his lead, his ball in his mouth. Nancy thought about what Mr Peabody had said as they strolled back to the cottage, both feeling much better for their walk. What skeletons did the Roths have? She had already discovered Will's secret but who else in that house might be hiding something? If she could find out what Lucy Roth's past looked like then maybe she could get closer to finding out the answer.

'All ready to go then, love?' Jane asked when Nancy came in. Charlie ran to his water bowl and lapped at it eagerly.

'I think so. You will be okay here on your own, won't you?' Nancy hadn't slept away from the cottage since university. 'I don't like leaving you here alone,' she added.

'As if I'm ever alone in this village! We need you to find out all you can about Lucy Roth. And I really think you will, I can feel it in my bones. I can't wait to hear all about it. Just be careful, won't you? And not just with Richard. This is a murder case. Lucy might have had a shady past, and you might run into it.' Her gran looked worried.

'I promise I will.' Nancy gave Jane a kiss as she heard a beep from outside. She wasn't as nervous as her grandmother – there was a frisson of excitement running through her. She had always wanted to solve a real-life mystery, and she felt certain that there was an important clue waiting for her in London, she just had to go down and find it.

'Don't forget your train snacks,' Jane added, going back to her breakfast. Nancy grabbed the Tupperware box from the counter, and picked up her bag.

'See you tomorrow, then.'

'Bye, love.' Jane gave her a cheerful wave.

Nancy left the cottage and climbed into Jonathan's car. The December rain fogged up the windscreen as they drove down to the station, Christmas music playing softly in the background.

'I'd like to know what sent Lucy to France, and into Harry Roth's path,' Nancy said, pulling out her notebook to jot her thoughts down. She always felt better writing things down; it helped to clear her head and focus.

'You mean did she go to Paris specifically to seek him out, or was it luck that threw a rich, eligible man into her path?'

'When you put it like that, it does sound like it could have been premeditated but how did she even know of Harry?'

'The Roths are very well known and not just in our area,' Jonathan replied with a shrug. 'I guess we need to try to find out as much about her background as we can. Did she need money? Was she in debt? That kind of thing.'

'Hmmm.' Nancy made more notes, her writing less neat than usual thanks to the rocking motion of the car. 'I keep wondering if someone we know really could have killed her? Out of the family, I mean? We know now that Will couldn't, and Harry seems so upset. I just don't think that's an act, he wouldn't have killed the woman he loved so much surely.' Nancy sighed. 'But then who are we left with? Annabel only came to stay to help her sister and niece plan the engagement party. Marcus Roth is very keen on keeping up their appearance as a family – murder goes against that completely. But Will was terrified of him finding out he was gay. And he made no bones about not being fond of Lucy. There's Jessica Roth who seems very cold and reserved; she definitely didn't like me and Gran being in the house, but she was clearly upset when Will was arrested so she must have some feelings. She might just be a snob who hated the thought her eldest son married a woman who worked in a bar.'

'We don't know a lot about Peter Roth,' Jonathan said, nodding along. 'I mean, he runs the family business now, not Marcus, so that could mean he also runs the family. But Marcus Roth doesn't seem the type to relinquish control to me.'

'He's so sweet about his wife, though. Would he really have hurt Harry's? The problem is, I really don't think any of them were happy about Lucy or liked her all that much. So that doesn't narrow things down. But to actually murder her...' She trailed off, frustrated.

'I guess we can't discount any of them at this point. Let's hope you can find something in London to help us.' Jonathan turned into the station car park and pulled up outside. 'Okay, here we are then,' he said. 'You got everything you need?'

Nancy put the notebook into her bag and nodded. 'All set. Thanks for dropping me off.'

'Of course.' He hesitated. 'I hope it goes well, Nancy. Keep in touch, okay?'

She was touched and leaned over to give him a quick kiss on the cheek. 'Thanks, Jonathan. See you when I get back!' She climbed out and gave him a cheerful wave, feeling a weird little lump rise up in her throat as she walked away from him.

Chapter Twenty-Eight

Richard was waiting for her just past the barriers when she arrived at the station in London. He wore dark jeans and a long coat, his hair sleekly gelled back. He lifted his hand in greeting when he saw her, breaking into a warm smile.

'How was your journey?' he asked, leaning down to kiss her cheek, and take her bag out of her hand.

'Pretty relaxing actually,' she said, following him through the station.

'How about some lunch before we start our sleuthing then?' he suggested, leading her to his car. 'I know a place you'll love.'

'Sounds good to me,' she replied, her stomach rumbling on cue. It wasn't raining in London – just grey and cold. There were people walking briskly everywhere she looked. They set off, and made slow progress as they met with traffic en route. She looked out of the window at the tall buildings leaning over them, thinking that it really was a world away from Dedley End.

'I can't believe you're here,' Richard said. 'In London, after all this time.' He smiled across at her.

'It's very different to Dedley End,' she said. 'But I know you love it here.'

'Well, I enjoy my work and there's so much to do,' he said. 'But I'd be lying if I said I wasn't lonely sometimes.

You're surrounded by people but it's not always easy to connect with them. That's why I'm so happy you came.' He gave her thigh a quick squeeze. 'I really hope you like this place,' he added as he parked down a small side street. He looked a little nervous, something she was unused to. The dynamic between them had shifted a little after their years apart, and she was sure that he could feel it too.

Nancy climbed out and followed Richard to a book-shop; she grinned at him as he opened the door for her, leading her through the books and into the back which was a small restaurant. It was decorated in deep blues with wooden booths and felt really cosy. Each table had a stack of hardback books on it with a candle on top as the centrepiece. 'This place is perfect,' she told him. They found a booth and sat down opposite one another.

A man came over to them. Nancy looked twice at him. He didn't look much like a waiter – he was an older man with a scruffy beard, ripped jeans, and he just sort of grunted at them as he handed them the menu.

'Thanks, Bill,' Richard said with a smile.

'You've been here before, then?' Nancy asked as the man shuffled away again and slumped at the desk to wait for something to do.

'A client told me about it. And I knew you'd love it as soon as I came here. Not only is it all themed around books but they employ ex-offenders,' he explained in a low voice. 'And give money to a homeless charity.'

'How interesting.' Nancy was surprised, if she was honest. Richard had never before been particularly phil-anthropic, so this was a turn up for the books. Looking down at the menu, she saw that even the food had a literary theme. He really had picked a place he knew she'd love. She was flattered and pleased. She was sure he hadn't been as thoughtful in the past so maybe it was true that he had changed for the better, that maybe they did have a future together after all.

'What do you fancy, then?' Richard asked her.

'I think I'll go for the Sherlock Holmes burger.'

'Sounds good to me.' Richard called Bill who shuffled over obediently, and ordered two burgers and soft drinks, as they both wanted to keep clear heads for their afternoon outing. 'So, fill me in on what's been happening since I last saw you.'

Nancy told him everything that had happened with Will. 'So, it's great news that we were right and Will is innocent but it means the suspect pool keeps on shrinking.'

'But that's what we want, isn't it? For the suspect pool to shrink until the killer is obvious.'

Nancy liked how he used the word 'we'; he seemed as invested in the case as her. 'True. As long as we are left with someone in the frame though! At least I feel like we might be getting somewhere by checking out where Lucy lived before she came to Dedley End. The more we know about her and her past, the better, surely?'

'I agree. We'll head there after lunch and see what we can uncover together.'

She smiled. 'I'm surprised you're taking this so, well, seriously, I suppose. I honestly thought you'd just laugh at me for even thinking that we could solve this murder.'

'I hate that you think that of me. I want to support you, especially in things that mean a lot to you. I know you want to find justice for Lucy, and that's admirable.'

'I find myself comparing it to what happened to my dad. Almost as though, if I can help catch the person responsible for her murder, it somehow makes up for the fact that I have never found out who was driving on that road with him that night.'

'You have nothing to feel guilty about,' he reassured her, reaching over to touch her hand.

'It's hard to believe that. I just don't want the same thing to happen to Lucy. And poor Harry, to live with not knowing who killed the woman he loved, you know?' She smiled, trying to lighten the atmosphere. 'Plus, my gran and I need to win the bet against Jonathan.'

He didn't smile back at that though, just looked thoughtful.

'What is it, Richard?'

'I've been thinking about the past a lot lately.' Richard leaned in a little closer. 'I know you thought that I looked down on where you live, that I hated Dedley End or something but it was never that. I was almost envious of it. You loved it there so much, and I wanted us to be together; I wanted you to come to London with me and I resented the village and everyone in it for stopping that from happening. I should have told you how I felt but instead I acted like a spoilt boy and put everyone's backs up. I wasn't very pleasant to your grandmother or your friends when I came that Christmas, I can see that now. I hoped that by making fun of them, you'd realise you should come and be with me, but instead, I just pushed you further away.' He sighed. 'I was twenty-one, about to be let loose on the world, and I was scared. I know I handled it all badly. I really did love you, Nancy, and it really hurt when you said you wanted to stay in Dedley End.'

'I still wanted to be with you.'

'I don't think it would have worked though, do you? But perhaps we were meant to take a break, to grow up a little, become the people we were meant to be? I'm glad you're back in my life again anyway.'

'It has been good to see you again,' she agreed. Their food arrived then and she thought about what he had said. It was a relief to know he had loved her and wanted them to be together, and she could see how it might have seemed that she had chosen her village over him. She had wanted to have both but maybe he was right, and that would have been impossible. Would it always be impossible? It made her feel a little sad but also a bit better about the past. As if she understood it, and him, much more. She bit into the burger and almost moaned. 'This is delicious,' she said, her mouth full.

Richard laughed, loud and hearty. 'I've never met anyone quite like you, Nancy Hunter.'

'Is that a good thing?' she asked, swallowing her food.

'I'm not sure. You might well have ruined me forever.'

Nancy popped a chip into her mouth, thinking that if he kept saying things like that to her, he might well end up doing the same thing to her.

Chapter Twenty-Nine

After lunch, and an obligatory browse around the book-shop, which ended in Nancy picking five books that Richard bought for her despite her protests, they drove east to the address that Natalie had given her. They found themselves on an estate full of grey blocks of flats rising up from the concrete. Richard parked outside the one where Lucy had lived. A light drizzle of rain fogged up the window as they looked out at it. 'Not exactly Roth Lodge, is it?' Richard said with a frown.

'Certainly seems like it was a big step up for Lucy,' Nancy said. 'Coming from this, and then moving to Paris, and ending up in Dedley End as a member of one of the country's richest families. It's like a Cinderella story or something.'

'She probably felt like she had gone from the gutter to the stars, but then look what happened to her,' Richard said with a shudder.

'Be careful what you wish for, I suppose,' Nancy said. 'Right then, let's find out what brought Lucy to Dedley End. And why she never left it again,' she added, darkly, before jumping out of the car.

Someone was coming out of the main doors to the flats so Nancy rushed forward to hold the open door, and she and Richard slipped in. 'I wonder if her flatmate still lives here,' Nancy said as they got into the lift to go to the tenth floor, and what had once been Lucy's flat.

'Only one way to find out,' Richard said. They got out of the lift and went up to the door, Nancy knocking on it briskly.

They waited for a couple of seconds before the door was opened cautiously, and a woman peeped out.

'What?' she asked, in a blunt voice, not seeming at all happy to see two strangers on her doorstep.

'We are investigating Lucy Roth's death,' Nancy told her. 'We believe she used to live here?'

She sighed. 'I already talked to the police.'

'We're not police,' Nancy said, quickly. 'The family have asked us to help them find who did this,' she explained, feeling guilty for saying it but hoping the end would justify the means. But Will had asked for her help, and Harry needed it, so it wasn't strictly a lie. 'Lucy was your friend – you'd like to see justice for her, wouldn't you?' she added, taking a big gamble that this woman even knew Lucy.

The woman hesitated and then swung the door open. 'Fine, come in.'

Nancy looked at Richard with relief. They followed the woman into the flat – an open-plan living area and kitchen, pretty much the size of the hallway at Roth Lodge. She perched on the arm of the sofa and stared at them. She looked about Lucy's age, a few years older than Nancy, with dark blonde hair pulled into a ponytail. 'I told the police that I hadn't heard from her in months. Not since she took off in the night and left me with all that month's rent to pay.'

'She was your roommate, then?' Nancy asked as Richard glanced around looking a little shocked to see how this woman lived. Perhaps he hadn't left behind all his snobbish ways after all. 'How did you know her?'

'She answered a Gumtree ad I placed for a flatmate. She seemed alright. We got on okay but you could tell she hated living here. Wanted bigger and better things, did our Lucy. As I said, took off and left me high and dry, and then the next thing I hear is from the police that she had been murdered.' She shrugged, not seeming all that bothered by the fact. 'I can't help you more than that, I'm afraid.'

'Lucy recently got married but we believe she used a fake maiden name, did you know her real name?' Nancy asked.

'She was Lucy Lewis to me.'

'Did she mention Harry Roth, or the Roth family at all to you?'

The woman shook her head. Nancy felt herself deflate – this felt like a complete waste of time. Either Lucy's former flatmate really did know nothing useful about Lucy, or she just didn't want to tell them.

'So, you didn't talk about her background much? Where was she working?'

'At a bar in the city. She wasn't a big talker. Kept herself to herself but she was clean and tidy, and quiet, so I had no complaints.'

Nancy looked at Richard who shrugged, looking as disappointed as she felt. He turned to go back out of the front door when another question came to Nancy. 'What about Lucy's family? Did she mention anyone in her life?'

'Only her mum.'

Richard paused, and Nancy leapt on that nugget of information. 'Her mum?'

'Yeah.' She nodded. 'She complained that the home her mum was in took most of her wages. I think that's why she could only afford to live here.'

'Do you know the name of the home, by any chance?' Nancy asked her eagerly. Finally, they had a breakthrough. The Roth family believed that Lucy had no relatives but that appeared to be a lie.

The woman frowned as she thought about it. 'I think she said it was called New Haven, and was a complete racket. But I could tell she cared about her mum, didn't want her in a crappy home, you know? This one cost a lot, but was worth it to her.'

Nancy noted down the name of the home on her phone. 'That's really helpful, thank you.'

'I'm not heartless, I hope you find who did it,' she said then, softening a little as she showed them out. 'I'll just be careful in future about collecting the rent.'

'Very sensible,' Nancy told her. 'Thanks for talking to us.' She and Richard left the flat and rode back down in the lift in a thoughtful silence. Outside, the rain had started to fall in earnest, slanting in a way that made umbrellas useless so they hurried back to Richard's car, and when they were safely inside, and dry, turned to one another.

'Well, that was interesting,' Nancy said. 'If she had to look after her mother then she needed money.' She leaned back against the seat. 'Maybe then she was killed for trying to get hold of the Roth fortune.'

Richard thought for a moment. 'Why Harry Roth, though?'

'What do you mean?'

'Why was he the rich man that she went after? She went to France suddenly as if she planned to find him there. There would have been enough rich men to ensnare here in London yet she chose to go after Harry. But why?'

'That's a very good question.' Nancy's phone started to ring then and she pulled it out of her bag. She didn't recognise the number, which was unusual. There were pretty much only three people who ever rang her, unless you counted annoying sales calls.

'Hello?' she answered, curiously.

'Nancy, it's Will Roth,' a posh voice replied. 'I wanted to call you to thank you for helping out with Harry. I told my family everything and he supported me. It went as well as I could have hoped. It really helped to have him on my side.'

'That's good news. I'm glad it's all out in the open.'

'Listen, I asked Natalie about where Lucy used to live for you but she said she'd already given you the address. I thought, of course you'd already got it!'

Nancy smiled into the phone. 'Actually, I'm in London this weekend with Richard. I'm going to find out as much as I can to try to help get to the truth.'

'Richard? He said you used to be an item.'

She could hear the grin in Will's voice.

'Well, I'm all for it. You and Richard looking up Lucy's past. Harry will appreciate it.'

'Keep it quiet for now, just in case,' she said quickly. She trusted Will and she really didn't think Harry's grief was at all put on but the fewer people who knew she was investigating the murder, the better, in her opinion – just in case.

'Okay. I hope we can put this to rest soon for all our sakes. Hopefully you'll find someone in her past that did this. It can't be any of us. I thought maybe it was but I just can't believe it. It must be someone Lucy knew before she married Harry, don't you think?'

'I hope so,' she replied, non-committally. Richard tapped his fingers on the steering wheel. 'I'd better go now, Will.'

'You've been a breath of fresh air ever since I met you, Nancy Hunter. Don't you stop now.'

She chuckled. 'I won't,' she promised, and hung up. 'That was Will Roth calling to thank me for my help. Although I'm not sure if I'm still helping or not. We still really don't know if Lucy purposefully went after Harry Roth, or what's happened to her mother. Will thinks it's someone outside of his family, but he would, wouldn't he?' She frowned, trying to fit the puzzle pieces together but failing.

'No one wants to think badly of their family.'

'Speaking of family, what about the revelation that Lucy did have a mother she was looking after? Let's look up the home.' They bent their heads over her phone as she typed 'New Haven' into Google. It was a private home for the elderly, specialising in dementia. 'Huh,' she said aloud when she read that. 'So, Lucy's mother needed specialist care.'

'It looks expensive; it must cost a lot to have someone there,' Richard said. 'Where is it?'

'Burley,' Nancy said, looking. 'That's about an hour from Dedley End. Hmm. Did Lucy make sure her mother was close enough for her to visit from Roth Lodge?'

'But her mother was in there before she met Harry.'

'We come back to the question – did she target Harry Roth? Arrange to meet him? Get him to fall in love with and marry her? For money?' Nancy sighed. 'I really thought Lucy loved him, I can't really explain why. But I did.' She hated to think of Lucy plotting to ensnare Harry but she supposed if she had done then it might explain why she was killed in the end.

'Do you think her mother is still there?'

'I wonder if I can find out? And if she is, then who is paying for her to stay there?' They looked at one another, stumped.

'Look, the day is running away with us and I have something booked for us,' Richard said. 'We can't do anything right this minute, anyway. Maybe you can tell the police about Lucy's mother and they can look into it?'

'Maybe,' she said, uncertain what the next move should be. She wanted to call Jonathan but she knew Richard wouldn't be thrilled by that so she'd have to wait until she got back to the hotel later.

'Come on, let me show you the sights, you deserve to relax,' he said, brightly, starting up the car. 'I'm going to take you to do something you told me you've always wanted to do. Let's have some fun.'

Nancy wasn't at all sure she could just switch off and have fun with the murder still hanging over her but he looked across at her, so excited that she relented. She had promised to let him show her the city after all. 'Okay.' He beamed at her and she forced a smile back.

As they drove away though, Nancy looked at the flat where Lucy had lived. She could never have known that marrying Harry Roth would end so tragically for her. Or could she? Had Lucy laid the foundations that had built up to her murder somehow?

That thought haunted Nancy as they drove back into the city.

Chapter Thirty

Richard had taken Nancy ice skating at the Winter Wonderland in Hyde Park, something that she had told him she had always wanted to do. She had gone ice skating a lot as a child and she loved it. She was flattered he had remembered that. The sun had set early so the twinkling lights from the tree in the centre of the rink had made her feel all Christmassy, and had indeed taken her mind off the last couple of weeks. She had enjoyed herself more than she thought she would.

Afterwards, they had looked at all the stalls, drinking mulled wine from plastic cups and then he'd taken her to see the lights on Oxford Street and she'd felt like a tourist looking at them in awe. Then they had wandered around Selfridges and Nancy had bought a selection of cakes to take home to her grandmother.

By then they were exhausted and ready for dinner so Richard drove her to her hotel so she could check in and change for the evening.

Her room was small but clean and bright and she perched on the comfortable bed, her feet aching from walking so much, her cheeks rosy from the mulled wine. She did feel better for relaxing. The festive atmosphere in the city had been cheerful and contagious. Thoughts of Dedley End and murder couldn't have been further away from her mind while she had been out in the thick of it but now she was alone in her hotel room, they all came tumbling back so before she had a shower, she pulled out her phone to call Jonathan with an update.

'Nancy! You won't believe what's happened,' Jonathan answered somewhat breathlessly. It sounded like he was walking quickly, noise of a road in the background.

'What?' Nancy cried, wrong-footed by how he had greeted her. She'd thought she had news for him, not the other way around.

'Well…' He drew out the word as if to build suspense. Nancy tapped her foot against the carpet impatiently. 'I just had a phone call from Natalie at Roth Lodge with the news. There's been a break-in. I'm heading there now to see if I can get anyone to talk to me. The police just drove past.' He sucked in a breath. 'But that's not all! Not only has there been a break-in but someone left a note.'

'A note?' she repeated, a little dazed from all the information.

'Natalie said the kitchen window was smashed in and there was a note left on the kitchen table. A blackmail note saying, "*Bring me Lucy's necklace, or there will be another murder*".'

'Oh my God,' Nancy replied, her mouth falling open.

'I know, right! And there was an address for where the Roths should bring the necklace to on Boxing Day at midday. All typed on a computer – totally anonymous.'

'What necklace are they even talking about?' Nancy asked him, trying to think if she'd heard it mentioned before.

'Harry bought it for Lucy for their wedding so Natalie says, and Lucy wore it a lot. It's made of sapphires and diamonds – kept in the safe, worth a fortune. Here's the most important news, though: Lucy was meant to be wearing it on the night she was killed but she changed her dress at the last minute to red and it didn't match so she didn't wear it.'

'So?'

'So, the person who killed Lucy could have been after the necklace. That's the motive. When they realised she didn't have it, they could have threatened her to give it to them, she said no, they panicked and threw her over the railing. They came back again to try to find it, and now they're threatening to kill again if they don't get it.'

Nancy's eyes widened. 'Wow.'

'Exactly. This changes the whole investigation. And points us away from the family. After all, it's their necklace, they wouldn't need to steal it. It's not like they need the money or anything. So, it must have been a guest or someone managed to get into the house uninvited after all. Or there was more than one person involved.' Jonathan sounded excited but Nancy shook her head.

'It all sounds rather convenient to me.'

'You're suspicious?'

'Why have they waited until now to come back for it?'

'Don't forget there have been police all over the place. Natalie said the family had gone to visit friends for lunch – the first time they've really all left the house alone since the murder. The killer must have been watching the house, and seized the opportunity. Right, I'm here, I can see DCI Brown. I'm going to see if he'll tell me anything. Call you back later!' He rang off in a hurry.

Nancy let the phone fall onto the bed with a frown. She felt rather deflated herself. If it was all true then their investigation would be over. The police would stakeout the spot the robber had marked for the necklace drop, and that would be it.

Was the murder really nothing to do with Lucy's past or the Roth family, after all? It was all just to steal a necklace? She was frustrated that she wasn't there with Jonathan to find out more but there was nothing she could do tonight. She would have to wait for more news from him.

She got up and went into the bathroom, turning on the shower, and slipping out of her clothes. She had really thought she'd made a breakthrough finding out about Lucy's mother but now it all seemed to have been for nothing. She hadn't even managed to tell Jonathan about it.

After she had showered, she put on the dress she had brought with her, her black court shoes, and styled her bob, adding a touch of make-up and perfume. Glancing at her reflection, Nancy was pleased. She looked pretty but not as if she had made too much effort, either. The exact effect she wanted. She sighed though: Jonathan's phone call was playing on her mind. She felt confused and frustrated by this development. She thought about Will Roth saying he couldn't believe one of his family were responsible for the murder. It almost felt like someone was making certain that the police looked in another direction, to make sure the family would no longer be suspects. Nancy was not sure what to believe anymore.

Her phone lit up with a text from Richard then saying he was waiting in the lobby for her, so she had to push the murder aside for now. Putting her phone in her bag, she slipped out of the room to meet him. Her stomach fluttered a little with nerves about spending the evening alone with Richard.

'You look gorgeous,' Richard said, grinning as she stepped out of the lift and into his path. He had changed into a dark suit, and she breathed in the scent of his aftershave as he gave her a kiss, this time gently on her lips, sending a surprising thrill through her.

'This way.' He led her out of her hotel into a waiting taxi and took her hand in his as they drove through the city. The taxi pulled up outside their destination quickly and a uniformed doorman stepped forward to open up the taxi door.

Nancy climbed out and looked up in wonder. 'The Ritz?'

'Because of that book you loved when we were at uni.'

Nancy was surprised he'd remembered that. The novel about a murder at The Ritz by Thomas Green had been published when she was at uni and she'd loved it, it was one of her all-time favourites and after reading it, she had longed to go to the hotel and see all the scenes in it come to life. 'Richard, I can't believe this.'

He grinned as she tucked her arm through his and they stepped through the doors into the lobby, her heels clip-clopping on the shiny floor, a sparkling chandelier above them. A stunning Christmas tree stood in front of them, stretching up to the ceiling, and looking dazzling.

Nancy felt as if she had gone back in time as they were shown through to the restaurant, gold shining wherever she looked. They were taken to a table right in the centre of the room and she looked around at the other patrons – all dressed up to the nines, a rare sight nowadays, and one that filled her with joy.

'Some champagne, sir?' their waiter asked as they sat down.

'Most definitely,' Richard told him, and he melted away to fetch it. 'A good surprise, then?' He looked across at Nancy, raising an eyebrow.

'A lovely surprise,' she confirmed with a smile. 'Thank you. This is the perfect way to spend my night in London.'

'I hope you think the company is perfect too,' he said. Their champagne arrived and was poured into two crystal glasses. Richard raised his once they were alone again. 'Here's to us.'

'To us,' she replied, and they gently clinked glasses. She took a sip and was greeted with light, delicious bubbles. 'I could get used to this,' she said with a laugh.

'I'm glad,' he said, looking pleased. 'So, how do you feel about our mission earlier? Do you still think Lucy's mother holds the key to it all?'

'I did but now I'm not so sure.' She told him about Jonathan's call and the break-in at Roth Lodge. 'So, it seems it might be nothing to do with the family after all.'

'If that's the case I'm relieved; I've hated to think of such an old family wrapped up in something so sordid, but I can see by your face you're not at all convinced.'

She smiled. He really did know her well. 'It just seems so perfect coming so soon after Will's arrest – as if someone is trying to make sure the family are no longer suspects. But maybe I'm just reading too much into it. Perhaps I'm just disappointed that we didn't solve the murder in the end.'

'You have great instincts; if it doesn't feel right then maybe it isn't.'

'I'll have to see when I go back, I guess.'

Richard sighed. 'I wish you didn't have to go back. Selfishly, I know.'

'Dedley End is my home,' she reminded him, firmly. The Ritz was wonderful, but it was a fantasy. It wasn't real life. Real life for her was back in the Cotswolds, and they both knew it.

'I know that now,' he said, quickly. He reached for her hand, and she let him take it. 'I've been thinking about that. Don't say anything tonight, okay? Let me just say this and then think it all through, okay?'

'Okay,' she replied, cautiously, taking a sip of champagne.

'I hadn't realised how lonely I've been here, or how much I've missed you. Being with you today has been so lovely. I don't want to lose this again. I want you in my life. I know that you love Dedley End and you don't want to live in London. Right now, my job is here but the Cotswolds really aren't all that far away. I could work a bit from home now, too.' He took a deep breath. 'I could move to be with you. I could get us a place together. It could be right in Dedley End if you want. And I could stay in London maybe four days a week and spend the rest of the time up there with you,' he finished all in a rush.

Nancy stared at him. She couldn't believe it. The words she had longed for him to say, five years after she had been hoping to hear them. 'You'd really do that?' she asked after a moment.

He nodded. 'I want us to be together, and this seems like the perfect solution. In time, I could find a job closer to you, or even set up my own firm one day. It doesn't matter as long as I have you.'

'Bloody hell,' she said, unable to think of anything else to say.

Richard laughed. 'That wasn't quite the reaction I was hoping for but I know this must be a shock.'

'You've only just come back into my life. It is quite a shock.' She drained her glass dry, and he quickly topped it back up.

'I know. That's why I don't want you to say anything now. You need to think about it. Of course you do. But it's not a straight no, is it? Do I have some… hope?'

He looked so vulnerable that Nancy squeezed his hand, and nodded. 'Definitely. There is definitely hope.' She felt light-headed from both his words and her champagne, and the fact that she was at The Ritz.

He leaned over the table and kissed her on the lips. 'You've just made my night, Nancy Hunter.'

Chapter Thirty-One

It was Christmas Eve when Nancy arrived back in Dedley End. She had caught an early train, worried about there being disruptions later especially as a cold front was heading towards the Cotswolds, and the weather forecasters were even talking of a possible white Christmas.

Richard had had to work so she hadn't seen him since early that morning when he had given her a kiss goodbye as she slept in her hotel bed, slipping out to change before going to the office. He had thoughtfully arranged for a room service breakfast of scrambled eggs, toast and tea to be sent up for her, though.

Thoughts of the night before kept popping into her mind and she smiled to herself, blushing a little, as she remembered Richard's kisses and touch, and the way he had held her as she slept. She felt rather like a teenager again. It was hard not to get carried away by the feeling but she was trying as hard as she could to keep a clear head so she could think about Richard's proposal rationally. Having him in Dedley End could be a dream come true but there was the small problem that she knew the people she loved best in the world were not his biggest fans. But surely that would change once they really got to know him, and if she loved him?

That was the real question though, wasn't it? Did she love him? She had once, and last night had brought her close to it again but she really wasn't sure of her feelings.

The train slowed then as Woodley station came into view. She looked out on the platform and saw Penelope's car in the car park next to it. Penelope herself was leaning against it, her hands in her pockets, her breath showing on the air. Her little girl Kitty was inside the car fast asleep, and then there was Jonathan – a few steps away from her, talking on his phone. Nancy was happy to see them all. She heaved her case down from the rack and stepped off the now stationary train.

Walking out of the gate, she waved to Penelope who rushed forward and gave her a tight hug. 'I've only been gone for the night,' Nancy said with a laugh when Pen released her.

'It feels like ages! So much has happened. Plus, it's Christmas Eve, and it wouldn't be Christmas in Dedley End without you! Come on, let's get you home.' She wrapped an arm through Nancy's and led her towards the car. 'So, how was the big smoke, then? You came back in one piece, at least. How was Richard?' Penelope looked at her, raising an eyebrow in anticipation.

Nancy smiled when she was finally allowed to get a word in. 'I had a lovely time, actually. He took me to The Ritz, and it was wonderful!'

Penelope watched her more carefully. 'You're blushing... oh my God!' She yanked them both to a stop before they reached Jonathan. 'Did you sleep with him?' she hissed.

Nancy glanced at Jonathan but he was still on the phone and thankfully didn't appear to have even noticed them yet. 'Yes, I did,' she said, sheepishly.

'And?'

'And it was pretty great.'

Penelope squealed, catching Jonathan's attention. He turned and finished his call, smiling over at Nancy. 'I want all the gory details later,' Penelope hissed as Jonathan strode over. Like Penelope, he was wrapped up against the cold, his hair messy from the wind, his nose slightly red. He was, as usual, a little bit scruffy, but to Nancy, he looked just like home.

'The wanderer returns then,' he said with a grin, grabbing Nancy's bag and putting it in the boot of Penelope's car. 'There have been some interesting developments. Will Roth just called and has requested our presence at Roth Lodge as soon as possible. He couldn't get through to you on the phone.'

'I didn't have a signal on the train. That sounds intriguing.'

'Doesn't it? Want to stop off at the cottage first, though? We bought your gran breakfast this morning and she's dying for all the big city news.'

'We'd better, then. And it might not hurt to keep the Roths waiting a little bit,' Nancy told him.

Jonathan grinned. 'Make 'em stew, I like it.'

'Can we go please, it's bloody freezing!' Penelope called out of the window as she waited in the driver's seat.

'You had a good time though, did you?' Jonathan asked as he opened the back seat, Nancy heading around to sit beside Pen.

'I did but it's good to be home,' she replied, sincerely, earning another grin from him.

Kitty opened her eyes then. 'Is Santa here yet?'

Penelope chuckled. 'Not yet, darling.'

As they headed back towards Dedley End, a swirl of sleet started up outside. The Christmas lights in the village were twinkling through the grey light of the cloudy day, the sky above growing heavier by the minute, making the suggestion of snow seem more like a promise. The lights were on a much smaller scale than the ones Nancy had just seen in London but no less magical to her eyes.

'What was The Ritz like?' Penelope asked her. 'I'm so jealous you got to go there!'

'Like something out of a book. So elegant and magical. We had the most divine champagne, and the food was out of this world. It just felt so fancy and grown-up eating there,' Nancy told her, smiling across at her. She caught Jonathan's eyes in the rear-view mirror but he looked away. 'We had found out something interesting about Lucy Roth earlier but with the whole necklace news, I don't know if it's still relevant. It felt so at the time, though.' She twisted around to look at Jonathan who met her gaze this time. She told him about Lucy's mother being in a home. 'It looks expensive; you'd need a lot of money to have someone in there for as long as it seems like her mother has been there, I reckon.'

'Which may explain why she went after Harry Roth,' Jonathan agreed. 'So, she was a gold-digger, after all?'

'Perhaps. But it looks like that wasn't the reason for her death after all, right?'

'You look unconvinced.'

'I still feel like I'm looking at a puzzle with a piece missing,' she said.

'There's still time for us to find that missing piece.'

Penelope pulled up outside the cottage. She turned to Nancy. 'I need to pop to Tesco and get some last-minute bits then get this one home for an early bath and bed because I bet she'll be up at the crack of dawn.'

'I can't wait for my presents,' Kitty agreed from the back.

'I don't blame you,' Nancy said. 'You'll both be round early tomorrow though, right?'

'We wouldn't miss it for the world,' Pen promised, leaning over to give Nancy a goodbye kiss. After the first year Ollie was away, Penelope and Kitty had always spent Christmas Day at the cottage and Nancy hoped that the tradition would never end. She climbed out and she and Jonathan waved them goodbye.

'You'll be here this evening, won't you? For our usual Christmas Eve shenanigans?'

'If you can call watching *The Muppet Christmas Carol* with a tub of Quality Street shenanigans,' Jonathan replied, with a grin.

'A tradition you started,' she reminded him. 'I don't know why you'll never admit how much you love it.'

'I've got a reputation to keep up,' he said, picking up her case for her and leading the way into the cottage. She smiled as she followed, glad that nothing was changing this year. It might after her conversation with Richard but she didn't want to think about that right now. The thought of not living at the cottage in the new year and having a place of her own with Richard was so hard to picture. The cottage was home.

Charlie jumped up joyfully at the sight of her when they walked in, and she bent down to hug him, smiling as he licked her cheek. 'Hey boy, did you miss me?'

'In here!' Jane called from the kitchen.

Nancy left her bag and coat in the hall. 'Come on, Charlie,' she said to the dog, following Jonathan on through. 'Hi, Gran,' she greeted her.

Jane sat at the kitchen table with tea and the newspaper, the radio playing in the background and the light on to shut out the gloomy morning. The familiar set-up was welcoming and Nancy bent down to give her a hug.

'How was your trip? Sit down, the tea in the pot should still be warm. Jonathan, grab the biscuit jar, would you? I always need tea and biscuits after travelling.'

'I had a great time, Gran, and I definitely need tea and biscuits!' Nancy sat down. Charlie plonked himself on her feet so she leaned down to stroke him, pleased at how happy he was to see her. Jane poured a cup of tea for her and Jonathan, who brought the jar shaped like a hedgehog from the counter and put some chocolate digestives on a plate. 'I can't even get comfy though; apparently the Roths want to see me and Jonathan.'

'Really, why?' Jane asked in surprise. Jonathan updated her on what Natalie had told him and Will Roth asking them to come to the house. 'Well, I never. I didn't see that coming. Can I come too?'

Nancy looked at Jonathan who shrugged. 'I don't see why not. If they need our help then it's up to us who we bring along.'

Jane smiled at him. 'Thank you, dear. I don't want to be left out if we're about to solve the case.'

'I have my reservations though...' Nancy filled her grandmother in on what she and Richard had discovered down in London.

'Her poor mother,' Jane said. 'I hope she isn't all alone, and that she's being cared for. But surely now we have the note from the people after the necklace, it can't be to do with her?'

'I don't know,' Nancy replied with a sigh. 'I just felt that her mother might be the key, you know?'

'She still could be,' Jonathan said but he looked doubtful. 'Let's see what the Roths say.'

'Do they want you to write about the necklace being stolen, do you think?' she asked Jonathan.

'Will said I would have the scoop once they found out who was trying to steal it but made me promise to keep this all a secret until then. He was quite cryptic but said he needs our help. I thought it was all over, to be honest,' Jonathan said with a shrug as he munched on a biscuit.

'Something tells me it's far from over,' Nancy quipped, taking a sip of tea.

Chapter Thirty-Two

Jane, Nancy and Jonathan piled into his car and drove up to Roth Lodge once they had finished their tea and biscuits. The sleet was turning into snowflakes now, making it hard to see the twinkling lights, and the Christmas tree was barely visible on the green as they drove past it. Despite the unpleasant weather, the village was bustling as people hurried to pick up the last bits they needed for Christmas. Nancy was glad that she had stocked up at the supermarket earlier in the week and had everything they needed as she was looking forward to retreating into the cottage once she left the house on the hill, and not emerging again until after the festivities were over. The excitement of the past couple of weeks, not to mention the romantic drama with Richard, had left her feeling like she needed some quiet, cosy time at home, and she couldn't wait.

'You haven't said much about London,' Jonathan noted as they drove through the now familiar gates of the mansion. 'Your trip didn't make you want to run away from our village for the big lights of the city, did it?' He spoke lightly but didn't look at her, and Nancy wondered if he was actually worried she might do that.

'At the moment, there's more intrigue here than London,' she replied, matching his lightness of tone.

'How was it being with Richard?' Jane asked, leaning forward from the back to ask.

'It was nice,' Nancy said. 'He left me with a lot to mull over though,' she admitted as Jonathan parked outside the mansion. They both looked at her expectantly. She decided she might as well tell them; perhaps their reaction would help her know what to think about it. 'He wants us to try again, and he's willing to move up here to be with me.'

Jonathan's eyebrow quirked. 'Blimey. And how do you feel about the idea?'

'I really don't know how to feel, it's all very... sudden. He told me to think it over.'

'At least he's not pushing you,' Jonathan said, staying very neutral.

'He seems to finally be taking your feelings into account,' Jane said with a nod. 'Very admirable. Perhaps he really has changed for the better.'

'But what do I do?'

'We can't tell you that, love,' her gran said kindly. 'You have to follow your heart in these situations.'

Nancy just wished her heart wouldn't be so confusing about what it wanted.

Jonathan unclicked his seatbelt. 'Right then, let's get this over with, shall we?'

Nancy nodded, feeling a little bit disappointed, although she wasn't sure why. She and Jane followed him out of the car and walked up to the door but then Nancy paused, noticing something in her peripheral vision.

'What?' Jonathan asked but she shushed him and darted to the side of the building. He and Jane followed her curiously, and they all peered around the house as raised voices drifted on the wind towards them. Nancy frowned, trying to see through the sleet and she could just make out two figures striding across the lawn, gesticulating as they talked.

'Marcus and Peter,' she hissed to the others. They crept forward to listen and they watched as the two figures stopped abruptly, facing one another, their voices rising again enough so they were able to hear.

'This family's reputation is being dragged through the mud!' Marcus shouted. 'I won't stand for it, I tell you!'

'Father, please, he can't help the way he feels. He was so scared to tell us, he almost was charged with murder. Have some empathy, for God's sake. With all we've been through, I hardly think—'

'It's not just Will's bombshell,' Marcus cut off his son briskly. 'This whole murder is still hanging over us. The police seem useless. At least now we seem to be getting somewhere with the necklace. But when is it all going to end? If your son had kept a sensible head on his shoulders and not fallen for that common hussy, none of this would have happened! You need to keep a tighter rein on both your sons, Peter. I'm wondering if either of them are the sort of men we want to head up the family business.'

'You can't seriously be considering cutting them off,' Peter replied, shocked. 'They are excellent businessmen.'

'I am considering everything at this point. And I'll do what I think is best for this family!' Marcus strode off again across the lawn, Peter hurrying after him, their voices fading quickly as they walked away.

'Well.' Nancy leaned back and looked at the other two. 'I didn't think Marcus was capable of losing his temper like that, I must say. He seemed so kind and gentle.' She shook her head.

'We knew there was a reason Will had kept his sexuality from them, and there it is,' Jonathan said, shaking his head. 'In this day and age, they really think that hurts their reputation? And blaming Harry for bringing the murder to their doors... do you think he'd really cut them off?'

'I think from what we just witnessed he'd be more than capable of it,' Jane replied. 'Fancy shouting at your own son like that.' She glanced at Nancy, no doubt thinking of her own lost boy.

'But he seems to think the necklace was the reason for the murder so I guess that rules him off the suspect list? Could have been a bluff, though.'

'You still don't believe it was all for a necklace?' Jonathan asked her.

'I don't know, I just felt sure it was someone Lucy knew. But I suppose it could be both.'

'What do you mean, love?' Jane asked.

'Well, what if Marcus has threatened that before? To cut the family off from the money, I mean. What if this necklace was taken by one of the family? Because they wanted to be sure they'd have money,' Nancy suggested.

'That puts the whole family, minus Marcus and Will, back on the suspect list then,' Jonathan said with a sigh. 'It's possible. Money makes people do funny things. All I know is we need to find out the truth and fast because someone could be going down for this murder soon, and I for one would really like it to be the actual killer.'

Nancy and Jane agreed and they walked back to the front door to officially announce their arrival.

Frank, the butler, opened the front door. He looked furtively behind them as he did so, as if he was worried that they were being watched by someone. Nancy supposed that they could very well be. 'They're waiting for you in the drawing room,' he said, leading the way, walking briskly. They hurried after him, and he opened the door with a flourish. Everyone in the room fell silent, all eyes turning to the three of them. 'I'll leave you to it,' Frank said, hurriedly stepping back and closing the door again. Nancy looked at the others, feeling like they had been trapped in there.

The drawing room looked different from when they had seen it at the party, the furniture was back in the centre, and some of the Roth family were seated in front of them. Behind them, a tall silver and gold decorated Christmas tree stood proudly.

'Thank you for coming,' Will Roth said from the armchair, not batting an eyelid that Jane was there – but then she had been with Nancy prior to his arrest. And perhaps the family felt like they needed all the help they could get today. 'We didn't know who else to turn to. Please sit.' He gestured to the one of the sofas where they perched. Opposite them on the other sofa sat Harry, his mother, and aunt. Peter and Marcus Roth were clearly still outside and Nancy wondered if they'd been purposefully kept out of the room by the others.

'I think that Natalie told you about our break-in the other day,' Will began again once they had sat down. They all nodded. 'We naturally called the police straight away. They want to do a stakeout to catch whoever it is. They told us to find a similar-looking necklace that they would plant at the spot, and then they plan to have it watched so they can apprehend whoever is behind this when they arrive to claim it.' He leaned forward. 'The only problem is that we had another letter that evening – the person who wants the necklace knew we had called the police and told us that if we did it again, they wouldn't hesitate to hurt someone else.' He picked up the letter and handed it over to them.

They bent their heads together as Nancy held it up so the three of them could read it. The letter was typed and anonymous but the threat was clear. The blackmailer had provided a different location on the same day and time and expected the family to leave the real necklace there, and this time, not tell the police about it.

'They're clever,' Nancy observed. They had predicted the Roths would go the police, and wanted to be sure they would get their hands on the necklace and be able to escape.

'*Clever* isn't the word I would use,' Jessica Roth said, coldly. She turned to Will. 'I really don't understand why you've brought them here. What can they do?' She waved her hand dismissively at them.

'Are you happy to let Lucy's killer walk away scot-free?' Harry cried from the other side of her. 'If we do what this person says, they will take the necklace and run, and Lucy will never get justice. At least this way we have a chance to catch them.'

'We thought that they won't be looking out for you, they won't know who you are, so you could stake out the spot, and see who it is, and then we can call the police and catch them,' Will continued to Nancy, Jane and Jonathan as if none of his family had interrupted him.

'We don't care about the necklace,' Harry added, to which his mother tutted. 'For goodness' sake, Mother, we can afford to lose it. I just want to know who's behind all this, once and for all.'

'We understand, though,' Annabel said gently, 'if you think it might be too dangerous for you. We certainly don't want anyone else getting hurt.'

Will nodded. 'Of course.'

'I know this spot,' Jonathan said, taking the letter from Nancy. 'I used to go fishing there with my dad when I was a kid. I know a place where we could watch but not be seen.'

'All you'd need to do is observe, and get any details you can – their car, what they look like, and so on. We're not asking you to give chase or anything. But if they think there are police anywhere nearby then they just won't turn up,' Will said, encouraged by Jonathan's response.

Jonathan turned to Nancy. 'What do you think?'

She felt all their eyes on her. She was still suspicious about the necklace being the true motive for Lucy's murder but what better way to either prove or disprove that than by being the ones waiting for this supposed robber? 'I'm happy to help,' she said with a smile at the Roths. Best to let them think she was still very much on their side. She looked across at them lined up in front of her, knowing that one of them – or Peter – still could be behind all of it. She wondered what kind of person you had to be to not only be able to extinguish someone's life but keep the fact you were the one who had done it hidden.

Evil or desperate? A cold-hearted killer, or someone just seizing their opportunity?

'Will this actually work?' Jessica asked, turning to her son. 'They knew we'd gone to the police, after all. What if they realise we've told someone else now?' She looked genuinely worried beneath her usual chilly demeanour.

'I don't think you have much choice,' Jane said. 'They will get away with this if you do what they say. Besides, who would suspect us?' She chuckled a little.

'Gran, you have to let us two do this alone,' Nancy said, quickly. She didn't want her grandmother getting hurt.

Jane looked at her and sighed. 'I suppose you're right. No one will suspect a bookseller and a reporter now, will they?' she said, turning back to the family.

Nancy was surprised her gran hadn't put up a fight about joining the stakeout. 'We will make sure we aren't seen.'

Jonathan nodded in agreement. He was always confident that he could pull anything off. That confidence was contagious. She was nervous, of course, and she didn't relish the thought of coming close to a murderer but it was hard not to feel a tiny thrill about this. Nancy was going to be involved in a stakeout! Something that surely only proper investigators did. She tried not to get carried away but she was already wondering if she could buy binoculars anywhere before Christmas.

'See, Mother?' Will said. 'Nothing to worry about.'

But Nancy could tell by their faces that none of the family agreed with him at all.

Chapter Thirty-Three

'Well, naturally, I won't be staying at home,' Jane said cheerfully once they were safely back in Jonathan's car, driving back to the cottage. The afternoon was turning into evening and the snow was falling in earnest now – soft white flakes dusting the village like icing sugar. It looked as Christmas card-perfect as it did every year; you'd never have believed a murderer was living there. 'I pretended, though, in front of the family. If you're right, Nancy, and they are still behind it all somehow it was better that they just expect you two to be carrying out this stakeout, thinking that I'm safe and sound at home.'

'That's where I want you to be!' Nancy cried as Jonathan chuckled. She shot him a glare from the passenger seat.

'What? She had me fooled, too. You two are dangerous, I swear.'

Jane smiled, looking smug. 'I can be a third pair of eyes, the more the merrier. And I'll be safe. I'll stay way back in the car and just keep an eye out for you two.'

'You haven't driven in six months,' Nancy reminded her. Her gran still had her dad's old car and she wasn't sure it was even still road-worthy.

'Fine. You can drop me off nearby or something. And I'll bring Charlie along. You know he'd never let anyone hurt me. Honestly, sometimes it's like you're my grand-parent and not the other way around,' she tittered at Nancy whose mouth dropped open. Jonathan burst out laughing, and this time she elbowed him.

'Ow! Listen, it's obvious that whoever's behind this has got the inside scoop on everything that's going on: they knew about the police plan, they knew when the family would be out to try and take the necklace again, and they knew that it was in the house in the first place. It might be one of the family or someone they know, we have no idea, but if we can have the upper hand for once then so much the better. Because right now we need it,' he said, more sensibly, once he had stopped laughing.

Nancy scowled but had to admit they were both right; she was just worried. She wanted to protect her gran, who was her only family left, after all.

'It'll be fine, love, we will finally find out who killed Lucy soon. And before that we have Christmas to celeb-rate,' Jane said, reaching out to squeeze her shoulder.

'I just hope we're not walking into a trap, that's all,' Nancy mumbled.

–

Once the evening drew in, Nancy tried to push away thoughts of the Roths and focus on enjoying a cosy Christmas Eve in the cottage with Jane and Jonathan. It was an annual tradition for the three of them to spend the evening there. They had done so ever since Jonathan's parents had retired to Spain. He always spent time in summer with them over there but he spent the Christmas break with Nancy and Jane, and they all enjoyed the tradition. The fire in the living room was roaring, Jane was in her armchair with a blanket draped over her legs, and Jonathan was pouring drinks in the kitchen. Nancy was curled up on the sofa eating a mince pie. Charlie was snoozing in his basket close by, and the contentment in the room was high.

'I'm so ready to just eat and drink and not move from this sofa,' Nancy sighed.

'Don't forget the Quality Street!' Jane called out to Jonathan.

'Got it!' He walked in a minute later with a tray of drinks and the sweets. 'You've got enough food for the whole village, I think.'

'Better too much than not enough,' Nancy said, taking her glass from the tray. 'And we need to make the most of Christmas now that we have to be on a stakeout on Boxing Day,' she added, trying not to worry about it all over again.

'It'll do us good to get out of the cottage. I always put on about five pounds this time of year,' her gran replied, reaching for the Quality Street tin.

'Let's just promise now that there will be no heroics, okay?' Nancy said, eyeing the other two. 'If we really do see this guy, we call the police, we don't approach him or anything or try to catch him ourselves. If he's killed once…'

'You sure it's a man then?' Jonathan asked with a grin. 'Women can kill too, you know,' he added, cheerfully.

'Oh, I know plenty of women think about killing people, I've had some thoughts in that direction myself,' Nancy muttered.

'It's definitely a good idea to be sensible,' Jane agreed. 'We are just there to observe, aren't we?'

Jonathan nodded along but Nancy wasn't sure she trusted him to stick to their agreement. He wanted that front page splash. He held up his drink. 'Let's have a toast then. To watching but not catching a killer!' He winked at Nancy who sighed but raised her glass along with her grandmother, and then took a long, much-needed, drink from it.

They settled in for the evening watching Christmas films and eating and drinking far too much as usual. The cottage was super warm and cosy, and they all curled up in their chairs, contented and festive as the snow continued to fall outside. Nancy found herself wondering what it would be like next year if she was with Richard. Would her gran and Jonathan come to their house? She just couldn't picture Richard in the scene with them.

But was that a sign or not?

Penelope phoned just as Nancy was starting to drift off for a nap. 'Pen? Everything okay?' she mumbled into her phone.

'More than okay! Guess what?' Penelope cried, even more cheerful than usual. 'Ollie just came home! He surprised us!'

'Oh wow, I'm so pleased for you,' Nancy said with a smile.

'He was suddenly given three days' leave, I still can't believe it.'

'That's such good news.'

'Is it okay if he joins us tomorrow?'

'As if you even have to ask!' Nancy wished her a lovely evening then hung up and told the others what had happened. 'This Christmas is just full of surprises.'

'It will certainly not be one we forget in a hurry,' Jane said, switching off the film. She turned to her granddaughter. 'I thought we lived in a place where nothing ever happens!'

'Not anymore,' Nancy replied with a laugh. 'Not anymore.'

'Well, if we're going to have a full house tomorrow, I think we need a good night's sleep,' Jane said, getting up. 'Sleep well, you two!'

Jonathan and Nancy wished her goodnight. 'I'll just sort Charlie out,' Nancy said, letting the dog into the garden. Jonathan stayed over every year so he could drink with them. After the dog came back in, he went to his basket ready for bed, and Nancy made up the sofa for Jonathan.

'I'm so happy that Ollie has come home,' she said as she passed him a blanket. 'I know how much Pen misses him.'

'I so admire him for what he does,' Jonathan said, flopping onto the sofa bed. 'It must be hard for them though, being apart so much. Remember at school, how they were joined at the hip? I used to tell him he was under her thumb, and he said I should be so lucky to be under the thumb of a woman as amazing as Pen one day.'

'I want what they have one day,' Nancy said with a smile.

'You will. Me, on the other hand…' He shrugged. 'Mrs H was right – this Christmas really has been a crazy one, hasn't it?'

She moved to the door, yawning, ready for sleep. 'And it's not over yet. Night, Jonathan. I hope Santa brings you something nice,' she said with a chuckle before turning out the light and heading up to bed. 'If you're on the good list, that is,' she called back.

'Most definitely not,' he called back, cheerfully.

Chapter Thirty-Four

Nancy awoke on Christmas morning to a blanket of white outside her window. She looked out at the snow covering the village with an excited smile. The sight of a white Christmas drew her back to the past and when she was a child, living down the road with her father. She tried not to dwell too much on how sad it was that he wasn't here to enjoy it but it was hard. She remembered building a snowman with him before he died and bounding into his room to open up her stocking. She felt an ache in her heart when she thought back. She knew she should count her blessings – she had her wonderful grandmother after all, not to mention all her friends in Dedley End, but it was still painful thinking about what she had lost.

Her phone vibrated with a message breaking into the flashback of the past.

> Merry Christmas, Nancy! Hope you have a lovely day and you like your present. So looking forward to spending New Year together. Love Richard xxx

She went back to her bed and reached for the gift box she had put under it, having been unsure if she would want to open it in front of anyone else. Richard had sneaked it into her bag when she had left London, making her feel bad for not getting him anything.

Opening up the gold paper, she pulled out a bottle of Chanel No. 5. She had never worn it before but opened it up and gave herself a spritz. It was stronger than her usual vanilla scent and she wasn't sure if it suited her but she sent back a message saying thank you and that she would see him for New Year as she had already promised him she would.

Putting her phone down, Nancy pulled on her slippers, and shuffled downstairs, trying to be quiet in case Jonathan was still asleep in the living room. The cottage was toasty thanks to the heating coming on early, and the garden from the kitchen window was a picture-perfect wonderland. She turned the oven on and then the kettle before going to the fridge and taking out the turkey, glad she had bought an extra-large one now that Ollie would be joining them.

Her thoughts drifted over to Roth Lodge. Would they be celebrating Christmas this year? Surely not, with the murder hanging over them and the stakeout tomorrow? Then again, Harry was really the only one grieving over there. She couldn't believe the Roth Christmas was ever as cosy and cheerful as theirs was at the cottage, based on what she knew of the family, and she felt rather sorry for them. Then she shook her head. They had made that house and family what it was, she knew that she shouldn't waste her sympathy on people who didn't deserve it. She was determined to have a wonderful day with her friends and family and she only wished that the Roths could know what that was like.

'God, what time is it?' Jonathan came in, rubbing his eyes, his voice groggy. 'And how much did you let me drink last night?'

'I could ask you the same thing – my head hurts. It's seven but I wanted to get the turkey done early as nothing else will fit in this oven,' she replied, sliding the turkey inside. 'Coffee?'

'Please.' He sat down at the table in his T-shirt and jeans, barefoot, his hair a crumbled mess, stubble lining his chin but somehow the look worked on him. Nancy was certain her bob was standing up in all directions but he had seen her looking worse. She brought over coffee for him and tea for her – she could never bear anything but English Breakfast in the morning.

'Have you looked out of the window?' she asked as she sat down opposite him.

He turned. 'I haven't seen a white Christmas in years,' he said, his voice filled with childlike wonder. Turning back, he smiled at her. 'By the way, Merry Christmas, Nancy, my partner in crime – literally, now.' He raised his mug and she leaned over to clink hers against it, wondering why their exchange felt strange after just texting Richard. Nancy thought about the two men in her life.

'Something on your mind?'

She hesitated, but then the stairs creaked, and she heard her grandmother getting up to join them so she threw on a smile. 'Only that I need to warm up the croissants I got for breakfast.'

By the look on Jonathan's face, she'd failed to convince him but he said nothing as Jane appeared and she jumped up from the table to make them all breakfast.

Early on Boxing Day, Nancy and Jonathan sat side by side on a blanket on the grass. It was freezing. The snow had ceased but it lay soft and powdery as far as the eye could see. They were by the river at the fishing spot where Jonathan had spent a lot of his youth. They had chosen a place half obscured by trees, but which afforded them a clear view of the large willow tree where the Roths had been told to leave the necklace in the letter. It was under the tree, wrapped up in brown paper. A couple of miles away, the police were waiting by another spot where a fake necklace had been planted.

Nancy squinted to see if she could see her gran and Charlie on the bench over on the other side of the river but she couldn't; the willow tree obscured them from direct sight, which she was relieved about. Her gran told her not to worry, saying no-one would be looking out for a solitary old woman with a dog, anyway. She'd even brought some knitting with her – lent to her by Gloria – despite the fact she didn't know how to knit.

'So glad Gran made us bring this,' Nancy said, drinking tea from the thermos Jane had given her. Even in her duffle coat, scarf, gloves and thick boots, she shivered. She poured out some tea for Jonathan into a plastic cup, and he drank it gratefully. She reached up and touched the new pearl earrings she was wearing. They were a gift from Jonathan to match the pearl necklace she had been passed down from her grandmother – one of her most prized possessions. She had been incredibly touched by the thoughtful and personal gift and was still a little taken back by it. It was hard not to compare to the perfume Richard had given her, even though she was really trying not to.

'And your present has come in useful too,' Jonathan added as he waved the fingerless gloves she had given him, along with the watch that she and Jane had gone halves on. He was always writing in his notebook and his hands were always cold in winter and he was always late so they had been perfect gifts. The watch had been her gran's idea. She didn't like to admit it but she was fond of Jonathan, and actually thought of him as a surrogate grandson, despite despairing over his behaviour half the time. Nancy knew that when his parents had moved away, she had promised to keep an eye on him, and she always took her promises seriously.

'Do you think they're really going to show up?' Nancy frowned, trying to see anything on the horizon but there was nothing ahead but clear sky and water.

'If they want the necklace, they will.' He leaned back. They had arrived an hour early just in case, planting the necklace Will had given them before hiding in their current spot. He yawned. 'I hope they're on time at least, we're going to freeze out here soon and there's turkey leftovers at home.'

Nancy liked that Jonathan thought of her cottage as home. 'I don't know what it is about Christmas that we can even think about more food,' she replied with a smile but the thought of turkey sandwiches was getting her through the cold. 'It was a lovely day yesterday, wasn't it?'

It had been a quintessential Dedley End Christmas Day. Penelope and Ollie had come round for lunch with Kitty who was full of the joys of the season, thanks to her gifts from Santa and the snow, after which they had gone for a walk across the village green, played board games, and then slumped in front of the TV as it grew dark munching on cheese and biscuits and yet more chocolate.

'It was perfect,' Jonathan agreed. 'Heads up,' he hissed, leaning forwards. Nancy sat up straighter and watched as a car turned into the small car park by the river opposite them.

'Told you we should have got some binoculars,' Nancy said as she strained to see.

'I don't know where from around here,' he replied.

Nancy made a mental note to order a pair online. Although she supposed after this, she would have no need of them. Still, it was good to be prepared just in case for the future, right? She pointed as a figure got out of the car. 'Write down the number plate,' she said. Jonathan nodded and noted down the make and colour of the dark Ford car, and its number plate. The driver emerged dressed in black, a hood up, making it impossible to see who it was. 'A man, though,' he whispered as the figure drew closer. The figure was tall and stocky and Nancy nodded to agree that it looked like a man. He walked briskly to the package and grabbed it.

'Come on!' Jonathan pulled Nancy up with him and started to run towards his car, parked behind a tree. Nancy hurried to keep up with him.

'We're supposed to just call the police,' she said as she climbed in beside him. 'What will Gran say?'

'You can do that while I follow him,' he said, turning on the engine. 'We'll just watch to see where he goes.' He rolled forwards, and they watched as the figure got back into their car with the package and started to drive away at speed. Jonathan set off in pursuit with Nancy hastily putting her seatbelt on then calling the police station.

'Heading towards Woodley,' Jonathan said as the car in front turned left, and he drove quickly after them.

'Can I speak to Detective Chief Inspector Brown? It's urgent… yes, I know he's not at the station, can I have his mobile?' Nancy sighed in frustration as the person at the police station kept trying to fob her off. 'The Roths got another letter; they're at the wrong stakeout. This is urgent! Fine, fine, get him to ring me back then.' She hung up. 'I don't even know if he'll get the message. Should I just call 999?'

'Let's see where they go,' Jonathan said, turning quickly off into another road after them.

'I hope Gran is okay, why won't she have a mobile?'

'She still can't even work your microwave, let alone a phone. She's fine with Charlie, don't worry,' he replied.

There was a car on the other side of the road. As they passed the driver Nancy and Jonathan were chasing, the car veered across the road into their lane. Nancy gasped as Jonathan swerved off the road into the ditch to avoid a collision. 'Bloody hell!'

Nancy felt a flash of terror. She wondered if this was how her father had felt when his car had headed straight for that tree that night. Her heart pounded in her chest.

Their car screeched to a halt, the tyres squealing in protest against the grass. They both turned around to see the car on the other side of the road get back on the right side and disappear out of sight. The man who had the necklace also faded out of view in the opposite direction.

'Are you okay, Nancy?' Jonathan asked her urgently, slightly breathless.

'I think so. That was really close,' Nancy said, shaken, feeling even more strongly that she never wished to learn to drive herself. She jumped out, needing to get some air. He did the same.

'Are you all right?' a frantic voice called. They saw Jane walking up the road, Charlie at her heels. When he saw them, he barked and ran towards them.

Nancy waved. 'We're okay,' she called back, relieved that they appeared to all be in one piece. 'It's okay, boy,' she said as Charlie jumped up at her. 'Sit down, we're okay.' Nancy looked and saw the road they were on backed onto the side of the river where Jane had been sitting.

She joined them, breathless. 'I saw what happened. That other car came right towards you.'

'Definitely trying to stop us following whoever took the necklace,' Jonathan said, kicking the ground in frustration.

'Who was that? And how did they know we'd be here to follow them? I was right, wasn't I? It's still one of the Roths behind all of this,' Nancy cried, equally as frustrated. They had been so close to catching the killer.

Jonathan nodded. 'It must be. There's no way that was a coincidence. They wanted to make sure we lost that other car, and only the family knew we were going to be here today. Did you get a look at them? I was too busy trying not to crash.'

Nancy shook her head.

'I did,' Jane said now her breath was back. 'I saw a glimpse of a headscarf, and sunglasses. The car… it was red. I didn't recognise it. But it was definitely a woman driving it.'

'She could have killed us,' Jonathan said, shaking his head. 'Why did they ask us to do this stakeout if they were going to sabotage us?'

'Only one of them is the killer.' Nancy's phone began to ring. 'Hello? Oh, Inspector Brown, better late than never. Can we meet? We have a lot to tell you.'

'That's an understatement,' Jane muttered under her breath.

–

'You're telling me that you decided to bring the real necklace to a completely different spot to our stakeout, and that the two of you did your own stakeout that not only failed completely but almost caused you to have a car accident?' DCI Brown was furious. He paced around the Roths' living room, having gathered the family along with Jonathan and Nancy, and DC Pang, his face red with anger. They had dropped Jane at home. There was no point in everyone there finding out she had been with them too. Nancy wanted her back in the safety of their cottage. She looked at the family watching the inspector. One of them had lured them into a trap. But which one?

'We had to,' Will tried to defend himself. 'They said they would kill someone else. They knew we'd gone to you!'

'So now, not only have you lost the necklace but we have no chance of finding out who took it,' Brown continued as if he had never spoken.

'Lucy can't wear it anymore so it doesn't matter,' Harry muttered.

'What about the car – you can't track it?' Jonathan asked DC Pang.

'We have. It's stolen. We have no idea who took it or where it is now. We're trying to find it but there's no CCTV around, and the area was dead because it's Boxing

Day so I very much doubt we'll find any witnesses,' DC Pang replied dully.

Brown threw his hands up in the air. 'You should not have organised this by yourselves. And you two...' He spun around to glare at Nancy and Jonathan, standing by the door, both wanting to get out of there as fast as they could. 'Running around the village like you think you're bloody Sherlock Holmes and Miss Marple. I've a good mind to charge you both with obstruction. This is it, you hear me? If I see either of you anywhere near this house or the police station then I will arrest you!' He turned back to the Roths. 'If anyone contacts you again, you are to tell me straight away.'

'I can assure you...' Marcus began, throwing his family a despairing look.

DCI Brown waved his hand impatiently, cutting him off, which earned him a shocked look from Marcus, unaccustomed to being interrupted. 'Enough. I've had it up to here with this case. I don't know how I'm supposed to do my job in this village, I really don't.' And with that, he marched from the room, DC Pang hurrying after him.

'What an odious man,' Jessica Roth broke the stunned silence a moment later. Despite how she felt about Mrs Roth, Nancy quite agreed with her.

'I'm sorry I got you two into trouble,' Will said to them. 'I really thought we were doing the right thing.'

Marcus Roth stood up. 'Nothing happens to do with this case without you discussing it with me from now on.' He turned to Nancy and Jonathan. 'Frank will show you out. I trust this will put an end to any further involvement on your part too. Let's all leave this to the professionals, and get back to our lives as much as we can.'

Nancy and Jonathan could not protest – they followed Frank out, and found themselves shut out of Roth Lodge, likely for good.

'I'm sorry, Nancy, for pushing for your help in all this. I shouldn't have got you involved. I would never have forgiven myself if you had been hurt today,' Jonathan said miserably, as they walked back to his car.

'I just don't like the thought of giving up when we're so close,' she said, climbing into the car. 'But I suppose we have to.' She hated feeling like a failure. She had been so sure that they could solve this but instead, they seemed to have made it even harder for the police to do so. She looked out of the window at the house on the hill as they drove away, sure it was watching her right back but with a mocking smile.

Chapter Thirty-Five

Nancy, Jane and Jonathan weren't too thrilled about making their usual Boxing Day evening trip out to the White Swan for a drink but as Ollie was home, they knew Penelope would be disappointed if they didn't join them. And perhaps a G & T would cheer them all up. It was worth a try, they decided and they would have just dwelled on it at home anyway.

Jonathan offered to drive Jane to the pub then drop his car off at his flat. Nancy said she'd rather walk, knowing she both needed to call Richard, and that she couldn't face being back in a car again so soon after that near miss, so she set off alone, saying she'd meet them there.

It was early evening but the village was already coated with darkness, the Christmas lights shining merrily through the clear, crisp night. The snow had stopped but remnants of it dotted the pavement as Nancy strolled from the cottage. She decided to walk around the green, a longer route to the pub, and pulled out her phone to call Richard as she walked. The village was quiet and the peace helped to settle her disturbed nerves. What a couple of weeks it had been! She had never felt so frustrated in her whole life. It felt impossible that they even had a shot of solving Lucy's murder now – the police had banned them from getting involved again, and the Roth family would no longer welcome any of them in their house again, which was particularly galling as one of them appeared to have tried to run them off the road earlier.

It felt as if the only thing that they could do was to drop the whole thing, and that was the last thing she felt like doing. She was angry that someone had tried to hurt them, it having brought back her father's crash, but also because the murderer was likely full of glee and relief that it looked as if they were going to get away with killing Lucy Roth after all.

'It's lovely to hear from you,' Richard said when he answered her call, his good humour going a little way to help restore hers. She wasn't used to feeling deflated, and wanted to shake herself out of it but wasn't sure quite how to do that. 'How was the stakeout?'

Nancy had texted him updates over the past few days, keeping him up to speed with everything. 'A complete disaster! They got away with the necklace and we didn't see who it was, and they used a stolen car.' She sighed. 'The police are annoyed that we didn't tell them about the new location, and the Roths seem to have given up too. Basically, we've been told to stay out of it all.' She decided not to mention the car driving at them, she knew how much he would worry if she did. She shut her eyes to try to shake off the memory of it. It felt like it would haunt her for a long time though.

'But you still think one of the family is involved?'

'I do but I have no way to prove it.'

'What about what Lucy's roommate told us about her mother?'

'I just don't know. If she's in a home for people with dementia, I'm just not sure how much help she can give us. I wouldn't want to distress her.' Nancy walked over some snow, hearing it crunch beneath her boots. 'But I would like to know who's paying for her stay there now.'

'You sound upset. Are you okay?'

'I just hate to give up on things,' she replied. It was silly because solving murders wasn't exactly on her CV but she cared about getting Lucy justice, and about proving to everyone that she could do it, and that was hard to just let go of.

'I know but it sounds like you might have to, darling.'

Nancy was startled by his use of 'darling'. 'Maybe,' she said, dully. She paused, noticing a figure walking ahead of her, over the grass towards the recycling bins the council kept there. She thought she recognised her. 'Actually, I need to go. Thank you for listening.'

'Anytime. Take care, okay? I'll see you at New Year,' he said, hanging up.

Moving forward, she walked briskly and intercepted the woman. When she reached her, she saw it was Mrs Harper. 'Good evening,' she said, surprised to see the Roth housekeeper there.

Mrs Harper turned, two black bin bags in each hand. 'Oh! Nancy, is that you? You startled me.'

'I'm just walking to the pub,' Nancy said, falling into step with her.

'Oh yes, I might go in later to see Jenny. Honestly, you won't believe the rubbish the Roths have accumulated the past couple of days, our bins are overflowing and they're not collected for another week. It's ridiculous! So, I've had to bring these here,' she explained as they reached the bins.

'I bet they get sent so much for Christmas,' Nancy said. 'Here, let me take one, they look heavy.'

'Thank you. Yes, so many cards and gifts, especially this year, all of them fishing for information, of course.'

'I suppose the family just want to be left alone now,' Nancy said, throwing a bag in.

'They do. The police have agreed that they are able to go home now but Marcus has asked them to stay to celebrate Christmas tomorrow as with all the necklace business, they didn't get a chance on the actual day. The police are still looking for whoever stole the necklace so thank goodness, we can try to get back to normal now. Will and Harry will be off to London next week, and of course Annabel will be heading back to Cornwall. And I can get the house in order, it's such a mess.' She threw her bags into the bin too.

'I suppose they'll want to clear out Lucy's things too?'

Mrs Harper sighed. 'Yes, we've been making a start. Harry got very upset, the poor love. Natalie is doing most of it. God knows what we'll do with it all. She liked to shop.' They began to walk back towards the road.

'Did she have any family who might like it?' Nancy asked, thinking of Lucy's mother but obviously unable to let on that she knew about her.

She shook her head. 'No, she had no family, bless her. An orphan and all her friends are back in France so I think most of it will go to charity. I think Natalie might like something though, she was quite fond of her.' They reached Mrs Harper's car then. 'Thank you for helping, my dear. Have a lovely evening!'

Nancy waved, deep in thought, as she entered the High Street. Mrs Harper had confirmed that the Roths still seemed to think that Lucy had no family. It was so strange. Nancy felt worried for Lucy's mother even though they had never met, but if Lucy really had kept her existence a secret then there were two questions. The first was: why would she not want her new husband and his family to know about her? Was she ashamed of her? Perhaps she really had married Harry for his money to help pay for her mother's care at the New Haven nursing home? And if that was the case, the second question was: who was paying for that care now?

'There you are!' Jonathan called from across the road. 'I've been to my flat already, did you get lost?' He crossed over to join her, smiling at her.

'No, I actually met with someone rather interesting…' As they walked towards the White Swan, Nancy told him about her encounter with Mrs Harper. 'We know Lucy had a mother who was in a home in Burley so why did she not tell the Roths that? And what if the home throws her out, now that her daughter isn't paying for her care?'

Jonathan frowned. 'All very perplexing, isn't it? There must have been a reason why Lucy kept it quiet from them. I mean, unless her mother died since she left London? That's a possibility.'

Nancy nodded. 'It is, but surely if her mother had died after she met Harry, she wouldn't have been able to hide her grief that well? And why not just tell him that? There's more to this, there must be.' They reached the pub and Nancy paused. 'We could go to DCI Brown and tell him what we know…'

'We could,' Jonathan agreed, hovering by the door. They looked at one another. 'Or…'

'Or we could go to Burley, just to see if she's still alive. I mean, why waste his time if she isn't still there?'

Jonathan shook his head. 'We don't want to make him any angrier with us, though. We did say we'd stay out of it.'

She smiled. 'We could just want a little break. It's a lovely town, after all. We could bring my gran and stay in a hotel for the night. It would do us all the world of good.'

'When you put it like that, how can I argue?' He pushed open the pub door, light and voices breaking the quiet night, and they stepped into the warmth.

'You can never argue with me, Jonathan, because I'm always right.'

Chapter Thirty-Six

'There you are!' Penelope called to Nancy and Jonathan from a table at the back of the pub. It was full of villagers, the fire roaring, and conversation lively, everyone in good spirits after Christmas. They joined her, Ollie and Jane at their table; a gin and tonic and a pint of beer already waiting for them. Kitty was with her grandparents for a couple of hours. 'We thought you'd got lost or something.'

'Is it even possible to get lost in Dedley End?' Jonathan asked as he shrugged out of his coat and sat down next to Ollie.

'I was helping Mrs Harper; she was throwing out rubbish into the recycle bins on the green,' Nancy said, sitting down next to Pen.

'Not on the phone to Richard then?' her friend asked with a sly smile.

'I spoke to him too, yes,' Nancy said, with an eye roll. She took a grateful sip of her drink.

'Richard? As in…?' Ollie asked, looking at his wife.

'Nancy's ex who went off to live in London? The very same,' Pen told him.

'Are you back together?' he asked, raising an eyebrow.

'No,' Nancy said, quickly. A little too quickly, she knew.

'He wants them to be, though,' Jonathan said, taking a gulp of his pint.

'He was more polite at the tree night than I remembered him being,' Jane spoke up. 'Perhaps he has grown up, eh?'

'I think he has,' Nancy agreed, her mind wandering to his suggestion that he move into the village. She still wasn't sure if it was something she wanted. She had enjoyed seeing him again, there was still a spark there, and he did seem to have changed, but something was holding her back; she could feel it and she knew it was best not to ignore it.

'I suppose there is a lack of decent, eligible men around here,' Penelope said.

'Hey!' Jonathan cried at her.

'I did say decent,' Pen told him, pointedly.

'I can be decent,' he argued with her. 'Nancy, help me out here?' He turned to her with a raised eyebrow.

'I'm as neutral as Switzerland,' she replied, really not wanting to be drawn on Jonathan's eligibility status. 'Besides, neither of us have time for dating, we still have a murder to solve,' she added, changing the subject. 'With that in mind, Gran, how do you fancy a trip to Burley with us?'

'Burley? I've not been there for twenty years! Used to have lots of lovely market stalls in the High Street, they did.'

'Still do,' Penelope said. 'We went a couple of years ago.'

'That's right,' Ollie agreed. 'It's worth a visit.'

'Perfect!' Nancy smiled. 'We can go tomorrow and stay the night.'

Jane narrowed her eyes. 'And why the sudden desire to go to Burley, or would I rather not know?'

'We want to visit an old people's home there,' Jonathan said.

Jane turned to him, furiously. 'I would hope if you're thinking of putting me in a home, you'd at least have the courtesy to talk to me about it first!'

'No, Gran,' Nancy said, putting her hand on her arm. 'Not you! We think that Lucy Roth's mother is there despite the fact she told the Roths she was an orphan. Remember her roommate who I met in London? She said Lucy's mother was in a home there. It's our last lead – our last chance to get justice for her. The police have all but given up.'

'But they did tell you two to stay out of it now,' Jane said, uncertainly.

'Now, Mrs H,' Jonathan said with a grin. 'When have we ever done what we've been told to do?'

'You'd make a rubbish soldier,' Ollie told him with a chuckle.

'You have to help us, Mrs H,' Jonathan pleaded, ignoring him. 'We can't give up now, we're so close.'

'And you don't want to have to give Jonathan fifty quid, do you?' Nancy added with a smile.

'Hmm, well, that's true,' Jane conceded. 'But how do you propose we even get to see Lucy's mother, if she is there, anyway?'

'You can say you're an old friend. Neither the home or the police can prove otherwise, can they?' Nancy said. 'And you'll enjoy looking around the market stalls, won't you?'

Jane shook her head. 'I must be mad but I would like to get some nice chutney.'

'I'll drink to that!' Jonathan said, raising his pint. They then all toasted 'nice chutney', something that could surely only happen in Dedley End.

–

Early the following morning, Nancy got up to make a much-needed cup of tea. The weather had turned chilly again and a layer of crisp frost had spread across the grass outside. She yawned nosily, having not slept well after coming back late from the pub. She leaned against the kitchen counter as she waited for the kettle to boil, and remembered she had left her phone in the living room last night. She went to get it and stared at the screen in surprise. There were five missed calls, three text messages, and a voicemail.

All from Richard.

She played the voicemail as she went back into the kitchen, wondering what was up with him. She had left her phone on silent in her bag at the pub so hadn't seen any of his calls or messages and had stumbled in late and more than a little tipsy, so she had just collapsed into bed.

'Nancy, it's me. I'm worried now. You're not responding to any of my calls or messages! And it's late…' Richard sounded really anxious. 'Please let me know you're okay? With everything that's been happening there, I won't be able to sleep until I know you're safe.'

Nancy felt bad. He was obviously imagining all sorts of things with the murder still hanging over them. She quickly called him.

'Nancy?' He picked up straight away. 'Are you okay?'

'I'm fine! I'm sorry, I had my phone in my bag on silent all night – we were all at the pub so I didn't realise—'

'The pub?' He cut her off, angrily. 'I'm almost in Dedley End. I drove up, I was so worried about you.'

Nancy was taken aback. 'I didn't know, I'm sorry. We had spoken earlier, I didn't think you'd call again. Wait – you're driving here?'

'I wanted to wish you goodnight,' he replied crossly. 'And when you didn't answer, I was worried. I'm just coming into the village. Come outside, and we'll talk.' He hung up abruptly, leaving her staring at her phone. She knew that her involvement in Lucy Roth's murder might make Richard more worried about her safety than usual but it felt like overkill to drive all the way up to the Cotswolds to check on her. She had checked in with him yesterday as well, hadn't that been enough? She wasn't sure whether to find this sweet or somewhat annoying? Sighing, she walked to the front door and wrapped her coat over her pyjamas, stepping outside, just as Richard's car pulled up.

She went over and sat in the passenger seat, feeling the anger coming off him in waves. 'I really didn't see any of your calls until this morning, I went straight to bed when I got in last night.'

He shook his head. 'You were in the pub enjoying yourself while I was pacing my flat imagining all sorts of things that could have happened to you!'

'I'm sorry. But I'm fine, as you can see.' She touched his arm, and he reluctantly met her gaze. 'You didn't need to drive all the way here.'

'I was worried about you,' he said, defensively. 'I can't help feeling protective of you, especially with you involved in this murder case.' He took a deep breath. 'Look, Nancy, maybe you could leave it all now? The police asked you to, didn't they? I would feel a lot better if I knew you were safely off the case.'

She withdrew her hand. 'I can't do that. I'm going to Burley with Jonathan and Gran to visit that nursing home Lucy's flatmate told us about.'

Richard sucked in a breath. 'Why can't you just let the police do that?'

'They don't think the family is involved anymore but they're wrong!'

He snorted. 'Now suddenly you know more about solving murders than the police? Nancy, come on! It was sweet at first that you wanted to do some digging into it all but this is getting a bit silly, now. Leave it to the professionals, babe.'

'Don't call me babe,' she snapped, her patience evaporating. It had always annoyed her when he had called her that in the past. 'This is all too much. You've come back suddenly into my life, talking about us moving in together, and now you're telling me what to do, and turning up here because I didn't answer my phone!'

Richard looked stricken. 'I'm not telling you what to do, I'm just worried.' He grabbed her hand. 'Nancy, please, can't you see, I'm in love with you? I love you. I never really stopped. And seeing you again, I just know that we belong together.'

Nancy was torn. What he was saying was romantic and what she had wanted to hear from him when they were together before, but now she was uncertain. She had been so flattered by his renewed attentions but she remembered a couple of times at university when he had been over protective. Once, he'd tracked her down when she'd been having drinks with people on her course, saying he was worried when she hadn't come back to their halls at her usual time. Another time he had insisted on taking her to her exams and waiting outside for her even though they lasted a couple of hours. He'd even come along to every meeting of the Agatha Christie Appreciation Society despite never having read one of her books just so they weren't parted for one evening a month.

She had forgotten how claustrophobic she had felt with him on those occasions, but she felt it again now. This all felt too much, too soon. She wasn't sure how she felt about him but he was saying all these things about them being together forever. She felt trapped, if she was being honest with herself. But she didn't want to hurt him either. Why had everything become so complicated? She squeezed his hand. 'I need time. I'm not where you are yet. Please don't push me.'

'I can't lose you again,' he said, leaning in to kiss her. She returned the kiss but still felt uneasy. When they drew back, he smiled. 'You just drive me crazy.'

Nancy raised an eyebrow, unsure she could ever drive anyone crazy. 'I have to do this, Richard. I have to see this thing through. We're so close now. You have to trust me, okay? I'll be fine.'

Richard sighed and let her go. 'I wish you'd let me go with you.'

'I won't be alone – Jonathan and Gran will be with me.'

'Jonathan,' he said, dismissively. 'How can I trust him to keep you safe?'

'I don't need him, or you, to keep me safe. I just need you to trust me, okay? Richard?' she prodded, determined not to give way on this.

He looked at her, sensing her resolve. 'Fine. But can you call me, please? Let me know you're okay. Otherwise I'll worry the whole time you're gone.'

Nancy wondered whether he was more worried about the murder or the fact she was going with Jonathan. 'I'll let you know I'm okay,' she agreed. 'Do you want to come in for breakfast?'

'That would be great. I need to head back for work but really could do with a coffee. I'm glad you're alright.' He stroked her hair. 'Just be careful, and take care of yourself. For my sake as much as yours now.'

'Come on, I need tea,' she said, opening the door, keen to get out of the close quarters, and back in her own space. She supposed she should be touched that he cared about her so much but something about his behaviour was niggling at her. He had been so supportive of her investigating the murder, helping her in London and everything, and now he wanted her to just forget it. Why, though?

Was it really because he was worried for her, or was there another reason? But Nancy had no idea what that could be.

Chapter Thirty-Seven

It was dry, albeit freezing cold, when Jonathan, Nancy and Jane headed towards Burley to spend the night. They left Charlie with Penelope looking after the bookshop; she needed the distraction now that Ollie had left again for his station abroad. The town was about an hour away from Dedley End and had delightful cobbled streets winding through it, a good selection of independent shops, and one hotel perched on the edge, overlooking acres of lush green grounds.

The Burley Hotel was in a former stately home, richly furnished and filled with original details such as ornate ceilings, and grand fireplaces which had the effect of transporting the three of them back to another time. Nancy was in her element – she felt like a heroine in a Georgian romance as she walked through the rooms. They had booked in to stay for a night, Nancy and her grandmother sharing a larger room, Jonathan in a single. After storing their bags, they went down to reception where Jane and Nancy waited for Jonathan to bring the car round from the car park as the market was too far away to walk to.

As they stood in the grand lobby, Nancy's attention was caught by a man standing just outside. He was about fifty with a scruffy beard, wearing old jeans, his hand in his pocket, staring straight at them. He didn't look like someone who would be staying at the hotel. Nancy wasn't quite sure why he was unnerving her so much. Perhaps because he seemed slightly familiar to her? His gaze quickly moved when he realised she had clocked him but she couldn't shake the feeling he had been watching her. When Jonathan pulled up, the man faded away, and Nancy told herself she was just being paranoid. With everything that had happened lately, it was hardly surprising.

Jonathan drove them to the centre of Burley, finding one of the last spaces just to the edge of the pedestrianised main street, full of stalls and people. The sun was out, shining down on the cobbles, and the atmosphere buzzing.

They had planned to shop in the morning, have lunch, and then head to New Haven nursing home in the afternoon to find out all they could about Lucy Roth's mother.

'I don't know why we don't come here more often, this is lovely,' Jane said, looking round happily.

'Look, there's a chutney stall.' Jonathan led the way and they examined the array of chutneys, marmalades and jams, Nancy smiling at how sweet he could be to Jane.

She paused by a stall, casting her eyes over the silver jewellery, when something in her peripheral vision made her glance up. Her heart flittered. The man from outside the hotel was right there in the market! Now she was sure she wasn't being paranoid. He must have followed them. When they made eye contact, he turned and faded into the crowd.

She hurried over to Jonathan and Jane and said in a low voice, 'I think someone is watching us.'

'Who?' Jonathan asked promptly.

'There was a man at the hotel and I've seen him just now, here in the market. He looks vaguely familiar too.

What if it was the man who picked up the Roths' neck-lace?'

'You think he followed us here?' Jane asked, looking around nervously.

'I'm not sure but I think so,' Nancy said, goosebumps bubbling up on her arms under her coat.

Jonathan looked around. 'I can't see him now but let's keep an eye out. We'll confront him if he does it again. Don't worry, he can't do anything out here with so many witnesses,' Jonathan said.

'I'm not sure that's a comforting thought,' she replied, dryly.

'What do we do?' Jane asked, biting her lip.

'Just carry on as normal,' Jonathan said. More loudly, he added, 'Nancy, would I prefer apple or mango chutney with my cheese and biscuits?'

Nancy stepped forward to choose the one she thought he'd like best.

Jane watched them and then chuckled. 'Sometimes you two act like an old married couple, you know that?'

Jonathan made a half choking, half coughing sound, and Nancy elbowed him in the side. He picked up a chutney to buy, and Nancy turned to look over her shoulder but there didn't seem to be anyone watching them any longer.

The sooner they got to the bottom of this murder, the better, for both Lucy Roth, and Nancy's nerves.

–

The New Haven nursing home stood just out of the town, a large white stone building, low-lying in the hills. Jonathan parked out front, and they made their way inside.

Everything was clean and bright, the walls white, the floor shiny wood, plants and pictures brightening up the reception where they were greeted warmly.

'Looks pricey here,' Jonathan muttered as they walked up to the front desk.

'No wonder Lucy struggled to afford to pay for her mother's care here,' Nancy said. It made her feel better to see what a lovely place it was. She had been sure that Lucy had cared for her mother and this proved it. She had lived in that tiny flat in London working and giving most of her money to this place. Could Nancy now blame her for being attracted to Harry Roth's money? Will Roth had labelled Lucy as a gold-digger but maybe she was simply someone who longed for the security money like theirs could provide. That was surely understandable.

Nancy stepped forward to the desk. 'My grandmother's friend is here, and we were wondering if it would be possible to see her, please?' she asked the receptionist, a middle-aged woman with a neat bun and glasses perched low on her nose. 'Mrs Lewis?' They were hoping that Lucy had used the same fake name for her mother as well as for herself. If not, then they'd fail at the very first hurdle. Nancy held her breath.

The receptionist smiled brightly. 'Oh how lovely, Mrs Lewis rarely gets visitors these days.' Her smile faded. 'Not since...'

'How is she doing – after losing Lucy?' Nancy prompted her. At least the home knew that Lucy had died, which begged the question who was funding her mother's care there now.

'As well as can be expected. Some days she remembers and gets quite upset, and then on other days she asks when Lucy is coming for her next visit. It's very difficult. Sign in here, please, and I'll just buzz for someone to take you on through.'

They signed in and waited for someone to take them to see Mrs Lewis.

'She didn't seem worried about who would pay for Mrs Lewis's care here now,' Nancy said in a low voice. 'Only that Mrs Lewis is upset over her daughter's death – hardly surprising.'

'Lucy must have left a will. Perhaps she had more money than we think.'

'But then the Roths would have known about her mother and that she had inherited her money, right?'

Jonathan frowned. 'Right,' he agreed, looking just as puzzled as she felt about it.

A man in a white uniform came into reception then and led them down a winding corridor until he stopped outside a room, and opened up the door.

'Hi, there, Pam, you have some visitors today.'

'I do?'

The care worker stepped back to let Jane, Nancy and Jonathan in. The room was fairly large with a wide window letting in lots of light. There was also a bed, wardrobe, desk, TV and door open to a private bathroom. Mrs Lewis sat in the armchair by the window, a blanket draped over her, a book, glasses and mug of tea on the table beside her. She looked up in surprise, and then smiled at them. She had tidy grey hair, great skin for her age, and bright eyes which reminded Nancy of Lucy. You could see that Mrs Lewis had been beautiful like her daughter. 'Just give me a call if you need anything,' the man said before leaving them alone.

Jane was staring at the woman. 'Hi there, I'm Jane. Jane Hunter,' she said with a smile. 'She looks so familiar,' she murmured under her breath to the other two before stepping over. 'Mind if I sit?'

'Of course. Have we met before? My memory isn't so good nowadays.'

Jane sat in the chair beside her. 'We have. I come from Dedley End.'

Mrs Lewis smiled. 'I haven't been there in so long. Lucy said she'd take me once the weather gets warm. I'd love to see it again. I've missed it so much.'

They all exchanged looks at this interesting titbit. So, she had been in Dedley End? Then Lucy must have known about the Roths before she met Harry. Nancy saw Lucy's mother glance at the windowsill where photographs were lined up in frames so she wandered over to have a look. There was one of a younger Mrs Lewis with her daughter, smiling, and she thought how sad it was now to see such a happy photo.

'That's Lucy,' Mrs Lewis said, watching Nancy. 'Do you know her?'

'We only met once,' Nancy replied. She looked at the next photo. It was of a group of people standing on the grass, a large house rising up behind them. She peered at it, letting out a little gasp. Jonathan immediately came over. 'Isn't that…?' She picked it up. 'Mrs Lewis, this house – it looks so familiar to me.'

'Oh, yes, I work there as the housekeeper. Such a grand house, Lucy is always begging me to let her come with me to work but the Roths don't like it. Such a lovely house, it is.'

'You work – you worked at Roth Lodge?' Nancy asked. She took the photo over to her. 'Who is in this photo with you?' She pointed to it, hoping that the woman would remember.

'Well, there's Louisa Roth and her husband Marcus, they're my employers, and that's their son Peter with his wife, Dolly, lovely woman,' she replied, smiling happily.

'Dolly?' Nancy interrupted, her eyes catching Jonathan's. 'Did you say Dolly?'

Mrs Lewis nodded. 'That's what everyone calls her. It's not her real name, though, I forget what it is. I'm sorry, my memory isn't so good these days.' She smiled apologetically. 'And that's her sister there, too. It was summer. A garden party. The garden parties there were always my favourite, you know.'

It was Jane's turn to gasp, then. 'I know who you are. I remember now.' She leaned forward. 'You're Anne Walker.'

Chapter Thirty-Eight

A change overcame Mrs Lewis in an instant. She jumped up in her chair. 'You mustn't ever say that name! Never again!' she cried, frantically. 'Never, never, never!'

'It's okay, we won't, I promise,' Jane said quickly, looking horrified at her sudden distress.

'I'll get help!' Jonathan hurried from the room as Nancy tried to calm Mrs Lewis down but she had no success. Clearly agitated, Mrs Lewis kept repeating 'never, never, never,' over and over again.

'It's okay.' The care worker who had shown them in was back in the room in a flash, Jonathan following him. 'What's going on then, Pam? No need to get upset, is there? Come on, let's sit down, shall we?' His voice snapped her out of it a little bit. She stopped talking but her face was still twisted in distress. He turned to Nancy.

'You'd best head off, it'll be a while before she calms down and then she might well just fall asleep.'

'Does this happen a lot?' Jonathan asked as they moved towards the door.

'If she gets upset, yes. Often if she remembers something in the past or her daughter,' he said as he helped her back into the chair. 'She can even hurt herself. You did the right thing in calling me. I'll look after her now, don't worry.'

'I'm sorry we upset her,' Nancy said, feeling awful about it. The woman had only just lost her daughter and now they had caused her even more distress.

'I'm sure she was grateful for your visit,' he said, reassuringly.

They walked out thinking that seemed to certainly not be the case at all. Nancy went up to the receptionist as they left, one thing niggling at her. 'I think we upset Mrs Lewis,' she said to the woman. 'We mentioned her daughter. I think she remembered that she had died and became distressed.' She was aware of Jonathan and Jane hovering, wondering what she was doing.

The receptionist nodded. 'Yes, it's been very hard for her. Lucy was her only visitor so we've asked some volunteers to sit with her. It's not the same, though.'

'I'm not sure if you're able to tell us but we're quite worried about her. As Lucy was her only family...' Nancy leaned in closer. 'Is it still okay for her to stay here now? I mean, does she need any help with the cost of her care now?'

'Ah. No need for you to worry although that's very kind of you, not being family or anything.' She also leaned closer. 'The Roth family are taking care of it now.'

–

Nancy, Jonathan and Jane went back to their hotel to try to make sense of everything that had happened during their visit. They found a quiet table in the lounge and ordered themselves drinks.

'I hardly know where to begin,' Jane said, leaning back in her chair with a frown.

'As soon as you mentioned her real name, she became so distressed,' Jonathan said. 'Clearly, she was meant to

283

keep it secret. We can assume Lucy told her to. But why the hell did they need to change their name in the first place?'

'Language,' Jane chided him, mildly.

'Gran, how did you know her?'

Jane sighed. 'I never thought her name would cause such a reaction or else I would never have said it. It was that photo at the Roths' garden party. I couldn't help it; it all clicked into place when I saw that. I was at that very garden party.'

Their drinks arrived then so they waited until they were alone to speak again. 'So, who is she then, Gran?' Nancy asked. She and Jonathan leaned in to listen as Jane spoke in a low voice to make sure no one else could hear.

'Anne Walker was the Roths' housekeeper before Mrs Harper. She grew up in Woodley and was hired by Louisa Roth, Marcus's wife, who has since passed, as you both know. She lived in at the house like Mrs Harper does now. She was pleasant, well known by the village, as the family were back then – we'd see them out and about, all of them pleasant to say good morning to.' Jane took a sip of her sweet tea before continuing. 'I think she'd worked for them for a few years by the time the garden party came around. It must be over thirty years ago now. They had held a party annually for a few years by this point, every summer, and they usually invited pretty much the whole village as well as their more well-to-do friends and business associates. My husband came along with me, obviously.' She sighed at the memory. Nancy knew how much she still missed him. 'I think I have told you about this garden party before but now you've met Anne, I'll tell you the full story. It all started out wonderfully. The garden looked spectacular and they had so much food and drink, a band playing, lots of stalls too – it was a real event, everyone was excited.' Her face clouded over.

'What went wrong, Gran?'

'Suddenly, Marcus Roth came storming out of the house. His wife was with him, Peter and Jessica too – they hadn't been married that long at this point, and you could tell Marcus was furious. He ordered Anne to go into the house with them. Everyone was staring as they all went back inside and maybe half an hour later, Frank – the butler, as you both know – came out and said the party was over because there had been a theft at the house. Well, we were all shocked and we all cleared out, wondering what had happened. Later, it was said that Anne had stolen money from the family so they had sacked her on the spot and banished her from the house. I don't think they told the police, just tried to hush it up but it changed the family, for sure. That was the start of them drawing away from the village. And they never held a garden party again.' Jane shook her head. 'I suppose they were embarrassed about the scene caused that day. And perhaps they didn't know who to trust after that, either.' Jane let her words sink in for a moment. 'Just eight months later Harry Roth was born, and now we know that two years later Anne Walker had a little girl – Lucy, who would one day marry him.'

'And that little girl is now dead,' Jonathan said. 'And her mother has lost herself.'

'Is it all because of that garden party?' Nancy wondered. 'Anne Walker called Jessica Roth "Dolly". And I've seen that name before without knowing who it was.' She reminded them of the book that Annabel appeared to have taken from the Roths' library and the inscription she had found inside it – *For Dolly – I will never forget this summer. Forever yours, John.* 'Who is John? And why did Annabel hide that book from me?' She sighed in frustration. 'What does it all mean?'

'And,' Jonathan added. 'Why does the Roths' current housekeeper believe that Lucy has no family yet someone in the Roth family is now paying for Anne's care at the home?'

'Whoever killed Lucy must be paying for the home now,' Nancy said. 'Out of guilt, I suppose. I mean, it seems like losing her job completely ruined Anne's life. If that's so, then how could they also kill her daughter? We still don't have a motive, do we?'

'Perhaps Lucy found out what the Roths did to her mother and that's why she married Harry, to get her own back on the family finally,' Jonathan suggested.

'That does make sense,' Nancy agreed, slowly. 'But why was Lucy so angry? I mean, if her mum stole money then you can understand her being sacked.'

They looked at one another, the facts slowly coming together like the pieces of a puzzle.

'Or she didn't. Could one of the Roths have framed her? But who and why?'

'Dolly?' Jonathan suggested. 'AKA Jessica Roth?'

'I never warmed to that woman,' Jane said. 'But why would she need to frame Anne Walker for stealing? Jessica didn't need money, surely, she was married to Peter and had access to the family fortune.'

'We're missing something,' Nancy said with a sigh.

They slipped into silence, trying to work out what could have driven the wealthy and respected Jessica Roth to destroy her housekeeper like that.

'You said the book was signed by someone called John, maybe he was her lover?' Jonathan said, suddenly. 'Perhaps she was having an affair.'

'Oh my God!' Nancy cried, banging the table, and making the other two jump in surprise. Suddenly, things were finally becoming clear. 'Gran, you said that Harry was born just a few months after that garden party?'

Jane nodded. 'That's right.'

'So, she must have been pregnant at the party. What if Harry isn't Peter Roth's son? What if he's the product of her affair with this John? What if Jessica killed Lucy to protect that secret?'

Chapter Thirty-Nine

Nancy lay back in the bathtub of their hotel en suite, her body covered by bubbles. What a day! Her head was whirring with all they had discovered. It felt like finally they were getting close to the truth. But now they needed to decide what to do with it. Her grandmother was all for calling DCI Brown and telling him everything but Nancy was worried about doing that. She wasn't sure they had any actual proof Jessica Roth had killed Lucy and thought Brown would laugh at them, or worse, arrest them for interfering again. And she certainly didn't want to tip Jessica Roth off in case she did something else to cover her tracks.

Her phone buzzed from the edge of the bath and she looked at it cautiously. She had already answered five texts from Richard assuring him she was okay, and had promised to call him before she went to sleep, so she was relieved to see it was Penelope ringing her, and not him.

'Hi,' she answered the call on speakerphone.

'It's me,' Pen said, sounding far less cheerful than usual.

'Are you okay?'

'Yeah, it's just hard now that Ollie has gone. I can't wait for you guys to come back from Burley. Thank you for leaving Charlie with us though, it's made Kitty really happy.'

'I'm glad. And we'll be back first thing in the morning, I promise.'

'Well, maybe you can take my mind off of things – what's happening with the case?'

Nancy smiled at the word 'case' as if they really were detectives. She caught Penelope up with everything they had found out.

'Wow! So Lucy could have married Harry to get revenge for what happened to her mother. But why did Jessica frame Lucy's mother in the first place?'

'Maybe she knew about Jessica's affair? Jessica certainly wouldn't want any of her family to find that out especially if we're right and Harry isn't Peter's son. Perhaps Lucy was threatening to tell Harry the truth about it all. We still don't have the whole story, I'm sure of that.' Nancy sighed.

'How can you get the whole story though? Without Jessica telling you, I mean?' Penelope whistled. 'Can you really prove that she killed Lucy? I mean, are you going to the police now?'

'Well, that's just it. I'm not sure we can actually prove it. I don't know if the police would even take us seriously.'

'Honestly, it's hard to believe this is all real, it's like something right out of an Agatha Christie book, isn't it?'

Nancy sat up then suddenly, throwing bubbles over onto the polished floor. 'Pen, you're right! It's just like out of a novel…'

'What are you talking about?'

'We need to do what they always do at the end of a murder mystery novel – we need to gather everyone together, and tell them who we think did it. If it really is Jessica she'll either confess or give herself away. She'll have to, with everyone's eyes on her.'

'And if it isn't her?'

'The truth will still out,' she replied, confidently. 'Whoever did it won't sit back and let us blame her, surely?'

'I don't know. If they're capable of murder then I reckon they'd be capable of letting someone else take the flak for it.'

'It's the only thing we can try. There's no more evidence, and the police won't believe us. It always works in books, Pen.'

'Books aren't the same as real life, Nancy,' Penelope reminded her.

'I wish they were,' Nancy said, wistfully.

Pen chuckled. 'I know. Well, I say go for it. What's the worst that could happen?'

'We get arrested? The Roth family sue us for libel? The killer turns on us?'

'Crikey. Well, don't put yourself in danger. It's not worth it.'

'No, I know.' Nancy thought for a moment. 'I've had an idea but we'd need your help.'

'Anything! I need all the distraction I can get right now,' Pen said, quickly.

'Brilliant. Let's meet up as soon as we're back in Dedley End then. It'll all be okay, Pen,' she added, thinking of Ollie, and everything that was going on in the village too. She was quite looking forward to a more peaceful New Year now.

But first they had a murder to get justice for.

—

They decided to have dinner at the hotel before an early night so they could set off first thing for the village, and the house on the hill. Nancy slipped on a black skirt and polka dot blouse after her bath and went down with her gran, who had put on a long dress, to the grand dining room where Jonathan was seated at a table wearing what he deemed his 'smart' jeans, and a denim shirt.

'No wonder you never meet a nice girl, Jonathan, you dress like a scarecrow,' Jane commented as she sat down. Nancy stifled a laugh.

'Hey, this is smart for me,' Jonathan protested. 'And anyway, if a woman doesn't like me for who I am then she's not right for me. Don't you agree, Nancy?'

'I think I should stay out of this,' she said, as she sat down next to him. She smiled though; she quite liked his shabby dress sense, although she'd never admit that to him. She tried to picture him at The Ritz having a meal but the image just wouldn't come. A place like that just wasn't Jonathan at all. She had to wonder if it had really been her, either.

'Well, do we drink to solving a murder?' Jonathan asked the other two once their waiter had brought drinks, and their starters, over.

'I don't know; we're really banking on getting a confession out of Jessica Roth, and maybe that will just be too easy?' Nancy was nervous about counting their chickens just yet.

'Okay, let's just drink to teamwork, then. We found out more than the police managed to anyway. We have our suspect, and hopefully we'll catch her in the end.' He held up his drink, and the others clinked his glass with a chorus of 'Teamwork.' 'Mind you, don't think I'll be handing over fifty quid unless we can actually get Jessica Roth behind bars.'

'We're definitely going to win this bet, aren't we, Gran?'

'I should coco. Although I really shouldn't be encouraging you to compete, look at what happened when you were kids!'

'What do you mean?' Nancy asked.

'When you had that competition with Penelope when you were children.'

'Oh my god, I remember!' Jonathan cried, waving a slice of garlic bread in the air. 'We both wanted you to pick us as your best friend, remember? So you told us to race to the big tree on the green and the winner would be the chosen one, so to speak. So we did it, and I was winning but Pen grabbed my jumper and pulled me over. Trouble was, she's always been un-coordinated and she tripped as she did it, and we both fell onto the ground in a heap! I got a grazed knee, and she knocked her elbow, and we all trooped home feeling sorry for ourselves, and you never did declare a best friend.'

Nancy burst out laughing. 'I can't believe you remember that! We were only, like, seven. Although you should have known better, being older than us. Wow, some things never change then.'

'So, just who is your best friend, Nancy?' He grinned across the table at her, making her cheeks grow warm.

She shook her head. 'I think I'd better take that one to my grave.'

'Very sensible, love, very sensible,' Jane agreed. 'But I wish you wouldn't use that expression, not with a killer still on the loose.'

Nancy looked at Jonathan and despite her grandmother's serious tone, they both burst out laughing.

'I should have put a stop to your friendship back then,' Jane muttered, giving them both a despairing look.

Chapter Forty

'I think there's a car following us,' Jonathan said suddenly as he drove Nancy and Jane back to Dedley End the following morning. They'd enjoyed a large cooked breakfast at their hotel before setting off in a cheerful mood. Now they looked at one another worriedly.

Nancy swivelled around to look behind them – there was a dark, small car behind them and she could just make out the male driver – and his scruffy beard.

'I think that's the man who was following us yesterday,' she said, turning back to Jonathan. 'I still feel like I've seen him before – have the Roths sent him to keep tabs on us?'

'Oh dear, what do we do?' Jane asked. 'Can you lose him, Jonathan?'

'I've got a better idea,' Jonathan said as they passed a road sign. 'Just hold on.' He suddenly flicked on his indicator and pulled into the left lane, heading for the next exit, an earlier one than they needed. He checked the mirror again. 'He's following,' he said as they pulled off the motorway.

'Do you know where we are?' Jane asked, looking out of the window. 'Is it wise to leave the main road?'

'I had to do a story in this village once,' Jonathan said. 'If I'm remembering rightly, there's a dead end up here. He'll have to stop.'

'Why do we want him to stop?' Jane cried.

'Because we're going to talk to him,' he replied, grimly. 'Right, hang on, I'm going to speed up.'

'This feels like a bad idea,' Jane muttered worriedly.

'I think we need to know who he is, Gran. Don't worry,' Nancy said. She felt nervous herself but she trusted Jonathan. She gripped her seat as Jonathan hit the accelerator, turning right sharply and taking them into a lane that led to an entrance to a farm. He screeched to a halt by the farm gates, and hopped out of the car, Nancy right behind him. Jane followed at a slightly slower pace.

The car following them turned into the lane then and before he could work out what was happening, was forced to make a sudden stop just behind their car.

Jonathan marched over and banged on his door. 'Get out if you don't want us to call the police!' he yelled through the car window.

The man reluctantly switched off his engine and rolled down the window. 'I'm not getting out,' he growled at Jonathan.

'Why are you following us?' Jonathan demanded.

'I'm not… just got lost,' the man mumbled, folding his arms across his chest defiantly.

'I remember who you are!' Nancy cried then, stepping forward. 'I met you in London. You worked at that restaurant! The one that was a bookshop too,' she explained, inspiration striking just when she needed it to. 'When I went for a meal with Richard,' she added, frowning. 'Bill, isn't it?' She remembered Richard explaining that the restaurant employed ex-offenders, and how impressed she had been. She was less impressed now.

'Why are you following her?' Jonathan asked again. 'I mean it, I'll call the police right now if you don't start explaining yourself.'

Bill looked startled, and nervous. 'Look, I didn't mean any harm! I was just keeping an eye on you. No need to get the police involved or anything. I just needed the money.'

'Someone paid you to follow her? Who? Why?' Jonathan pressed him, leaning on the car, trying to look menacing which he couldn't really pull off, but the police threat seemed to have done its work.

'Richard,' Bill blurted out.

'Richard?' Nancy repeated, dumbstruck.

Jane reached out to hold her arm. Nancy leaned against her grandmother, grateful for the support.

'Are you sure?' Jonathan asked Bill with a frown.

He nodded. 'Yeah, mate. I'm sorry, I needed the cash. Just told me to watch you, and tell him what was going on.'

'Why, though?' Jane asked him, confused.

He shrugged. 'Said she might get into trouble,' he said, nodding at Nancy. 'And…'

'And?' Jonathan prompted him when he trailed off.

'And wanted to know if there was anything going on between the two of you.' Bill jabbed his finger towards Nancy and Jonathan.

Nancy let out a gasp. Jonathan looked at her again, also then dumbstruck.

After a moment of silence, Bill cleared his throat. 'Look, mate, I've told you what I was doing, now can I go?'

'Fine but if we see you again, we will call the police,' Jonathan answered him, seeing that Nancy was still struggling for a response. The man sped away without so much as a backward glance, leaving them standing in the empty space looking at one another, stunned.

'Well, I never. Are you okay, love?' Jane asked Nancy.

'I don't know,' she replied, slowly. 'I can't believe it! He paid someone to follow me. Turning up at the cottage the other morning because I didn't answer my phone and now this... But why?'

'You don't think...' Jonathan began, nervously. 'Could he be involved in the murder? I mean, he was at the party, he does know the family, he might know who did it or...' He trailed off, not wanting to finish the sentence.

'Surely not,' Jane said in shock. 'He helped you in London though, didn't he?'

'Yes but afterwards, he was keen I stopped investigating. And now he's having me followed. Maybe he was happy for me to be looking into it when I wasn't finding anything out but now we're close to the truth, he's trying to stop me?' Nancy shook her head. 'No, I'm sure Jessica is behind it. What would Richard have to gain from killing Lucy Roth? It makes no sense. But why then was Bill following us?'

'Richard was always rather controlling, wasn't he?' Jonathan said, shifting his feet uncomfortably.

'Is that what you thought?' Nancy hadn't known that Jonathan had noticed some of the things that had bothered her about Richard in the past.

'When he came here for that visit years ago, he seemed to be, yeah. That's why I didn't warm to him. And he didn't like it that you cared about your gran, and us. He seemed annoyed to have to spend time with other people, wanted to just be with you. I don't know, Nancy, I don't want to say too much, I know you like the guy.' He rubbed his hair and looked at Jane helplessly.

'I know what Jonathan means. I never fully took to him if I'm honest but he never did anything like this when you were with him before. So, I don't know.' Jane sighed. 'Turning up at the cottage because you didn't answer your phone was rather far-fetched, and now this… maybe he has taken trying to protect you too far. He really can't be involved in the murder, though, can he, love?'

Nancy didn't know how to answer. Suddenly, nothing seemed to make sense. 'I'll have to talk to him and find out.'

'Well, not alone, just in case,' Jane said quickly.

'We'll be there with you,' Jonathan agreed.

Nancy smiled weakly. 'Thank you. I suppose we should get home then?'

Jane rubbed her arm. 'Yes, let's get home.'

'What a few days,' Jonathan muttered, heading back to the car.

What a few days indeed, Nancy thought. She shivered and pulled her coat tighter around her. She felt like the cold had seeped into her bones. Would she ever feel warm again? She really didn't know.

–

When they got back to Dedley End, they headed straight for the bookshop after dropping off their things at the cottage, eager to check on it and see Charlie and Penelope, and have a cup of tea too, of course.

'Home sweet home,' Jane said with a smile when they walked in. 'I'll put the kettle on!'

'Hello, boy,' Nancy said with a laugh as Charlie bounded over to them, jumping up and trying to lick her face. 'Did you miss us? We got you some treats at the market.'

'It's been quiet today,' Penelope said, leaning on the counter with a smile. 'He hasn't had many people to make a fuss of him.'

'We missed you,' Nancy told Charlie, sitting on the window seat. He jumped straight up to sit with her. 'It feels like we've been away for a week, not just a night!'

'I want to hear all about it.'

'Wait till you hear what happened on the way back,' Jonathan told Pen, sitting in his usual armchair. He filled her in.

'God, that's so shady,' she said. 'What is Richard playing at?'

'I really don't know,' Nancy said. Charlie put his head in her lap as if he knew she needed his love.

'Right, tea's up.' Jane handed around the teas and sat down behind the till. 'Oh, look, here's the vicar.'

The door opened with a merry jingle and in walked Rev. Williams with a cheerful smile for them. 'I just wanted to drop off this cake from Gloria, she wanted you to try it, Jane. A new recipe,' he said, holding up a tin.

'I really don't know how we don't all end up morbidly obese here,' Jonathan said with a chuckle.

'I'm finding it harder and harder,' the vicar replied, patting his belly. He placed the cake down on the counter. 'Why all the long faces? How was Burley?'

'Eventful,' Nancy replied dryly.

'Things have been pretty eventful here too,' Rev. Williams replied, leaning against the counter. 'I've just had Harry in the church again, and it was quite hard calming him down, between us.'

'What was wrong?' Jane asked him.

'Will is due to go back to London tomorrow, and wants Harry to come too. They need to get back to work. Harry feels he's let Lucy down as they still haven't found her killer. He feels guilty just going back to life, I suppose. I told him there was nothing to do but that. He was very upset, you know.'

'They're going back to London?' Nancy and Jonathan looked at one another.

'That's right, and his parents are off to the Caribbean for New Year, I think. His aunt too, will be going back to Cornwall,' the vicar replied.

'We can't let them all leave!' Nancy cried, sitting up suddenly. Charlie let out a disgruntled noise as he was forced to lift his head off her.

'We'd better get round there now,' Jonathan said. 'But are we sure about this? You don't want to call DCI Brown?'

'Not yet. He won't believe us, Jonathan, and you know it.'

'And Richard?' he asked, uncertainly.

'If he's involved then we'll find that out. The killer will want to take down everyone else they can with them, I bet.' She couldn't believe he was involved but she also wasn't one hundred per cent sure that he wasn't, either. She could see that he was controlling, like Jonathan said, and had definitely tried to manipulate her into getting back with him, but was he capable of murder? She surely couldn't have loved anyone capable of that. The answer though, whatever it was, would be found at Roth Lodge as she had always suspected. She turned to Pen. 'Are you still okay to help us?'

Pen nodded vigorously. 'You bet,' she said.

'Well, what are we waiting for?' Nancy demanded, jumping up.

'What's going on?' the vicar asked them all, confused.

'We'll have to fill you in later. We need to close the shop for a bit,' Jane said, standing up, her eyes lighting up with excitement.

'Gran, are you sure you should come?'

'I'm not missing out on this!' Jane told Nancy firmly. The murder appeared to have made her feel ten years younger. 'Come on then, it's time to catch a killer.'

Chapter Forty-One

They passed Harry as he walked up the driveway to Roth Lodge, hands his pockets, head ducked, cutting a rather forlorn figure. They pulled up outside the grand house, and Jonathan, Nancy and Jane climbed out of the car, waiting for him to reach them.

'Hi, Harry,' Nancy greeted him gently.

'What are you doing here? If my grandfather sees you, he'll hit the roof,' he said, looking up in surprise, having apparently not noticed their car passing him.

'We've come to talk to you all. We think we know what happened to Lucy,' Nancy said. 'But it's tricky to prove. We were sort of hoping if we gather you all together, the killer will have to confess.'

Harry arched an eyebrow. 'Seriously? This isn't a TV show or a book, Miss Hunter. If you honestly have information on the crime then just go to the police. I've enough to deal with right now, I don't need you making things harder.' He turned to go, and then paused with a sigh. 'I suppose I'll bite – who do you think is the killer then?'

'Your mother.'

He threw his head back and actually laughed. 'Well, I must say, I didn't expect that. You know it's no one in this family. It was the person who stole Lucy's necklace.'

'That was a red herring,' Nancy said. 'We can explain everything, Harry. I promise.'

'There's no way that my mother...' He trailed off. 'God, I'm not thinking straight. Even I just wondered but no, it's impossible.' He opened up the front door, hesitating before seeming to make some internal decision. He looked back at them. 'The police aren't getting anywhere, and if you really think there's more to this than a robbery then you'd better come in.' Hope had entered his eyes; it was impossible to miss.

'We just want to get justice for Lucy,' Nancy said.

'Don't blame me if this goes horribly wrong,' he said, stepping back to let them into the hall. 'Wait in the drawing room, I'll gather everyone.'

'I was expecting him to throw us out,' Jane said as they walked in, a little surprised at having been allowed entry. They walked into the drawing room, and Harry went off to find his family. The three of them stood awkwardly in the middle of the room as they waited for the Roths to come in.

Nancy was nervous. Harry had made an excellent point. She had treated it all a little like she was in a TV show or a book, but this was real life. If they were right then they were about to face an actual killer and try to get them to admit it – were they crazy to think that they could actually pull it off?

'Maybe we should think about—' Nancy began but the door swung open, and in strolled Will, cutting her off. He looked much better, she noted, now that all suspicion had been removed from him and that his secret was out in the open, but also, she assumed because he would soon be back in his beloved London.

'What's all this about news on the murder? I knew you would carry on sleuthing!' He sat down in the armchair, gesturing for them to also sit, which they did on the sofa opposite him, the three of them squeezing in together, not wanting to be mixed with the Roths.

The door opened again and in came Harry, followed by his mother, and then Marcus Roth. 'My father is at the office in London,' Harry explained. 'And Aunt Annabel is packing upstairs, her taxi will be here soon to take her back to Cornwall.'

Nancy thought it was a shame that Annabel wouldn't come down as she had actually been counting on her reactions to help propel Jessica into admitting everything. But perhaps it was just as well if she was kept out of it; she was going to be so shocked and upset when she found out the truth about her sister. Harry sat down, and Jessica regarded them coldly, perching on a hardback chair at the edge of the room, crossing her arms with pure resentment floating like a cloud around her. Nancy couldn't meet her piercing gaze, it was too unnerving.

'I thought I told you two to leave us alone,' Marcus Roth said as he walked in, glaring at Nancy and Jonathan. He looked confused to see Jane there. 'My family have been through enough. And making Harry think there's been some kind of development is just cruel. You can see how much he's still suffering!'

Nancy understood why Will had been so nervous to tell his grandfather about his boyfriend – the way he spoke and looked at them was enough to make her want to flee with her tail between her legs but she had had enough of men trying to get her to do what they wanted. 'We know the truth,' she said, firmly, addressing the room. 'We know who Lucy Roth really was.'

'What do you mean?' Harry asked, leaning forward, and looking hard at Nancy.

'Tell them, Gran.'

Jane faced the Roths. 'Her maiden name was not really Lewis – her real name was Lucy Walker. Her mother, Anne, was your old housekeeper.'

Jessica Roth let out a whimper as her family gasped, and took in the revelation. Nancy jumped on that sound. 'And you knew that, didn't you, Jessica?'

There was a tense silence. Heads swivelled in her direction.

'Mother?' Harry asked, finally. 'You knew that?'

Jessica sighed, playing with her necklace and then lifting her eyes to meet the gaze of her eldest son. 'I found out, yes. That's why Lucy first threw herself in your path. She had some bee in her bonnet that we'd treated her mother unfairly, and caused her to have a breakdown. She has dementia now and lives in a nursing home, and Lucy thought we should pay for that.'

'She blackmailed you, didn't she?' Nancy pressed her. You could hear a pin drop in the room as Jessica nodded, slowly.

'What are you talking about?' Harry cried. 'She wouldn't have done that!'

'I received a letter, Harry. After the two of you came home married. Threatening me, demanding money from me. I paid, but then I got another one. They were coming every few weeks, it was getting out of hand,' she said, shaking her head. 'And then I found out who was doing it. Annabel caught Lucy red-handed writing a letter.'

'No,' Harry said, shaking his head.

'What did the letters say?' Marcus cut in smoothly then. 'You said she was threatening you – about what?'

'She believed that we'd sacked her mother unfairly, that we'd caused her health problems, that we should give money for her care,' Jessica replied.

'Why wouldn't she say anything to me?' Harry said. 'Her mother worked here?'

'It was before you were born,' Marcus confirmed. 'We caught her stealing from us so we had to dismiss her.'

'But why would Lucy come back for revenge? If her mother was a thief?' Will said, looking at Jane, Nancy and Jonathan for some clue.

'We don't think that she was,' Jane said.

'There was more to it,' Jonathan added. 'Are you going to tell them, Jessica, or shall we?'

Chapter Forty-Two

'Her mother didn't really steal the money that day,' Jessica admitted, seeming to sense that she was backed into a corner. 'She lost her job because, well, because of me.'

'What do you mean, Jessica?' Marcus asked, tensely.

'I took the money from the safe that day. When you found it had gone missing, I didn't know what to do. If I had told you the truth then you would have thrown me out.' Her voice wobbled. 'Annabel said that Anne could easily have taken it. She told me I should tell you all it was her. And I didn't want to, I felt so bad but I went along with it.' A tear rolled down her cheek.

'You decided it was better to save your own skin,' Nancy supplied the words for her, coldly. She had no sympathy for the woman in front of her. Lucy's mother had been blameless. She also had sympathy for Lucy trying to get some justice for her – it was hard not to.

'Why would you have stolen the money?' Marcus asked, incredulously.

'It was because of John, wasn't it?' Jane prompted.

She looked at them, shocked. 'How did you know?'

'A book – it's inscribed from John to Dolly, and I know that's what you used to be called. Your sister tried to hide it from me when I was looking at the library. Trying to protect you, I suppose,' Nancy said.

Jessica nodded, miserably. 'He gave me that for my birthday. Said the romance was unexpected in it. Like ours was.' Her eyes glistened. For once, Nancy saw a glimpse of the woman behind the cold exterior.

'I don't understand,' Harry said. 'What has all of this got to do with my Lucy?'

'I'm so sorry, Harry,' his mother said. 'I really am. I never meant for anyone to get hurt. It's all my fault!'

'Tell us the full story, Mum,' Will said then. 'Help us understand.'

'Okay.' She wiped her eyes. 'When I was young, I was madly in love with this man from our village called John, but my parents didn't approve. He didn't come from a good family, and they didn't think he was going anywhere in life. Instead of fighting for him, I gave him up. He joined the army and disappeared from my life. And then I went to university and met Peter and got married, and John just became a memory.' She took a breath then, looking down at her lap, perhaps finding it too difficult to meet her family's eyes. 'After we'd been married for a while, I literally bumped into John. I was just out shopping, and there he was. We spoke; he'd left the army as he'd been injured, and he was living close by. It was so strange seeing him again. All those old feelings, they just came flooding back. I know it was wrong but we couldn't help it – we began an affair.' Her cheeks coloured as she revealed that to the room.

'Oh, Jessica,' Marcus said, heavily.

'Blimey,' Will said. Harry said nothing but he'd gone very pale. Nancy's heart went out to him. Not only had he lost his wife, but he was about to find out that his own mother had been the one responsible.

'I couldn't help it, I fell back in love with John. I knew it was wrong but I couldn't stop. And then he begged me to come away with him. Said we could make a new life together abroad somewhere. I still loved Peter but I was swept up in this romance with John. I hadn't felt like that since I was a teenager. I felt like I had to follow my heart.'

'You were going to leave Dad?' Will asked in surprise. It was always strange finding out your parents were people in their own right, and both he and Harry looked so shocked that their mother was an adulteress. Marcus was seething in the corner, seemingly unable to speak, he was so angry.

Jessica nodded. 'But then I realised I was pregnant. And I panicked. I had no money of my own. I married Peter before I'd ever had a job. I moved in here and Peter supported us. I had nothing of my own. And I couldn't ask my parents – they would have never supported me leaving Peter. John had some money but not much, not enough for us to make a new life quickly, and especially not one that would support a child too,' she went on. 'So I decided to take some money. I knew there was a lot in the safe so on the day of the garden party, I arranged to meet John. There was so much distraction, I was able to go into the study, open the safe, and take the money without anyone seeing me.'

'I can't believe it,' Marcus said, finally. 'But why didn't you leave?'

She sighed. 'I did but when I got to the station, John wasn't there. We didn't all have mobiles then, I had no way to contact him. I went to a phone box and tried his flat but there was no answer. I waited for ages but he just didn't show up. I was devastated. I called the house and spoke to Annabel who begged me to come home, so I did. But when I arrived, Marcus had discovered the money had gone. And that's when Annabel encouraged me to say Anne had taken it. She even…' She broke down, dissolving into tears. '…Planted it in Anne's bag.'

'God, mother,' Will said, shaking his head.

'So, you ruined Lucy's mother's life all to protect yourself?' Harry said. 'I don't think I blame Lucy for wanting revenge, to be honest.'

'I can't believe you let me sack Anne,' Marcus said, coldly.

'I stopped you calling the police,' she cried, pleading with them. 'You don't know how guilty I felt.'

'Hang on,' Harry said, suddenly then. 'You were pregnant?'

His mother nodded, her sobs growing louder.

'Oh my god. Does that mean my father isn't really my dad? This John is my real dad?'

'I'm so sorry,' Jessica said between sobs. Her cool, calm demeanour had disintegrated. Nancy realised then it had been a mask. To protect herself from ever getting hurt again like John had hurt her back then.

'So, Lucy blackmailed you for money, threatening to expose your affair, and the fact that Harry's father isn't Peter Roth?' Jonathan said, clearly keen to get back to the facts. 'Money for her mother's care in the home?'

Jessica nodded. 'I've been paying for her care ever since Lucy…' she trailed off. 'Lucy wasn't good for this family. She wanted to break us all apart. I couldn't let that happen, could I?'

There was silence as everyone let that sink in. Nancy knew it wouldn't be long before they joined up the rest of the dots. That Jessica had had to silence her, to stop her from revealing the truth forever. And had pushed her to her death.

But then Nancy frowned. Everything made sense up to a point. But it was a big point. There was one last piece of the puzzle, and she couldn't yet solve it. 'But how did Lucy know that Harry wasn't Peter's son? If her mother didn't? You said that no one knew you were pregnant at the garden party?' Nancy said. Jessica nodded. 'So how could Lucy have possibly known?'

Chapter Forty-Three

Jessica looked up at her. 'I don't know,' she said. 'But in her blackmail letters, she knew, and she kept threatening to tell everyone. Annabel caught her red-handed writing one,' she said, looking confused. Her sister's name kept cropping up, Nancy realised. 'Annabel said we had to protect the family from Lucy. God. Did she lie to me? But why?'

Nancy leaned forward. 'Jessica,' she said, urgently. 'Where is Annabel?'

'Packing,' Jessica said. 'There's a taxi booked for her. She's going home to Cornwall.'

Nancy looked at the others. This hadn't gone as expected at all. Jessica had confessed to her past misdemeanours, but not to murder. It all led back to her being blackmailed over the past. Nancy had been sure that was why Lucy had been killed. But had Lucy really been blackmailing Jessica or not?

'We need to talk to Annabel,' Nancy said, standing up. Things were slowly clicking into place. She had thought she knew what had happened to Lucy that night but now it seemed it had been a very different story.

'I'll help you find her,' Will said, jumping up too.

'Stay here,' she said to the other two. She didn't trust the Roths left alone. As Nancy passed Jonathan, she gave his foot a little tap with her boot. He looked up at her, quizzically. She gave him a nod, and he nodded back. She had to trust that he had caught her meaning. It was time to put their plan into action.

'Be careful,' her gran hissed from behind her. Nancy nodded but didn't look back.

Will led the way out of the drawing room, up the staircase and along the corridor, glancing at the railing as they passed it, no doubt remembering Lucy standing there on the night of the party. Nancy, too, felt a shudder as she thought of the lifeless body in the hallway. Whatever they found out today, even if they did bring the murderer to justice, Lucy was still dead. It was such a tragic waste.

They went into the bedroom where Nancy had found the Agatha Christie book inscribed to Jessica, confirming as she had suspected that it was Annabel's room, and she had been the one to snatch it from the library. To protect her sister? Or, as Nancy now wondered, to protect herself somehow?

Annabel looked up in surprise when Will pushed open the door. She paused as she tried to zip up her suitcase. The room was empty of her things now, two bags on the bed ready to go. She even had her coat and shoes on. She looked just as she always had – clean and neat, unassuming, ordinary. The last person you'd suspect of telling lies. But that was exactly what Nancy now suspected.

'Is my taxi here?' she asked, finishing up closing the suitcase. 'I'm ready.'

'We need to talk to you first,' Will said. 'We're all in the drawing room. Mum's really upset – she needs you.'

'Why? What's going on?' Her eyes flicked from her nephew's serious face to Nancy hovering in the doorway. 'I do really need to go, I can't miss my train.'

Nancy took a chance. 'She's confessed,' she said, earning herself a sharp look from Will. 'To Lucy's murder. She needs you!'

'What?' Annabel stared at them. 'Are you serious?'

'We know about her affair with John, and that Lucy was blackmailing her because of what happened to her mother as a result. Harry knows that Peter's not his real father. Jessica said that once she realised it was Lucy black-mailing her, she had to silence her.'

'Oh my God,' Annabel said. 'I can't believe it,' she said but she glanced at her watch, and Nancy caught the movement. She looked like she was more interested in the time than her sister. And Nancy was sure now that she knew why.

'You have to come,' Will said, frowning, confused about why she didn't seem more shocked. 'I mean it can't be true, can it? That my mother killed Lucy?'

'Well, Lucy was threatening her. I mean, I caught her writing one of the letters blackmailing your mother for more money. And she said that she wouldn't rest until everyone knew the truth about Dolly's affair, and who Harry's father really is. I mean, she wanted to destroy us all!'

Will shook his head. 'But I was arrested for her murder. So what? My mother just sat here hoping I'd go down for what she did?'

'No,' Annabel said, quickly. 'We didn't want that. That's why we staged the break-in – and the note about the necklace. We thought if the police realised it had been a botched robbery then they would stop suspecting the family of killing Lucy. And it worked, didn't it?'

Nancy looked at Annabel, remembering the woman driver her gran had seen on Boxing Day. 'It was you,' she realised. 'You almost drove into our car to stop us following whoever picked up that necklace.'

'I'm sorry about that. I just wanted to scare the two of you off. Protect Jessica as much as I could.' She didn't meet Nancy's eyes, though. She was sure that Annabel was lying. There was a beep from a car outside, and Annabel went to the window to look down onto the driveway. 'That's my taxi. I don't see what more I can do for my sister,' she added, speaking quietly as if to herself, and not them.

'You can tell the truth,' Nancy said, sharply.

Annabel turned to her, narrowing her eyes. Suddenly Nancy could see a glint of ruthlessness beneath the meek, quiet exterior. 'If my sister has killed someone then it has nothing to do with me,' she said, heading for the door.

Will stood in her way. 'How can you say that? For one thing, she did this because you told her that Lucy was blackmailing her!'

'But that wasn't true at all, was it?' Nancy asked her.

'You're coming with us. Now!' Will grabbed his aunt's arm but she managed to shake him off and darted out of the door. 'Jesus!' Will barrelled out after her, Nancy hot on his heels. They followed Annabel as she hurtled down the stairs by the kitchen and out into the hallway, her eyes on the front door.

'Going somewhere?' Jonathan stepped out of the drawing room and stood in front of her, stuffing his phone in his pocket. 'I think we need a chat with you, Annabel,' he said.

'Get out of my way, you meddling little—'

'Enough.' Everyone froze at the deep bark that came from the doorway. Marcus Roth stood there, his face like thunder. 'I've had enough of these games. Annabel, join us in the drawing room. At once, please.' He turned and marched back into the drawing room. Jonathan hurried after him, and after hanging her head, Annabel reluctantly followed too.

Nancy looked at the front door before following with Will, hoping Jonathan had been able to make the call. It had all seemed clear once they had found out who Lucy Roth had really been but now she really wasn't sure why she had been killed after all.

Jane sighed with relief when she saw Nancy come into the drawing room; Nancy gave her a reassuring smile but didn't go over to her. Instead, she, Jonathan and Will stood near the door, blocking Annabel's exit.

Jessica Roth, seemed to have stopped crying. She looked up at her sister. 'Why did you tell me that Lucy was the one who was blackmailing me? It wasn't true, was it?'

Annabel just shrugged.

Nancy stepped forward. The only explanation to it all came to her then. 'Because Lucy found you, didn't she, Annabel? Writing one of your blackmail letters?'

Chapter Forty-Four

Jessica sucked in a breath. 'You wrote the letters?'

Annabel sighed. 'Yes, okay? I wrote them! And she found me writing one, and threatened to tell you. The meddling girl.'

'How dare you!' Harry spluttered, standing up. He advanced on Annabel but his brother strode over and placed a hand on his shoulder. 'What had she ever done to you?'

Annabel ignored him. 'After she threatened me, I had to tell Jessica that she was the one blackmailing her instead. I'd worked out who Lucy really was, you see. When I came to stay to help with the party and I met her for the first time, I knew instantly. She looked so much like her mother. I was surprised no one else had seen it. I confronted her and she admitted Anne Walker was her mother. Said she had targeted Harry. Thought that she could get her hands on the Roth money to make up for her mother being fired but the stupid girl only went and fell in love.' Annabel's tone was full of scorn as if Lucy had lost all sense in her eyes. 'I told her I'd keep her secret. It was too perfect. I wrote the first letter that night demanding money from Jessica.'

'I always wondered why Lucy had stayed here for six months. She came for revenge but fell in love and she had enough money for her mother's care, and that was enough for her. She wanted to fit in with this family despite how hard you all made it for her,' Nancy said, shaking her head.

'She really loved me?' Harry said, hardly daring to believe it.

His aunt sighed. 'Yes. She begged me not to tell anyone who she was, didn't think you'd ever believe that she loved you if you knew who she really was, so I agreed, and pretended I was her ally in the house. Unfortunately, she found me writing one of the blackmail letters. She knew I was making out that they were from her. She was furious about it, saying I shouldn't be doing that to my sister. Like she actually cared that I was hurting you, Jessica. After the way you treated her!'

Jessica had the grace to look ashamed about that. 'But why were you sending the letters in the first place? Why were you blackmailing me? I don't understand.'

'No. No, you never did, did you? You hooked Peter Roth with your good looks, bagged yourself a rich husband, while I struggled along in my tiny cottage in Cornwall. At first you gave me money when I asked but then I became too much of a hassle, didn't I? Despite the fact you have millions! You didn't want me to have what you had.'

'That's not true,' Jessica said, coldly. 'I was at the end of my tether. First, you ran through all of our parents' inheritance and then you kept wanting money from me. All to feed your gambling habit, and I'd had enough of it!'

Nancy was surprised at that. 'You gamble?' She thought of the phrase 'it's always the quiet ones' and thought that was pretty apt in this situation. Annabel was turning out to be a much darker character than her outward appearance suggested. Nancy felt they had all been blind to it. Even her own sister hadn't realised the lengths she would go to to serve her own interests.

'She is almost bankrupt,' Jessica said. 'And yes, I was sick of it. Always promising she'd get help, that she'd change, but it never stopped.' She faced her sister. 'You had everything from our parents' house. You promised you'd live quietly in Cornwall, that you wouldn't gamble again but it lasted only a couple of months, didn't it? Then you started back up again. I've given you thousands over the years. I even said you could come and live here but you said no because you knew you'd have to give it all up. You knew Marcus wouldn't stand for your "little habit", as you like to call it. So, don't tell me I didn't try to help you. Cutting you off was a last resort, the only thing I hadn't tried. Don't you see, I wanted to help you? I wanted you to stop it!'

'You don't understand,' Annabel said quietly. 'The people I owed. I couldn't just not pay them. They needed their money. They were waiting only because they knew I was here and who my sister is but they were getting impatient. I knew I couldn't hold them off for much longer. So, yes, I resorted to blackmailing my own sister. I was that desperate, can't you see? I was afraid for my life!'

Jessica shook her head. 'Why didn't you just tell me?'

'I didn't think you'd believe me.'

'Are you insane?' Harry rounded on Annabel. 'You did all this for money! Between us we have more than enough, why didn't you just tell us what was happening?'

'She enjoyed it,' Jessica said. 'She enjoys manipulating people. Playing games. Having the upper hand. Power. She always has. That's why she likes gambling. Only at that she never wins.'

'I win at other things though, don't I?' Annabel practically spat at her sister. 'You thought you could run off with John and leave me, and all this money? Well, I wasn't going to have that. I went to see him. I told him you didn't want to go with him. That you never loved him.'

This time, Jessica was the one who jumped up and ran at her sister, slapping her hard across the cheek. The noise of the slap rang out in the room, shocking them all.

'You bitch,' Jessica hissed as Marcus grabbed her and pulled her back. Annabel laughed. Loud and hard. They all stared at her. She looked like she was enjoying herself.

'You didn't win at one thing,' Nancy said, stepping forward. She couldn't bear the look of triumph on Annabel's face. 'You didn't get away with killing Lucy.'

'I thought...' Harry trailed off, looking at his mother.

'As if she'd ever have had the guts,' Annabel scoffed before realising she had pretty much just confessed.

'No, Annabel did it to protect herself,' Nancy said. She thought about what Natalie had told them at the pub. 'Before the police came, it was you that went into Lucy's room. What did you do there?' Nancy asked.

'I told Jessica I was hiding the evidence of the blackmail letters,' Annabel said, a little smugly. 'To make sure the police didn't find out what Lucy had done and come up with a motive. But really I was making sure Lucy hadn't hidden any of them in there as evidence against me.'

Will turned to his mother. 'Wait, so you knew Aunt Annabel had killed Lucy?'

'You told me you killed her to protect me,' Jessica said, glaring at her sister. 'To protect our family. But it was all just to protect yourself.' She turned her back on her sister and sat down slowly, as if exhausted.

'You killed Lucy,' Harry repeated, staring at his aunt.

'Fine. Yes, I killed her. She told me she was going to tell Jessica it was me behind the letters and not her. She came into my room before the party, told me that once it was over she'd tell my sister everything. She didn't want to upset Maria by doing it beforehand.' Annabel snorted. 'She cared more for all of you than you cared about her. I knew I couldn't let her do it. When I saw her go upstairs alone, I followed her. She was just standing there looking over the railings. Everyone else was in the drawing room. We were completely alone. I saw my opportunity and I took it. I had no choice.' She moved towards the doorway. 'But good luck proving it.'

'I think you'll find it's you that needs the luck,' Jane told her as she looked behind Nancy at something.

'Oh, really, Mrs Hunter? And why is that?'

'Turn around,' she replied.

Annabel did – just as DCI Brown, DC Pang, and three uniformed policemen walked in, followed by Penelope. Jonathan had called her on Nancy's signal. She had been waiting outside the police station and on receiving Jonathan's call, had brought DCI Brown up to date with everything. They had all hurried to Roth Lodge to catch Lucy Roth's killer, arriving just in time to witness Annabel confessing to the crime.

As DCI Brown read Annabel her rights, her hands cuffed behind her back, Pen gave Jane, Nancy and Jonathan a thumbs-up sign.

Chapter Forty-Five

'This hurts me,' Jonathan said as he handed Nancy a fifty-pound note. 'More than you know.'

'Oh, I do know, and that makes me very happy. Very happy indeed,' she replied, pocketing it with undisguised glee. They were gathered in the Hunters' cottage as evening settled over the village.

Jane, Nancy and Jonathan had just returned from the police station after giving their statements to DCI Brown. The inspector had told them again that they should have kept him informed of what they had found out and warned them that they had risked everything by confronting Annabel, but once he had finished scolding them, he then begrudgingly thanked them for finding out that she was the killer. The police had found and arrested the man who had picked up Lucy's necklace – he had been one of the men Annabel owed money to so had taken it as payment, helping her to throw everyone off the scent of the true murderer in the process. But not for long. She was now safely behind bars, and the whole of Dedley End was reeling from the news.

Penelope joined them at the cottage after her own debriefing with the police and having collected Kitty from her grandparents. Kitty was on the floor playing with Charlie while the four of them had a cup of tea and a biscuit at the kitchen table.

'We did tell you we'd find the murderer,' Jane said, smugly. 'See? All those murder mysteries came in handy after all. I wonder what your father would say,' she added to Nancy.

Nancy smiled. 'I think he'd be proud of us. I am. We got justice for Lucy and I'm so happy she can now rest in peace.' She was happy too that Lucy had loved Harry, after all. She had thought she wanted revenge but had chosen love instead. Nancy wished she could have known Lucy in life but instead had to make do with finding out the truth of what happened to her.

'I wonder what will happen to the Roths now?' Penelope asked, smiling at Kitty squealing with delight as Charlie licked her.

'I think Will and Harry will escape to London as soon as they can,' Jonathan said. 'I wonder if Peter will stay with Jessica once he finds out about her affair? And finds out that Harry isn't his. Marcus might very well cut Harry off.'

'I don't know. I think they'll do all they can to avoid more scandal,' Nancy said.

Jonathan stood up. 'Well, I need to head to the office and write up my article. I don't think my editor can quite believe he has an eye witness account of it all.' He grinned and then turned to Nancy. 'When did you realise it was Annabel after all, and not Jessica?'

'When she said that Lucy had threatened to reveal the truth about Harry. There was no way Lucy could have known about him not being Peter's real son. And I don't know, I always felt that Lucy had loved Harry really, and the idea of her being with him just for revenge… it just never felt quite right.'

'Well, Annabel is certainly manipulative. I would never have guessed she was behind it all,' he said. 'Just goes to show what secrets people can hide, huh?'

'I must say I did enjoy our investigation, even if it was nerve-racking at the time. All in all, though,' Jane said, sipping her tea, 'I'm quite looking forward to things getting back to normal around here.'

'I don't know,' Jonathan said as he walked to the door. 'Perhaps we've all changed for good.' He glanced at Nancy before slipping out.

'Tomorrow morning we'll be back in the bookshop, won't we, love, and we can put this all behind us?' Jane said to Nancy.

Nancy gave her a small smile but inside, her heart sank a little bit. It wasn't that she didn't love the bookshop but after the excitement of the past couple of weeks, Dedley End going back to its normal pace was going to feel, well, rather dull. Their village was usually safe and sound so there didn't seem much hope that anything like this could ever happen again. Nancy knew she should feel relieved about that but she couldn't quite make herself feel that way.

'At least it turned out that Richard had nothing to do with the murder,' Pen said, trying to cheer Nancy up.

'True, but that doesn't mean what he did was acceptable. No, before we can get back to normal, there is one more thing I have to do,' Nancy said, checking her phone. 'And I'm not much looking forward to it.'

'It'll be okay. You're doing the right thing.' Jane gave her hand a quick squeeze.

'I know.' Nancy had asked Richard to come and see her. They needed to talk. Having someone follow her was unacceptable. It wasn't about looking out for her or keeping her safe, but keeping tabs on her. She had allowed Richard to sweep her up with his enthusiasm about a second chance for them but she knew now that they were no longer right for one another, and maybe they never had been.

When Richard arrived, she took him into the living room alone. Jane had already made herself scarce – going round to see Gloria to eagerly discuss the solving of Lucy Roth's murder. There really was nothing else that anyone in the village would want to discuss and the Hunters, along with Jonathan and Pen, were destined to be guests of honour everywhere they went for the foreseeable future.

'What was so urgent? I thought you were coming to me for New Year?' Richard asked as he sat down on the sofa, looking at her quizzically.

Nancy perched in the armchair. 'I'm not coming to London for New Year,' she told him. 'I know that you paid someone to follow me,' she explained, as calmly as she could.

'What are you talking about?' he cried, indignantly.

'Don't bother trying to deny it,' she told him. 'I spoke to Bill. I recognised him from the restaurant you took me to.' She shook her head. 'Why would you do that?'

He sighed, running a hand through his hair. 'I was worried about you, okay? Running around getting your-self involved in murder, for God's sake! And I'm miles away. I just wanted to protect you.' He looked at her, pleadingly. 'I just want to protect you.'

'No, no you don't. Following me without my consent is not protecting me, it's controlling me. You wanted to keep tabs on me.'

'No! I really thought you might get hurt. I tried to get you to stop but you wouldn't so I had to do something. I love you!'

'That doesn't mean you can control my life. That's not love!'

'The problem is, you just don't feel the same way. If you loved me then you would have been touched by what I did,' he flung at her.

'You're wrong. I'd never want to be with someone who feels like they have the right to have me followed. I want to be with someone who trusts me, who lets me live my life how I want to live it.'

'Like Jonathan, I suppose?' he asked, his voice bitter, a sneer suddenly crossing his handsome features like a cloud blocking out a sunny day.

Nancy's patience evaporated. 'Jonathan is one of my best friends. I haven't even seen you for five years – if we were going to be a couple, don't you think we would have been by now?' she demanded. 'There was a reason that we broke up. I thought maybe we deserved a shot at getting our happy ending but there is no future for us. We're just different people, Richard. I'm sorry but this time, it's really over. For good.'

Richard got up and went over to the armchair, kneeling down beside her. 'Think about this, Nancy. You can't really want to let go of us? I know how broken-hearted you were when we broke up before. I know that you love me. We belong together.'

'I was hurt and upset, of course I was – we'd been together for three years – but that was a long time ago. I'm a different person now. I don't love you now, and I realise that we were right to end it back then. We don't belong together. And I don't think we ever did.'

Richard stood up abruptly. 'You just lost the best thing you've ever had, you know that, don't you? Who else is going to want you with your annoying grandmother in tow? Who else would offer to live in this Godforsaken village with you? You're going to end up an old spinster.'

Well, he had finally shown his true colours. Any sympathy she had felt for breaking up with him disappeared in that moment. Nancy stood up too. 'I love living in this village, and my grandmother is a wonderful woman, and I have amazing friends who love and support me. It's you I feel sorry for. I think it's time you left.'

'Oh, don't you worry, I can't wait to get out of here!' He stalked out into the hallway and flung open the front door. Turning back to glare at Nancy, he decided he needed to have the last word. 'And if you're waiting around for Jonathan to notice you, you're delusional. He'll never love anyone but himself, let alone his dowdy book-selling friend,' he flung at her before walking outside.

Despite knowing his words came from anger and hurt, they still stung Nancy as she watched him climb into his car. She comforted herself for a moment by slamming the door shut, blocking him out of her life, hopefully for good.

Chapter Forty-Six

No Dedley Ending to this story — bookshop owners solve Roth murder!

Nancy stared at the headline on the front page of the *Cotswold Star* newspaper in disbelief. It had just dropped through the door of the cottage. It was morning on New Year's Eve and she padded to the door in her dressing gown and slippers from the kitchen where she and Jane were drinking tea and eating toast together. She knew Jonathan had spent the time since she had last seen him writing his article on the Roth murder, but she hadn't dreamed that it would focus on her and her grandmother.

> *Nancy Hunter, along with grandmother Jane, was certain the police were following the wrong lines of enquiry, and after tirelessly investigating the crime they discovered the true culprit was Annabel Anderson, sister of Jessica Roth. They then went on to extract a confession from her. Read on for our exclusive eye witness report!*

'What's that, love?' Jane asked as Nancy walked back into the kitchen reading the article Jonathan had written.

'The paper. Jonathan's article is on the front page, and it's all about us solving the murder.' She slid the paper over the table to her gran.

'Well, I never!' Jane picked it up to read.

'Jonathan helped but he plays that down and focuses on you and me. Makes a better story, I guess.'

'Excellent publicity for the bookshop,' Jane said. She looked at Nancy and smiled. 'You always knew one of the Roths had done it, and you got Annabel to confess. I'm so proud of you! Front page and everything.'

'If you hadn't remembered Anne Walker though I would never have joined up the dots. We make a good team.'

'We do indeed!' She read on as Nancy looked at the front-page article. It would surely be a big boost for Jonathan's career. Given how well known the Roths were, the article would be widely read, even perhaps picked up by the nationals, and that could change everything for him. He had talked about promotion but she now wondered if job offers from London might very well flow in too. Would he want to take them?

Nancy's phone rang. When she answered, she was surprised that it was Frank, the Roths' butler, requesting her presence at Roth Lodge to speak with Marcus. Somewhat reluctantly, she agreed. She really could have done with not having to go back to the house on the hill for a long time after all that had happened but she was intrigued as to why she, and she alone, had been summoned by the patriarch. 'What can he want?' she asked her grandmother after she had hung up.

'He probably just wants to thank you properly. I don't know why he didn't ask me and Jonathan to come along as well.' She looked a little put out.

'It's a little strange. I'd better get ready then.'

'Make sure you're home in time for tea before you go to the party at the pub,' Jane reminded her as she got up to go and have a shower. 'You'll need to line your stomach, I know what New Year's is like there.'

Nancy smiled. 'I'll be back in plenty of time, hopefully this won't take long. Are you sure you won't come for the party?'

'I'm past staying up to see the New Year in,' Jane replied, shaking her head. 'But you go and have fun, you deserve it, and no doubt will be the guest of honour. I suspect everyone will want to buy you and Jonathan drinks tonight.'

Nancy went upstairs to get ready, a spring in her step. It had been awful witnessing a murder but she had helped to solve it and she did feel rather proud of herself. She couldn't deny that she had a taste for it now; it would be hard to go back to everyday life. But she loved her life and she was sure she would be perfectly happy for it to carry on as it always had done. It was almost time for a new year and that meant a fresh start, and she was looking forward to it.

—

The walk to Roth Lodge was a cold one and Nancy's cheeks were pink by the time she reached the front door. The wind was bitter as it whipped around her face but she was glad she had walked, needing to clear her head. It really had been the most dramatic month and she was looking forward to the party at the pub, cheering in the New Year, then having the bank holiday off to rest before returning to the bookshop. She felt like she could sleep for a week. She hoped Marcus Roth wouldn't keep her there for long.

Frank opened up the front door quickly. 'Thank you for coming, Miss Hunter. Oh, you must be freezing,' he said, frowning when he realised she had come on foot. She stepped eagerly into the warm hall. 'Let me take your things, and then I'll get some tea brought in for you.'

'Thank you,' she said, gratefully, handing him her coat and scarf. He led her past the drawing room to a small room she hadn't been inside before.

'I'll send Mr Roth in,' Frank said as he swept away, leaving her in what she realised must be Marcus Roth's study. It was a small room, facing the vast back garden, with a large, dark wooden desk, a bookshelf filled with books to the side, a rich red carpet and heavy drapes at the window. Nancy sat down in the leather chair on the other side of his desk to wait. It was a masculine, and somewhat intimidating, room. Her eyes wandered to the bookshelf where various family photographs were perched with the books.

'Ah, Miss Hunter, Nancy, thank you for coming,' Marcus said from behind her then. 'Don't get up,' he added, seeing her move. He walked round and sat down behind the desk. He nodded at her. 'I trust you're well?'

'Yes, thank you,' she said, a little amused at his formality but perhaps the room demanded it of him.

'I read Mr Murphy's article,' Marcus said, tapping the newspaper in front of him. 'A well-written piece, and full of praise for you, as it should be. We really are most grateful to you for getting to the bottom of everything. Of course, it has all been very trying and things have been revealed that – well, let's just say it will take time to get back to normal. But I do wish to apologise for trying to stop you looking into the case. I put my faith in the police when it turns out, my faith should have been in you all along.'

'I hold no grudge, Mr Roth. I think the police just looked at the cold, hard facts whereas I tried to get to know the people.' Nancy shrugged, wanting to be modest. 'And, of course, my gran and Jonathan helped too. We make a good team, I suppose.'

He nodded. 'I also wanted to apologise for stopping your work on our library. I know you have a lot going on but I thought maybe you would like to come back and continue it. I know before you weren't keen on being paid for your work but now there is also the matter of a reward for finding out who killed Lucy too.' He reached into his desk drawer.

'Oh, no,' Nancy said, quickly. 'We didn't do it for any reward.'

'I know, which is what makes it all the more remarkable but I would still like to pay you for your work. You acted like a private detective and should be compensated accordingly, and you could consider it an advance for your work on the library too, and any books you buy for us.' He slid a cheque across the desk towards her. 'I know how tough it is to keep a small village bookshop going in this day and age so I want you and your grandmother to invest it in your business. We want to make sure it stays open for years to come, now, don't we?' He sat back a little, smiling.

Nancy's eyes flicked to the cheque on the desk in front of her, and she did a double-take. 'Fifty thousand pounds? You can't be serious!' she cried, unable to hold in her feelings. The figure was inconceivable to her.

There was a swift knock on the door, and they both turned to see Will in the doorway. 'I thought I heard you, Nancy.'

'Good, Will. Come in and tell Miss Hunter here she must accept this money. As a thank you for everything she's done for this family,' Marcus said quickly, waving him closer.

'It's just too much,' Nancy protested. 'I really couldn't accept it,' she said, pushing the cheque back towards him.

Marcus stood up and moved around the desk, knocking a photo on the bookshelf as he moved. 'Oh dear, I really must sort this room out.' He straightened it. 'Ah, Louisa, my dear wife. Nancy, she would have wanted me to give you even more. I just know it.' He saw them watching as his voice dropped to a softer tone. He cleared his throat. 'Because of the bookshop, you know, as a fellow book lover and all that,' he added, quickly.

Nancy glanced at the photo. It was strange to see him becoming so emotional at the mention of his wife, especially now she had seen how stern he could be. He must have really loved her. She did look pretty in the photo with long, wavy hair, perched next to a vintage sports car, smiling at the camera. Something about the image sent a jolt through Nancy. 'That's quite a car,' she said.

'Oh, Granny loved that car, didn't she?' Will said. 'And then she had to get rid of it. I can't remember why?' He turned to his grandfather with a frown. Marcus Roth had gone deathly white. The colour had drained away from his face as he stared at the two of them.

Nancy looked at the photo again, and then she realised what it was that had struck her. 'That scarf,' she said, aloud. Louisa Roth was wearing a vivid yellow and blue silk scarf in the photo. And Nancy had seen it before. She stared in shock. The only clue at the scene of her father's car crash had been a scarf found near his car. A yellow and blue silk scarf. An expensive scarf. From Liberty London. The same scarf that Louisa Roth was wearing in that photo. Nancy's blood ran cold.

Marcus moved in front of the photograph and pushed his cheque towards Nancy again. 'You must accept this. Tell her, Will,' he said, hurriedly. Will looked uncertainly back and forth between the two of them.

'It was her,' Nancy said, slowly, looking up and meeting Marcus's scared eyes. 'That night, the night of my father's car crash… your wife, she was driving the car. Wasn't she? She fled the scene and left my dad there to die. Alone.' She felt like the world had slowed down as she waited for him to speak. The horror on his face said it all, though. She stood up abruptly, pushing the chair back with a piercing scrape. 'And what? You thought you'd try to buy me off with this?' She grabbed the cheque in anger, and ripped it in two.

'Grandfather?' Will cried. 'This isn't true, is it?'

'I didn't know it was your father,' Marcus said then, his eyes on Nancy. 'Not until I read the article that Jonathan had written, where he said you lost him sixteen years ago. So I looked up the report on the crash. The fact that the only evidence was the scarf found at the scene. And I knew then.'

'Are you saying it's true?' Will asked, shaking his head.

Marcus sighed and went back around the desk, sinking heavily into his chair. He put his head in his hands. 'My wife was a wonderful woman but she was battling a lot of demons. She used to drink sometimes. It got worse and worse. I tried to get her help, to make her stop but I couldn't. When Anne Walker stole from us, we shut ourselves off from the village. It was only ever meant to be temporary until the scandal died down but Louisa's drinking became out of control; there was no way I could hide it from anyone. So, we kept away from the village. I know everyone thought we had lots of visitors, that we thought ourselves too good for the village, but we didn't. We would attend business functions in London without my wife – that was it. No one ever came here.' Marcus sighed. 'And then that night happened. I hid her keys but she found them. She went driving in no fit state to do so. When she finally came home, she was hysterical. It took most of the night to calm her down and only then did she tell me what had happened. She told me that it had been raining hard, and dark, and it had been so hard to see. She had rounded a bend too fast and ended up on the wrong side of the road. She said the car came out of nowhere. She tried to swerve but she couldn't – and then the other car managed to but...' he trailed off, his voice cracking.

'He drove straight into a tree,' Nancy finished for him.

'Jesus Christ,' Will whispered.

'She said she got out but it was clear that the other driver hadn't survived. She panicked, and she drove off. But she never got over it, Nancy. I know that's no consolation.' Marcus looked up. 'My wife didn't die of cancer like I told everyone. She killed herself.'

Chapter Forty-Seven

Nancy had no idea how to feel.

Louisa Roth was responsible. She had caused the crash that had killed her father when Nancy had been just ten years old, changing her life forever in an instant. She had been drink driving, and she'd fled the scene in a panic leaving Nancy and her grandmother not knowing all these years what had happened that night.

After that, Marcus said he'd retired from the family business, holed himself up at Roth Lodge, and kept everyone away to make sure no one ever discovered the truth. Maria's party was the first time he relented and then death had struck once again.

Nancy walked through Dedley End, not noticing that it had begun to rain, feeling numb. She had burst out of Marcus's study after he had told her everything, and had run out of the front door, moving as fast as her legs would carry her until the house on the hill was finally out of sight. Then she had slowed to her current pace, walking aimlessly, the rain drifting down on top of her shoulders as she tried to make sense of all she had found out.

'How could she?' Nancy said aloud in horror. How could anyone walk away from a scene like that? What if her dad hadn't been dead after all? What if she could have saved him if she had only called for help? Tears rolled down her face then, mingling with the rain, the pain in her heart making it difficult to breathe. She stopped at a bus stop and sank down onto the wet bench, unable to go any further.

And then there was the revelation that Louisa had been so haunted by the accident that she had taken her own life. The look on Will's face. It was clear none of the family had known. Marcus had hidden it all from them, for all these years. Trying to protect everyone. Well, their reputation anyway. That seemed to be all the Roths truly cared about.

He had kept the house shut up from visitors until the night of the party. Was the family cursed? It appeared so. Death and destruction seemed to trail in their wake. She hadn't ever felt so sorry for Lucy as she did in that moment. For choosing a family so twisted to marry into. And her father too, for getting in their way all those years ago. Both taken from this world far too soon by the damaged and dangerous Roths. It was just too tragic.

She couldn't believe that Marcus had tried to buy her off once he realised that it had been her family his wife had destroyed. As if any amount of money could make up for that! Nothing could bring her father back. He was gone forever. It had been sixteen years but the pain came back to Nancy as fresh as it had been on the day her grandmother had told her the tragic news of the car crash.

'Nancy!' A car pulled up alongside the bus stop and someone jumped out. 'Get in the car – you're soaked. Please?'

Nancy looked up through her tears to see Jonathan bending down, taking her hands in his. 'She left him to die alone,' she said to him.

'Will called me,' he said, gently. 'He told me everything. He was so worried about you. I've been looking everywhere for you. Please, will you come and get into the car? You're soaked.'

She let him help her up and then he led her to the car where she sank into the seat as if in a dream. He closed the door and hurried around to climb in beside her. He shut his door and they sat for a moment in silence; the only sound was the rain pounding on the roof of his car.

'I can't believe it, after all this time,' Nancy said, turning to Jonathan with her tear-stained face.

'I'm so sorry, Nancy. I can't believe it either. That someone could just walk away like that.' He reached over the gearstick to squeeze her hand. 'All this time Marcus Roth knew the truth but kept it from everyone. Will said his wife took her own life. One night and so much tragedy.'

'All this time I wondered, you know, was it my dad's fault? Did he cause the accident? Was it his fault that he hit that tree? But now I know that he didn't. God, what am I going to say to Gran?'

'I'll come with you, I'll help you tell her,' Jonathan promised. He reached for her and wrapped an arm around her shoulders. She leaned into him, resting her head against him.

'Thanks, Jonathan,' she whispered, so glad he was there with her.

'I'm always here for you,' he whispered back. 'Always.'

And then he planted a soft kiss into her hair.

—

After the revelations of the morning, neither Nancy or Jane were in the mood to go to the White Swan for the annual New Year's Eve party. Their friends refused to let them see in the new year alone though. So Jonathan, Penelope and Kitty, Rev. Williams and Gloria gathered in the cottage to be with Nancy and Jane, and Charlie, of course. Neither Nancy nor Jane wanted to spread more gossip about the Roths around the village but they told Pen everything, and when the vicar and his wife popped in to check on them, they couldn't hide the truth. And, Nancy reasoned, why should they? The Roths had thought they were above justice for years but the truth was out. They had destroyed many lives in their years in the village but Nancy was determined that they would never do so again. She hoped that they might finally leave Dedley End now. She certainly didn't want to see any of them ever again.

They sat in the cosy living room of their cottage, the log fire cracking, all with a drink in their hand. None of them felt merry at all, but they felt better to all be together at least. Kitty was curled up with Charlie reading while the grown-ups talked in low voices about the events of the past few weeks until Jane cleared her throat, and all eyes turned to her.

'We shouldn't be sad,' she said, firmly. 'That's not what my George would have wanted. We should focus on the fact that we now know what happened to him. It was a dreadful accident, one that we all wish we could change the outcome of, but we can't. At least we know now that he wasn't to blame, it wasn't his fault, and we now know who was responsible. It's New Year's Eve and we should look forward as much as we can. It's what George would have wanted, wouldn't he, Nancy?'

She nodded. Her dad had always been an optimist. He opened a crime bookshop when everyone said there was no way it would be a success. He raised his little girl alone after his wife left them. And he did it all with a friendly smile on his face.

'You're right, Gran. We know the truth finally, and now hopefully he can rest in peace. Along with Lucy Roth. There's been too much tragedy in our village. It's been a hard few weeks but we will get through it, and we'll get through it together, because that's what we do in Dedley End.'

'Hear, hear,' the vicar agreed, raising his glass. 'I say we drink to George Hunter and to our beloved village.'

'And to a happy and healthy, and crime-free New Year,' Jane added.

'Well said, Jane,' Pen agreed. 'We can't go back, only forward!'

'Here's to the New Year,' Jonathan added. 'One that brings us everything we want.'

They all raised their glasses, clinked them, and took a long sip. Even Kitty drank from her orange juice. Charlie let out a bark in agreement, which made them chuckle.

Jonathan cleared his throat then. 'So, I have some news actually,' he said. 'I've had a job offer from a paper in London,' he admitted. Nancy held her breath, wondering what she would do if he left their village. 'But I've turned it down. My editor gave me a promotion – I'll be assistant editor at the *Cotswold Star* and I can write whatever stories I want to write. I don't want to be anywhere but right here in Dedley End.'

'I'm definitely going to drink to that!' Penelope said, taking another gulp.

'Well done, young man,' the reverend said, reaching out to shake his hand.

Jonathan looked across at Nancy who smiled. 'The village wouldn't have been the same without you,' she told him.

'Even I might have missed you,' Jane said, making them laugh.

'Congratulations,' Gloria told him. 'And what about you, Nancy? What are your plans for the New Year?'

'To make Dedley Endings bigger and better than ever,' she replied. 'I thought that maybe we could start hosting some events. It's something Dad always talked about but we never got them off the ground. I think it would be fun. And maybe start a book club up too. And something for the kids in the holidays. Now the bookshop has had some great publicity, courtesy of Jonathan, we should make the most of it. And I know the village would enjoy the events and it might bring in people from further afield too.'

'It's a great idea, love,' Jane agreed. 'George did always want to do that.'

'Maybe we could start up a cold case club, we could solve more crimes...' Jonathan began.

'I think we were lucky to solve two crimes this Christmas, and that's more than enough for a lifetime,' Nancy told him. He looked disappointed. 'I'm sure Dedley End will go back to exactly how it was before – perfectly safe and sound.' On one hand, she would be relieved but she understood his disappointment too. Now they'd had a taste of excitement, it would be an adjustment for everything to go back to its quiet, peaceful way again.

'Don't jinx it,' Penelope warned her.

'It's almost midnight!' Kitty cried, excitedly.

'Put BBC on,' Jane told Nancy.

Nancy turned the TV on and they watched the countdown to midnight followed by the chimes of Big Ben and the dazzling firework display over London.

'Happy New Year!' they chorused to one another. A round of hugs and kisses and handshakes followed as 'Auld Lang Syne' rang out.

Nancy looked around the room at the people she loved and knew that whatever the next year would bring, everything would be okay because she would have them beside her.

Epilogue

Six Months Later

Nancy looked up from her book when the bell sounded on the door of the Dedley Endings Bookshop, and smiled when Jane, her grandmother, walked inside.

'Just on my way to the fete committee meeting, I wondered if you fancied me picking up fish and chips on my way back?'

'Sounds perfect.'

Jane glanced around. 'It's quiet in here today.'

'The school rush has long gone, I'll be closing in twenty.' Nancy waved the book she was reading. 'Thought I'd carry on with this, I want to finish it before the fete.'

'I still can't believe he's coming.' Jane's eyes danced with excitement. 'Right, I'd better go, otherwise Gloria will have my guts for garters.' She marched out with purpose, her short grey hair bouncing as she walked.

Nancy smiled to herself – her gran loved being involved in all of Dedley End's events and the annual summer fete was one of her favourites. It would be held on the village green and there was extra excitement in the air this year as Nancy had found them a guest of honour to speak there, and she could hardly wait. She looked around her bookshop, passed down by her father, and smiled with pride. Nancy, a lifetime lover of books, was finally going to meet an author in real life!

She left the counter where the till was. 'Almost time for our walk,' she said to her beagle dog Charlie who was in his usual spot on the window seat looking out at the village passing by. She went over to the new bulletin board which they were using to publicise upcoming events. They now had a weekly Storytime for children and a monthly book club, and now finally an author event. She went over to the poster they'd had made to announce the talk at the fete. She frowned. Someone had written on it in Sharpie. She looked around. It had been a busy day so she hadn't noticed anyone hanging around the poster.

Walking right up to it, she leaned in to look at it more closely.

You will pay for what you have done.

Nancy gasped when she read what someone had defaced the poster with. Was this a joke? Or something serious? Her pulse sped up.

It was written right next to the name of the author who was coming to the fete – Thomas Green. One of Nancy's all-time favourite crime authors. It had been ten years since he'd last published a book so everyone was excited for his new novel and the promotional tour he was doing for it. The fact that he wanted to return to the Cotswolds, where he had grown up, for the first stop was the icing on the cake.

Nancy's eyes moved lower. That wasn't the only thing someone had done with their Sharpie.

At the bottom of the poster was a headshot of Thomas and whoever had written the warning words had also put a big black permanent cross through his picture.

344

But who would have done this? And what did it mean? Was Thomas in trouble? Surely, he would be safe coming to Dedley End?

Then Nancy thought about how six months ago there had been a murder in the village. She had helped find the culprit, along with her gran, and her best friend, local reporter Jonathan Murphy. But everything had been quiet since then. No crime of any kind had been committed. And the family responsible for the murder had fled the village.

So, it was a shock to find this threat on the poster. Nancy had no idea if it was real or not but she couldn't pretend it wasn't there.

Despite thinking that after solving the murder at the house on the hill at Christmas she would never be troubled by a crime again, it appeared to be knocking at her door once again.

Nancy was glad she was alone in the bookshop because although she was horrified by what she was looking at, she was also a little bit excited.

Acknowledgments

Thank you so much Lindsey Mooney and Keshini Naidoo for loving this book and taking a chance on a new direction with me. I'm so excited to work on this new series with you both!

Thank you so much to the whole Hera and Canelo team for all your hard work on my books, I love working with you all.

As always thank you to my agent Hannah Ferguson for your continued support, and the whole team at Hardman and Swainson for looking after me and my books.

I love the cover for this book so much so a huge thank you to Cherie Chapman for designing it.

Thank you so much to my copy editor, Jennie Ayres, and proofreader, Vicki Vrint.

A big thank you to everyone reading this! If you have read my Glendale Hall series, thank you so much for trying something new with me, and if this is the first book of mine you've bought, a huge hello – I really hope you all enjoy reading it. Without the support of you lovely readers I wouldn't have had this opportunity to write a murder mystery and I'm so grateful to you all. To anyone who has messaged me to say they have enjoyed one of my books, it really does mean the world to me.

Thank you so much to book bloggers, reviewers, and retailers for all your support for my books, I really do appreciate every review, every social media share, and every bookshop that stocks them. I really hope you love Dedley End as much as you have loved Glendale Hall. A huge thank you to my book squad on Facebook, I really do appreciate you guys. Thank you so much George Lester, Lisa Swift, Kiley Dunbar and Anna Bell for all your support.

Thanks so much to my mum for watching so many murder mysteries with me over the years! Some of my characters in this book are named after my favourite cosy crime and murder mystery TV shows and books so a huge thank you to them for inspiring me to write my own.